B. C. BURGESS

descension

the mystic series

bandit publishing

This book is a work of fiction. Any references to historical events, real people, or real locales are used fictitiously. Other names, characters, places, and incidents are the product of the author's imagination, and any resemblance to actual events or locales or persons, living or dead, is entirely coincidental.

Second printing.
Bandit Publishing
Flower Mound, TX

Edited by Kelly Schaub
Cover Designed by Sarah Hansen
at OkayCreations.net

ISBN: 978-0-9886951-4-6

For my Mom.

Without you, neither my world nor
Layla's would exist.
Thank you for all you do.

Acknowledgments

Though I wrote the book, it took a small army to bring it to life. My love and appreciation overflows for all of them. To my mom – thank you for being my biggest fan and unofficial editor. To my sister, Lisa, and my friend, Amy – you gave me much more than financial support. I'll always remember your loving encouragement and will strive to pay it back and forward.

To my avid readers – you are my cheerleading squad and lift my spirits when I'm low; especially you, Aunt Leona. You and your enthusiasm make me smile.

To my editor, Kelly Schaub – thank you for guiding little ol' me around the pitfalls of writing long after you fulfilled your contractual promise.

To the creator of the beautiful cover, Sarah Hansen, and my new website, Carrie Spencer – thank you for breathing new life into the series.

And last but not least, to my amazing husband and son – without your support and patience, I wouldn't have been able to finish this book. You've given me a gift beyond measure, and I'll always hold it close to my heart. I love you guys.

Prologue

Present Day—Maine

Power begets gold; gold spawns power. On both accounts, Agro was a rich man. For over sixty years, his supremacy had been matched by few and stymied by none. Not because there weren't attempts. Defiance and disputes were around every corner—ignorant fools willing to die for pitiful beliefs, powerless bleeding hearts too stupid to let bygones be bygones. Both were laughable and completely welcome. Agro enjoyed crushing the insignificant lives that got in his way. It was one of life's more rewarding pleasures, a fulfillment few received and even fewer accepted, a delight Agro embraced like a long lost child.

As for gold, he'd always be willing to add another priceless piece to his immense collection of artifacts, and in his opinion one could never have too much money to play with. But even in a world where desires could be fulfilled with the wave of a hand, not everyone had the wits to gather the treasures he'd obtained.

It hadn't always been that way. As an adolescent, Agro was forced to earn his possessions by toiling away at degrading jobs, accumulating a scant collection that would shame a vagrant. By seventeen, he'd abandoned humble restraint. Armed with deadly determination, he set out on his own, building his life around a new set of rules—rules that hundreds would follow by his twenty-fifth birthday.

Now, wise and robust at eighty, he commanded a slew of subordinates willing to plunge daggers into their bellies to please him, a mere snap of his fingers could part all the wet thighs in his camp, and his fortune would make a Texas oil tycoon piss his boots and lower his Stetson in shame.

Yes, Agro had been reaping the rewards of his ways for decades. His desires were now handed to him. Not on silver platters, but diamond trays. He'd thrown the silver he'd plundered over the years to his soldiers, raising morale and solidifying loyalty.

And the most loyal of the peons was approaching.

As the familiar footfall grew louder, Agro lowered his goblet, turning his orange eyes to the entrance of his spacious tent. His second in command, an obedient brute with more brawn than brains, stepped through the canvas flaps, dropping his gaze to the antique Persian rug.

"Sir," he greeted.

"Farriss," Agro returned. "To what do I owe your sudden appearance?"

"Garran Bram is here to see you," Farriss replied.

Agro shrugged. "Probably came to beg for more time."

"He says he has some interesting information to divulge. Something you'd want to know."

"Is that so?" Agro murmured, raising one eyebrow. He couldn't imagine what useful information a lowlife such as Garran could possibly hold. Nevertheless, his interest spiked. "Very well. Bring the boy in."

Farriss hurried from the tent, and Agro filled an alexandrite encrusted goblet with wine as he waited, thinking a bit of useful information might add intrigue to an otherwise dull day.

Farriss returned, roughly pushing a derelict wizard draped in a shabby brown cloak. Or perhaps it was a white cloak caked in dirt. The malnourished man dropped to his knees and stared at Agro's feet with wide eyes, his forehead sprouting beads of sweat, his larynx quivering over a rapid pulse.

Agro enjoyed the ambiance of fear surrounding the cur, but there was no excuse for his pitiful hygiene. A magical sweep of the hand would improve his appearance tenfold.

"Farriss," Agro said, watching his company's greasy, black hair.

"Yes, sir?" Farris replied.

"You may go."

The brute bowed then took his leave, and Garran trembled, offending Agro's senses with his stench.

Agro scrunched his nostrils and retrieved a sprig of sandalwood from a side table, wafting it between him and the riffraff. "Do you have your penance, Garran? You've owed me for over a month now. Not many people get away with that."

Garran's shaking turned violent, intensifying his stink. "N-no, sir. I've n-never had that kind of m-money."

"That's because you piss it away gambling."

"The fucking hexless rig their competitions," Garran cursed.

"Perhaps you should have considered that before squandering your money on their games and impregnating one of their bitches," Agro scorned. "I got you out of a jam. I don't do those things for free. I scratch your back, you scratch mine. Hypothetically of course," he added, observing Garran's dirty and jagged fingernails.

"Of c-course, sir," Garran stuttered.

Agro rolled his eyes as he sipped his wine, continually waving the fragrant twig. "Farriss says you have something interesting to tell me. Is this an attempt to pay your debt?"

"Y-yes, sir."

"Look at me when I'm talking to you."

Garran snapped his head up. "S-sorry, sir."

"And stop stuttering. It's getting on my nerves."

"Y-yes, sir."

Agro set his goblet aside. Then an ivory smoking pipe appeared in his hand. "Well, get on with it. What's so interesting?"

Garran gulped, watching as Agro lit his pipe with a flaming fingertip. "I heard a rumor," Garran revealed, "that you once lost something dear to you."

Agro's gaze wandered as he tried to recall something he'd held dear, but nothing came to mind. "What are you babbling about?"

"A child, sir," Garran explained. "A child you wanted but couldn't get."

Agro puffed the pipe as he thought. Over the years, there had been many children he wished to obtain but couldn't, and he was always slightly disappointed when one evaded recruitment. But his only true regret had come twenty-one years earlier, when he'd lost the one child he wanted most. His blood still boiled when he thought about what that child could have contributed to the Dark Elite—or, as their enemies like to call them, the Unforgivables. Agro smiled every time he imagined a burnt and bloody victim whispering the dreaded nickname —*Unforgivables*. It did have a certain ring to it.

He sobered and turned his attention to the vermin at his feet. "There have been many children I've wished to procure and didn't. You'll have to be more specific."

Garran eagerly nodded. "Yes, of course. You're under the impression this child was never born. You believe it died in the womb..." He trailed off as Agro narrowed his eyes on him, but after a quick breath, he hurriedly continued. "I heard a man say you'd been fooled. The child was safely delivered and lives to this day."

The pipe and sandalwood vanished as Agro leaned forward, nostrils flaring in anger and disgust.

Garran shrank back, trembling again. "I'm s-sorry, sir. I don't mean to imply you're a fool or anything. That's what the man said."

"What man?" Agro seethed. "Where did you get this information?"

"He wouldn't say his name," Garran answered. "I was in a tavern in New Hampshire, minding my own, when he sat down and bought me a drink."

Agro stood and began pacing, fidgeting with the smoky quartz encrusted in the platinum buckle of his gold belt. "What else did he tell you?"

Garran fearfully watched Agro's agitated gestures, clearly torn between begging for his life and fleeing for it. "He said it had been twenty-one years since the great Agro had been taken for a fool. And I defended you, sir. I said nobody calls Agro a fool. Agro's a good man who helps little people like me out of tight spots. But the stranger just laughed and said you'd been hoodwinked."

Agro stopped pacing when he heard the time line. "What else did the stranger say?"

"He told me you believe the child dead, but she's alive, living somewhere in Oklahoma, in a hexless community."

Agro turned his back on the snitch, muscles rolling. If what the stranger revealed was true, he *had* been taken for a fool. Rage swelled, burning his eyes and lungs. So the child was alive—a twenty-one-year-old female living in a non-magical community in Oklahoma. But who was the stranger in the tavern? It had taken a great sacrifice to ensure the child's safety. So why, twenty-one years later, would someone blatantly reveal the secret? Who was this unknown third faction who'd discovered the truth when he, the great Agro, had not? And why had the man freely passed such valuable information to a worthless rat like Garran Bram?

"What did the stranger look like?" Agro quietly asked.

"He was young, sir," Garran answered, "early twenties, with fair skin and short hair—light brown or dark blonde, however you flip it. And he had a short mustache and goatee. I never saw his eyes. He wore sunglasses the whole time."

"Useless information," Agro hissed. The unknown wizard could have easily transformed his appearance before revealing his secret. Only his eyes would have been genuine, the color and detail of the iris, but he'd wisely kept them hidden.

Agro turned, looking down at his unpleasant company. "Did the stranger give you any more information about the child?"

"No, sir, only what I've told you."

"Did you share this with anyone else before bringing it to me?"

Garran's eyes widened as he hurriedly shook his head. "No, sir. Of course not. I came straight to you."

Agro tapped a fingernail to his temple, considering a plan of action.

"I've done well, right?" Garran asked, starting to relax.

Agro looked down. "Yes, Garran, you've done well, which bestows in me the tiniest tinge of regret for what I must do next."

Garran's hopeful expression wrinkled in confusion then flexed in fright as Agro raised a palm. Garran opened his mouth to scream, but the shriek died in his throat as his body solidified into a horrifying ice sculpture with terrified eyes and a twisted mouth. Agro's hand fell to his side, and the frozen man shattered. With one more flick of the wrist, the shards flew from the tent.

Pity, Agro mused. Then his goblet and pipe reappeared as he called for Farriss.

Chapter 1

Present Day—Oklahoma

Layla Callaway—young, healthy and desperately desolate; lost in a forsaken and pessimistic chasm bereft of pleasure and purpose. Her descension into the lonely belly of the debilitating beast had taken three years, three years of emotional pain and nail-biting fear. Though she remained cognizant enough to discern the depth of her despair, hope had dwindled, taking with it the motivation to resurface.

Not even dipping into childhood memories could stem Layla's grief. Rich as they were, lavish with love, happiness and peace, all of them co-starred Katherine—Layla's mom, best friend, and lone relative—and Katherine was gone, dead for two months, though a massive stroke had smothered her lights three years earlier, leaving her an invalid.

"Three years," Layla brooded, sitting at Gander Creek's lone stop light.

The light turned green, and she tapped the gas pedal of her Taurus, creeping past thrift shops, general stores, and meandering people. She eventually cleared downtown and sped up, wistfully sighing at the steely gray clouds rolling in from the west.

Oklahoma's severe weather was one of the few things Layla still managed to appreciate—the untamed power that humbled the soul, intrigued the mind, and awakened the senses. But while Katherine's death hadn't stifled Layla's love of storms, it had dulled the excitement she got from them. No longer could she and Katherine sit on the porch together, acting like giddy children as they watched the clouds swirl with ferocious grace, counting the seconds between strikes of lighting and clacks of thunder, goading each other into more intense anticipation of whipping wind and beating rain.

As usual, Layla's memories took a sad turn.

Giant raindrops occasionally slapped her windshield as she parked behind the local diner, recalling the night she found her mom unconscious on the floor. The image would forever be burned into her mind, haunting her dreams nightly. A medical team managed to revive Katherine, but her nervous system was shot. Her brain, however, was a thing of mystery not even three years could unravel. Even the expensive doctors in the big cities couldn't answer Layla's questions about Katherine's mental capacities, so for three years, Layla acted as her mom's caregiver, unsure if she understood words, remembered the past, or recognized her daughter's voice and face. Nevertheless, Layla always treated Katherine as if her brain worked fine, and she flatly refused the option of a nursing home. What was three measly years, after all, compared to all the wonderful years Katherine took care of her? At least the time she'd spent nursing her mom gave Layla focus and purpose. With that purpose dead and gone, life was empty.

Layla tied her jet black spirals into a long ponytail then pulled in a deep breath, trying to straighten her shoulders, but she only got them halfway there before giving up. Oh well. Time to go to work, bad posture and all.

She tugged at the knots in her apron strings as she entered the diner, shuffling alongside an outdated bar displaying the usual greasy spoon delights. "Damn apron," she murmured, struggling with a particularly stubborn knot as she stepped into the break room.

"Surprise!"

Layla cursed and jolted, dropping her apron to clutch the door jamb. When she regained her wits, she looked around, finding two of her co-workers—Travis Baker and Phyllis Carter—next to a homemade cake with the words *Happy 21st B-Day* written across the top.

"Is today the third?" Layla squeaked. "Of March?" She was in bad shape. She'd forgotten her own birthday.

Travis pulled Layla into a hug as he threw Phyllis an *I told you so* look. "Hell, Layla," he gently chided, leaning back to find her face, "you've gone and forgotten your twenty-first birthday." His tone brightened as he wiggled his eyebrows, trying to make her laugh. "I think it's 'bout time ya had a night out. Ya know, paint the town red. This place could use some color, and ya need to get outta your funk. First, I think, we'll get ya drunk. Then we'll find a farmhand willin' to fulfill all your naughty desires."

In many ways, Travis was a paradox. A country boy born and raised, he worked on the family farm until his dad passed away. Strapped for cash, his mom sold the land, moving Travis to town when he was seventeen. Now, at the age of twenty-three, he still adorned his reed thin, six-foot frame in tight Wranglers and leather boots, and he could easily pass for a star on the professional bull rider's circuit, but not everything was as it seemed with Travis. Yes, he could handle a ranch and all its inner workings, but he wouldn't do it without an MP3 player filled with show tunes. Travis was an admitted homosexual—the only one in town.

Layla had witnessed Travis face persecution in Gander Creek too many times to count. He was shunned daily by its small-minded citizens, and she often wondered how much longer he could put up with it. He stayed for his mother, whose health had waned following a heart attack, and if Travis was anything at all, he was devoted to his mamma. So he remained in a town where most people passed unfair judgment, tossed about slurs, or simply leered at him in disgust.

Layla adored Travis. He was the closest thing to a friend she had, and he was the one person who could bring a genuine, if halfhearted, smile to her face.

"It's sweet of you to offer me a compliant farmhand, Trav," she sarcastically replied, flashing him the elusive smile. "But getting drunk and felt up like a dairy cow isn't everyone's favorite brand of medicine."

"Lord knows it's mine," Phyllis disagreed, swooping in for a hug. "Used to be anyway. Now-a-days it's a hot bath and a good book. But I'm an old woman, honey. You're young and gorgeous."

Layla felt many things, none of them young or gorgeous, but as a perpetually doting woman, Phyllis always said things like that. The plump, fifty-four-year-old was widowed young and childless, and she remained that way, perfectly content to spend her days toiling at the diner only to return to an empty home. She was her own pleasant company, she claimed in defense, and Layla believed it. Phyllis was an unceasingly positive person and likely hummed a happy tune every time she walked through the house.

"It's not like you're ninety, Phyllis," Layla pointed out. "You could spend the next twenty or thirty years getting your udders felt up."

"Amen to that," Travis advocated.

Phyllis rolled her hazel eyes behind thick glasses. "Shoot. That would mean puttin' down my book and exercisin'. 'Sides, I'm fond of my jelly rolls and the sweets that put 'em there."

"Ya know," Travis teased, nudging Phyllis with a bony elbow, "some men like more cushion for the pushin'."

Layla's blush flared, and Phyllis smirked, shooing Travis away with a bejeweled hand. "Anyway," she diverted, smiling at Layla, "happy birthday, hon. I made your favorite cake—dark chocolate ganache with mocha icin'."

Layla patted her stomach. "Mmm… Are you trying to make me fat?"

"You could stand to put some meat on your bones," Phyllis lectured.

"Well that cake should do the trick," Layla countered. "Thank you."

"My pleasure. Now, Travis somehow talked me into lettin' him pick out the gift. But…" She held up an index finger, warning Travis not to interrupt. "I must admit, he did an excellent job."

Travis' mouth fell open. "Why, Phyllis, if ya keep up those compliments and your yummy cookin', I just might put a ring on your finger."

Phyllis rolled her eyes but giggled like a school girl. Travis had a way of boosting a woman's confidence.

"So what did you get me, Trav?" Layla urged.

Knowing Travis, it was something entertaining and thoughtful. He usually blessed her with humorous limericks written on paper flowers or napkin butterflies, and on a few occasions, he'd brought her foreign candies provided by his vast collection of internet comrades.

"Well I'm not givin' it to ya, missy," he refused with a grin, "unless ya agree to have a drink with me after work."

Blah. Layla didn't know what a bar was like. She'd never been in one and had no reason to dislike them, but she had absolutely no interest in seeing the people who patronized the local watering hole. It catered to an uncomfortable combination of town drunks, town gossips, and people she'd gone to high school with, all of whom knew about her mom's death. Gander Creek was a small town where the only topics of discussion were religion, the weather, the deaths, and the gay guy who worked at the diner, so she knew the subject of her personal life had been on the wagging tongues of its bored citizens. She'd be foolish to place herself in a social setting with any of them. If they didn't bombard her with heart-wrenching sympathies, or avoid her altogether, they'd ask her what she was doing with herself these days, and sadly, she'd have no answer.

"How about this?" she suggested. "You buy the booze, and we'll drink at my house. You should come, too, Phyllis. We'll play cards or something."

Layla could tell Travis wanted to argue. This plan negated the part of his that got her felt up by a farmhand, but he must have thought better of it, because he sighed and grabbed her gift off the table.

"Only you wouldn't give a damn 'bout bein' carded on your twenty-first birthday. Here," he said, gray-blue eyes sparkling with pride as he handed her a neatly wrapped package.

Layla returned his smile then looked down, a blush heating her cheeks as she carefully tore the wrapping paper from a green velvet box. For some reason, getting gifts from someone other than her mom always flustered her; she never felt like she sufficiently expressed her gratitude, so her anxiety spiked when she saw the jewelry box. Surely Travis hadn't bought her jewelry. But he had. He'd bought her the most beautiful necklace she'd ever gotten her hands on.

A wide braid of platinum coiled over a large, oval stone, which initially shone vivid emerald green, but a closer inspection revealed a wave of emerald swirling atop deep black and darker shades of green, like liquid in motion.

Layla's chest tightened with a mixture of guilt and gratitude as she bowed her head over the necklace, presumably to examine it, which she was, but she viewed it through the blossoming tears she was trying to hide. She hadn't been a very good friend to anyone in so long, and she'd never been the kind of friend Travis and Phyllis deserved, yet here they were, giving her beautiful jewelry. She took a shaky breath, fighting the threatening waterworks.

Travis noticed and leaned over, looking for her hidden face. "Green's one of your favorite colors, right? I thought it'd go great with your eyes."

"Not to mention that tan skin of yours," Phyllis offered, rubbing Layla's bicep.

Travis was right on both accounts. Green was one of Layla's favorite colors, and since her eyes were also emerald green, the necklace would go great with them. "It's beautiful," she squeaked, feeling weak and foolish. Her head was saying she didn't deserve something so beautiful, but it would be rude for her mouth to repeat it. "What kind of stone is it?" she asked, relieved it came out clearly.

"Mawsitsit," Travis answered, "a type of Burmese jade. I searched the internet for three days tryin' to figure that out, but ended up havin' to take it to an appraiser."

"They didn't tell you what it was when you bought it?" Layla asked.

"I found it at a thrift store," he explained. "An old man was droppin' off some costume jewelry when I got there, but he didn't have a clue what he was givin' up. Mawsitsit's a pretty pricey stone." He looked from the necklace to Layla's face. "So ya like it?"

"I love it," she answered. "It's perfect. And you're right about green being my favorite color." She looked up, trying to convey appreciation with an enthused smile. "Thank you. Both of you." She was thankful for much more than the impromptu party, cake and gift. Layla owed them a thank you for her sanity. If she didn't have Travis, she might have detached from reality altogether, and since Katherine's stroke, Phyllis was the only person to offer motherly encouragement.

"I'm glad ya like it," Travis approved. "Phyllis might've killed me otherwise."

"Darn tootin'," Phyllis confirmed, always quick to give Travis a hard time.

Layla smiled at their banter as she held out the necklace. "Will one of you help me put it on?"

"You do that," Phyllis told Travis. "I'll serve the cake. We got just enough time for a piece before our shift starts."

Layla turned and lifted her ponytail, letting Travis nestle the mawsitsit in the hollow of her throat. Once the chain was fastened, she turned and tilted her chin up. "How does it look?"

Travis whistled and raised his eyebrows. "Do I know how to pick 'em or what? I hate to boast, but I was right, it matches your eyes perfectly."

"You love to boast," Phyllis corrected, passing out huge pieces of cake. "But he's right. The necklace looks lovely."

"Thank you," Layla murmured, turning her attention to her plate.

A moment of silence passed as they ate, and as usual, Travis finished first. "Phyllis, my sweet, if I ask ya to marry me, will ya bake me goodies every day?"

"What would I be getting' outta the deal?" Phyllis smirked.

Travis shifted his shoulders back. "A young stud of course."

"Hmm… What are hound dog stud fees up to these days?"

Travis smiled as he bowed his head, yielding to the witty comeback. Then their boss walked in.

"Happy birthday, Layla."

"Thanks, Joe."

"I sat tables one, three and nine," he announced. "I'll let you guys fight over 'em."

"You guys finish up," Layla offered. "I'll take their drink orders." She gave her leftover cake to Travis then retrieved her apron, dusting it off as she left the break room.

The rest of her shift proceeded without incident, and she was in a fairly decent mood thanks to the surprise party and the storm raging outside vapor shrouded windows. Not only did she admire Mother Nature's mysterious beauty and strength, the torrents of rain kept the dinner rush to a minimum. Bad for tips, but good for stress.

Shortly after midnight, she clocked out and patiently waited for Travis and Phyllis to do the same. Then the three of them worked out a game plan. Phyllis would follow Travis to his house so he could drop off his car. Then they'd head over together.

Great, Layla thought. This would give her time to clean. She hadn't hosted company since the day of her mom's funeral, and her messy house proved it.

Once home, Layla scrambled to pick up dirty clothes, junk mail, and unread newspapers. When the doorbell rang, she was finishing the dishes. "Come in," she shouted, drying her hands on her t-shirt.

A few seconds later, Travis and Phyllis entered the kitchen, each bearing five bottles of alcohol.

"What did you do," Layla asked, "rob the bar on your way here?"

"No," Phyllis laughed, discarding bottles on the counter. "Travis' liquor cabinet."

"I like to entertain," Travis explained. "And I didn't know what the birthday girl prefers,"

Layla eyed him suspiciously. "I think all this would do a pretty good job of getting me drunk."

"I'm merely givin' ya options, sugar. So, juice or pop?"

Layla scanned the array of liquor bottles and mixers. "Juice."

"How 'bout you, Phyllis?" Travis asked.

"I'll have what Layla's havin'," Phyllis answered, seating herself at the kitchen table with a deck of cards.

Travis mixed three identical drinks, garnishing Layla's with a birthday bow. Then he joined them at the table for a game.

By one o'clock, the liquor had relaxed Layla more than she'd been in… well, she couldn't remember. And by two o'clock, she was downright tipsy.

Travis and Phyllis observed Layla's mellow mood and decided to take advantage. "So…" Travis hesitantly began, "what's next, sugar?"

Phyllis shot him a disapproving look, and he apologetically shrugged, but the reprimand was unnecessary; the broad question flew right over Layla's tipsy head. If she hadn't been drinking, she might have noticed the shift in body language or the sudden tension in the air. As it was, she assumed Travis was talking about the game they were playing.

"I don't know, Trav. It's your turn."

Travis contemplated his hand. "So…" he started once more. Then he cleared his throat and looked at Layla. "I know ya don't like talkin' 'bout your personal life, Layla, but you're my friend, and I like to think I'm your friend. And as your friend, I wanna know how you're doin' and what you're doin'. You've been cooped up in this house for too long. Ya did the right thing by your mom, but she's…" He trailed off, looking embarrassed.

Gone. He didn't have to say it. Layla knew. And he was right, about all of it.

Layla kept her eyes on the table, sad and ashamed. "You are my friend, Travis. You, too, Phyllis. The only friends I have. And you do have the right to ask me how I'm feeling and what I'm doing." She took a deep breath, forcing herself to look Travis in the eye. "I'm sorry I gave you the impression you shouldn't." She felt awful that Travis and Phyllis thought they had to tip toe around her. She never meant for it to be that way.

Phyllis laid a hand on Layla's arm. "I remember when ya first started workin' at the diner, honey. I looked at ya and thought that girl can do anything she wants; she's goin places. Ya were so outgoin' and spirited, not to mention the most gorgeous thing I'd ever seen. Now I know all your plans were pushed aside when your mom got sick, but now's your chance to start fresh."

Layla stirred her cocktail into a cyclone, trying to remember the carefree girl from her past. Once upon a time there were things she dreamed of doing, places she wanted to see, and relationships she yearned to form, but it had been so long since any of them were a possibility, they'd become delusions.

"If ya don't mind me askin'," Phyllis continued. "How's your finances?"

"Well," Layla answered, "I don't know, but I'm meeting with my mom's lawyer Monday to figure it out. She had some money set back for me, but I don't know how much, and the house is paid for, but I don't have a clue what it's worth. Other than that, I have about three thousand in the bank."

Travis was wiggling in his chair, waiting for Layla to finish. "Hey, didn't ya say somethin' one time 'bout wantin' to live in California?"

Ever since Layla could remember, Katherine talked about moving to the west coast following Layla's high school graduation. She'd make up bedtime stories about visiting the ocean, where they'd meet beautiful people and live a fairytale life. But the stories were distant dreams now; they'd floated away with her mother's spirit.

"California?" Layla asked, raising an eyebrow at Travis. "Are you trying to get rid of me?"

"No, but if you lived there, I could visit. I've always wanted to see California."

"Well plan a vacation and book a motel, because there's no way I can afford a move to the west coast. The cost of living there is ridiculous."

"Whatchya wanna do then?" Travis countered. "I know there's better out there for ya than a dirty diner off the highway. No offense, Phyllis."

"None taken," Phyllis assured. "Layla's way too good for the diner."

"See?" Travis pressed. "Even Phyllis agrees with me. So what is it ya wanna do with yourself now that ya got nothin' keepin' ya here?"

Layla considered this as she flipped through her cards, but the alcohol hindered her thought process, and not even a lame excuse for a life plan came to mind. She had to give them something. They were looking at her with hopeful expressions, desperate to help.

"I don't know," she finally replied. "It's been a long time since I've thought about stuff like that. I guess I'll wait until after I talk to my mom's lawyer then weigh my options. I have a lot to consider in the meantime."

Phyllis gave her a motherly smile. "We're not tryin' to rush ya, honey. We just want ya to be happy. You've always been so sweet and responsible. We think it's high time ya acted selfish. Time to do what's best for Layla."

"Thanks," Layla mumbled. "I'd be in awful shape if it weren't for you guys. And I promise to make an effort to... move on with my life." She meant it, but didn't have high hopes for the endeavor. "Now," she added, anxious to abandon the subject, "can we get back to this game so I can kick your butts?"

She did, in fact, kick their butts. Then she thanked them for everything as she walked them out. After watching Phyllis' taillights disappear, she stepped inside and shuffled to her room, falling into bed partially clothed and fully scatterbrained. She was alone again, left with nothing but her thoughts, and her head was full of them.

Could she really turn her old, empty and sad life into something new, purposeful and happy? What was holding her back? Her mom was gone, she'd never known her father, and to her knowledge she didn't have any other living relatives. She was a lone woman. The only permanence in her life was a lonely house full of sad memories, a dead-end job, and a couple of co-workers she was lucky enough to call friends.

Her thoughts faded as she drifted to sleep, and for the first time in three years, she had a dream that wasn't a nightmare.

She stood naked on the edge of a cliff, towering over a gray ocean, waves crashing below as wind whistled through the forest behind her. The only source of light was the moon, its rippling reflection littering the sea with diamonds.

Layla wasn't fazed by her uncharacteristic nudity, nor was she afraid of standing on the cliff's edge. She was euphoric—peaceful yet charged, every nerve ending, bone and hair follicle crackling with intoxicating energy.

The wind picked up, tickling her bare skin like delicate, cold fingers, twisting and lifting her onyx curls. She tilted her face to the sky and closed her eyes, concentrating on the tingling of her body as she inhaled salty air. She felt as if she could walk off the cliff and fly to the massive moon. A mere jump away, it serenely floated atop endless water, a beacon of peace tempting her to take the leap.

Her lids slowly drifted open… and she was deeply disappointed to see the clock on her nightstand. She slammed her eyes shut, trying to retrieve the dream, but it was too late. She was wide awake.

Chapter 2

When Layla's alarm clock buzzed Monday morning, she blindly pushed several buttons then tossed it on the floor, dreading the meeting with her mom's lawyer—a man she'd never met. As she stumbled out of bed, closing the curtains on sunshine and birdsong, her feet felt like they were coated in cement.

Layla didn't know Katherine had a lawyer until after the stroke, when a man named Gerald Greene called to tell her about the $1,000 check she would start receiving every month. Apparently Katherine had arranged a contingency plan, making sure Layla would be provided for in the event of her incapacitation. When Layla asked Gerald where the money was coming from, he said he couldn't tell her. She'd wondered, so sadly, what kind of sacrifices Katherine made to build that nest egg for them—a wise investment despite its price. If not for that money, Layla would have had to work overtime, leaving Katherine in the constant care of strangers.

A month after Katherine's death, Gerald called again, offering his condolences and suggesting they meet. Katherine had left something in his possession, instructing him to give it to Layla upon her death, along with what was left of their nest egg. Convinced it would yield little more than emotional turmoil, Layla procrastinated for another month before committing to a meeting. Now it was time to pull her head from the sand and irritate wounds that would never fully heal.

As she backed her car out of the driveway, she cursed herself for being so weak. Whatever Katherine bequeathed must have held value or she wouldn't have gone through the trouble of a lawyer. She could have kept it at the house like everything else she owned. Layla would have found it, eventually, once she found the guts to explore Katherine's bedroom.

The lawyer's office was in a neighboring town twenty minutes away. As Layla drove the barren stretch of two lane highway, she watched the bland scenery, trying to focus on anything besides the impending meeting.

Some would say Oklahoma's a pretty state, and Layla somewhat agreed. She liked driving for miles without seeing a house, and she appreciated the views of rolling hills and riverbeds, unobstructed by people and their projects. Livestock, on the other hand, was plentiful. A person couldn't drive from one town to another without seeing cows and horses. They might even spy a herd of buffalo or llamas. But Layla was tired of it. She'd lived in Gander Creek her entire life, and the wheat fields, rivers and livestock no longer held interest.

Layla's critical evaluation of Oklahoma occupied her mind until she reached the strip mall housing Gerald Greene's office, at which point unease washed over her. After parking the car, she closed her eyes and counted to twenty, trying to find composure and strength.

"This is stupid," she berated, exiting the car on surprisingly sturdy legs.

Odds were she'd sign her name then be given a small chunk of money—no emotional torment involved. And it was highly unlikely the money would lead to any life changes, because Katherine had never been a wealthy woman. She'd lived payday to payday on a secretary's salary; she'd bought a small, two-bedroom house two decades before and never considered moving; she clipped coupons, shopped discount stores, and drove sensible cars. Not the types of things people sitting on a mountain of cash do.

When Layla reached the lawyer's door, she filled her lungs and swung it open, taking a large step inside. The waiting room was much like every other waiting room—a couch, padded chairs, a coffee table complete with magazines.

A woman popped her head up from behind a long counter. "Hi there. What can I do for ya?"

"I'm Layla Callaway, here to see Gerald."

"Of course," the woman replied, "Come on back." She rose from her chair and led Layla down a short hallway, glancing back often. "I'm Dolores—Gerald's gal Friday. Layla's here," she announced, walking through an open door.

"Oh good," a man replied. "Come on in."

Layla obeyed, rounding the corner to find a husky man of about fifty stretching his hand across a cluttered desk. "It's good to finally meet you, Layla. Katherine always boasted about her little girl."

Layla managed a small smile as she shook his thick hand. "It's nice to meet you, too, Gerald."

"Would you like something to drink? Water or coffee?"

Due to Layla's nervousness, she'd forgotten her coffee that morning, and she'd been regretting it since pulling out of the driveway. "Coffee would be nice."

"How do ya drink it?" Dolores asked.

"Lots of cream and even more sugar."

Dolores nodded and left, closing the door behind her, and Layla's nerves flared as the latch clicked into place.

"Take a seat," Gerald offered, seating himself. "I'd like to tell you again how sorry I am for your loss."

Layla nodded as she sat, never sure what to say to that. Thank you? It's okay? Neither of them fit.

"I'm aware you have no idea what to expect today," Gerald continued. "Katherine was very specific about her privacy, but everything she told me is now yours to know."

Layla considered this as Dolores returned with a steaming cup of coffee.

"I only put two sugars in," she said, handing over the mug, "but I brought more."

"Thank you," Layla replied, eying the extra sugar. As soon as Dolores made her exit, Layla picked up the packets and added them to her cup, sipping as she stirred. The brew wasn't sweet enough or strong enough, but it was acceptable and appreciated. Coffee was one of her favorite things in the world, and she hadn't gone a day without it in over five years.

She let the hot liquid warm her throat and belly then continued the conversation. "How long has my mom been a client?"

"Almost twenty-one years," Gerald answered.

Layla's mouth fell open as a few drops of coffee slid over her fingers. She couldn't believe her mom had known this man for twenty-one years, yet she knew nothing about him.

"Katherine came to me in April of '89," he elaborated. "You were with her then, so I guess I have met you, but you were just a tiny thing, only a month old."

"What did she ask you to do?" Layla pressed.

"She hired me as a financial adviser. She'd come into some money and wanted it wisely managed. She also gave me this." He held up a manila envelope. "She told me it contained information she wanted you to have once you turned eighteen and had graduated high school. She fully intended to give it to you herself, so my instructions were to keep it until she came and got it, or until her death. If she died before you turned eighteen and graduated, I was to keep it until then."

"What's in it?"

"I don't know. Katherine never told me."

"So you've had that same envelope for twenty-one years?"

"Yes, the envelope's the same, but its contents have changed."

"How so?"

"In the spring of 2001, Katherine removed a sheet of paper and added several more."

Layla's brain kicked into gear, trying to figure out what was so important yet interchangeable. Why did she have to be eighteen and out of school to see it? And why didn't Katherine tell her about it after graduation?

"The last time I saw your mom," Gerald went on, "was shortly before your graduation, around your eighteenth birthday. She told me she'd come back for the envelope soon… as soon as she could muster the courage." His bushy, gray eyebrows furrowed as he hung his head. "I never saw her again."

As Layla watched Gerald's expression, a feeling of awe rushed over her, respect for the woman Katherine had been. Here was a man who had little contact with Katherine, so little Layla had never met him, yet he grieved the loss.

Gerald straightened his shoulders and cleared his throat. "When I found out she was ill, I started sending the checks per her request, but I still couldn't give you the envelope. Three conditions had to be met. You were eighteen and done with high school, but Katherine was alive. I think, above all, she wanted to be the one to give it to you, and this plan was a last resort."

Layla cleared her throat, trying not to sound as weak as she felt. "I'm sure that's the case."

"So here we are," Gerald said, lifting his palms. "I'll need you to sign for the envelope and the money."

"Where did the money come from?" Layla asked.

"That's one thing I can't tell you," he refused.

"Why not?"

"Because I don't know. Katherine wouldn't tell me. I used to tease her by asking if she robbed a bank."

He chuckled, wiping his thick mustache, and Layla took a sip, avoiding the polite gesture of laughing with him. "How much is there?" she asked.

Gerald quickly sobered. "You'll be signing for $773,000."

Layla choked, spilling coffee down the front of her shirt, and Gerald jumped up, rushing to an attached bathroom.

"I guess I should have warned you," he said, returning with a hand towel.

"You think?" Layla blurted, absently dabbing her chest. She wasn't mad about her shirt, but her mind twirled like a twister and her lungs felt too tiny to hold air. "Where did she… How did she…"

"I don't know, dear. She never told me." He reached over the desk, retrieving the mysterious envelope. "Perhaps it explains in here."

Layla took the envelope, but didn't open it. That's something she'd do in private. "What now?" she murmured. "I don't know what to do with that much money. I can't walk out of here with $700,000 in my pocket."

"$773,000, and yes, you most certainty could attempt to walk out of here with hundred-dollar bills falling out of your pockets, but I don't advise it."

"What would you advise?" she asked.

"Well, there are a couple of sensible options. I had my bank prepare a check, or, to avoid roadblocks, we could shred the check and electronically transfer the funds. Either way you'll need to speak with your bank about it. The FDIC only insures up to $250,000, so your bank will probably suggest you open additional accounts or place the overflow in secure investments. If they don't sufficiently explain your options, I'd be glad to offer my legal knowledge on the subject, and I could walk you through any paperwork that comes along with it."

Layla didn't trust herself enough to carry around a piece of paper worth more than half a million dollars, so she quickly decided on the second option. "If you could transfer it, I'd really appreciate it."

"Sure. I'll run by the bank at lunch. It should be done by two."

"Do you need my account number?"

"Is it the same one your mom used?"

"Yes."

"Then I already have it." He shuffled through the documents on his desk then cleared a spot in front of her, laying out the paperwork. "Sign here, here and here. If you have any questions, just ask."

"What about taxes?" she returned. "Don't I owe someone something for all this?"

"You did, but Katherine asked me to take care of it for you. The details are on the top page. It shows the original amount and itemizes the taxes and penalties."

Layla took his word for it and barely glanced over the forms as she signed them. He gave her copies then placed the originals in an overflowing file cabinet.

"So that's it?" she asked, looking up with wide eyes.

"Almost," he answered, handing over a stack of twenty-dollar bills. "Katherine wanted me to give you some cash to leave with. You're supposed to buy yourself something right away, no ifs, ands or buts."

He chuckled again. "I miss your mom, Layla, she was a happy woman. I liked to call her Miss Sunshine."

"Miss Sunshine," Layla mumbled. "It fits." Katherine had been a very happy and positive person.

Gerald showed Layla to the front door, insisting she call him if she had any questions. Then she walked into the sun, dazed by the recent turn of events. She was halfway to her car when she remembered the money in her pocket. Katherine had wanted her to take advantage of her new found wealth immediately. This contradicted Layla's sense of frugality, but it had been a last request. Besides, her shirt remained soaked in coffee.

She glanced around the strip mall, finding the kind of places she generally avoided because of their prices. After a moment's hesitation, she pushed her shoulders back and marched across the parking lot. She entered the first boutique she came across then halted inside the door, scanning their expensive selection. Unimpressed, she nearly backtracked, but then she spied a clearance rack and bee-lined toward it.

Because the sales clerk was pushy and Layla was a pushover, the shopping spree yielded a skirt she would never wear, but it also provided two pairs of practical jeans and three casual shirts, one of which she wore out of the store.

As she tossed her bags in the car, Layla realized it was the first time she'd bought new clothing since her high school graduation. She felt good about her purchases, but couldn't ignore the guilt—a result of the money she'd spent and the fact that she felt good for a change.

Dark clouds once again shadowed the sky and Layla's heart by the time she toted her bags into the house, following a photo-lined hallway to her bedroom. She tossed the sacks on her bed, and the manila envelope slid out, drawing her undivided attention. She froze, staring at it like it was a spider with foot-long fangs. Then she gathered the guts to snatch it up, quickly marching it down the hallway so she wouldn't lose her nerve and toss it in a closet.

Instead, she tossed it on the kitchen table and started a pot of coffee, rummaging in the refrigerator for an apple as it brewed. This was something she'd done nearly every morning for the past five years, so she'd perfected the process, finishing the last bite of her sliced and peeled fruit when the percolating came to a halt. After generously adding sugar and cream to a steaming cup, she sipped and sat in front of the envelope.

For a few minutes she just stared at it, steeling herself for what was inside, but when the steam quit rolling from her mug, she set it down, opening the envelope with fumbling fingers. Swallowing a thick lump, she reached inside, pulling out several sheets of notebook paper—a letter in her mom's handwriting.

After a deep breath, she laid it flat on the table and read.

My dearest Layla,

If you're reading this letter, it means my life on earth is over, and it means it ended far too soon. You must be so sad and lonely right now. I hate thinking about it. I never want to leave you.

Layla started crying on the first line, so she stood and found a box of tissues. Once back in her chair, she took another deep breath and continued.

Before you, my life was so empty and sad, but then you came along, filling me with the purest love imaginable. I couldn't have asked for a more perfect daughter. I've always loved you, from the very beginning, but with each passing year my admiration and love grows. You shower me in joy, purpose and peace, and I wouldn't be complete without you. Thank you, my precious baby girl, for making my life rich and wonderful.

Layla wiped her eyes and blew her nose, thinking she'd never make it through five pages of emotional upheaval, but she had to try.

Having said that, I must reveal the true purpose of this letter and convey my deepest apologies. I've lied to you, Layla, over and over again.

This caught Layla completely off guard.

I'll tell you the story as I know it and pray you'll understand. So, here it goes. As you know, my parents died when I was seventeen, leaving me without a family. But what I'm about to tell you is something I've never discussed with you, and for good reason. It's horrible, and I'm so sorry I'm writing it down for your eyes. I wouldn't do it if I didn't feel you deserve a solid explanation. So brace yourself, and please forgive me for what you must read.

After my parents died, I lived on my own in a tiny apartment in Seattle. For three years I would walk to a plastics factory, work a ten hour shift, walk home, eat, sleep then do it all over again. I had no friends, no goals and no ambition. My life was empty and my routine was dragging me down.

The woman Layla was reading about sounded nothing like the mother she knew.

One night, on my way home from work, I was feeling careless. I wanted to do something different, something exciting, so I slipped into a bar off an alley.

Stupid, I know, and as soon as I did it, I regretted it. There were only four patrons, all men, and one glance told me they were bad news.

Layla's heart thumped harder and faster.

When they saw me, smiles lit up their drunk faces, and I knew I was in trouble. I was on my way out the door when the first one caught my arm, and the next thing I know, I was in the air, held by all four of them. The bartender came around the counter, and I begged him to help me, but he just laughed and locked the door.

No! Tears blurred the words, burning Layla's eyes as panic churned her stomach and twisted her heart, like she was there, in that grungy bar, watching it all.

I'll spare you the details. No one should have to hear them, least of all you. Once they finished with me, they threw me in a dumpster, thinking I'd be dead before sunrise.

Layla chocked back a sob, trying to shake the image of her mom's battered body lying in a dirty dumpster.

I thought I was dead. I thought I was in hell, but I managed to live long enough for a garbage collector to find me. I was a critical care patient for three days, and when all was said and done, I had a new nose, a new jaw, permanently damaged vision, a few broken bones, and a barren uterus.

Layla went back, read that last sentence again… then again, head spinning. A barren uterus? Did this mean she was adopted? Was that why she never knew her father? Katherine claimed he didn't want children, so she'd let him off the hook. Well, that would still ring true if she was adopted.

Layla was a mess—confused, shocked, heartbroken over her mom's horrifying experience. She couldn't put anything into perspective, so she got up and refilled her coffee. She tapped her toes on the linoleum and drummed her fingernails on the counter, scared to keep reading, but she couldn't rest until it was over, so she sat and grabbed a tissue.

I can't imagine how you must feel, so I have no words of wisdom. I guess I'll just get on with my explanation.

Because I lived to testify, the five men were sent to prison . . .

Good! But they should have been severely beaten, castrated and locked in a dumpster.

. . . and I ran from city life, ending up in Ketchum, Idaho, a small town I remembered from childhood ski trips. I lucked into a secretarial position at an accounting firm, but outside of my job, I was a hermit, guarded against the world. I fell into a mundane routine, which suited me just fine. I'd learned what happens when you go looking for trouble. You find it.

But as the years crept by, I yearned for the one thing I couldn't have. For ten years I thought of nothing but the baby I'd never be able to carry. Finally, when I turned thirty, I decided to adopt. I didn't have the thousands of dollars it would cost, and they frowned on single parenthood, but I had nothing but lonely time on my hands and couldn't be deterred.

Of course she couldn't. When Katherine went for something, a little discouragement never stopped her. Layla loved that about her. Layla loved everything about her.

I'd finally found a purpose, something to work toward, something I wanted more than anything, so I began saving money for adoption and lawyer fees, and I researched every aspect of being a mom and a dad.

To help finance my goal, I put the garage apartment behind my house up for rent, but Ketchum's a small town, and for eight months the apartment stayed empty. Finally, in the summer of '88, a woman knocked on my door to inquire about my rental. And I have to tell you, Layla, she was beautiful, the most perfect looking woman I'd ever seen. Hair like an obsidian waterfall and flawless, olive toned skin. It was one of the hottest days of summer, and she was on foot, yet there wasn't a drop of sweat on her. I was struck dumb as she spoke to me, like I was meeting a movie star.

She told me her son and daughter-in-law were newlyweds expecting a baby, and she wanted to rent the apartment for them. I hesitated, concerned about being a landlady to people I hadn't met. Then she offered me two years rent money up front and I couldn't refuse. The money was enough to hire a lawyer, which was the first step in having a baby of my own. Once the deal was made and she had the key, she told me they would be arriving late that night and insisted I not wait up for them. I was intrigued, and the next day, when I met them, I was amazed.

Their names were Sarah and Chris, and they were so beautiful and so in love. My bitter past had led me to form an unkind opinion of the male population as a whole, but Chris changed that. He was unlike any man I'd been around. He treated Sarah and their unborn child like they were more precious than the air he breathed, and not a minute went by where he wasn't anticipating Sarah's needs.

I must admit, I was jealous.

Of course she was, Layla sympathized. Sarah had everything Katherine wanted and lost.

But it didn't stay that way for long, because Sarah's heart was as golden as Chris'. She was so kind, gentle and soft spoken, and they both treated me like family, something I'd been missing for years. I found myself dipping into my adoption fund to buy Sarah and her unborn baby gifts, and I did it without any regret at all, because I loved them.

When Sarah was around four months pregnant, she fell ill, and things took a sad turn. At first she and Chris didn't tell me what was going on, and I didn't ask. Even though I was closer to them than I'd been with anyone in fourteen years, sometimes they still felt like strangers, like they lived in a different world than the rest of us. But as the months went by, Sarah got worse, and they finally told me she suffered from a rare heart condition that had no cure. Of course I had questions, but again, I didn't voice them. I just watched from the sidelines as Sarah's illness destroyed her. It destroyed Chris, too. They both waned physically, and it wasn't uncommon to find them crying.

When Sarah was around eight months pregnant, her and Chris' parents visited, and everyone's mood was grim in a time that should have yielded great joy. They never said it, but their expressions told me Sarah wasn't going to live. I prayed nightly for her and the baby in her belly, but only half my prayers were answered. A week after their parents' arrival, Sarah died giving birth to a healthy baby girl.

Layla's mouth fell open. Was she the baby girl? Was this woman, Sarah, her birth mother?

Chris' and Sarah's parents left with the body, but he and the baby stayed. What happened next changed my life in so many ways.

Chris confessed that he and Sarah hadn't been completely honest about their lives, revealing the real reason they moved to Ketchum. He explained, vaguely, that they'd been hiding from a dangerous group of people who wanted to take their baby away. He assured me it had nothing to do with government authorities, but he couldn't go into detail about the situation. I had to believe him, Layla. I couldn't mistrust someone who held such an intense love and devotion for his wife and child. It was obvious how much he cared for them, always, so I didn't press for more information.

He told me he had something important to do, something absolutely necessary, and he didn't think he'd be able to come back. That's when he made me the sweetest offer I'd ever been made. He wanted me to adopt his baby. He wanted me to take her and keep her as my own.

I couldn't believe it, Layla.

Neither could she.

My own precious child. My dreams were finally within reach, literally. But I had to think about the baby's well being, so I tried to talk him into staying. I offered to help with the obstacles of being a single father, but that wasn't why he was leaving. It was killing him, all of it. Sarah's death and his decision to leave crushed him. His pain and regret were obvious.

Then why? Why would he leave his newborn with someone he'd known less than a year?

So I agreed. I adopted a beautiful baby girl with soft tan skin, shiny black curls, and emerald green eyes. I became your mother that day.

Yep, that was her all right. So she was adopted. Her whole life had been a lie. She wasn't sure how to feel about that.

Your dad was adamant about your safety. He asked me to change my last name—at the time it was Moore—and leave Idaho without telling anyone where I was going.

This was getting weirder and weirder.

I agreed. It was the least I could do. I was getting so much in return. He provided me with birth certificates, social security cards, and enough money to live on for years. And he provided you with even more.

So that's where the mysterious money came from. Her… she had a hard time thinking the word *dad* . . . had left the money before leaving her.

He wanted you to have the opportunity to meet your family someday, but he asked me to wait until you're grown before revealing the truth. He wanted you to be a normal kid and graduate high school without carrying this burden around, and he feared your safety would be greatly compromised if you searched for your birth family as a child. Because of that danger, he couldn't be specific about how to locate them, and I'm sure you'll find the clues as cryptic as I found them. But he insisted too much information could lead to unsafe circumstances, so I didn't object.

Why? Why was it so unsafe for her? What could possibly pose such a threat?

This is so hard to explain in a letter, Layla. I plan on telling you this myself someday. This is just a precaution, in case I don't get the chance.

She hadn't gotten the chance. The tears returned.

I love you so much, honey, and since you're reading this letter, I know you're without a family right now. But you do have one out there somewhere, and I promise they love you very much. I saw the love in their hearts every second I was around them, and I firmly believe your safety was their top priority. Giving you up was a desperate attempt to shield you from a dangerous and sad situation, so I know your family misses you and wants you back. I'm sure they'll understand if you can't or don't want to find them, but I urge you, Layla, take what little information I can give you and at least try.

So she had a family out there, somewhere, waiting for her to find them? The absurd idea sank in slowly, very slowly.

Here's what I know. Your parents and grandparents admittedly gave me false names, but remember them anyway, because your grandparents will. Their names, as I knew them, were Chris Callaway (your father), Sarah Callaway (your mother), Jack and Susan Callaway (your dad's parents), and Paul and Dianne Klein (your mother's parents).

(I chose the name Callaway as our new surname when I adopted you. I thought it fitting and fair, and your father wholeheartedly agreed.)

Chris never told me where his parents lived, but he admitted that Sarah's parents lived somewhere near Portland, Oregon. He and Sarah had a home in the area before moving to Ketchum. Portland was where he wanted you to start your search.

"That's not much to go on," Layla huffed.

I know, cryptic, but according to your dad, necessary.

There's a picture included with this letter. The two in the photo are your mom and dad on their wedding day.

Layla reached into the envelope with a shaky hand, slowly pulling out a four-by-six photograph.

The man was muscular and statuesque. His pitch black hair hung straight, shiny and smooth, and his square jaw matched his angular nose. His emerald eyes seemed to smile, and his olive toned skin was darkened further by a summer tan. He was the epitome of tall, dark and handsome.

The woman was petite yet toned, with thick spirals of glossy, golden hair cascading to her hips. Her soft pink lips and cheeks contrasted beautifully with her flawless, ivory skin, and her round eyes were bright aqua blue. She had both arms around her husband's waist, her body turned toward him, and he had one arm around her shoulders, the opposite hand holding her forearm. They both smiled beautifully at the camera, like it was a loving relative looking back at them, like it had said something sweet and entertaining.

Layla stared at the picture for a long time, studying every detail—the timeless clothes and carefree hair that looked nothing like other wedding photos she'd seen from the outrageous eighties. The Grecian wedding gown could have been purchased yesterday or a thousand years ago, and the man wore the ever stylish combination of khaki and white.

When Layla's eyes roamed back to the letter, it felt like someone else turned her head. Like a dream, she had no control or influence over herself or her surroundings.

Beautiful, aren't they?

Yes, the two in the photograph were the most beautiful people Layla had ever seen, which made it harder to believe.

And so clearly in love.

That hadn't escaped Layla's attention either. Chris and Sarah looked like poster children for happiness and love.

Your dad told me not to show that picture to anyone, and he wanted you to be very cautious about whom you show it to when and if you search for your family. So the best advice I can give you about the photo is use your instincts, because they're usually spot on. If it feels fishy, swim away.

The only other clue I can give you is the oddest of them all.

"More mysteries," Layla sighed.

Perhaps it will turn out to be the most useful.

Layla's eyes narrowed as her interest spiked.

Your dad told me he and your mom enjoyed visiting Cannon Beach, a coastal town west of Portland. From the pictures I've seen, it's a cute community with great ocean views, so you'd like it. I hope we get to go there together. Anyway, he said to tell you that if you ever make it there, a place called Cinnia's Cannon Café has really good coffee, the best coffee.

Coffee? Out of everything her . . . *dad* could have told her, could have given his advice on, he tells her where to get a good cup of coffee? Well, she did like coffee, a lot, but that wasn't the point, damn it. She could make her own damn coffee.

Rationality failed her.

So there you go. I know this is a pitiful attempt at an apology, and an even worse attempt at an explanation. Hopefully I'll be able to tell you this in person. I hate to think of you finding out this way.

Please forgive me. Forgive me for the lie you've been living, and forgive your birth family, too. I know they love you. You were put in my care as a last resort, and I'm so glad you were. I know that's selfish of me, but I can't imagine my life without you in it. I would have lost myself years ago if you weren't blessing me with your hugs and kisses and smiles. They mean everything to me. So whatever you decide to do, be happy. You deserve it, because you've made me the happiest woman in the world. I wasn't the one who gave you life, but you're the one who gave me life, and I sincerely hope I've been the mother you deserve, regardless of my dishonesty.

I love you so much, my dearest Layla, and I'll miss you like crazy when I'm gone.

Love forever and always,
Mom

p.s. Good luck with your search. I know you can do whatever you set your mind on.

Layla stared at the last sentence for several seconds, watching the words blur as tears swamped her vision and grief squeezed her heart. Then she moved the letter out of the way, laid her cheek against the cool table top, and cried. She didn't stifle her sobs, gasps and tears. She didn't even blow her nose. For too long she'd held it all in. The dam had burst.

She stayed that way for hours. Sometimes the sobs would turn to whimpers and the rivers of tears would dwindle into trickling streams, and sometimes her chest heaved with emotion, making it hard to breathe. By five o'clock her eyes were dry, albeit swollen and burning, and oxygen was making a steady journey to her lungs.

She peeled her face from the table's Formica surface then slowly turned her head, careful not to upset the kink in her neck. Emotion and new found knowledge weighed heavily on her body and mind, so she lethargically rose to fix a fresh pot of coffee.

She'd have to read the letter again. There was no way around it. Disjointed information rolled in her head like marbles. She could barely make two plus two equal four, let alone add up the fact that she was adopted. It didn't help that she was starving, so she made a sandwich, poured a glass of milk, and sat down, bravely picking up the letter.

She thoroughly read it six more times, and each time the tears flowed less and less. By the seventh, they hadn't come at all.

The information was clear in her mind, but there were too many missing pieces to draw conclusions. Why did her birth parents hide?

What, exactly, had led to her diminished safety? Where did her father go? Was he still alive? If so, why didn't he come back? So many unanswered questions, so many mixed emotions.

Layla picked up the photograph and reexamined it, viewing it differently, with believing eyes the exact same color as her father's. Now that she'd properly absorbed the letter's disclosure and accepted it as true, she could clearly see the resemblances between herself and them.

She had her father's jet black hair, emerald green eyes, and tan skin, and her eyelashes were as thick and black as his but as long as her mom's. She also inherited her dad's wide set mouth, but aside from that and her coloring, she looked just like her mom. Plump and curvy lips, corkscrew spirals, unusually round eyes, a small nose, a slender jaw that led to high cheek bones, and a short and petite frame. Layla wondered, though, who passed along full breasts and curvy hips, because her mom wasn't nearly as shapely as her. Nonetheless, it was obvious these two strangers were her parents.

So what was she supposed to do about it? Go on a wild goose chase halfway across the country? What did she have to go on? Six fake names, the broad location of Portland, a photograph she wasn't supposed to flash around, and a recommendation for good coffee.

And what if, by some miracle, she succeeded? What did she expect to find? Her mom was dead. And her dad, well, if he wasn't dead, he was probably a deadbeat. Safety be damned; Layla couldn't imagine one scenario that would justify a father willingly leaving his newborn with no plans to return.

Her safety—another vague and aggravating issue. It seemed she could be in danger if she tried to find her long lost family. Apparently she'd been skirting danger her entire life. If the threat was real. Katherine claimed the adoption was a last resort, necessary for Layla's safety, but there wasn't any proof. Furthermore, Layla had no idea if *anyone* in her biological family still lived. Her grandparents would probably be around sixty years old. If death hadn't already claimed them, they were likely beset with health problems.

Grandparents . . . she'd always wanted grandparents.

No, she couldn't do that. She couldn't imagine herself with the extended family she'd always wanted. It would be one thing to go to Oregon to see what she might find, but to go hoping for a miracle—that would be begging for disappointment. The clues were too cryptic.

Layla thought her head might explode. Maybe she needed to sleep on everything. Maybe tomorrow would bring the rationality eluding her tonight.

She took a shower, letting the hot water soothe her achy neck, but it didn't wash away her thoughts—thoughts of Oregon and the ocean; a good cup of coffee in the coastal town of Cannon Beach; a grandma and grandpa; maybe even aunts, uncles and cousins.

Layla shook her head under the spray, trying to dispel the castles in the sky.

She lay in bed looking at her parents' faces by moonlight for hours that night, memorizing every detail. When exhaustion finally defeated her brain, she dreamed vividly.

Relaxed and peaceful, she stood barefoot on smooth rocks, facing a choppy, gray ocean and stormy skies, watching seagulls swoop and waves crash. Stones clacked behind her, and she tensed and twirled, finding the stunning faces of her birth parents. They smiled as their eyes widened, and for a moment, Layla was blinded by their beauty and the bright, golden haze swirling around their bodies. They each had an arm extended, and when Layla looked down, she found them holding out steaming cups of coffee.

Layla jolted awake, and it took her a moment to remember what she'd been dreaming about. Once the vision reformed, all she could think was, "How weird?"

Chapter 4

Layla awoke Tuesday feeling groggy and scatterbrained, but after an apple and two cups of coffee, which she drank while staring at her parents' wedding photo, she found the energy to wash up and make a few phone calls.

Every move she'd made since waking up, she'd made while thinking about her mom's letter. The facts were straight in her head, and her options were clear, but which to choose was not.

She could disregard what she'd read and continue her life as it was, with a few financial changes, or she could go to Oregon armed with nothing but vague clues. If she was honest with herself, going to Oregon was exactly what she wanted, but she was hesitant to open herself up to more disappointment. What she needed was an outsider's perspective, so she invited Travis and Phyllis over.

Thirty minutes later, they arrived, Phyllis with homemade bruschetta and Travis with orange juice and champagne.

"What's that for?" Layla asked, pointing out the beverages.

"Mimosas," Travis answered, "to celebrate my first official invite to your house."

"I've invited you before," Layla countered, pulling dishes from the cabinet. "Haven't I?"

"No," Travis replied. "Unless ya count your birthday, when I pretty much invited myself."

"Oh. Sorry."

"Don't be," Travis insisted, bracing himself to pop the cork on the champagne. "So what's the occasion?"

"I met with my mom's lawyer yesterday."

"Oh yeah. How'd it go?"

"I'll show you," Layla offered, carrying the plates to the table. "Let's sit."

Phyllis passed out bruschetta as Travis mixed mimosas, and Layla fidgeted with Katherine's letter, bracing herself to let it go.

"What's that?" Travis asked.

"A letter from my mom," Layla answered. "I want you guys to read it and tell me what you think."

Travis and Phyllis froze, raising incredulous eyebrows.

"Are ya sure?" Phyllis asked. "You're such a private person."

"I'm sure," Layla answered, handing over the letter, "but I want you both to finish before saying anything."

Travis and Phyllis looked at each other. Then Travis shrugged and placed the letter between them.

Layla sipped her drink as she watched their expressions, guessing where they were in the plethora of information. When they finally met her stare with sympathetic gazes, neither of them spoke, so she broke the silence.

"Crazy, right?"

Travis nodded, mouth still hanging open, but Phyllis had more tact. "How are ya, honey, really?"

If the question had been asked after the first time Layla read the letter, she would have answered with a sob, but now that everything had soaked in, she was coming to terms with it. Sort of. "I'm okay," she answered, and Phyllis narrowed her eyes. "Really," Layla pressed, "I am. Yesterday was rough. I kind of had a break down the first time I read it."

"Good," Phyllis approved, patting Layla's hand. "Sometimes all it takes to deal with somethin' is a good cry."

"Maybe. You okay, Trav?"

He hadn't moved an inch. "Uh… yeah," he replied, shaking his head. "Man, Layla, I'm sorry. I just can't believe it. That must've been hell for ya to read."

"Yeah, but the seventh time was easier."

"Ya did this to yourself seven times?"

"Yeah."

"You're a masochist, Layla."

"You're one to talk, Trav."

Travis shrugged because he couldn't argue. "So how do ya feel?"

"I've gone through every emotion in the book," Layla answered, thumbing the pages of the letter. "I'm sad, confused, amazed, among other things." She didn't tell them she was hurt, because she wasn't sure she had a right to be, and she didn't tell them she was hopeful, because she was too damn hopeful.

Travis got to his feet and moved behind her, wrapping skinny arms around her shoulders. "I'm sorry, sugar. Is there anything I can do to make it easier?"

"I'm glad you asked," Layla replied, "because I need an outsider's perspective. I've come to terms with the fact that I'm adopted, but what to do next is what I can't wrap my mind around."

"Do ya know your options?" Travis asked, taking the chair next to her.

"For the most part."

"Are ya leanin' toward one in particular?" Phyllis asked.

"Yes," Layla whispered, "but I'm not sure it's the best idea."

"Ya wanna go to Oregon, don't you?" Phyllis concluded.

"Yes," Layla confirmed, "but I'm scared. What if I drag my butt all the way there, turn my world upside down, and there's nothing there to find?"

"But what if there is?" Phyllis countered. "Life's nothin' if ya don't take chances."

"What's the last chance you took?"

"I let Travis drive me over here."

Layla smirked at Travis' guilty grin. Then she sobered and looked down. "I keep telling myself I should go, just to see the place, that I don't necessarily have to search for anything, but I'm worried a dead end will crush my hopes no matter what I claim my motivations are. Oregon's a long way to go to be crushed. I could manage it much closer to home."

"Do ya still consider this home?" Phyllis asked.

Layla wasn't sure anymore. Home wasn't the house or town. It was her mom. "I guess I don't," she answered, "now that I think about it."

"Instead of thinkin' of reasons to go," Travis offered, "ask yourself if there's a reason to stay. If not, go. If not to Oregon, somewhere else. Unless you wanna live the rest of your life in Gander."

Layla wrinkled her nose. "Eww. Not so much."

"Did your mom leave ya enough money to make a move to the coast?" Travis asked.

Layla was uncomfortable telling them exactly how much money was in her bank account; she felt guilty having so much. "There's enough to go pretty much anywhere."

"There ya go," Travis said. "If ya don't wanna mess with Oregon, there's always California."

Phyllis shook her head. "Look, Layla, if ya wanna know the family you've lost, ya shouldn't let fear get in the way."

"So you think I should go?"

"I think you got less to lose and more to gain by goin'. Do like ya said, just go see the place. Ya can't lose somethin' ya don't have to begin with. If there's nothin' to find, you'll be in the same position ya are now. If ya don't try, it'll eat at ya forever. You'll always wonder what might've been."

"You're probably right," Layla mumbled. "But say I do find them. Then what? What if they're horrible people who didn't give a damn about me and fed my mom those lies to make her feel better?" An awful thought struck her, sucking the breath from her lungs. "What if they hate me for killing my birth mother?"

Travis quickly took her hand. "If that happens, I'll personally kick their asses all the way to New York."

Layla knew Travis wouldn't hurt a fly. He was the jester, not the knight. Nevertheless, she appreciated the sentiment. "Thanks, Trav."

"I don't think that's somethin' to worry about," Phyllis offered. "If that were the case, the clues wouldn't hold any truth at all. If they didn't want ya, they wouldn't give ya a way to find 'em."

"I guess that makes sense," Layla agreed, her fear of rejection subsiding, but the fear of loneliness remained, along with the supposed danger. "I don't know what to make of all this danger stuff. It's weird."

Phyllis' eyebrows drew together. "It doesn't explain much about that, does it?"

"No," Layla huffed.

"But it does seem to imply the danger's pretty much passed," Phyllis assumed. "Now that you're grown and all, the risk is minimal. Isn't that the impression you got?"

"Yeah," Layla answered, staring at her untouched bruschetta.

"I'm not sure ya should let a small risk stand in the way of findin' your family," Phyllis added. "I hate to think of ya in danger, but no one's messed with ya in twenty-one years. Why would they start now? And what's the chances you'll cross their paths in your search? Don't seem likely to me."

The raw truth—Layla feared being alone far more intensely than she feared the unexplained danger. "I won't know anybody there," she whispered. "At least I have you two and my job here, and I know my way around. I would be completely alone in Oregon. I'd be lost." She was embarrassed to admit her fear, and her face showed it.

Phyllis smiled and patted her hand. "You're an amazin' person, Layla. You've overcome so many obstacles in your short life already. If anyone can do this with grace and dignity, it's you. It'll be scary in a strange place with no one to turn to, but you've faced scarier things before, and you're still kickin' to tell the tale."

That was true. Layla couldn't think of anything more terrifying than finding her mom on the floor after the stroke. It had been hell, the worst hours of her life, but she'd made it through to sit and ponder the mysteries of her past over mimosas.

"If fear is the only thing holdin' ya back," Phyllis asserted, "there's nothin' to discuss. I'm not gonna let ya give up somethin' important just 'cause you're scared."

"She's right," Travis agreed. "If this is what ya wanna do, we're gonna make sure ya do it. So, is goin' to Oregon what ya want?"

"What about California?" Layla replied, trying to stall.

"California's a helluva lot closer to Oregon than it is to Oklahoma. And you're stallin'." He knew her too well. "I'm not gonna let ya make excuses, Layla. If Oregon is what ya want, come hell or high water, I'm gonna get ya there."

Layla wasn't sure if she was ready to commit, to leave the only life she knew in search of one she'd missed, a life she could still know, or may never know. The odds of finding that distant life were not on her side, and the probable failure still scared her.

Travis scooted closer and leaned forward, taking both of her hands. "I know this is a big decision, Layla, but puttin' it off ain't gonna make it easier. It'll only make it harder. If ya wanna find your family, ya hafta grab this opportunity by the balls, 'cause everyday things change, places change, and people die. If what your birth family told your mom is true, they've been waitin' on ya for three years. Are ya really gonna make 'em wait longer?"

Tears welled up in Layla's eyes as her throat and hands tightened. For Travis to be so heartfelt and serious was a testament to how much he cared about her. He liked to keep things light. "What about work?" she asked.

"We'll pick up the slack 'til Joe finds a replacement," Phyllis offered.

"But the house would be a hassle to clean out and sell," Layla murmured.

"We'll help," Travis countered, "and if ya list it with an agent, ya won't hafta deal with the sale."

Layla gnawed on her bottom lip. Was she really going to do this? "I would need a place to stay."

"We'll have one by tomorrow," Travis replied, eyes victoriously flashing. "Come on, Layla, if it wasn't scary, it wouldn't be as excitin'. If all ya do is go and see some new things and places, that's okay. It's still an adventure. And maybe you'll get more than ya bargained for. Maybe you'll get a family."

"What about you?"

"What about me?"

"I would miss you."

"I'd miss ya, too, sugar, but I got my own plans for gettin' the hell outta Dodge. They're just on hold right now. In the meantime, I need ya to do this for me, so I can live vicariously through you."

"Me, too," Phyllis added. "I can think of nothin' better than seein' Oregon through your eyes."

They were good, Layla thought, mildly amused. "You guys aren't playing fair," she observed, and Travis winked.

"Do we ever? So whatchya think? To Oregon?"

They made it sound so easy and natural, like it was destiny calling her home. Once her decision was made, adrenaline flooded her veins, inciting goose bumps and jitters.

She gave Travis a nervous and excited smile, finally taking the leap. "To Oregon."

Within a week, Layla was out of excuses to stay in Gander Creek. The house was empty and on the market, and almost everything in it had been donated to charity. Packed in Layla's car were her clothes, a few sentimental tokens of her mom, small kitchen appliances, and a huge box of photo albums, framed pictures, and home movies.

Layla had enlisted Gerald Greene's help to sell the house, requesting he take his fee out of the profit before donating the rest to charity. And she'd hired him to pay her bills and collect her mail until she could provide the post office with a proper address.

Her car had new traction tires and fresh oil, the gas tank was full, and the console overflowed with toll booth change. She'd gotten rid of the old manila envelope, but the letter and photo were tucked inside her glove compartment.

Travis and Phyllis huddled in their jackets, hiding their ears from dawn's chilly bite as they stood in Layla's driveway, waiting to see her off.

"Ready?" Travis asked with a grin.

Layla tried to return his smile, but knew it was weak. "Yeah. I think."

"Are ya excited?"

"That's definitely one of the things I'm feeling."

"It's gonna be great," he assured, "and if ya don't like it, Gander Creek will still be here."

"I guess it will," she conceded. "That's a little reassuring."

Phyllis moved in, giving Layla a big hug. "Call us when ya get a chance, or if ya need anything. We wanna hear how things are goin'. Remember, we're livin' vicariously through you."

"I will," Layla agreed. Then her throat clogged as she looked at Travis. "You'll come visit me, won't you?"

"Well yeah," he answered. "That's the deal."

Tears swarmed Layla's lids, blurring his face. "I love you, Travis. I know that sounds silly, because we've never said that before, but... well, you're my best friend." The tears spilled over as she choked back a sob. She'd never realized how much she counted on seeing him at work, or contemplated how much he soothed her when she needed it most. He'd become an infinitely important person in her life without her noticing or acknowledging the fact.

He wrapped his long arms around her, and she buried her sad and ashamed face in his chest. "I love you, too, Layla," he whispered. "I don't know anyone else like ya, and I'm gonna miss ya somethin' fierce."

"Good. Then you'll come see me sooner."

"As soon as I get the chance."

He squeezed before letting go, and Layla wiped her face. "I want both of you to visit. If money's the only thing holding you back, I'll buy the plane tickets."

They nodded their agreement. Then the three of them stood silent and still, sadly watching one another.

"Well," Layla finally breathed, trying to look brave as she opened the car door, "I guess I'm going to Oregon."

"You'll be fine," Travis soothed.

"She'll be more than fine," Phyllis encouraged. "She'll be great. Call us when ya stop so we know you're safe."

"I will," Layla agreed. "Bye, Phyllis."

"Bye, honey."

Layla fought more tears as she looked at Travis. "See ya, Trav."

He squeezed her shoulder and kissed her forehead. "See ya, sugar. Drive safe."

She nodded then quickly got in the car, afraid she might change her mind any second. She stared at her house for a moment, absorbing its details and the memories made within. Then she gave Travis and Phyllis a sad wave as she backed out of the driveway, indefinitely leaving the only home she'd ever known.

Chapter 5

After two long days on the road, Layla left Twin Falls, Idaho for her third and final stretch. Anxious to get the tiresome journey over with, she was gone by eight in the morning, entering Oregon by ten. Then she gained an hour when she entered western time.

The beginning of her trip through the Wallowa Mountains was uneventful—a divided four-lane highway winding through rocky, snow-patched hills, bypassing the occasional town and dipping into canyons. Then her ears started hurting as she ascended Cabbage Hill into the Blue Mountains, ominously nicknamed Deadman Pass. The moniker made her nervous enough to pull over at a rest stop on the summit, determined to learn more about the descent she faced. Plus, she needed gum. Her ears were about to explode.

As she filled her travel mug with coffee, luck would have a man in uniform doing the same, so she told him she was from Oklahoma and asked if her traction tires would get her down the mountain. He assured her the west side of the pass was clear of ice, took the time to check her tires, and even offered to follow her down the mountain, insisting his patrol took him that direction anyway.

Icy or not, Layla was relieved to have a lawman following her down the steep and dangerous road, especially when she took the two hairpin curves on a six percent downgrade. It was a terrifying experience, worsened by the signs reading *Runaway Truck Lane—1 mile.*

The cliffs eventually opened to safer roads, the friendly officer exited the interstate, and Layla's anxiety quieted. Surely the most perilous part of the trip was over. The thought was further reinforced when the interstate flattened and straightened, eventually meeting the Columbia River and following it west.

For a while the lands to the south were flat and Layla could see for miles, but the further west she traveled, the more uneven the earth became, rising to her left and occasionally her right, trapping her in earthen corridors.

When she saw a sign for The Dalles—a large city near an enormous dam—her anticipation spiked. She knew from researching the trip she'd soon enter the greener half of the state, and after driving through brown mountains and canyons for over eight hours, she was ready for the vegetation rich scenery that differed so vastly from the wheat fields of Oklahoma.

When a smattering of trees cropped up on the hills to the north and south—tall, skinny timber that reminded Layla of rock candy—she shifted in her seat, itching to go faster, anxious to see what lay in wait. She didn't have to wait long. Soon the lands were lush as far as the eye could see, which wasn't far when the timber encroached both sides of the highway. Suddenly, the three day trip was completely worth it, if only to gaze upon the greenest land she'd ever seen.

Signs advertising the Columbia Gorge Scenic Highway came into view, and Layla glanced at the clock—shortly after five. According to research, she'd lose the light around seven, which meant she had plenty of time to take the detour.

The diversion turned out to be one of the best decisions of her life.

The historic route scaled the cliff—narrow, curvy and shadowed by immense trees that looked skinny, but only because their majestic height gave the optical illusion. Dogwoods and oaks that Layla would have considered large in Gander Creek were dwarfed in the gorge, looking more like brush than trees.

Right beyond the timber—dark, mossy and moist—towered layers of volcanic rock. Once in a while the road opened to picnic areas, affording views of slender waterfalls trickling down the cliff face, but Layla bypassed them, knowing Oregon's tallest waterfall was around a few more bends.

She reached Multnomah Falls about an hour before sunset, ignoring her bubbling anticipation long enough to organize the backpack she carried in lieu of a purse. After double-checking she had her camera and keys, she walked to the visitor's center and purchased a day pass to the state parks.

Well worth it, she decided, finally approaching the pool at the bottom of the two-tiered waterfall. High above her, a bridge spanned the bottom half of the cascades, boasting a much more enticing view, so Layla snapped a few pictures of the pool then hiked up the cliff, patiently navigating through tourists to claim a prime spot on the catwalk.

Awe-inspiring in its uncontrived glory, the falls sprung from the depths of Larch Mountain and powerfully rushed down its basalt cliff face, casting a cool mist that moistened Layla's cheeks. She watched for a long time, reveling in its raw force. Then she closed her eyes, blocked out the tourists' chatter, and listened to the roar.

A peaceful moment, to imagine being the only human presence among untamed nature, but Katherine's aching absence kept it from being perfect. Every step Layla took toward the west coast felt like a step away from the woman who'd inspired her to make the journey, like she was forsaking her old life for a new one that no longer included Katherine.

Layla shook the sad musing from her head and opened her eyes, snapping several picky pictures of the falls. Then she returned to the gift shop, loading up on postcards for Travis and Phyllis. As she walked to her car, she stared at a post card featuring her next destination—the Crown Point Vista House.

By the time she reached the observatory, the sun was melting into the western skyline, casting half of the octagonal Vista House in bright orange light. The two-story building was beautiful, with stained glass windows and a domed roof, but the panoramic view of the gorge was better. Across the river, the Cascade Range rose into orange-vanilla clouds, and the water below couldn't decide if it wanted to reflect the sunburst on the horizon or the inky blue twilight flowing from the east.

Layla snapped more pictures, knowing her mediocre camera would never do the view justice. Then she climbed into her car once more, pleased by her impeccable timing. She and Travis couldn't have planned her trip across Oregon better.

By the time she refueled and entered Portland, the skies were bereft of sunlight, a medley of dark blues and purples, and she was a nervous wreck as she followed her memorized directions. She did her best to maintain the speed limit, yet other cars flew by like she was riding her brakes. She almost missed her exit to Morrison Bridge—one of eleven spanning the Willamette River—and had to cut someone off.

"Whoops."

She winced and glanced in the rearview mirror. The driver was undoubtedly pissed, but everyone drove bumper to bumper and zipped across lanes of traffic, so Layla easily forgave herself the goof.

After crossing the river, it was a straight shot to her downtown hotel, and she breathed easy for the first time since entering the city, but when she circled the block to find the parking garage, she found it full.

"Now what?" she mumbled, circling the block again.

Crowds of pedestrians, zooming bicycles, and colorful streetcars simultaneously intrigued and disoriented her, and it had started misting, turning everything into a grayish blur that glaringly reflected the city lights.

Layla drove to the next block, then the next. Then she followed the one-way streets back around, finding another full parking garage.

"What's wrong with you people?" she grumbled. "Don't you know it's a weeknight?" Apparently they didn't care, because there wasn't one parking spot within three blocks of her hotel.

She expanded her search, steadily moving further away from where she wanted to be. By the time she found a parking garage willing to take her, she'd lost count of how many blocks she'd gone.

She couldn't scramble out of her seat fast enough once she cut the engine. The damn car felt like a spaceship manned by foreigners who didn't believe in two-way streets.

She opened her trunk, laying eyes on the large suitcase she'd packed for the hotel, and her shoulders sagged. "No way," she decided, stuffing one day's worth of clothes in her backpack.

After slipping on a hoody, she slung the pack over her shoulder and marched into the rain, which was colder than she thought it would be.

Five Portland blocks felt like ten Gander Creek blocks, and her fingers were going numb, but she was sure the hotel was around the next corner. When she took a left and looked up, finding a clothing store where her hotel should be, her heart sank and she spun around, clueless where she went wrong.

"Oh no," she breathed, eyes stinging. "Oh shit." She suddenly felt tiny and weak—a foolish fish swimming in a sea of sharks.

She dazedly noticed she was holding up foot traffic and moved beneath the boutique's awning, blinking back tears as she dug her cell phone from her pocket. She could have asked one of the pedestrians for directions, but she was on the verge of bawling and didn't want to do it to a stranger, so she dialed Travis' number with fumbling fingers.

"Hello," he answered, and Layla nearly sobbed his name.

"Travis."

"Hey, sugar. What's wrong?"

"I'm lost."

"Where?"

"I don't know. That's the point. I couldn't find a place to park and had to drive forever down these damn one-way streets, and I thought I knew my way back to the hotel, but I get here and it's clothes and I don't know where I went wrong."

"Layla," Travis interrupted, "breathe."

Layla obeyed, squeezing her eyes shut as she took a deep breath.

"So you're somewhere near your hotel?" Travis asked.

Layla opened her eyes and looked around. "I think so."

"That means ya made it," Travis praised.

Layla rolled her eyes. "Yes. Now I'm lost in the rain."

"Ya like the rain."

"I do," she whispered, "but it's cold. Can you help me?"

"I'm a man of many talents," he boasted. "Is there a coffee shop nearby?"

Layla furrowed her eyebrows as she looked down the block, finding a café across the street. "Yes!" she exclaimed, wondering how he'd found her so quickly.

"Good," he approved. "Go get a cup of coffee while I wait for my laptop to boot up."

Layla slouched. "I'm a mess, Travis."

"Without coffee," he countered, "yes ya are."

Layla sighed and trudged to the café, answering Travis' stream of questions about her trip.

"Then it's as pretty as they say?" he asked.

"Prettier," she confirmed. "Hold on. I'm going to order."

Layla tucked her phone in her pocket as she ordered and paid, averting her teary gaze from the clerk. Then she returned the phone to her ear as she walked outside, sipping the hot brew. "You there, Trav?"

"Yep, and I got my computer goin'. What's your cup say?"

Layla read him the name of the café then waited as he searched her out.

"You're only a block away," he said.

Layla's held breath burst from her lungs. "Really? Which way?"

"South. Take a left outta the coffee shop."

Layla turned and headed south. "You're a lifesaver, Travis. You have no idea."

"I'll stick with ya in case I'm wrong," he offered.

"Thank you," she returned. "What would I do without you?"

"You'd look that café clerk in the eye and ask for directions."

"Smartass," Layla smirked, rounding another corner. "There it is! You found it!"

"Glad I could help."

"You did, enormously. I was ready to jump in the car and backtrack to Oklahoma."

"Don't ya dare," Travis objected. "Ya gotta give yourself more than one day. You're gonna be great, Layla, once ya start figurin' things out. Ya got more to offer than Gander Creek can hold. Give the coast a chance to bring out the best in ya."

"*You* bring the best out in me," Layla countered. "I'd literally be lost without you."

"Then I'll be your personal GPS. Just promise me you'll give Oregon a fair chance. I'll need a place to stay when I get there."

"Right," Layla laughed, knowing his encouragement had nothing to do with a place to stay and everything to do with his big heart.

She entered the lobby of her hotel and walked to a couch, peeling off her wet hoody as she finished her conversation. "I really do appreciate this, Travis. I'm warm and dry because of you."

"Anytime. Now go stretch out in your comfy bed, 'cause I know your legs are cramped."

"A little," she confessed. "Keep your phone handy tomorrow. I'll probably get lost again."

"I'll be sure to do that. Sleep tight, sugar."

"You, too, Trav. Goodnight."

"Night."

Layla hung up and stared at the phone, wishing she could show Travis how much he meant to her, but she'd missed her chance to be the friend he deserved. Now all she had was long-distance words.

Exhausted, she followed Travis' advice and stretched out in bed as soon as she got to her room, lazily wiggling out of her damp jeans. After throwing them in a corner, she reached over the side of the bed and pulled two photographs from her backpack.

For a long moment she stared at the one of her and Katherine, wishing she was there. Then she stared at the picture of her birth parents, wondering why they were never there.

When her eyelids grew wet and heavy, Layla tucked the photos under her pillow and turned off the lamp, quickly falling into a dreamless sleep.

Layla took her time getting out of bed Friday morning, but once up, she didn't lounge around. After taking a hot shower and dressing in comfortable layers, she shoved her dirty clothes in her backpack so she'd remember to transfer them to her laundry bag. Then she left the room empty, hoping she'd find a closer parking spot the next time she returned.

Bypassing the coffeepot in the lobby, she headed for the café she'd visited the night before, unwilling to gamble on something as vital as quality coffee. Supposedly the best brew in the world was about an hour away, but she refused to make the drive to Cannon Beach without a jolt of caffeine. Besides, she wanted to get more familiar with the area around her hotel before venturing too far away from it.

So that's what she did. All afternoon she wandered from block to block, memorizing business names, street names, and most importantly, parking garage locations. Though she was busy learning, she kept her pace slow so it wouldn't feel like work, taking time to window shop, people watch, and park hop; and she found a stationary store where she could mail out Travis' and Phyllis' postcards. When her stomach started growling, she got a pamphlet from a real estate office and searched out a casual restaurant, looking over local listings as she ate.

She spotted a few properties in Cannon Beach—gorgeous photographs included—and suddenly yearned to see it in person, to sip the best coffee in the world as she walked beside the ocean.

"Would you like a to-go box?" the waitress asked, snapping Layla out of her daydream.

"Um . . . no thanks," she answered, jittery with unexplained urgency. "Do you know what time it is?"

"Four-thirty," the woman answered.

Layla's mouth fell open. She had no idea she'd been wandering the streets that long. She quickly stood, digging a tip from her pocket. "Do you know how to get to Cannon Beach from here?"

"Sure," the waitress answered, pulling a notepad from her apron. "You'll want the Sunset Highway." She jotted down a few directions then handed them over. "Is that understandable?"

Layla scanned the paper then looked south. "That way?"

"Right," the waitress confirmed. "Follow the Oregon Zoo and Beaverton signs if you get confused. You'll pass them on your way out of town."

"Thanks," Layla returned, grabbing her backpack. Then she headed for her car, determined to reach the coast before nightfall.

As she navigated her way out of Portland, bypassing the zoo and a few city suburbs, she wondered if *Cinnia's Cannon Café* would still be there. Any number of things could have happened in the past twenty-one years—demolition, foreclosure, takeovers. It could be a *Starbucks* by now. She told herself she didn't care as long as there was decent coffee, but she knew it was a big, fat lie. She couldn't deny her deep desire to see where her mom and dad had once sat drinking their favorite brew. When she wondered what they liked in their coffee, she cursed and turned up the radio.

Her ears felt the pressure rise as she left Willamette valley behind, following the narrow highway into the Coastal Range. Colossal trees lined the road—cedars, firs, spruces and hemlocks—and their greedy canopy blocked the waning sun, dimming the two-lane path and casting the undergrowth in murky green shadows.

When the timber finally thinned, the sun broke through, practically blinding her despite the partly cloudy sky. Having been in the shade so long, tunneled by towering trees, the daylight and openness was like a wave of air, like when she'd lay on the bed as a child and let Katherine spread a cool sheet over her. She couldn't see the ocean yet, but the oxygen leaking through her vents suddenly smelled salty.

She followed the signs into Cannon Beach and kept driving west, looking for water, which she eventually spied in the distance, through gaps between buildings.

Unsure where to go, she followed the foot traffic onto North Hemlock Street, passing shops and restaurants that looked more like houses than businesses, and she kept glimpsing the ocean at intersections. A road lined with inns ran closer to the beach, but Layla was keeping an eye out for one business in particular. After driving for several blocks without finding it, she sighed and searched out a parking lot, trying to deny the disappointment. With only an hour of daylight left, she didn't want to waste time chasing coffee shops in the sky.

When she exited the car, bitter wind whipped her ponytail around, and she quickly grabbed the long locks, pulling them in front of her shoulder as she raised her hood. Though she couldn't see the ocean, she could taste it in the shockingly salty air, and she could hear its waves crash against the shore. She leaned against her car and closed her eyes, wondering what it would be like to stand on the beach when her senses were so overwhelmed at a distance.

"Why speculate?" she mumbled, opening her eyes. Then she joined the pedestrians on the sidewalk.

She quickly found a café… but not the one she was looking for, so she kept walking. A few window displays tempted her, particularly the ones advertising fudge, but she wanted to find a good cup of coffee—the best cup of coffee—then go see the beach.

After another three blocks of crushed hopes, she decided to give it a rest and backtrack, visit a different café and perhaps ask about the one eluding her.

She headed for the next crosswalk, wanting to explore the other side of the road, but when she reached the corner and glanced around, she finally found what she'd come for.

Larger than she expected but as charming as she'd imagined, the L shaped building sat on a corner lot, a wooden deck stretching from one corner to the other, providing seating and scenery with cedar tables and overflowing flower beds. The smaller side of the L was devoted to a quaint bookstore simply named *Enid's,* while the bigger portion of the building had a large, white sign curving over the entrance—*Cinnia's Cannon Café.*

Layla froze. She couldn't make her feet move. A huge lump consumed her throat and her stomach knotted. After all these years the café survived, keeping memories made within its walls alive.

She tried to force the lump down, but her mouth was too dry. This is stupid, she scorned. There was good coffee in there and she was standing outside, afraid to move. She took a deep breath, trying to relax. Then she forced her feet forward, one shaky step at a time.

Chapter 6

The café was perfect, exactly the way a coffee shop should look—cocoa and cream color scheme, round wooden tables and high-back stools, comfy couches and chairs facing a wood burning fireplace. And the aromas were heavenly. Layla wanted coffee before walking in, but after getting a whiff of the place, she needed it like an addict needs their fix.

The shop was busy and being tended by only one woman, who handled the pressure well, every move perfected and immeasurably graceful. She was around Layla's age, but slightly taller with an outgoing attitude, and she was gorgeous, an unusual bright spot amidst mundane kitchen gadgets. Her long, blonde hair hung straight and smooth from a flawless part, boasting honey-gold undertones, and she had a friendly face, with round cheeks and a big smile exposing perfect teeth.

When the line advanced, giving Layla a closer look, her mouth fell open. She'd never seen eyes like the clerk's before. Around the pupil, ran a thin ring of pastel green, which was encircled by a darker ring, then another. They continued that way, subtly changing hues, until they reached the outer iris, a dark layer of forest green. They had to be contacts, Layla concluded. No one has eyes like that.

When the man in front of her left with his order, Layla approached the counter, trying not to stare as the clerk wrote something down on a notepad.

"One second," she murmured, still focused on her memo.

She'd only said two words, yet she had the most beautiful voice Layla had ever heard.

"Take your time," Layla replied, ridiculously in awe of the woman.

The clerk whipped her head up, scanning Layla with narrow eyes. Then she smoothed her scowl and warily smiled. "Hi."

"Hi," Layla returned, completely confused.

The clerk's forehead creased. "What can I do for you?"

Layla cleared her throat, answering in the clearest voice she could muster. "Large coffee and um…" Damn, she'd forgotten what she wanted. She threw a quick glance at the hand painted menu. Oh yeah. "A piece of the chocolate-hazelnut torte. Please."

The clerk's odd expression stayed in place as she repeated the order.

"Yeah," Layla confirmed, torn between looking at the counter and staring hard into the strange woman's multicolored eyes.

The clerk totaled up the tab then expertly fixed the coffee and dessert, glancing up often. Layla tried to pretend she didn't notice the looks, but found her own eyes constantly shifting toward the weird and wonderful woman.

Once Layla had her purchases and her change, she offered the clerk a small smile. "Thanks."

"You're welcome. Have a good night."

"You, too," Layla mumbled. Then they both furrowed their eyebrows at the same time, sharing one last look of confusion.

Layla turned and scanned the room, quickly choosing a corner table with a clear view of the entire store, including the counter and the woman tending it.

The dessert was excellent—silky smooth and sweet—and the coffee was, in fact, the best she'd ever had. As she ate, she imagined what her parents would look like sitting at each table, but most of them were occupied, and aside from the stunning clerk, no one could compare to her lovely mom and dad.

Until he walked in.

Layla's gaze was roaming over the front door when it swung open, revealing a man so gorgeous her breath caught in her chest. Her reaction surprised and embarrassed her, but she couldn't look away as his tall, bronzed body moved with strength, grace and purpose to the counter.

Instead of entering the queue, he moved behind the bar and began helping the clerk. All Layla could see then was his back, but she didn't mind. She took her time examining his head, shoulders, torso—and by leaning to the left—his hips, butt and legs. He wore a white t-shirt, brown cargo shorts, and flip-flops. Inappropriate for the weather, but fantastic for the view.

Layla cocked her head to the side, appreciating his relaxed style and fine form. Then her gaze returned to his upper half, quite content to do so. White cotton rippled over muscle as he worked. And his thick hair—the color of which was strikingly similar to a pot of strong coffee held up to the light—shimmered in loose waves, sweeping over the nape of his neck.

Just as Layla wished she could see his face again, wondering if it was as beautiful as she remembered, the last customer in line walked away. The female clerk moved to the handsome stranger, and he leaned in, letting her whisper in his ear.

She must be his girlfriend, Layla concluded, swallowed by an unexpected wave of disappointment. Not that she would ever, in a million years, have the courage to talk to someone who looked like him. He could easily be a famous face and paired far better with the stunning clerk.

Layla tried to force her gaze away, but the attempt was unsuccessful and quite pitiful. She really didn't want to look away. He might disappear.

Suddenly, he straightened and turned, staring right at her.

Layla gasped and looked down, heat flooding her face as her heart thundered. It felt like he'd x-rayed her, peered straight into her soul, and she didn't dare look up again. Instead, she watched the coffee at the bottom of her cup, mortified to be caught ogling and worried she'd offended his girlfriend.

Layla wanted to leave immediately, run far away from the ridiculous situation and forget it ever happened. She shouldn't have come, except… well, the coffee was excellent. Damn. She'd blown her chance for a refill.

She took a deep breath, working up the courage to raise her head and leave, but her concentration was blown to bits when a deep voice spoke, quickening her hasty pulse.

"Would you like a refill?"

Layla snapped her gaze up, locking eyes on the most magnificent man she'd ever seen. His front was so much better than his back. "Um… yeah, sure," she stuttered, feeling like a complete idiot.

He took her cup, a small smile curving over his strong jaw. "I'll be right back."

Layla figured he was laughing at her in his head, but she couldn't bring herself to mind. The tiny smile sent pleasurable goose bumps across her chest and neck.

Once he walked away—for only then did Layla have the brain capacity to ponder anything at all—she wondered what her problem was. Sure, he was the most crush-worthy man she'd ever seen, but she'd lived twenty-one years without getting silly over a guy. Melting like butter when he was near made her feel weak and ridiculous.

When he returned, she looked at the table, sliding figure eights across its polished surface, trying not to make her attraction obvious, but most likely achieving the opposite affect. Who sits around staring at a table while tracing invisible figure eights? Loonies and people trying not to look at something, that's who.

He sat down in the chair across from her, but he didn't surrender her coffee. He just watched her with intense brown eyes that were so dark the pupil and iris were barely distinguishable.

"How do you drink it?" he finally asked, holding up her cup.

"Sugar and cream," she answered, voice cracking.

He gave her another small smile, and Layla couldn't tell if humor or sympathy played on his lovely lips.

"You'll have to be more specific," he said, picking up the cream.

More embarrassed than ever before, Layla couldn't quit blushing, and her palms were slick with sweat. She wiped them on her jeans and ordered herself to pull it together. If she got any worse, he'd think she escaped a nuthouse.

"I'll do it," she offered, taking the cup. "I use a lot of sugar."

He stayed seated, watching her add the condiments. When she poured the sugar, he raised a dark eyebrow, one corner of his full lips twitching into a smirk. "That is a lot of sugar."

Layla shrugged, trying not to stare at his mouth. "We all have our vices. Mine's really sweet coffee."

He wouldn't look away long enough for her to take a drink, and she felt stupid just sitting there, so she straightened her shoulders and met his stare. "Do you always sit and visit with your customers?"

"I don't work here," he replied.

"Then why are you working?" she asked.

"I'm not. Earlier I was helping a friend. Now I'm a customer sitting with a beautiful woman."

Layla glanced around the table, half-expecting to find a pretty lady. Then she returned her suspicious gaze to the handsome man. "You're not a customer," she said, pointing out the empty table in front of him.

His smile widened, and dimples appeared below chiseled cheeks.

Now that's not fair, Layla thought, absolutely blown away by the pristine package in front of her. How perfect can one person be?

"Would it help if I got a cup of coffee?" he asked.

"Help what?" she returned.

"Make you more comfortable sitting with me."

So her embarrassment was obvious. Great. "Maybe, if you tell me who you are and why you're sitting here."

"Then I'll get some coffee," he said, smoothly rising from his chair. "Be right back." He walked behind the bar and helped himself, ignoring the pointed looks the clerk threw him.

Layla wasn't sure what to make of everything. Why was this beyond gorgeous man giving her the time of day? And why was the beautiful clerk reacting so strangely? Layla was stumped; therefore intrigued.

When the handsome man started back, Layla looked away at nothing in particular, waiting for him to sit before looking forward.

His gaze stayed on her face as he added a small amount of sugar to his cup. Then he sipped and set the mug aside. "Now, what was it you wanted to know?"

It took longer than it should have for Layla to remember what he was talking about. "Who are you?"

"That's right." He flashed dimples as he reached across the table. "My name's Quinlan, but most people call me Quin."

Layla tentatively accepted his hand, and his large palm enveloped hers, but his touch was warm and gentle, sliding tingles up her arm to her stuttering heart. "It's nice to meet you, Quin. My name's Layla."

He frowned, his hand and pupils contracting. Then he let her go and looked at his coffee. "It's nice to meet you, too, Layla. Do you have a last name?"

"It's your turn to answer one," she countered.

His smile returned as he looked up. "I guess it is. You wanted to know why I'm sitting here, right?"

She nodded, and he answered without a moment's hesitation. "Because I'm intrigued by you."

Layla furrowed her eyebrows, withholding a sarcastic snort. "And what about me intrigues you?"

"Nope. Your turn again."

Layla puckered, and Quin grinned. "What's your last name, Layla?"

"Callaway," she answered.

He looked away again, and Layla took a drink, trying to decipher his reactions. "I'm not satisfied with your previous answer, Quin. Why are you sitting here?"

"Do you want me to leave you alone?"

"No," she answered, way too quickly, and her cheeks flushed as she bowed her head.

"I wanted to meet you," he explained, quite simply and with much more confidence than she could ever achieve.

"Oh," she mumbled, slowly looking up.

He caught her gaze and held it. "I'm in here a lot and I've never seen you. Are you from around here?"

That depends on how you look at it, she thought. "No, this is my first time here."

"Here in Cannon Beach? Or here in *Cinnia's*?"

"Both. It's my first time in Oregon."

"Are you on vacation?"

"You ask a lot of questions, Quin."

"Am I bothering you?"

"Not really." It was a lie. He was bothering her, in very interesting ways.

She cleared her throat, determined to hold a decent conversation with someone other than herself. "Do you live in Cannon Beach?" she asked, keeping her voice steady. A little too steady. It seemed forced. *Damn it, Layla, get over yourself.*

"No," Quin answered, leaning forward, and Layla's lungs froze. "I live northwest of Jewell, a logging community between here and Portland."

"I saw the junction," she noted.

"Junction?" he repeated.

"Yeah, the Jewell Junction. On the highway from Portland?"

"Right," he mumbled. "Is that where you're staying? Portland?"

"For now," she confessed. "I moved here on a whim, so I don't have a place yet. I'm at a hotel until I figure out where I want to live."

"Is that what you're doing in Cannon Beach?" he asked. "Looking for a house?"

She hesitated, somewhat suspicious of the handsome man's motives. "No. I'm here for the coffee. I was told *Cinnia's Cannon Café* has the best."

"*Cinnia's* has a good reputation," he confirmed. "It's been around for years."

"That's what I've heard."

"So you drove to the coast just to try *Cinnia's* coffee."

"Well, I also wanted to see the beach."

"Did you see it?"

"From a distance."

"Do you have a warmer coat in your car?"

Layla glanced at her hoody, thinking the question odd. "Yes," she answered, looking back up.

“Good.” He took her cup and stood. “I’m going to refill our coffee. Then we’ll go to the beach and watch the sun set.” And without another word, he walked away.

Chapter 7

He didn't give her a chance to say no. Not that she would have. Layla knew it was careless to go off with a man she'd just met, but she didn't sense a threat. Quin's reactions were weird, sure, but he'd been perfectly nice and polite. Besides, she wasn't ready to walk away and never see him again, so she put her backpack on and headed for the counter.

Because she was purposefully looking away from him, Layla didn't realize he was quietly speaking with the clerk until she was within earshot. She tuned out the whispers and turned away, flustered and guilty, but then Quin called her name.

She slowly turned back, cheeks flaming. "Yeah?"

"This is Brietta," he said, "a close friend of mine."

Brietta smiled as she held out Layla's fresh coffee. "It's nice to meet you, Layla."

"You, too," Layla returned, accepting the cup.

Quin walked around the counter, and only then did Layla realize exactly how tall he was. His pecs were right in her line of sight, his sturdy shoulders several inches above her head.

"Ready?" he asked, covering her entire shoulder blade with a large palm.

"Um . . . yeah," Layla mumbled, trying to gather her wits. "Bye, Brietta."

"Bye, Layla. See ya, Quin."

"See ya," he returned, guiding Layla out of the café.

As they walked to her car, he remained remarkably close without actually touching her, and his gaze rarely left her long enough to look where he was going. When they crossed the street, one of his palms lightly touched the small of her back, shooting tingles up her spine and vibrating her shoulders. She was sure he felt her tremble, but he didn't mention the ridiculous reaction.

"How long have you been in Oregon?" he asked.

"Yesterday," she answered.

"Not very long then. Have you seen anything you like?"

She looked up, blushing as she met his stare. "Yes. I've enjoyed everything, even the drive from Idaho. I took a detour to the Columbia Gorge Scenic Highway and stopped at Multnomah Falls. Then I hit Crown Point at sunset. It was amazing—looking out at the gorge as the sky changed colors. Portland's nice, too. There's tons of stuff to do, but I'm not used to crowded, one-way streets and no parking." She paused her nervous rambling, embarrassed. "Anyway, I'm sure you've seen it all a million times, but I think it's fantastic."

"It's a fantastic state," he agreed. "Have you seen anything else of interest?"

"Well, I walked around downtown Portland for about five hours today, so I saw more than I can recount."

As they approached her car, she hit the unlock button on her key-ring, and Quin took a big step, opening her door.

"Oh," she breathed. "Thanks."

"You're welcome. What did you think of Multnomah?"

She forced herself to maintain eye contact, smiling despite her flushed cheeks. "It was fantastic," she answered. Then she slid into the driver's seat, trying to remember if a guy had ever opened a car door for her. The limo driver at her mom's funeral. That was it. Until now.

Quin opened the passenger door and climbed in. "We're only a few blocks from a beachside parking lot," he said, glancing at the stuffed backseat. "Since we're here to get your coat, we might as well drive. Take a right out of here and follow the signs advertising Haystack Rock."

"Will we see it?"

"Yep. So you've only been in Oregon for two days, right? Including the drive in."

"Right."

"And you've seen downtown Portland, the Columbia River Gorge Scenic Highway, the Sunset Highway, and Cannon Beach."

"Yes. Now I'm visiting the Pacific Ocean for the first time in my life."

He smiled, exposing killer dimples. "Really?"

"Yes. I've seen the east coast a few times, but I've never been this far west."

"You've been busy, Layla. Do you always do a lot in a little amount of time?"

"I don't know. It didn't seem like a lot. Maybe I accomplished more because I didn't have anything slowing me down."

"Like what?" he asked, flipping through her CDs.

"I was by myself," she answered.

"Other people slow you down?"

"Well," she mumbled, flustered by his interpretation, "it always slows things down when there are others to consider. I'm on my own, running my own schedule."

"Is that how you like it?"

"Not necessarily, but that's what I'm used to." She cleared her throat, quickly changing the subject. "Have you always lived in Oregon?"

"Yes. Well, I moved to Alaska for about a year when I was a baby, but other than that, yes."

"Same town?"

"Same place, same house."

Layla threw him a sideways glance. "You still live with your parents?"

"I do. Does that worry you?"

"May I ask why?"

"Because I don't need to move," he answered. "I have a great relationship with my parents and all the freedom and privacy I want. Until I have a reason to go, I'll stay."

"You guys don't get on each other's nerves and fight about petty stuff? Like most families?"

"We don't fight," he claimed.

"Ever?"

"Nope."

"That's unusual."

"Maybe," he conceded, "but it's always been that way for me. I'll move out when I need to. In the mean time, I enjoy living at home."

If he was telling the truth, sincerely unashamed that he enjoyed his parents' company, Layla found that he lived with them endearing.

"Liz Story?" he asked, holding up one of her CDs.

Layla looked over, cheeks flushing. "She's a pianist."

"I know," Quin replied. "She plays beautifully. I'm just surprised to find her in your selection. Have you heard George Winston's *Autumn* album?"

Layla looked over, baffled by his knowledge of American pianist. Then she reached out, pushing play on her George Winston CD.

"Guess that's a yes," Quin said, returning her music to her center console. "Do you play?"

"I wish," Layla replied, "but I had too much going on to squeeze lessons in as a child, and I didn't want to learn if I couldn't devote myself to it. You?"

"A little," he answered, pointing out her turn, "but I'm by no means devoted."

After parking next to the beach, Layla grabbed her coat and exited the car, determined not to sit around long enough for him to open her door. She slipped the jacket on as she walked around the bumper. Then she paused at the open passenger door, curiously tilting her head.

He'd removed his shoes and was tucking them in a black leather bag tied to his waistband. When he straightened, he ran his gaze from her head to her toes.

"You should leave your shoes in the car," he suggested.

"We haven't made it to the sand," she objected.

Quin ignored her protest and knelt, undertaking the task himself. "Lift your foot," he instructed, patting the top of her right shoe.

Oh—my—god. This beautiful man was removing her stinky shoes and socks. "I can do that, you know," she challenged.

"Just lift your foot," he returned, grinning up at her.

She reluctantly obeyed, blushing like mad as he slipped off her shoe. His hand slid over her ankle, and she rolled her eyes at the sky, refusing to look as he searched for the top of her sock. When his fingertips brushed her leg, her heart raced and her throat swelled.

"Here," he said, laying her sock flat on the cement, "stand on this while I get the other one."

Layla did as she was told. "The ground's freezing," she pressed.

"You won't be on it for long," he countered, removing her other shoe, and Layla furrowed her eyebrows, wondering what he meant.

Once she was barefoot and standing on two socks, he straightened, sweeping her off her feet as he rose. By the time she found her wits, she was cradled against his chest, her flaming face a mere inch from his. She barely breathed, ignoring the lump in her throat lest he notice her gulp it down.

She'd never met anyone like him, an extraordinarily gorgeous gentleman, and she couldn't believe he was holding her in his arms on a beach in Oregon. The moment was surreal, something a person reads about in books or sees on movies, but never actually experiences, yet here she was. Unless she was having a vivid and fantastic dream.

"Put your arms around my neck," he instructed.

"What?" she squeaked, eyes widening.

"Hold on to my neck so I can pick up your socks."

Layla hesitantly wrapped her arms around his neck, taking a big, shaky breath filled with his earthy scent—leather, amber and cedar… and a hint of citrus.

She barely felt movement as he tossed her discarded footwear into the passenger seat and closed the door.

"How are your feet?" he asked, returning his arm to her back.

Layla lightly cleared her throat as she reluctantly loosened her grip. "Chilly, but tolerable."

"Tell me if that changes," he insisted, leaving her car behind.

Despite the fact that he was barefoot and never looked where he was going, he navigated over rocks with ridiculous ease. "You're stunning, Layla," he noted, like it was something people said every day. "And the longer I look at you, the more beautiful you become."

Layla tried to maintain eye contact, but couldn't.

"You're not used to compliments," he concluded.

"No," she confessed, looking back up. "Not ones like that."

"That's too bad," he scowled, but then he raised his eyebrows. "We'll have to change that."

Layla's cheeks flamed, and he grinned, overtly amused by her embarrassment. "Should I keep carrying you?" he asked.

Layla looked down, surprised to see sand. "I'll walk. Until my feet succumb to frostbite."

"I'll warm them up when I give you a ride back," he offered, lowering her legs.

Layla smiled and wiggled her feet into silky smooth sand, receiving a chill when the freezing silt slipped between her toes. It felt wonderful despite the cold, or perhaps because of it. "Now I see why you told me to leave my shoes in the car," she conceded, walking toward the water. "This feeling is definitely worth the shock."

"I think so, too," he approved. "Everyone should try it at least once."

They quickly approached the high tide line, outlined by lumps of dark kelp, so they halted, looking out at the turbulent ocean. The sun had fallen beyond a line of deep purple clouds, a mere sliver of electric orange peeking from stormy depths, and Haystack Rock—a towering basalt monolith—was cast in pitch black shadows, contrasting beautifully with the colorful horizon.

"Wow," Layla breathed, grabbing her ponytail so the wind would stop toying with it.

"We missed the final plunge," Quin noted. "You would have had a more detailed view ten minutes ago."

"It doesn't matter," Layla replied. "This is perfect. Well," she added, wrinkling her nose, "a little fishy."

Quin smiled and breathed deep. "Can't avoid that. You'll want to be careful if you come here alone. Keep your eyes peeled for sneaker waves and debris. It's common for entire trees to wash up."

"Sounds dangerous," Layla mumbled, looking east for the moon, but she couldn't find it through the clouds.

"It can be," Quin confirmed, tucking his hands in his pockets.

Layla looked back to the horizon, watching the sun's final flicker fade into the sea. Then Quin's voice broke through the chorus of crashing waves.

"Why did you move to Oregon, Layla?"

She abandoned the ocean view, tilting her head back to find a better one. In the dark, Quin's eyes were like shiny, onyx marbles framed by black velvet lashes. "I heard it's a nice place to live," she answered, short of breath.

"Where were you living?" he asked.

"Oklahoma."

"That's a long way away. Don't you have people there who'll miss you?"

"Sure. My friends Travis and Phyllis will miss me."

"No family?"

"No."

His forehead creased, but he didn't press for an explanation. "Still, that's a big leap of faith—moving halfway across the country for no reason."

"Is it not a leap of faith even if you have a reason?" she countered.

He pulled his right hand from his pocket and slowly reached up, halting an inch from her face. Then he moved his fingers to a spiral that had escaped her ponytail. "I guess it would be. Did you have a reason?"

"I wanted to get out of Oklahoma," she answered, more enraptured by him than the world's largest ocean.

"And you heard Oregon was nice," he returned, raising a skeptical eyebrow.

Layla chewed her lip, wondering how much she should divulge. Then she took another leap of faith. "I recently found out I have family here."

"There it is," he approved. "Are you here to see them?"

"Um . . . not really. I don't know their names, let alone their addresses, so I'll probably never meet them. It was just time for a move, and Oregon was as good a place as any." She glanced at the ocean then back to his face. "Better actually."

They silently watched each other for several seconds, Layla's heart beating madly as Quin wrapped a curl around his finger, sending chills through her scalp. When goose bumps tickled her spine, she shivered, and her cheeks flamed as she tore her gaze from his.

"What about you?" she asked. "Do you have family here? Besides your mom and dad?"

"I have a very large family," he answered.

"That's nice."

"I think so."

Layla liked that he spoke politely about his family. She felt it spoke volumes about his maturity. "Do you work anywhere?" she asked. "Besides the café?"

He laughed, and Layla grinned at the sand, wondering how such a strong man could sound so sweet.

"I work with my parents," he answered. "You could say we're contractors, but we also design and decorate the spaces we construct."

"The whole nine yards, huh? Did you go to college for that?"

"No. I've been involved in the business my entire life. After I graduated high school, my parents made me a partner."

"Do you like it?"

"Sure. It's creative work, and I get all the days off I want."

"That is a perk," she laughed. "Do you think that's what you'll always do?"

"Unless something better comes along. What about you? Do you have a career?"

Embarrassed by her answer, Layla looked away. "No. I was a waitress for three years before moving. Not a career waitress, a diner waitress."

"Did you like it?"

"I didn't hate it. I worked with the friends I mentioned—Travis and Phyllis, so it was a pretty easygoing atmosphere."

"It helps to like the people you work with."

She nodded her agreement. Then there was another lull in the conversation, but Layla soon swept the uncomfortable silence away. At least she found it uncomfortable. He seemed content just staring at her. "I haven't asked what your last name is," she remembered.

"Kavanagh," he answered, "with a K."

"How old are you, Quinlan Kavanagh?"

"I turned twenty-two last Saturday. You?"

"I turned twenty-one on the third."

"Happy late birthday," he offered.

"You, too," she returned.

He gently pulled his forefinger from her hair then took her cheek in his large palm. "Do you have to go back to Portland tonight?"

Layla swallowed, trying to breathe evenly. "If I want to sleep, I do."

"My aunt owns an inn here," he revealed, "right down the street. She would gladly give you a free room."

"I don't want to impose."

"You wouldn't be," he insisted. "You'd be doing me a favor."

"How so?"

"I want to see you tomorrow."

Layla's heart stuttered then raced. "Um . . ." She didn't want to seem too willing, but the idea of seeing him again was her idea of heaven. Besides, she was dreading the dark and curvy drive back to Portland. "Okay, but I'm paying for the room."

"That's not necessary," he assured.

"Yes it is," she argued. "I won't stay otherwise."

"If you must," he caved, "but she's going to give you a discount."

"Fine," Layla sighed, feigning annoyance.

Quin laughed as he glanced at her car. "I guess you have clothes with you?"

"Everything I own is in there," she confirmed.

"If you're missing something, we can stop by one of the shops."

Layla offered him a knowing grin. "That won't be necessary."

"I'm going to try one more time," he quietly persisted, moving a little closer. "Then I'll give it a rest. Will you let me buy you breakfast at *Cinnia's* in the morning?"

Layla didn't have to think too hard about that one. "Throw in a cup of coffee and it's a deal."

Quin's dimples deepened, and Layla stared at them for a long moment before looking to his eyes. What she found in their dark depths captured her undivided attention, and the rest of the world melted away. Until a damn yawn obstructed the gorgeous view.

"Ready for your ride back?" he asked, reaching into his bag.

Layla didn't want the night to end, but the thought of seeing him in the morning made it easier. Plus, her feet were freezing, so she nodded her agreement.

In the blink of an eye he'd swept her into a cradle hold. Then he knelt, bracing her weight on his knee as he wrapped her feet in a piece of black velvet, which was the same temperature as his body—weirdly warm in a wonderful way.

Layla knew she must look like a fool as she gawked at his handy work, but she was blown away by his oddly thorough and romantic demeanor. By the time she shook her dumb expression away, he was lithely carrying her across the beach, watching her face instead of his path.

Quin showed Layla to his aunt's seaside inn then dug her largest suitcase from her trunk, carrying it through a wide, wooden arch into a quiet lobby.

A tall, slender woman occupied the stool behind the desk, absorbed in a leather bound book, and she, like everyone else Layla had met that evening, was incredibly beautiful. What's with this place, Layla wondered, feeling like she'd stumbled into a secret commune of models.

"Hey, Quin," the woman greeted, barely glancing up. Then she did a double-take, snapping her book shut as she scanned Layla from head to toe.

"Dion," Quin returned. "This is Layla. She needs a room for the night."

"Sure," Dion murmured, blindly picking out a room key. "Nice to meet you, Layla."

"You, too," Layla offered, wondering why everyone looked at her weird when they were the anomalies.

Dion's intrigued gaze never wavered as she handed the key across the desk. "Room 203."

"She insists on paying," Quin said, taking the key, "but she'll accept a discount."

"Oh," Dion mumbled. "Thirty dollars?"

Layla dug into her bag, coming out with two twenties. "Keep the change. I know these rooms are more than forty dollars."

Dion threw Quin a glance then placed the money in the till. "Need anything else?"

"Yeah," Quin answered, pointing behind the counter. "Do you have one of Morrigan's CDs back there?"

Layla looked at him in confusion, but apparently Dion knew what he was talking about, because she swiveled on her stool and opened a drawer of CDs. "Here it is," she said, passing him a plain white case with the name Morrigan hand-written across the front.

"Great," he approved, smiling at Layla. "Ready?"

Layla nodded and waved goodbye to Dion. Then she followed Quin to the second level.

"Who's Morrigan?" she asked, pointing at the CD.

"The best pianist I've heard play," he answered, unlocking room 203.

Layla's mouth fell open. "And you *know* her?"

"Yep," he confirmed, holding the door open.

Layla entered the room and slowly spun in a circle, scanning the tidy yet cozy décor. With its high ceiling and unique furnishings, the elaborate space felt more like a master bedroom than a hotel room.

"Is Dion your aunt?" she asked, admiring the framed art work.

"No," he answered, laying her suitcase and room key on the bed. Then he walked to a corner desk, propping Morrigan's CD against a stereo. "My aunt's name is Karena. She tries to avoid working nights. What time would you like breakfast?"

Layla looked at the clock—half past eight. And it would undoubtedly take her a while to fall asleep. "How about nine?"

"Great," he agreed, showing himself out. Once he was in the hallway, he turned and pointed toward the threshold. "I'll be here at 8:45."

"I'll be ready," she replied, stunned by the night's events. She felt like she was dreaming. Perhaps she was. Maybe she'd still be in Portland when she woke up. As she watched Quin's alert and shiny eyes, she sincerely hoped not.

"Goodnight, Layla Callaway," he whispered.

"Goodnight, Quinlan Kavanagh," she returned.

He grinned and reached for the doorknob, giving her a heart-melting wink as he shut himself out.

Quin stared at Layla's closed door for a long time before walking away, trying to absorb and accept reality. Not an easy thing to do when reality had once seemed impossible.

The further away he traveled, the quicker his steps became, his muscles tense and edgy as he leaped over a railing and down the stairwell. He had no idea how this would play out, which pissed him off. One wrong move and she could flee.

He was within sight of the front desk, but he didn't slow down.

"What's going on, Quin?" Dion asked. "Who is she?"

"She's harmless," he assured. "But you need to keep this meeting to yourself. If she leaves, call me. See you tomorrow." Then he was out the door.

He looked around, finding the parking lot deserted, so he dug into the bag at his waist, pulling out a black velvet cloak much larger than the satchel from which it came. Within seconds he was bathed in black, practically invisible. Then he shot into the air on wings of magic.

A profusion of thoughts swarmed his head as he flew northeast, and he paid close attention to all of them, determined to handle the situation as wisely as possible.

He knew it was her as soon as she said her name; though he'd already been clued in by her honey voice and astounding beauty. Further questioning was unnecessary, but on this he couldn't be negligent, so he'd found out more, and all of it fit. After twenty-one years of silence, Layla had returned.

Quin had been dreaming about the mysterious Layla his entire life, but his dream Layla never had a face, just a magnificent blur of beautiful colors. The real Layla's face did not disappoint. Exceeding even his greatest expectations, her heavenly visage soared beyond the realm of imagination.

Quin's thoughts drifted to the past, to his earliest recollections of the dreams—a comforting rainbow of soothing hues with a lovely little voice that couldn't enunciate words. As he got older, he overheard his parents talk about Layla and somehow knew they were one and the same—his dream girl and the lost girl. When her musical coos became enchanting words, she confirmed her identity, and from then on he called her Layla.

In more recent years, she'd wreaked havoc on his sex life. Understandably, his dates didn't like him mumbling another woman's name in his sleep. But while other women came and went, his dream girl remained. He and his mysterious Layla grew up together, and more than anything else, the visions were a source of comfort in times of need.

Bringing his mind out of dreamland, Quin recalled the moments he'd spent with the real Layla; the way he'd reached out, half-expecting his fingers to move through her like they had in the visions, finding instead soft skin and silky spirals. He'd been mesmerized by the reddening of her pink cheeks when she blushed, and the flutter of long lashes over big, round, emerald eyes. She was perfection in the flesh, yet she clearly believed herself inadequate. She had no idea how beautiful she was. She had no idea what she was.

Quin closed his eyes, remembering how it felt to hold her in his arms, and his stomach flipped and knotted. He'd never been more determined, nervous or concerned. One error in judgment could destroy more than his dreams. Others were at risk.

The image of Layla's smiling face blessed the backs of his eyelids, but he needed to focus, so he tried to shake the stunning vision away. It didn't work, and he smiled, realizing her face was there to stay, eyes open or shut.

His home came into view, and he sobered, descending into a large clearing thickly surrounded by trees and dotted with houses. His entire coven was on the lawn, awaiting his arrival, and two of them—Caitrin and Morrigan Conn—rushed forward when he landed.

Caitrin was the first to speak, his deep voice lacking its usual serenity. "Is it true, Quinlan? Is she here?"

"She's here," Quin confirmed, dropping his hood, "at the inn."

Morrigan sobbed and wrapped her arms around Caitrin's waist, burying her face in his chest. "I can't believe it. She's here. She's finally here."

"I can't believe it either," Caitrin whispered, stroking Morrigan's curly hair. "Hope waned with each passing year." He rested his cheek on her head, anxiously meeting Quin's stare. "What did you discover?"

"Her name's Layla Callaway," Quin answered. "She just moved here by herself from Oklahoma and says she didn't leave a family behind."

Morrigan's emotional sobs paused as Caitrin's eyes narrowed. "She didn't mention a mom?" he asked.

"No," Quin answered, "just two friends she worked with. She confesses to having family here—says she recently found out about them—but she lacks names and addresses, so she doesn't expect to meet them." He paused, bowing his head as he pulled a deep breath into his tight chest, unnerved and awakened to feel such heartache for a woman he barely knew. "She's been through a hard time, Caitrin. She didn't say it, so I don't know what's happened, but I can tell she's struggling. She's sad and insecure, and she's spent too much time alone. It's what she's used to. We'll have to be careful not to scare her. You need to alert Serafin right away."

"Yes," Caitrin agreed, urging Morrigan from his chest. "How's my sweet peach?"

Morrigan straightened, trying to pull herself together. "I'm fine. Better than fine. I'm thrilled, but we can't mess this up. It will kill me."

Caitrin took her cheeks, touching the tip of his nose to hers. "We'll do everything in our power, Morrigan. I promise. Why don't you go phone Daleen? Tell her everything we know so far."

"Okay," Morrigan agreed, standing on her toes for a kiss. Then she soared across the lawn.

Caitrin watched her go then turned back, clearly agitated. "How are we going to do this?"

"I have no idea," Quin replied. "Has anyone here ever told the hexless what we are?"

Caitrin's niece, Enid Gilmore, spoke as she stepped from the nearby crowd. "I told a friend in high school."

"How?" Caitrin asked.

"I just told her," Enid answered. "Then I made a matchbook disappear."

"How did she take it?"

"She left the room and never spoke to me again."

The idea of watching Layla walk away made Quin nauseous. "Anybody else?" he asked, and his Grandpa Lann stepped forward.

"I told a college professor," he confessed, "after we polished off a bottle of absinthe together. I even turned his schnauzer blue, but he woke up in a stupor and thought he'd dreamed it all. I never corrected him."

Quin's twitchy hands clenched into fists. None of this was helping. He looked to the eldest member of the coven, his great-grandfather, Catigern Kavanagh. "What about you, Grandpa Cat?"

Catigern walked forward, running a hand through his salt and pepper hair as he spoke. "There's no easy way to tell the secret. I've heard many stories—most of them ending like dear Enid's . . ."

Quin and Caitrin cringed.

"But the elements of Enid's tale are quite different than those spinning this one," Catigern continued. "Layla's by no means average, and let's not ignore how remarkable it is she's here. That suggests she's accepted her adoption, among other things, so we shouldn't underestimate her acceptance of us. Our best option is to take the plunge and hope we surface without losing her. Skillful honesty and profound patience will be vital."

The lawn was silent for a long moment as everyone contemplated the consequences and benefits of taking the plunge. Then Caitrin swallowed and cleared his throat. "She should be given the chance to come to terms with what she is before meeting everyone."

"I agree," Quin advocated, "and we need to make it safe for her to take that time. What's the latest news on Agro?"

"He was spreading terror in the Allegheny Mountains two months ago," Caitrin answered, "murdered a pregnant hexless woman. That's the last anyone's heard."

"We need to make sure his dogs aren't lurking," Quin pressed. "If Layla crosses paths with the Unforgivables . . ."

"I know," Caitrin quietly growled. Then he took a calming breath and searched out Lann. "Do you mind making some phone calls, Lann? Map out the Unforgivables' movements the best you can. And get in touch with all of our contacts in Oregon and Washington; make sure they haven't caught wind of Agro or his miscreants."

"I'll do my best," Lann agreed, squeezing Caitrin's shoulder. Then he glanced at Quin, momentarily meeting his thoughtful stare.

As Lann flew away, Morrigan returned, alighting next to Caitrin and taking his hand. "They're leaving now," she said. "We can expect them tomorrow night."

Caitrin nodded his approval then looked at Quin. "You're seeing her tomorrow?"

"I'm taking her to *Cinnia's* for breakfast," Quin confirmed.

Caitrin stood quite still, contemplating his course, and not a soul interrupted or rushed him. After several minutes of deliberation, he kissed Morrigan's hand and looked at Quin. "Are you willing to tell her?"

Quin didn't have the slightest idea how to do it, let alone do it right, but he couldn't turn down the delicate task. Having no control over the outcome would drive him crazy. "Yes."

As soon as he answered, an objection rang out. "Wait a minute."

Quin looked over, unsurprised to find his parents, Kemble and Cordelia, walking toward him.

"I'm not sure that's the best idea," Kemble went on, stopping next to Caitrin.

The entire coven knew about Quin's reoccurring dream. And if they were looking at him closely, which most of them were, they would undoubtedly notice that Layla had already left her mark on him.

Quin understood their concerns; they were his own, but his apprehension didn't merit submission. "I'm not sure it's the best idea either," he confessed, "but I'm not going to refuse. If Caitrin's willing to let me do it, I wholeheartedly accept."

"She needs levelheaded support right now," Kemble countered, "not a boyfriend."

"I understand," Quin replied. And he did. He'd already considered everything running through his dad's head. "I know why you doubt me . . ."

"No, Quinlan," Cordelia interrupted, "we don't doubt you."

"It's okay, Mom. Your concerns are justified given the situation, but I'm very aware of them and have treaded as conscientiously as possible around her." He met his dad's searching stare. "Believe me, the last thing I want to do is scare her away."

"I know," Kemble replied, "but perhaps someone else . . ."

"Who?" Quin challenged. "She already knows who I am, and she trusts me enough to be alone with me. It wasn't easy getting her to relax. Ask Bri."

Everyone on the lawn looked at Brietta, who nodded. "It's true," she confirmed. "She was very skittish."

"And she remained guarded the entire time," Quin added. "A stranger with no apparent motivation for speaking to her would only scare her. She would be hesitant to accept anything they say." He paused, glanced at Caitrin then back to his dad. "I know a relationship would complicate things for her right now, but her interest in me is the only reason she agreed to stay in Cannon Beach. I don't like the idea of abusing her attraction, but it's the only leverage we have." The more he defended his point, the more he believed it.

Kemble remained skeptical, but Quin had convinced his great grandpa Catigern. "Quinlan's right," he advocated. "He's in the best position to break it to her gently."

Kemble didn't respond or relax. He just watched Quin's face and the air around him, thoughtful and concerned.

"If Caitrin will let me do this," Quin firmly decided, "I'm going to do it." He turned to Caitrin, looking between him and Morrigan. "And I'll do everything I can to make it easy on everyone involved, particularly Layla."

"I know you will," Caitrin quietly replied, pulling Morrigan's hand to his cheek. "Let us know if you need anything, and keep us updated on any unforeseen changes."

Quin nodded, glanced at his parents then walked away, already focused on his purpose.

"Quinlan," Caitrin called.

"Yeah?" Quin replied, turning back.

"You said she's sad, but…" Caitrin paused, clutching his throat as he watched the ground. "How does she look?"

Quin stared at him for a moment, remembering, seeing. Then he smiled. "She's beautiful, Caitrin, like a star in a storm. You won't be disappointed."

That night—the first night of the rest of Quin's life—peaceful rest was an elusive dream. Between snippets of exhaustion in which he'd have visions of the real Layla, he was alert and brainstorming ways to tell her the truth. None of his ideas were good enough, none of them fail safe, and it pissed him off that he couldn't guarantee an acceptable outcome.

He deeply feared her reaction to the confessions he'd make the following day; for not only would he reveal he knows her family, he'd reveal she descends from a powerful line of witches and wizards.

Chapter 9

Layla huffed and tossed a t-shirt across the bed then delved further into her suitcase, which lacked anything date-worthy.

She froze, stomach flipping. Was this a date? It seemed like a date. *Blah!*

She threw her hands in the air and sat on the bed, squeezing her eyes shut and counting to twenty. She wasn't used to feeling hot and bothered and needed to get a grip. She wasn't a school girl getting ready for prom. She was a grown woman going to breakfast with a handsome man. A very handsome man.

Her eyes popped open as she grabbed a pair of dark jeans, a white v-neck shirt, and the necklace Travis and Phyllis gave her. At least she had pretty jewelry to wear with her bland outfit.

After getting dressed, she looked in the mirror. Yes, the clothes were plain, but the platinum chain and emerald mawsitsit contrasted nicely with the white shirt.

She didn't own any makeup, so that was done, and she was leaving her hair down, so she ran her fingers through it and slipped a ponytail holder around her wrist. The waist-length spirals were hard to maintain, becoming a tangled mess more often than not, but she refused to cut them short. A weird quirk, she knew, but she'd been born with it, objecting to haircuts from the first attempt. According to her mom, she'd been a year old and cried harder than ever before when they snipped that first curl.

After looking in the mirror one more time, sighing hopelessly at the mundane outfit, Layla moved to the bed to clean her mess. As she shoved the last of the clothes in her suitcase, someone knocked on the door.

Her reaction was instantaneous and ridiculous—heart racing, palms moistening, cheeks burning. "Act your age," she hissed, slipping on a gray, button-up sweater. Then she exhaled and walked to the door, boldly swinging it open.

For the tiniest moment, Quin looked worried, but a smile quickly stretched from one dimple to the other. "Good morning," he greeted, eyes roaming from her head to her toes. "That necklace looks great on you."

"It's a pretty necklace," she replied, touching the gem.

He reached up, moving her fingers from the stone to her clavicle. "The necklace is lovely because you're wearing it. It's not wearing you."

Their fingertips quivered over her rapid pulse as heat flushed her entire body. "Thank you."

He dropped his hand, clearing his throat as he flexed his fingers. "Are you hungry?"

Layla waited as long as she dared before answering, trying to strengthen everything—nerve, knees, voice. "Yes," she replied, thrilled it came out clearly. "Let me get my bag."

"Leave it," he suggested. "Aunt Karena's having a two-for-one special this weekend."

"Is that right?" Layla smirked.

For so long Quin wondered what it would be like to kiss the mysterious Layla. As he watched her mouth, the urge to find out grew. "That's right," he returned. "It would be a shame to let it go to waste."

"Never mind the room going to waste in Portland," she countered.

She was *so* stubborn. He liked it. "We could check you out of that hotel and book this room for the week." He could be stubborn, too.

"Um . . ." she hesitated, glancing over her shoulder. "I'd prefer to start the day off with coffee."

He grinned and reached around her, grabbing her backpack off an entryway table. "Of course you would. Leave your luggage," he insisted, taking her hand. "If you want to go back to Portland later, it will still be here." Without waiting for her approval, he closed the door and led her down the corridor.

The café was only a few blocks away, so they walked, hand in hand —her watching the window displays as he watched her.

"It embarrasses you that I'm holding your hand," he concluded.

She met his stare for the first time since he'd taken it. "I'm not used to it," she confessed. "It's nice, though, just… a little weird."

"Why is it weird?"

"Because we just met. Most guys don't ever make this kind of gesture, let alone make it this early."

"What kind of gesture do you think it is?"

Damn. She was on the spot and her own mouth put her there. What if what she thought it meant was way off base? "Well," she weakly explained, "I see holding hands as a way to show you care about someone and want to keep them close."

He smiled. "That's an excellent way to put it."

"Then you see why I find it weird."

"No."

She sighed. "Really?"

"Really," he repeated. "It makes perfect sense."

She watched him for a long moment then looked at the sidewalk. "I've never met anyone like you, Quin. Most guys dodge their feelings, embarrassed to have them, let alone express them."

"I was raised differently."

"Hmm…" she mumbled. "It's refreshing." And unnerving and embarrassing and it made her feel all tingly inside. She lifted his hand, staring at their entwined fingers. "So you want to keep me close?"

He grinned. "You haven't noticed my attempts to keep you at my aunt's inn?"

She stopped walking, bringing him to a halt as well. "You're serious," she decided, slowly scanning his casually humored expression.

"Why wouldn't I be?" he asked.

Her face was hot again, so she looked down. "Why me, Quin? Why are you holding my hand?"

He reached out and took her chin, raising her gaze back to his. "You're the most beautiful woman I've ever met, Layla. I don't know you very well, but so far you're friendly, witty and wonderfully stubborn. Now you're blessing me with a chance to discover more, a chance I consider myself lucky to have, so if you're willing to let me keep you close by holding your hand, that's what I'm going to do."

Layla searched for signs of dishonesty, finding none, and her heart constricted then swelled. "Okay," she whispered.

He smiled and squeezed her hand. "Okay?"

"Yeah," she confirmed, trying to find her lungs, but she was experiencing so many new and unusual sensations, her vital organs struggled to keep up. She wondered if she was finally going through that raging hormonal faze she managed to skip as a teenager.

"Excellent," Quin approved, compelling her to walk. "So did you listen to Morrigan's CD?"

"Yes," Layla beamed, forgetting about her insecurities and worries. "It's amazing. Do you really know that woman?"

"Very well. I'll introduce you some time."

"I wouldn't know what to say," Layla countered. "It would be like meeting a rock star. Why haven't I heard of her?"

"She doesn't play professionally," Quin explained, leading her across the café deck, "just in her spare time."

"That's a shame," Layla replied, catching a whiff of the world's best coffee. "She's incredibly talented."

"I'll tell her you said so," he offered, holding the door open.

Apparently Quin was popular around the café, because the moment they entered, a male clerk waved them over. He was average in height, but brawny in build, and his light blonde hair was close-cropped, accentuating his bulky frame. He energetically drummed his hands on the bar, flashing a bright smile that pinched his cheeks and stretched into sparkling blue eyes.

When Quin and Layla approached, the clerk ceased his drum roll, but remained lively. "Hey."

"Hey," Quin returned. "This is Layla."

The clerk stretched his arm across the counter. "Nice to meet you, Layla. Banning Gilmore, but you can call me Bann."

As Layla accepted his hand, an odd tingle shot up her arm, but she hid her surprise well, not flexing her fingers until he'd released them. "Nice to meet you, too, Bann."

"Do you know what you want?" Quin asked, keeping his eyes on Layla's face as he leaned on the counter. "Besides coffee, of course."

"Of course," she replied, staring at his smirking lips. Then she tore her gaze away to scan the breakfast menu.

After taking their order, Banning disappeared into the kitchen, and Quin moved around the counter, helping himself to coffee while suggesting Layla pick a table. She chose the same corner she had the night before, sitting with her back to the wall, so it was like déjà vu when Quin sat across from her.

"You like this table," he noted.

"It brought me luck," she divulged, watching him add the perfect amount of cream and sugar to her coffee.

"I like that," he confessed, sliding her cup over.

"What?" she asked.

"That you found it lucky to meet me."

She smiled. "How do you know I wasn't referring to the discounted room at the inn?"

"Now you're breaking my heart," he feigned, lifting a hand to his chest.

Layla laughed then sipped her sublime brew. "I have to admit, it wasn't the room."

"No?"

"No." She raised her cup. "I *really* like coffee."

"I almost believe that," he laughed.

"You're wondering."

"About a lot of things," he confirmed. Then Banning appeared with a tray.

"That was fast," Layla noted, looking down at the sliced apple fanned out beside a perfect stack of pancakes. "Thanks."

"Sure," Banning replied. "Give me a shout if you need anything else."

"Okay," Layla agreed, and Banning returned to the counter, offering coffee refills along the way.

"He's nice," Layla said, watching him go.

"He's a good kid," Quin agreed.

"How old is he?"

"Seventeen."

"Really?"

"Yeah, but it's close enough to his birthday to round up." He paused, glancing over his shoulder. "Does he look older? He'd love to know that."

"He acts older," Layla explained. "All the seventeen-year-old guys I went to school with were more interested in booze and sex than anything else. Working the early shift on a Saturday was their idea of hell."

Quin frowned. "A lot of people choose unwisely when first given the freedom to. You need experience to learn the true value of your priorities."

"But then it's too late," she observed. "You've missed your chance to do it right, to spend your time wisely."

"Until the next time," he agreed, thoughtfully searching her face. "Is there something you missed?"

"As a teenager?" she asked.

"Sure."

"No. I was right where I wanted to be."

"And where was that?"

Layla's fork lay idle as she watched his move around his plate. "Oklahoma," she eventually answered.

"Oklahoma," he repeated.

She nodded her confirmation, and he grinned. "Clever."

Layla watched him eat, waiting for him to insist she elaborate on her clever answer, but he didn't, so she went back to her pancakes.

When Quin's plate was nearly empty, he motioned to hers. "I thought you were hungry."

"I was."

"You ate two pancakes and an apple."

"That's two pancakes more than I usually eat for breakfast."

"So you run on coffee."

"If only it were that easy."

He laughed, took another bite then set his fork down. A few seconds later, Banning appeared, gathering the dirty dishes and balancing them in one large hand. "I'll refill your coffee," he offered, gathering their cups.

Once he walked away, Quin leaned forward. "Will you be blessing me with your company for a while longer?"

He seemed nervous, which was odd considering he was the most confident man Layla had ever met, and for good reason. He was handsome, polite and extremely charming. "I don't have any plans," she answered, fidgeting with a napkin holder, "so if you have one, I'm in."

"I don't have a plan," he confessed, "but whatever I do will be more enjoyable with your company."

"Then I guess we need a plan."

"I guess we do. Anything in particular you'd like to see in Cannon Beach?"

"Not really. You're the local. Fill me in on the secrets."

"Secrets," he mumbled, leaning back in his chair as he ran a hand over his jaw. "So you're leaning away from tourist traps."

"I'd like to take advantage of the inside knowledge while it's available," she confirmed. "I can follow the brochures anytime."

"That's wise," he agreed, contemplating his options. "There's a slice of unspoiled nature about twenty miles away. It's not impressive enough for the tourists, but I like it. Would you like me to show you?"

More than anything, she thought. "Yes."

Banning returned with their coffee, and Layla smiled as she added cream and sugar. "Thanks, Bann."

"My pleasure. Maybe I'll see you again soon."

"You will if you keep serving coffee like this."

"It's been the same for thirty-three years. I doubt it'll change anytime soon."

"Then you'll definitely see me again."

"I look forward to it," he replied, smiling brightly. Then he turned to Quin. "Anything else?"

"Nope," Quin answered, offering Layla his hand. "Ready?"

"Sure," she agreed, and he pulled her to her feet, giving Banning an absent wave as they left the café.

Chapter 10

Barely visible through a looming canopy of branches, the cloudy sky shed little light on the rural road Quin led Layla to. She flipped on her headlights then glanced at him, deciding by his posture that he was uncomfortable riding with her.

"You could have driven," she offered.

He stared at her for a long time before responding. "I don't know how to drive."

"What?" she blurted.

"I don't know how to drive," he repeated.

Layla considered this, realizing she hadn't seen his car, nor had he mentioned one. So how had he gotten home the night before? Unless he stayed at the inn. But he wore different clothes—olive green shorts instead of brown, and his white t-shirt looked freshly laundered. His flip-flops were the same—dark brown and comfortable.

"How do you get around?" she asked.

"I walk a lot."

"Apparently. But how do you travel long distances?"

He didn't answer. He just stared at her for what seemed like ages.

"Take your next right," he instructed, breaking the heavy silence.

She slowed then turned onto a narrow road lined with giant Sitka spruces.

"Keep going on here until you hit a dead end," he added.

She threw him a tentative glance. "Did our conversation hit a dead end?"

"No. There are a lot of things I want to tell you, just not while we're driving."

"Does my driving scare you?"

"No," he laughed, "but I want you to be able to look at me when I tell you."

"Oh." That made perfect sense. "So where is it we're going?"

"It's a clearing," he answered. "There are dozens like it around here, many of them right off the highway, but this one's off the beaten path and undiscovered by tourists."

They were definitely off the beaten path, Layla thought, turning her car around at the dead end. She cut the engine and tossed her keys in her backpack, looking over to find Quin's jaw set.

"You okay?" she asked.

He wasn't. He was a mess of nerves and guilt. Nerves, because a lot of people were counting on him to do this right. And guilt, because he wasn't giving her a way to escape if he did it wrong. She'd have a hard time finding her way back from the clearing without his help.

He forced himself to relax, offering a somewhat dishonest answer. "I'm worried you won't like hiking without a trail." He paused, lips twitching into a smile. "I could carry you again."

"That won't be necessary," she refused, a grin curving from one red cheek to the other. "I'm pretty good at navigating the ground when I have shoes on."

Quin had no doubt. She was extremely graceful. And why wouldn't she be? That was one part of being a witch that needed no training. He tore his gaze from her face and removed his flip-flops, slipping them into his bag.

"Why do you do that?" she asked.

"I'd rather walk on earth than shoes," he answered, watching her gather her hair into a ponytail. "Why do you put your hair up?"

"It will get tangled if I leave it down."

"Hmm . . ." he mumbled, resisting the temptation to touch the contained spirals. "Are you ready?"

She looked him over, stomach fluttering like mad. "Yeah."

Navigating bulging roots, overgrown brush, and reaching tree limbs, Layla proved to be the lithest witch Quin had ever seen. If his stride hadn't been longer than hers, he would have had a difficult time keeping up. Considering her parentage, her astounding grace didn't surprise him, but it did captivate him.

"These trees are insane," she said, tilting her head back. "It's like looking up the side of a skyscraper."

Quin followed her gaze to the treetops. "They're wonderful."

"Yes," Layla agreed, skirting a small patch of yellow wildflowers. Then she sidestepped to avoid a cluster of shelf fungi protruding from a lichen covered tree trunk. She wrinkled her nose at the bright orange conks then glanced at Quin, blushing when she found his eyes.

"So," she mumbled, quickly looking away, "is Karena your only aunt?"

"No. I have two. Karena's my dad's sister, and my mom has a sister in Alaska. But I also have a great aunt."

"Close by?"

"Very close. My dad's entire family lives within five acres of each other."

"How many are there?"

"Sixteen."

Layla stumbled to a standstill. "You live within five acres of sixteen family members?"

"Yes," he confessed, carefully gauging her reaction.

"Wow," she breathed. "I can't imagine what that's like."

Quin took her hand, compelling her to walk. "It's nice. If you need something, there's always someone around to help. Another family shares the property with us, and we're as close to them as we are each other. You've met a few of them."

Her forehead wrinkled, so he elaborated. "Brietta and Banning are the youngest of them—brother and sister. There are six others."

"You share land with twenty-four people?" Layla asked.

"Yes," he answered.

She suddenly halted, narrowing her eyes on him. "You're not part of a cult, are you?"

"No," he laughed, once again urging her forward.

"Is it a religious group?" she pressed.

"No," he assured, "just two families who get along well enough to share land. Do you have a religious affiliation?"

"No," she replied, adamantly shaking her head. "I mean, I've been to church a few times, but organized religion isn't for me. Too much fire and brimstone. I say, as long as you're not hurting people, live how you want to live. Not a popular slogan in the Bible belt. Oklahoma's conservatives are glad to be rid of me."

"It's a good slogan," he commended, looking forward. "We're here."

Layla raised her gaze as they stepped into a small clearing divided in two by a bubbling stream. Springing from a cluster of rocks capping a plant covered escarpment, the water cascaded down slick moss then trickled across the clearing, disappearing into the dark crevices of a cracked boulder.

Layla stood silent and still, opening her senses to the water and birdsong as she watched misty beams of cloudy light flood the forest floor. "It's fantastic," she approved, smiling at her guide. "Very peaceful."

"That's one reason why I like it," he said, digging into his bag. Then he pointed toward a large boulder shaped like a jelly bean, its concaved side conveniently facing the water. "Do you want to sit?"

Layla scanned the thick, green moss carpeting the ground. "Isn't it wet?"

"Yes," Quin confirmed, pulling a compact raincoat from a small plastic pouch. "But I knew that."

"Hmm . . ." Layla smirked, watching him drape the thin plastic over the moss. "Do you always carry a brand new raincoat in your bag?"

"No. I usually get wet."

"How do you keep from freezing?"

He straightened, blatantly staring as she pulled the elastic band from her hair. Then he sat, nestling his back into the boulder's arch.

"It's a trick I learned as a child," he answered, patting the plastic to his left.

"That's all I get?" she objected, sitting next to him.

He flashed a smile as he took her hand. "For now."

Layla laughed as she looked at the creek. "So what else do you like about this place? Besides its peacefulness."

"Pretty much everything," he answered, playing with her fingers as he looked around. "Its undisturbed vegetation tops the list, along with its size and seclusion. With so much natural beauty packed into such a tiny space, you're guaranteed an entrancing view." He paused, looking from the waterfall to her face. "I like that you like it."

Layla's cheeks grew hot, so she dropped her gaze and fidgeted with a lost leaf. Quin remained silent, still playing with her fingers. Then he took her wrist and raised it in the air.

Layla looked over, finding him examining her hand. "What are you doing?" she asked.

"Admiring your hands," he answered.

She wrinkled her nose. "That's kind of weird."

"Why?" he returned. "They're nice to look at."

She skeptically searched her hand, looking for nice features. "They're okay," she decided, "now that I can wear my nails long."

"Why couldn't you wear them long before?"

Damn. Layla should have anticipated the question; he was so damn thorough. But she hadn't; now she was stuck. Unnerved and pressured by his continuous stare, she looked away, anxiously rubbing the side of her neck as she watched a bird hop from branch to branch. She'd never told the story to anyone and wasn't sure she could get through it without making a blubbering fool of herself.

"You don't want to talk about it," Quin concluded.

Layla swallowed, blinking back dreaded moisture. "I . . . I'm not sure how."

"Because it's sad?"

She nodded, still looking away.

"You don't want me to see you cry," he realized.

Layla smirked and looked forward, glad the move didn't jar any tears loose. "Isn't that kind of a buzzkill?"

"Maybe to some," he conceded, "but I ask questions because I want to know you. Why would I fault you for giving me the honor?"

Despite his assurance, Layla didn't want to bawl in front of him, so she took a deep breath before finding his eyes. "I kept my nails short for my mom. She had a stroke the year I graduated high school, and I don't have a dad or siblings or anything, so I took care of her. Until she died… about two months ago." She turned away, wiping her eyes before looking back. "See? Buzzkill…" Her voice trailed off as Quin's forefinger touched her lips.

"No," he countered, lowering his hand. "You made a difficult sacrifice for someone you love—a choice worthy of admiration and respect. I'm sorry you faced such tragedy alone. I can't imagine how much that must have hurt."

"It hurt like hell," she mumbled, licking her tingling pout. Then she cleared her throat and looked at the water. "But life goes on, right? I was a zombie when she was sick, and I got even worse when she died. It took two very good friends to make me realize I hadn't died with her."

"I'm glad you had them."

"Me, too," she agreed, picking up a twig and twirling it through her fingers. "They're the reason I'm getting a guided tour of Oregon from a good-looking guy."

"You think I'm good-looking?" he asked.

"Like you didn't know," she smirked.

"I hoped," he confessed, "but I didn't know."

Layla raised an eyebrow then shrugged. No point in denying the obvious. "I doubt there's a woman out there who wouldn't think you're gorgeous, Quin."

"You're not like other women, Layla."

"What makes you think so?"

"I don't think; I know."

"Yet you claim not to know I find you good-looking."

"That's just one reason why you're different," he explained. "It's obvious when other women find me attractive. With you, I can't be so sure."

"Just mildly sure," she returned, knowing her attraction hadn't gone unnoticed. Maybe she didn't throw herself at him like other women, but there was no way he hadn't figured out why she blushed every time he spoke.

"Sure," he confessed with a grin.

"I'm not a mystery, Quin. I can't help but be obvious."

"Why do you try so hard to avoid it?"

"Why does anyone?"

"Nice sidestep," he noted, dimples deepening.

She puckered and looked at her twig. "You're not the most obvious person either."

He'd been rubbing his thumb over her fingernails, but suddenly stopped, silently watching her for several seconds. Then he laid her palm on his warm knee, covering it with his warm hand. "What do you want to know?" he offered.

Layla boldly met his stare, determined to take advantage. "Do you treat everyone the way you treat me?"

"I'm not sure I understand the question."

"Are you always this polite and vocal about your feelings?"

"I like to think so."

"Then why aren't you married?"

"What?" he laughed.

Layla's gaze remained level as she elaborated. "A polite, good-looking guy who openly expresses how he feels. It reads like a fantasy personal add. I bet there are unattractive jerks everywhere using that line as we speak. So tell me," she insisted, wiggling her hand under his, "why isn't there a ring on your finger?"

He stared at his hand for a moment then found her eyes. "The women I've been with were great, but not what I was looking for."

"Really," she dryly replied. "Within two hours of meeting you, you introduced me to two incredibly beautiful women. I'm going to assume there are more. So what are you waiting for, your soul mate?"

"No," he casually answered. "I'll probably never meet her."

"You think she's out there?"

"Yes."

"You're serious," Layla realized. "You believe in soul mates."

"Yes," he confessed, "but not everyone's destined to find theirs. With work and forgiveness, the love between two people who aren't soul mates can be nearly as beautiful and just as fulfilling." He paused, watching her incredulous expression. "I guess you don't believe."

"I've never seen anything like that."

Quin could feel it coming—the perfect intro to an unusual subject. "There are a lot of things people don't see," he pointed out. "That doesn't mean they don't exist."

"But that's like saying anything's possible," she argued.

Quin's heart skipped a few beats, his free hand flexing as nerves erupted, twitching his entire body. Everything was riding on how he handled the next few minutes. "So you need proof to believe in something," he said, trying to keep his voice casual, but his anxiety was at an all time high.

Layla thought for a moment then nodded. "Yeah. In order for me to say I honestly believe in something, I need proof. I could consider a theory, and find it plausible, but that doesn't equal belief."

"So if I told you I have a pair of jeans at home," he teased, trying to ease his tension, "you wouldn't believe me?"

"Very funny," she laughed, "and completely off subject. Now, if you tell me there's a purple alien staying in your guestroom, we'll be back on track."

"I don't believe in purple aliens," he countered.

Layla tilted her head. "How can you believe in one and not the other?"

"You believe I have jeans, yet you dismiss soul mates."

"I've seen jeans, so I know they exist."

"So it's definite. For you, seeing is believing."

"I would have to say, yes, it's definite." She paused, chewing her lip as she looked down. "That doesn't mean I'm not open to ideas. I like to hear theories and form opinions. I just can't support them without proof, and I won't change my desired lifestyle based on blind faith."

"I think that's a strong and honest point of view," he commended.

"Maybe. Or maybe it's stubborn and contrary." She stopped spinning her twig and looked him in the eye. "What else do you believe in?"

He hesitated, terrified to come right out and say it. "A lot of things. There are a lot of secrets out there."

"But no purple aliens," she added.

"Not that I'm aware of," he confirmed.

She laughed and shook her head. "Okay. So what is out there?"

She'd done it again. She'd given him the perfect intro. After a deep breath, he took the plunge. "How do you feel about magic?"

"What do you mean?"

"Do you believe in magic?" he rephrased, barely breathing as he searched everything about her—face, posture, hands, the air around her.

"Are you asking if I believe magicians really do possess miraculous power?" she asked.

"No," he clarified. "I'm not talking about sleight of hand or smoke and mirrors, which is what you see at public magic shows. I'm talking about real magic. The kind the public doesn't see."

"You're forgetting," she replied, "I need to see to believe."

"Right," he mumbled.

"Do you believe?" she asked.

Quin maintained sober eye contact as he answered. "I do."

"Hmm..." she mumbled, curiously searching his gaze. Then she shrugged. "I guess that's no different than believing in soul mates, and since we can't prove each other wrong, it's a moot point."

Quin took a moment to memorize her smile before risking it. "What if I told you I could prove it?"

Her lips dropped as her forehead furrowed. "I guess I'd ask you how."

Quin filled his lungs then scooted around, sitting cross-legged in front of her. She pulled her knees from her chest, crossing her legs as well, and he took her twig, tossing it aside so he could have her hands.

"Layla," he breathed, meeting her stare, "I'm not like most people."

"I know," she smirked.

"That's not what I mean," he continued. "I'm saying I can do things other people can't."

She tilted her head, biting her lip as she watched his eyes. "Like what?"

"A lot of things," he answered, tightening his hold on her hands. He couldn't help himself. It took a great deal of restraint not to grip her like his life depended on it.

"Like what?" she urged.

Quin sighed and got it over with. "Like magic, Layla."

Stunned, confused and torn between laughing and backing away, Layla had to make sure she'd heard correctly. "Magic?"

"Yes," Quin confirmed.

"You're joking," she assumed.

"No," he insisted. "I'm very serious."

"Magic," she repeated, at a loss for something useful to say.

Quin nodded, and Layla continued to stare, unable to make heads or tails of his confession. Oh god. He was crazy. She was in the middle of nowhere with a crazy person.

Quin shifted, his fingers flexing around hers. "What are you thinking, Layla?"

"That you're crazy," she snapped, agitated by the whole damn situation. She glanced over her shoulder, wondering how to handle the handsome nutcase. Then she smoothed her ruffled feathers and looked back. "I'm sorry. That was mean. But . . . well, are you?"

"Am I what?"

Crazy, she thought. "Unwell," she answered. "Do you take meds and visit with doctors about your . . . magic?"

Quin smiled and shook his head. "I'm not crazy, Layla. I'm telling the truth. I can perform genuine magic."

Apprehensive about playing along, Layla looked down, weighing her options. She hated the thought of blowing him off—returning him to the café before walking away forever. But she couldn't sweep the subject under the rug and pretend his delusional behavior was normal.

"So," she whispered, trying to remain sympathetic despite her disappointment, "what kind of things can you do?"

"Just about anything," he answered, relaxing his grip. "Do you want me to tell you or show you?"

She raised an eyebrow, wondering how far he would take it. "Both."

"Okay, but don't let it scare you. There's nothing to be afraid of."

"Okay," she hesitantly agreed.

"Hand me that twig you were spinning," he instructed, releasing one of her hands.

Layla reached out, blindly finding the twig and handing it over.

"Don't be frightened," he pressed, softly kissing her hand. Then he placed it in her lap.

Layla touched her tingling knuckles, her heart and cheeks flooding with warmth. Damn. Why'd he have to be crazy?

Quin held out a hand, and the small stick lay idle in his large palm. "I can make this twig do pretty much anything I want without touching it."

"Show me," she insisted.

Keeping his gaze on her face, he took a deep breath and pointed at the twig, which floated into the air! Layla gasped, clapping a hand over her mouth, and the stick fell to Quin's palm.

"Are you okay?" he asked.

"How did you do that?" she demanded.

"Magic," he answered.

She shook her head, unable to find her lungs. "This is a joke. This has to be a joke."

"No," he countered, "it's magic."

The hair at the nape of Layla's neck stood on end, her eyes moistened, and her chest tightened. "Do it again."

"The same thing or something different?"

"The same thing."

Like before, he stared at her and she stared at the twig, watching it float from his palm. When it stopped and hovered, she leaned forward, slowly running her fingers along every side. There was nothing holding it there!

"I can't believe it," she whispered. "It's impossible."

"Do you want me to stop?"

"No," she blurted, bewildered and mystified, but unafraid and itchy with anticipation. "It's exciting. What else can it do?"

He grinned, a huge sigh deflating his chest. "What do you want it to do?"

"I don't know. Make it spin around or something."

As soon as she made the suggestion, the stick began rotating, each turn faster than its predecessor until it was a blur. When it stopped, it flipped upright, floating to eye level. Then one inch cracks split along the top and bottom. As the bottom pieces formed an upside down V, the top pieces formed a tiny heart. Then two thin strips of bark, one on the left and one on the right, slowly peeled away from the wood, stopping once they hung by a thread from the base of the heart.

Layla gasped, discerning a tiny stickman with two legs, flexible arms, and a heart shaped head. "That's amazing," she breathed, watching the earthen creature wave and bow.

"Hold out your hand," Quin instructed.

Layla eagerly obeyed, and the twig man hopped to the moss, picked a yellow wildflower then jumped into her palm. She barely felt the pressure of his miniscule feet as he stepped forward, raising the flower toward her face, but tingles slithered from her hand to her spine, reaffirming his magical presence.

Layla leaned in, smelling his offering. Then she grinned at Quin, finding deep dimples and twinkling eyes.

Chapter 11

"I still can't believe it," Layla whispered, in awe as she examined the stickman, which lay inanimate between her fingers. "What else can you do?"

Quin scooted to the spot beside her and took her hand. "Is this okay?"

Layla looked down, blushing through her answer. "It's better than okay. I feel like I've stepped into a fairytale."

"Then let's see some magic," he approved. "If something worries you, let me know and I'll stop."

"Okay," she happily agreed, wiggly with excitement.

"What's your favorite animal?" he asked.

She froze, nervously eyeing him. "What are you going to do?"

"I want to show you the magic," he countered, "not tell you about it."

She started to argue, but stopped when he pulled the back of her hand to his lips. "Just watch," he insisted. "What's your favorite animal?"

"Dogs," she answered.

"Any breed in particular?"

"Um . . . I have to go with spaniels."

Quin pointed to the waterfall, and Layla looked over, watching it hit the smooth rocks at the bottom of the embankment. As the droplets rebounded off stone, they conglomerated in mid-air, forming a King Charles spaniel!

Layla's mouth fell open. "That's . . It's . . ." She looked at Quin, who still held her hand to his smiling lips. "No way!" she exclaimed, returning her gaze to the liquid creature.

The dog bounded from the stream, flipping water droplets from its shimmery coat. Then it lapped at Layla's cheek, leaving it soaked. She burst into laughter, wiping her face with the sleeve of her sweater, and the spaniel skipped back to the brook, diving into the water with its tongue hanging out.

Layla's cheek was dry, and the dog had melted into the current, but she couldn't stop laughing. "That was incredible."

"Your laugh is incredible," Quin replied.

Layla immediately stifled her giggles, but couldn't erase her smile. "It's been years since I laughed like that."

Quin frowned, but then he smiled again, watching her profile as he laid his cheek on the back of her hand. "I'd say that makes me a uniquely lucky man. What's your favorite color?"

Surprised by the change of subject, it took Layla a moment to answer. "Oh. Um . . . green."

"Second favorite?"

"Blue."

"How about your favorite flower?"

"Lilies."

"Second favorite?"

"Roses."

"Hold out your hand."

Layla obeyed, and a blue and green marbled rose appeared an inch above her palm.

"Take it," he insisted.

As she picked the smooth stem from the air, a wide variety of lilies sprang from the moss, slithering over her shoes and around her ankles. "They're beautiful," she marveled, smelling the rose.

"Yes," he agreed, "but they're outshined. Let's see . . ." He scanned the clearing then pointed toward the brook, moving his finger up and down.

Layla anxiously looked over, finding a small section of the creek oddly bubbling. Then six narrow streams of water shot into the air like a circular fountain, jumping higher with each surge. Quin flicked his hand at each jet, and tiny lights ignited at their bases, alternating green and blue. With one more sweep of his hand, a large liquid rose bloomed from within the fountain, rotating to reveal its sparkling, blue and green petals. As if the moment wasn't enchanting enough, he whistled, and two black-capped chickadees soared from the forest, singing as they circled the tips of the bouncing jets.

Layla raptly watched the magic show, still mystified by the turn of events, still inclined to wonder if she was dreaming, but the fingers gently wrapped around hers suggested otherwise. More solid than the stone at her back and the earth below, Quin's hand felt like a harness safely suspending her between two shaky worlds—one of them hopeless, the other outlandish. She glanced at him, expecting to find his eyes, and sure enough, they were watching her, delving deeper than her surface. She blushed and looked at the fountain, wishing she had the guts to lay her cheek on his arm, to dip into his body heat and breathe his masculinity, but she'd never made a move on a man in her life and had no idea how to do it.

The lights at the base of the jets eventually vanished, the water stayed down, and the birds returned to the forest. "Wow," Layla breathed, shaking her head. "Crazy."

"Do you want to see something more impressive?" Quin asked.

"More impressive than that?"

"That's just the beginning," he revealed. "Magic goes far beyond stick people and fountains."

"I want to see," she beamed.

"I want to show you," he approved. "Do you want to take part in it?"

She hesitated, nervously biting her lip.

"You don't have to," he assured, "but if you want to, you should. It isn't dangerous."

"What will we do?"

Quin stood and helped her to her feet. Then he led her several steps away from the boulder. "Put your hands on my shoulders," he instructed.

"Like this?"

"Sure."

He wrapped his hands around her waist, and her heart raced, pumping feverish blood.

"You okay?" he asked.

"Yeah," she breathed.

He watched her face for a moment, fingers lightly flexing across her lower back. Then he smiled. "Remember, there's nothing to be afraid of, but if you get scared, tell me."

"Okay," she agreed, once again bewildered by how weird and wonderful he was, by the things he showed her and the way he made her feel—like she was floating.

"Still okay?" he asked.

"Yeah," she mumbled. "Why? Do I not look okay?"

He grinned. "Look down."

She did, squeaking and digging fingernails into his shoulders. They were floating three feet above the ground!

"I won't let you fall," he said, squeezing her waist. "You can relax."

She retracted her claws, but her grip stayed firm as she looked around. The sensation of standing on air was odd, supernatural and stomach flipping, but fantastic. "This is insane," she whispered. "We're actually flying."

"No," he corrected, "we're hovering. Flying will come later."

Her mouth dropped open. "You can fly? You can fly! That's why you don't drive!"

"Yes."

"You fly everywhere?"

"Yes. I guess you're okay with heights?"

Layla looked down and squeaked again. They'd risen another fifteen feet. She didn't feel threatened, but had a clear sense of risk, the thrill of uncertainty, like performing a well-practiced routine on a balance beam with no mats below. "I guess I am."

"Do you like to dance?" he asked.

"Um . . . yeah, but I've never danced with a guy."

He whistled, and the chickadees returned, singing a soothing tune as they perched on a nearby branch. Layla smiled at the winged creatures. Then she lost the view when Quin spun her around, cutting wide, lazy circles through the air. After giving her a few minutes to adjust, he quickened his pace and tightened his circles.

"May I pull you closer?" he eventually asked.

Layla nodded, speechless as she blushed from head to toe, spellbound by him and everything he did.

"I'm going to let go with this hand," he warned, wiggling his right fingers, "but you're not losing any support."

She nodded again, so he moved his right hand to her left, lifting it from his shoulder as he wrapped his other arm around her waist. After sliding her up his body, bringing her face even with his, he released her hand and covered her back, slipping his fingers under her hair.

Layla's oxygen intake was practically nil, her blood blazing as she stared him right in the eye, fingers and toes tingling. Was it possible to have weak knees when weightless? Apparently, because hers were jelly.

She swallowed a lump, and he smiled, gently urging her to tuck her blushing face into his neck. She easily complied, and as her trembling lips touched his skin, he burrowed his face through her hair, sweeping the tip of his nose across her clavicle.

Oh wow, Layla thought, eyes drifting shut as a thrill shot through her core.

Quin tightened his fingers around a tuft of silky spirals, chest expanding as he wondered if Layla's flavor was as bewitching as her scent. He yearned to find out, but his confession wasn't over, and he didn't know how she would feel about his lie of omission.

After several heavenly minutes, he pulled his face from her hair, sent the birds away, and returned to earth in more ways than one. When his feet found cool moss, he kept Layla in his arms, itching to squeeze tighter. "We're on the ground."

"I know," she whispered, prickling his skin.

He closed his eyes, withholding an aroused groan. "There's something else I need to tell you."

She breathed deep then abandoned his neck. "What's that?"

"Well," he hesitantly answered, "I haven't been completely honest with you."

She tilted her head and scanned his face. "Let me guess," she teased. "Karena's not having a two-for-one special."

"I wish it were that simple," he replied, lowering her feet to the ground, "but it's something more serious."

Her hands slid from his shoulders, and he cringed. "I haven't actually lied," he hurriedly continued, "I just haven't been forthcoming with the truth."

She bowed her head, watching him out of the corner of her eye as she shifted away. "The truth about what?"

"Several things," he answered. "Let's sit. It's not an easy story to tell."

She stayed tense, maintaining suspicious eye contact.

"Please, Layla."

She huffed and moved to the boulder, and Quin flexed his fingers as he followed, sitting down in front of her.

"I've already told you a few things about my family," he began, tentatively taking her hands, "but there's more you should know."

"Like what?" she coolly asked, and Quin could tell she'd donned an emotional shield, bracing herself for a blow.

"Well," he answered, "for one thing, they can perform magic as well."

Layla's eyes widened as she lowered her defenses. "All of them?"

"Yes."

"Brietta and Banning, too?"

"Yes, all twenty-five of us are magicians, or witches and wizards if you'd prefer."

"Witches and wizards?" Layla whispered.

Quin released her hand and pulled a drinking glass from his bag, summoning water from the stream with a flick of his wrist. "Yes," he answered, handing the glass over. "I'm a wizard."

Layla curiously watched him as she took a long drink. Then she shrugged. "I guess that makes sense. What else would you call yourselves?"

"That's not what I need to tell you."

"Oh."

Quin set the water aside and took her hands back. "As witches and wizards, we can read people's emotions by looking at them, and it works even better with other magicians. Having said that . . ." He paused, took a deep breath then slowly let it out. "…when Brietta saw you last night, she noticed something different about you, something that confused her."

"You're finally going to tell me why you sat with me," Layla mumbled, looking down.

Quin's stomach squirmed as he squeezed her hands. "Yes," he confessed, trying to find her eyes, but she was purposefully hiding them.

"Go on then," she insisted.

Quin didn't want to go on. He wanted to lift her gaze and tell her any man sitting with her was a blessed man, but he forced himself to stay on track. "Brietta had never seen anyone like you. It worried her, and she wanted a second opinion from a member of our coven. I was in the bookstore next door, so she called me."

Layla's shoulders rose with a shaky breath. "I see. She sent you to my table."

"No," he countered, giving into temptation and lifting her chin. "Brietta called me in there, but I sat down on my own accord. I told you the truth last night. I was intrigued by the most beautiful woman I'd ever seen. Why wouldn't I sit down?"

Her forehead wrinkled as she searched his eyes, and he could tell he'd soothed at least some of her insecurities.

"What about me intrigued you?" she pressed.

"Well," he answered, anxiously flexing, "I'm getting to that, but I feel I should warn you."

"About what?"

"About the things I need to tell you. They won't be easy to hear, let alone believe, but please try to keep an open mind and stay calm, and if there's anything I can do to make it easier, let me know."

She nodded her curious agreement, and he deeply inhaled, trying to slow his speeding heart. "I know why you're here, Layla."

"You invited me here," she replied.

"Not here in the clearing," he corrected. "Here in Oregon."

She narrowed her eyes. "I told you why I came here."

"Yes, but you didn't tell me all of it."

"How would you know?" she countered. "Is that something you can magically see about me?"

Quin felt her shields go up, but he didn't know how to soften the blow, so he grasped her hands tighter and ripped off the bandage. "I know why you're here, because I know your grandparents."

Her mouth fell open as she yanked her hands away, shocked, confused . . . and afraid. Shit. Quin ached to grab her hands back, but somehow managed to restrain himself.

"You… you what?" she asked.

Quin's chest and stomach tightened, muffling his reply. "I know your maternal grandparents very well. And I know your past, what drew you to Oregon."

Layla stood so fast she was on her feet before Quin realized he no longer held her gaze. By the time he jumped up, she'd turned her back on him and was staring into timber, intensely fidgeting with the sleeves of her sweater.

"That's ridiculous," she decided, spinning back around. "What makes you think that?"

Quin's heart squeezed as he dropped his guilty gaze. "You know my family shares land with another magical family."

"So?" she huffed, impatiently lifting a hand.

"Well, that other family is your family."

Her hand fell to her side, slapping her jeans, and Quin took a cautious step, hoping like hell she wouldn't flee. "You're a witch, Layla," he quietly added. "I knew it the moment I saw you."

Chapter 12

Layla thought her head might explode as heat scrambled her senses, making it hard to process what she'd heard. How could this be true? If Quin had told her this yesterday, she would have called him a lunatic and walked away. But after the morning she'd experienced, she could no longer turn her back on what she thought was impossible. The word had lost all credibility.

"I don't understand," she breathed, pushing the words through a tight throat. "What makes you think I'm part of that family? A magician . . . or whatever. You don't know me."

"I do know you," Quin insisted. "I know your mom and dad named you Layla, and that you were most likely adopted by a woman named Katherine Moore. I know your parents used the surname Callaway when they stayed in Ketchum, Idaho, and I know you were born on the third of March in 1989. I also know, without a doubt, that you're a witch."

Layla's stomach churned as he rattled off facts he shouldn't know, wouldn't know without knowing her. But even if he knew her family, one thing made absolutely no sense. "But I'm not, Quin. You got the wrong girl. I'm not a witch."

"Yes you are," he countered. "I can see it, and when you're ready, I can prove it. There's no doubt—you're a witch and always have been."

Layla's legs liquefied. "I need to sit."

Quin was at her side in an instant, summoning the raincoat as he helped her to the ground. Layla's butt crinkled the plastic. Then she pulled her knees to her chest and rested her forehead on them, her stomach swirling as her brain throbbed.

She stayed that way for about an hour, digesting everything he'd told her, doing her best to separate and evaluate all the bits and pieces, but information overload and oppressive disbelief hindered productive conclusions. How could it be? Proof or no proof, how was any of this happening? Maybe she'd entered another dimension when she drove into Oregon. Blah. None of it made any sense.

Quin sat silent and still as he watched Layla try to deal with the life altering news, hoping he hadn't messed up the most vital task he'd ever been set. When she finally looked at him, his heart and breathing paused.

Her face was calm, and its beautiful coloring had returned, but he could tell she remained confused and reluctant to accept the facts. When she spoke, her voice was hoarse, but her words were clear.

"Why was Brietta worried about me?"

The insignificant question surprised Quin, considering she probably had a million high priority questions burning her brain, but it also relieved him, and he breathed easy for the first time since descending from their dance.

"Brietta realized you're a witch as soon as she saw you, but she also saw something she didn't recognize. Until that moment, she'd never met an adult magician who doesn't know how to perform magic, so she didn't understand what she was seeing and thought it might be a trick. There's also the fact you were a stranger. We're somewhat familiar with all the covens in Oregon, and we rarely get unknown, magical visitors, so you threw us for a loop."

Layla harrumphed. "I'm pretty thrown myself. I had no idea."

"I know," Quin assured. "As soon as I sat down, I realized you were genuinely unaware, and when I learned your name, I knew exactly why."

"That's more than I know."

"Yes," he confessed. "You haven't had a very easy go at things."

"It wasn't always this confusing," she countered. "Before my mom's stroke, I led a happy and carefree life."

"That's what your parents wanted for you."

Layla's hand flew to her heart as she whipped her gaze to his, searching his eyes as if they held the most frightening and intriguing knowledge in the world. After taking a shaky breath, she looked away, plucking a lost conifer needle from the moss.

"So," she murmured, snapping the needle into tiny pieces, "my dad . . . is he dead?"

Quin wrapped his arm around her shoulders and tucked her hair behind her ear, sadly watching her profile as he broke her heart. "Yes. He died within a few weeks of your birth. I'm sorry."

Her needle was gone, so she fiddled with the sleeves of her sweater as she looked at the stream. "I didn't realize how much I'd hoped to find him. What were their names? I only know the fake ones."

Quin played with a curl as he answered. "Rhosewen Keely Conn and Aedan Dagda Donnelly. Your mom took his surname when they married."

"Those are nice names," she whispered, raising shaky fingers to her throat.

"I think so, too," Quin agreed. "Our coven holds your parents in the highest esteem."

She pensively cocked her head then met his stare. "So Brietta and Banning are related to me?"

"Yes. They're your second cousins, but with so many of us living together, we simplify things and just call them cousins."

"I forget how many you said there are," Layla mumbled. "In my . . . family."

"Eight," Quin answered. "Of the twenty-five people in my coven, eight are related to you by blood or marriage. Your dad's parents live in Virginia, so you have more relatives, but I don't know how many."

She shook her head, eyes wide and shiny. "I couldn't have imagined this outcome in a million years. I don't know how to handle it; where to go with it. What's a person supposed to do with information like this?"

"I can't imagine how you must feel right now," Quin offered, wishing he could do more. "You're handling it better than I would."

"There's so much I don't know," she mumbled, burying her face in her knees, "so much I don't understand." She was silent for a moment, then her voice muffled through denim. "Will you tell me more?"

"Sure," he agreed, getting things straight in his head. "Let's see... Your mom's parents are Caitrin and Morrigan Conn..."

"Morrigan," Layla repeated. Then she popped her head up. "The pianist?"

"Yes," Quin confirmed, smiling at the excited spark in her eyes. "That CD was recorded by your maternal grandmother."

"Wow," Layla breathed, laying her head back down.

When she didn't say anything more, Quin continued divulging information. "Your dad's parents are Serafin and Daleen Donnelly. I've seen them several times, so I can answer questions about their looks and personalities, but I don't know much about their lives in Virginia." He paused, waiting to see if she had questions, but she didn't comment, so he kept going. "Neither Rhosewen nor Aedan had siblings, so you don't have any aunts or uncles, but Caitrin has a sister, which would be your Great-aunt Cinnia..."

"Cinnia?" she asked, raising her head again. "As in *Cinnia's Café*?"

"The one and only," he answered.

Layla thoughtfully chewed her lip for a moment then murmured under her breath. "So the coffee was the most important clue."

"Clue?" he asked.

"You don't know?" she returned.

"Know what?"

"About the trail of breadcrumbs I was supposed to follow."

"Oh," he whispered, wrapping a spiral around his finger. "I know you didn't have much to go on."

"Apparently I had more than I thought," she countered, "but even if I had considered the possibility of a family member owning the café, I wouldn't have believed it. I've never had an aunt, let alone one who sells the best coffee in the world."

He smiled and swept a lock of hair across the tip of her nose. "You do now."

"So it would seem," she conceded. "What else do I have?"

"Well, Cinnia married a man named Arlen Giles, so you also have a great-uncle in the coven, and they had a daughter named Enid. She owns the bookstore next to the café. Enid married a man named Kearny Gilmore, and Brietta and Banning are their children."

"Let me make sure I got this straight," Layla said. "In your coven, my family includes my grandparents, Caitrin and Morrigan, a great aunt and uncle, Cinnia and Arlen, and my cousins, Enid, Kearny, Brietta and Banning."

"You have an excellent memory," Quin commended.

"I don't know how I'm remembering any of it," Layla countered. "My head is too full right now."

"Magicians have good memories," Quin explained. "We're better at compartmentalizing."

She straightened her shoulders and skeptically met his stare. "So you're telling me I can do those things you did?"

"With practice, yes, you can do much more than what you've seen."

"How is that possible, Quin? I've never done anything remotely close to that. I've been as normal as anyone my entire life."

Quin watched her emerald eyes, pink lips, and shiny spirals, wondering if she'd ever seen a mirror. "You're far from normal, Layla, but I get what you're saying." He paused, searching for the best way to explain. "In most cases, when a magician is born, their coven starts teaching them what they are and how to focus their energy on performing magic. It's exercised as much as anything else. Like crawling, walking and talking, magic is practiced and encouraged. A few things come naturally, aesthetic things like our good looks, physical grace, sharp memory, and artistic talent, but everything else takes practice. If a magical baby's never told what she is, never taught how to focus, perform and control her ability, she could live her entire life without realizing she possesses the gift. Above all, if someone doesn't believe in magic, there's no way they'll be able to perform it."

"How do you do it?" she asked.

"It's all in the mind," he answered. "The movements are merely for the benefit of realizing our goal."

"So you can do those things without moving?"

"Sure, but it takes more concentration."

She still looked confused, so he elaborated. "Using movements helps us take what is just a thought and turn it into something physical, which makes it more of a reality. That's the goal of magic, to take the idea we've formed in our head and make it a reality. With the fountain, I thought about what I wanted the water to do, and by pointing and moving my hand, it was easier to see it as real." He sighed. "Am I making sense?"

"I think I get it," she replied. "If someone's a magician, they can think of the outcome they want, imagine it as real, and it happens."

"A good summary," he approved, "but it's more complicated than it sounds. Figuring out how to achieve what you want is the hard part. Once you figure that out, it's easy. Your natural born ability kicks in and all that's left to do is strengthen the skill by finding quicker or more elaborate ways to achieve your goal."

Layla picked up the rose he'd given her, drifting it under her nose. "So you created the flower and the scent?"

"Yes," he confirmed. "I imagined every detail, from stem to petal to pollen."

"So you need to know the anatomy of your subject to create it?"

"Yes. Otherwise you end up with mutant flowers that quickly wilt. The greater your knowledge and imagination, the better the product."

"You have a good imagination," she commended, once again smelling her rose.

"We all do," he replied, holding out a hand, and another rose appeared—blue and green like the first, but with a slightly different scent. He offered it to Layla, and she happily accepted, grinning as she buried her nose in soft petals.

"I thought magic was supposed to be about spells and rituals," she said, picking one of the lilies he'd created—a bright pink stargazer, which she bundled with the roses.

"It is," he confirmed, gathering the nearby stickman and yellow wildflower. Then he took Layla's bouquet, magically adhering the stickman to the stalks before tying the stem of the wildflower around all four creations. "Even the easiest bit of magic we perform is considered a spell," he added, returning her flowers, "and sometimes spells are considered rituals; usually when they involve multiple people, objects or an extended period of time. But because our magic is so flexible, our labels are often inconsequential. Two people can bring about the same result by taking two completely different paths. You don't have to follow a rule book or memorize step-by-step instructions. You just have to use your imagination to figure out a way, and most importantly, you have to be specific about what you want—from stem to petal to pollen, and everything in between."

"So the only limit to magic is your own," she concluded.

"Pretty much," he replied. "But as easy as that sounds, you'll quickly learn there's more to it than meets the eye. It's all in the details. Miss even the tiniest component, and your spell will likely fail. Figure out the details, and the rest is magic."

"Hmm . . ." she thought, wiggling her lips. Then she raised an eyebrow at him. "Can you make these flowers live forever?"

"Only with daily care," he answered. "I would have to keep them hydrated and reverse the marks of time."

"Can you not create them so that they wouldn't need water?" she challenged.

Quin grinned at her ornery smirk, wanting to kiss it. "No, I cannot, but there might be someone who can. Can you think of a way?"

She scowled, but humor still tugged at the corners of her mouth. "I guess I deserve that."

"It wasn't a shot," he laughed. "You never know who has the answers you're looking for."

"I have no answers," she whispered. "I don't even know myself, let alone what I can do."

"Tell you what," he offered, reaching for her bouquet, "I'll keep your flowers alive until you figure it out."

Her cheeks and smile brightened. "Yeah?"

"Sure," he agreed, opening his bag, but before he could slip the flowers inside, Layla grabbed his hand.

"You'll crush them," she objected.

Quin couldn't help but laugh as he set the flowers aside and pulled the satchel from his waistband. "It has a spell cast on it," he revealed, reaching inside the bag. "It holds as much as I need it to, protects its contents, and makes them weightless. It's a highly detailed spell that requires regular maintenance."

When his hand emerged from the bag, a large pile of black velvet followed, and Layla quietly gasped. "What is that?"

"The cloak I wear when I fly at night."

"Oh. What do you wear when you fly during the day?"

"Whatever I want. We can conceal ourselves."

"What do you mean?"

"I can disappear."

Her mouth fell open. "Really?"

Quin laughed, surprised she still had the energy to react. "Really."

"Then why don't you disappear at night?" she asked.

"It's nice to fly without hiding," he answered. "The night gives us the opportunity. Would you like to see the concealment spell? Or not see, I should say."

"Yes," she eagerly agreed, watching him with unblinking eyes.

Quin stifled a laugh as he stowed the cloak and flowers and tied his bag to his waistband. Then he stood and took a few steps back. "Ready?"

"Yes," she answered. Then he was gone.

Layla jolted and nervously scanned the clearing, suddenly terrified she'd never see her magical guide again.

"I haven't moved," Quin assured.

She looked to the spot he'd been a moment before, and thought she saw a shimmer, but couldn't find it a second time.

His voice floated through empty air. "A non-magical person could spend all day in this clearing and not notice me, but you're different." A short pause then another shimmer. "Do you want to try out your magic to see me? This would be an easy start."

"*My* magic?" she squeaked, anxiety swallowing excitement.

"Sure," he confirmed. "It takes minimal focus once you know what you're looking for. It's how we know other magicians when we see them, and how we know what people are feeling. It's just a matter of opening your mind and eyes to what you know exists."

"How do I do it?"

"First, close your eyes and remember what I looked like standing here."

Layla obeyed and sighed. This vision pleased her.

"Don't focus on the details," he instructed, "but on the reality of it, that my body, without a doubt, occupies this space. Now, this is the important part. Shift your focus to the intangible aspects of being human—the ability to think critically and the capacity to feel on an emotional level. Those qualities occupy this space as much as my body does. Remember that, focus on it, then open your eyes."

He fell silent, but Layla kept her eyes closed, concentrating on the picture in her head. But it wasn't a picture, or even a memory. It was fact. The seemingly empty space in front of her was filled with Quin's body, heart and soul.

She slowly lifted her eyelids, silently repeating the verity of it. Then she sharply inhaled.

Quin's presence was validated, but she couldn't actually see him, just the lack of him. A multicolored, translucent mist swirled around the shape of his body, floating several feet in every direction.

"What you're seeing is my aura," he revealed, "an abstract look into my soul. All magicians can see them, from the moment they're born, and I'm sure it was the same for you. But while most magical babies have families who acknowledge auras, point them out and talk about them, you were raised by a woman who wouldn't have been able to see them no matter how hard she looked. Without her validation, you likely ceased to believe, and you must look for auras to notice them."

With every second that passed, his aura became clearer. Layla could distinguish different colors now, whereas before they were blurry and pale. "It's very pretty."

"I'm glad you like it," he replied, "because you'll probably see it from now on."

"Really?"

"Yep. Looking for someone's aura comes as naturally as looking for their face. Now that you know about them, you'll find them without even trying, and you'll quickly figure out how to read them."

"Read them?"

"Yes. You'll learn to recognize emotions, musings and magical power."

"Oh."

"I'm going to lift the concealment spell," he warned.

"Okay," she agreed, and his body filled the empty space inside the fog, which somehow sharpened his image instead of obscuring it.

"You really like it," he observed.

"Very much," she admitted. "I'm afraid to look away."

"Don't be. Give it a try. Look at the waterfall then back to me."

Layla watched him and his aura for another ten seconds before forcing her gaze away. Then she whipped it back around, already missing the sublime view. "It's still there," she beamed, searching the mist. It had gotten thinner, and the colors had dulled, but the longer she stared at it, the more vibrant it became.

Quin knelt and took her hand, scanning the air around her as he pulled her to her feet. "Would you believe me if I said your aura is the most beautiful I've seen?"

Layla looked from his colorful haze to his dark gaze. "I don't know. You say things like that a lot."

"Because I mean them," he assured. "Your aura captivated me the moment I saw you. It's unlike any before it, and it's only gotten better since yesterday." He paused as he searched her eyes. Then he moved a little closer. "I know hundreds of witches, Layla, and most of them have beautiful bodies, faces and auras, but they're average compared to you, and none of them have affected me the way you do. You're the only thing I've thought about since meeting you."

Layla didn't disclose that he was mirroring her feelings for him; she didn't have the courage and admired him for his.

A flash of green caught her eye, and she looked at the mist surrounding him. "Will I ever not see it?"

"You can make it go away anytime you want," he answered. "Just ignore it, pretend it doesn't exist."

"I don't want to," she blurted. Then she blushed and looked down, hiding her flustered face.

"Good," he whispered, pulling her palm to his heart, "because I don't want you to. But if you'd like, you can make it softer without losing it altogether. Just imagine what you want to see."

Trembling from head to toe, Layla doubted her ability to concentrate, but after a long moment of silence, her heart rate mellowed and her focus sharpened. She turned it to Quin's aura, imagining the mist fading, and the colors blanched. When she yearned to see it more clearly, the colors flared.

"You're advancing quickly," he noted.

"How can you tell?" she asked.

"Your aura," he answered. "I can see your power improving."

"Oh."

"Do you want to try something different?"

"I don't know," she mumbled. "The possibilities must be endless."

"We could try some elemental magic."

"Elemental?"

"Yes," he confirmed, waving his free hand through the air, and a breeze floated into the clearing, lifting the curls framing Layla's face.

"You did that?" she asked, glancing around.

"Yes. That was a form of air magic. You also have water," he said, motioning to the creek, and three liquid fish jumped from its surface. "Earth," he added, stretching his hand over the jellybean shaped boulder, and the moss quickly grew, veiling the stone in greenery. "And last but not least," he finished, raising his palm, "fire."

A perfectly round fireball with a diameter of at least seven feet shot into the air, halting and hovering near the treetops. Then it began slithering, constantly changing form until it had taken the shape of Layla's name—burning cursive letters stretching across the cloudy blue sky. When Quin closed his hand, the flames dissipated.

"Which would you like to try?" he asked.

Layla continued to watch the sky, mesmerized. "That one."

"Okay," he agreed, "but don't be disappointed if nothing happens. Out of the four, fire's the hardest to work with."

"Why?"

"Because it rarely has a base. I had air, water and earth at my disposal, but no fire."

"But that was fantastic," she countered, pointing toward the sky.

"It wasn't bad, but I'm a fire child, so it was easy."

She snapped her gaze to his face. "You're a what?"

"A fire child," he repeated. "All magicians know basic elemental magic, but each of us thrives at one element in particular. Mine is fire."

"Can you tell what mine is?" she asked. "By my aura?"

"No. That's something you'll figure out when you start reaching your limits."

"Oh," she breathed, shoulders sagging.

Quin reached up, lightly tapping her pout. "What's that about?"

"It's overwhelming," she explained, "how little I know."

"I see," he whispered, pulling her into a hug.

Layla's fingers flexed over his heart as she rested her cheek to his chest, her lungs stuttering as tingles slid down her spine to her fluttering tummy. The move felt monumental, like the earth's axis had shifted and nothing would ever be the same. Layla was a changed woman, enlightened as she stared at Quin's hand, inhaled his scent, and listened to his pulse.

"You've handled everything beautifully," he commended. "If you want to learn, I have no doubt you'll do it in record time."

"It's not just that," she countered. "There's twenty-one years of knowledge missing. My background, my parentage . . . my identity, it's all a mystery. I'm afraid I'll never catch up."

He leaned in, touching his lips to her hair, and her scalp buzzed with tickling energy. "I know some really great people who could shed some light on the situation," he noted.

Layla's bones softened at the idea of meeting her family. What would she say? *Hi, nice to meet you. I hear you're a bunch of witches and wizards.* Talk about inappropriate.

"No one's going to force you to do this," Quin added. "We know it's hard. If you need more time, take it."

What was to gain by keeping her head in the sand? Nothing, there was nothing to gain by avoiding the truth, but the things she could gain by facing her fears—abundant. "They know I'm here?" she asked.

"Yes."

"They know you're with me?"

"Yes."

"So what now?"

Quin leaned back and found her eyes. "That's up to you. Your family wants to see you when you're ready. They want you to join the coven and live the life you were born to live. They want to know you. But if these things aren't what you want, you're free to go on with your life as you please." He paused, taking her face in both hands as he moved a little closer. "But I should probably warn you—choosing not to join the coven doesn't necessarily get rid of me. Now that I know you, I have no desire to stay away from you."

"I don't want you to," she whispered.

"Good." He watched her lips for a moment then released her face, taking her hands instead. "I'm not rushing you, but I'm curious. Do you know what you want to do?"

She knew, and it only fueled her nerves. Making the decision hadn't calmed her at all. "Yes," she answered. "I want to meet my family, but not until I get some food and coffee."

A huge sigh whooshed from his lungs as his lips curved toward dimples. "Food and coffee sounds great." He held out a hand, and his water glass and raincoat flew from the ground. After offering her a drink, he drained the glass and tucked the items into his bag. "Ready?"

"Not quite," she refused. "I didn't get to try my elemental magic."

"That's right," he remembered, stepping behind her. "Close your eyes."

"You didn't," she objected.

"You won't always have to close them," he assured. "It's a beginner's tool, to help block out distractions and increase focus."

"Oh. Sorry."

"Don't be. Are you ready?"

"Yes."

"Are your eyes closed?"

"Yes."

"Raise your right arm, palm forward, straight out in front of you."

She obeyed, and he touched two fingers to her right temple.

"Start to imagine the fire here," he instructed. "Think about every detail—color, movement, sound, feel. Picture it as clearly as you possibly can. When you feel like the image is complete, nod your head."

Layla put the pieces of the blaze together in her mind, creating a surprisingly clear vision. Then she barely nodded, afraid too much movement would shake the image away.

Quin felt the tiny nod and quietly continued. "The goal is to transport that fire down your arm and out your hand. When I move my fingers, try to make the flames follow."

The slight pressure at her temple crept downward, and she mentally urged the blaze to follow. She was quite pleased that it did and nearly lost the image as excitement jarred her concentration, but she forced the pride to cede so she could maintain focus.

Quin's fingers slowly trailed over her jaw then down her neck, and heat penetrated inside and out. The inside burn was a result of the vision, while the warmth on the outside stemmed from his touch. As his fingertips made their way across her shoulder, the heat followed, flaring from her temple to the top of her arm. The trail was several degrees hotter than the rest of her body, but it was exhilarating rather than painful.

When Quin got to her wrist, he pulled his hand away, but stayed close. "When I count to three, take all that heat and push it from your outstretched hand as forcefully as you can. Make a point to imagine it traveling away from your body, not around it, and don't drop your hand until you're sure the heat's gone."

The warmth pulsed from Layla's head to her fingertips, and she thought of it as a single unit that couldn't be divided, so when a portion went, the rest would go.

Quin was at her ear again, whispering. "On three. One . . ."

She pulled in a deep breath.

"Two . . ."

She braced herself.

"Three . . ."

She mentally pushed then flipped her eyes open, finding an imperfect sphere of flames shooting from her palm. About the size of a large beach ball, it soared several feet then evaporated with a loud pop.

Layla was thrilled. She'd never felt anything like it. The flames had left, but their power still surged her body. She felt like she could do anything, like she could fly to Mars and find a cure for cancer, or dive to the depths of the ocean to solve world hunger.

"Wow," she breathed.

"To say the least," Quin mumbled, staring at the puff of dissipating smoke. Then he shook his head and looked at Layla. "I practiced magic for years before creating a fireball that big. Maybe you're a fire child."

"That felt wonderful," she beamed, vibrating from head to toe. "It still does."

"I can tell," Quin whispered. "You radiate emotions like body heat."

"What?" she asked.

"Never mind," he replied, smiling as he pointed toward her trembling body. "We like to call that post-power euphoria."

"Will it go away?"

"Yes."

Her smile fell, and he laughed. "You'll feel it again soon," he assured. "I still feel it often."

Layla brightened as she considered trying the magic again, but then her stomach growled.

"Let's go get something to eat," Quin suggested.

Layla bit her lip, afraid leaving the clearing meant leaving the magic. "I feel like everything I've learned this morning will cease to exist as soon as I walk away."

"That won't happen," he countered.

"I know. It's foolish."

"Not really. Everything you've witnessed here are things you've never seen anywhere else. It's natural to relate the two, but it's you who holds the magic, not the clearing."

"I guess," she agreed, reaching for the ponytail holder on her wrist, but Quin closed a hand around it.

"You don't have to do that anymore."

"What do you mean?" she asked.

"You're a witch," he answered. "Tangles are no longer a problem." He lightly ran his fingers down her curls. "If it gets messy, I'll show you how to fix it with magic."

"Oh. Okay. Thanks." She wrinkled her nose, wondering what other perks lay in wait. "How convenient."

"Let's go get some coffee," he suggested, giving her hand a squeeze, and she smiled as she squeezed back.

"Now you've said the magic word."

Chapter 13

George Winston's *Moon* flowed from the speakers as Layla drove into Cannon Beach, laughing at Quin's inexperience with vehicles. When he told her to park at *Cinnia's Café,* Layla stopped laughing immediately, her stomach somersaulting.

"We don't have to eat there," Quin offered. "I can fix something to-go."

The butterflies quieted. "Would you? I'm not ready to see anybody just yet. I'm sorry."

"Don't be," he insisted. "We don't want you to feel rushed. You'll meet everyone when you're ready."

"Thanks."

"You have to stop doing that."

"What?"

"Thanking me for every tiny thing. I'd like to make this easier on you, and there's nowhere else I'd rather be. Your thank yous are unnecessary. So, what do you like to eat?"

"I'm not picky. Well, actually, I kind of am."

"Most people are. How do sandwiches sound?"

"Good. I like turkey and mayonnaise."

"Veggies?"

"Yes. And don't forget my coffee."

"I wouldn't dare."

Layla parked behind the café, and Quin shifted in his seat, scanning the air around her as he reached for the door handle. "I'll be right back."

"Okay."

He stared for another twenty seconds then climbed from the car. When he disappeared around the wood-shingled corner of the café, Layla's anxiety spiked. At first she had no idea why. Perhaps she was worried Banning would come outside to see her. But to stop there would be a lie, because her nerves, she realized with certainty, stemmed from Quin's absence. She ached to see him again, and couldn't look away from the café for more than three seconds. All her thoughts were of him—the way he looked, smelled and sounded, the things he said and the way he said them.

The enlightenment swelled her throat, squeezed her lungs, and moistened her eyes. She'd known Quin less than twenty-four hours, yet she yearned to make him a permanent fixture in her life. She felt he'd already claimed an everlasting position, but this wasn't the case, which made her mouth dry and her palms sweaty. He could remove himself any moment; leave her with mere memories of the most amazing day of her life. He hadn't even kissed her. What made her think she had a claim on him? He wasn't hers to keep.

She drummed her fingernails on the steering wheel, trying to deny her feelings, but her unease grew as unwelcome questions charged her brain. What if he was only treating her kindly as a favor to her family? What if he planned to walk away as soon as he delivered her to her grandparents? What if she was nothing more than a task?

Blah! Her nostrils flared as she watched the café. She'd grown accustomed to taking care of herself and was rattled by the sudden and severe burst of need. What could she do about it? Walking away from him wasn't an option. He was the only person who knew her now. He knew her better than she knew herself.

She laid her hands in her lap, staring down at her magical palms. In one afternoon her life had drastically changed and would never be the same again. She'd been reborn and was starting from scratch, and she didn't want to face her new life alone. No matter how independent she'd been before, she needed someone now.

The passenger door opened, and she jolted, looking over as Quin slipped into the car. He was smiling, like he held an intriguing secret, but then he saw Layla's expression.

"What's wrong?" he soberly asked.

Normally she'd say *nothing* and change the subject, but he would know she was lying. Apparently the aura had its inconveniences as well as its perks. She looked at the haze of color surrounding him, which wasn't swirling like before. It was idle save for slight waves of vibration.

The mist pulsed when he said her name. "Layla."

"Yeah," she answered, looking at her hands. "I'm fine. I . . . I was just thinking about how different everything is. I feel like a whole new person starting from scratch."

"You're still the same person you've always been," he replied, "just with a little something extra."

"I know. I'm okay, really. I just have a lot on my mind."

"I'm sure," he mumbled.

Layla could tell he wanted a better explanation, but he didn't push for it. "Where's the food?" she asked, pointing at the cups in his hands.

"Inside," he answered, passing her coffee over. "I'll summon it when we get where we're going."

Layla sipped then sighed. He'd added the perfect amount of cream and sugar. "Where are we going?"

"Do you want to go to the beach?" he asked. "You'd have a better view this time of day."

"Um . . . Do you mind if we eat at the inn?"

"Not at all," he agreed, so Layla started the car, driving two blocks south, then one block west.

It wasn't until she parked that she remembered the inn was owned by Quin's aunt. "Who will be working the desk?" she asked, trying to sound casual, but with little success.

"Dion," he answered, watching her chew on her bottom lip, "the woman from last night."

"Is Dion part of the coven?"

Quin reached out, touching her pout with his thumb, and it slid from her teeth, resting against his fingertip. "No," he assured. "She's part of a coven that lives northwest of our community—good friends of ours. But they don't know anything about you or your past. With the exception of your dad's family, that information has never left our coven."

His touch soothed her more than his words, and it was his gaze that melted her muscles. "Oh," was all she could say, because she'd forgotten what they were talking about.

Her stomach growled, and Quin smiled as he dropped his hand. Layla watched him exit the car. Then she shook her head clear and followed suit.

To Layla's relief, Dion was on the phone and merely waved as they walked through the lobby. As soon as they reached Layla's room, she bee-lined for the bathroom, barely excusing herself with an inaudible mumble.

Quin smiled at her modesty as he walked to a table by the window, taking two plates from his bag and setting them side by side. When Layla returned, he pulled her chair out, waiting for her to sit before doing the same.

"You don't need to go?" she asked, pointing toward the bathroom.

"I went at the café," he answered.

"Oh. Just making sure there isn't a spell for that."

He laughed and shook his head. "Nope, nothing like that. But our willpower reaches higher levels than normal, so we can delay physical needs longer than non-magical people." He glanced at the empty plates. "Ready to eat?"

"If I had food," she teased.

He stared at her smile for a moment then cleared his throat. "Right, we need food. It's a hassle to pack and carry it everywhere, so we usually prepare it ahead of time then summon it."

"So there are sandwiches sitting at the café, waiting to be summoned?"

"Yes. I fixed them when I was there. And when I say fixed, I mean I put them together using magic. We can take a raw turkey and prepare it however we want in seconds, no appliances needed. Anyway, I made the sandwiches then performed a spell to preserve them until we're ready to eat." He held his hand over her plate, and a turkey sandwich with lettuce, tomatoes and mayonnaise appeared. When he covered his own plate, a roast beef sandwich materialized.

"You make it look so easy," she whispered.

"I've had twenty-two years of practice," he noted.

Her posture sagged, and Quin's straightened. "What's up?" he asked, sweeping her hair behind her shoulder.

"Is it going to take me twenty years to learn what you know?"

"No," he assured. "You'll catch up in no time."

She wasn't convinced, so he elaborated. "A child's magic is weak because they don't posses the same amount of patience and focus adults do. You're going to be able to skip most of the steps I took in my magical education."

This soothed her, so she picked up her sandwich, waiting for him to look away before taking a bite. He smiled, concentrating on his food in an effort not to watch her eat, and within ten minutes they were done.

"Do they do something magical to the food and coffee at *Cinnia's*?" she asked, watching him magically clean the dishes.

He shook his head as he returned their plates to his bag. "Besides the way it's prepared, no."

"It's really good," she noted, "better than normal."

"Cinnia perfected the process of selecting and brewing good coffee beans years ago, so her coffee's everyone's favorite. As for the food, it's as good at home. We always use fresh ingredients, and our gift helps us prepare them flawlessly."

"I see."

"But the smells are magical," he added. "Our food preparation doesn't generate the usual aromas, so they use magic to make the dining room smell appropriate."

"That's not fair," Layla humorously objected. "They're not giving people the chance to refuse their product. When I smelled the place, I was tempted to jump over the counter for a cup of coffee."

Quin laughed, shifting in his chair to face her. "I guess it's working."

"To say the least. That could be dangerous if they get another coffee addict like me in there."

"I'll have to warn them," he replied, taking her hands.

She looked at their entwined fingers, and Quin yearned to know what she was thinking. But even her silence, though unfamiliar and unnecessary, captivated him.

"What would you like to do now?" he asked.

"Hmm . . ." Layla hummed, quickly pushing the option of meeting her family to the back burner. So far her day had been stressful, but amazing and magical. She worried the magic would slip into the background once she came face to face with her past.

She found Quin's eyes, and by the dim light of the wall sconce they looked black, but they weren't frightening. They were warm and tender. As Layla stared at them, she realized her fear of watching Quin slip into the background outweighed her worry over magic.

"May I try some more magic?" she asked.

"Sure," he agreed, pulling her with him as he stood, "but we'll have to keep it mellow. We don't want to disturb the other guests." He led her to the side of the bed then he tossed the pale blue comforter aside, pulled back the sheet, and threw a pillow on top of the blankets. "This is a good example of how our gift makes everyday life easier. Most people make their beds, but we can do it in seconds without any physical work. Would you like to try?"

"Yes," she answered. "How do I do it?"

"It's the same theory I explained earlier. You have to visualize the result you want then realize it happening. I'll tell you the steps to take, but then I'm going to stand back and let you do it on your own."

"Why?"

"Because explaining as you go will distract you."

"Oh, okay."

"First, you'll close your eyes and get a good mental picture of the bed made the way you want it. Then you'll keep that image active while looking at the unmade bed. Theoretically you'll have two outlooks at that point—what you want and what is. Your goal is to take what is and mentally rearrange it into what you want. It will help to use your hands on this. If you want that pillow by the headboard, imagine it happening while using this motion." He swept his hand to the right, and the pillow floated to the headboard. His hand returned to the left, and the pillow followed, softly landing on the heap of covers. "Don't be embarrassed about your movements. They can feel awkward, but they really do help."

Layla nodded, and he swept her hair behind her shoulders. "Remember everything?"

"Yes, but that doesn't mean I'll be able to do it."

"I think you'll do fine, but don't get discouraged if it doesn't work. We have all afternoon to practice."

Layla couldn't think of anything she'd rather do than spend the day making magic with him. "Okay," she agreed, pushing her shoulder back, and he smiled as he stepped away.

Layla watched him for a moment then turned toward the bed, examining the sheets, pillows and comforter. Once she'd memorized the details, she closed her eyes, but instead of conjuring the image of the already made bed, she recalled the messy one. Her mind's eye looked closely, making sure the details were perfect. Then she imagined the steps she would take to put everything where it belonged. Once the bed was in ideal order, she held tight to the image and opened her eyes, determined to make it a reality. But the bed was already made!

She spun around. "Why didn't you let me do it?"

Quin laughed and pointed at the bed. "You did do that."

"But I . . . I didn't do anything."

"What did you think about when your eyes were closed?"

"I did what you told me . . ." She trailed off, realizing that was a lie. "Well, no, I guess I didn't. I imagined the messy bed. Then I made it in my head."

"That's amazing, Layla. You just performed magic a lot of practiced magicians have a hard time doing. When you saw the bed making itself, that's exactly what I saw. You did that without any movement at all."

Layla looked at the perfectly made bed, proud she'd succeeded, but disappointed she'd missed it. It didn't seem real. "I wanted to see it," she pouted, feeling ungrateful.

"Okay," he said, waving a hand, and the blankets pulled back, wrinkling once more. "Try it again, but leave your eyes open. It will be harder to imagine it clearly, but I have no doubt you'll succeed."

He stepped away, and Layla faced the bed, staring at the pillow that was two feet from where it should be. She imagined it rising, but it lay idle. She tried again. Nothing. She huffed and aimed her right palm at the stubborn pillow, imagining it rising as she slowly lifted her hand. The cushion wiggled then jerked into the air, and Layla grinned, softly squealing as she flipped her hand to the right. The pillow zoomed two feet, hit the headboard then fell into place.

Layla giggled, beyond elated. She would have jumped for joy had the mere idea not ignited her cheeks. Instead, she went on with her task, and within twenty seconds the bed was in perfect order.

Layla stared at her accomplishment through happy tears, a smile frozen on her face.

"See?" Quin said, laying a hand on her shoulder. "You're a natural."

She looked up at him then buried her face in his chest. "I can't quit smiling."

"Good," he whispered, wrapping her in a hug. "I like your smile."

She flashed it at him. "May we do some more?"

"We can do whatever you want," he agreed, sweeping her hair from her flushed face, any excuse to touch her, to capture the exhilarating energy bursting through her forgotten armor, to absorb a small yet astounding piece of a woman unlike any other. A small moment with her was worth a million moments with anyone else, and he would steal them as often as possible.

Chapter 14

Layla spent the rest of the day testing her magic, succeeding in every challenge presented. She magically remade the bed a few times then used her newfound skill to rearrange the room. Once she'd put everything back, she stunned Quin with her knowledge of botany as she conjured a bouquet of lilies and a small fichus tree, animating the flowers to tap dance and turn flips on the tree's leaves.

Quin showed her how to perform magic on herself as well. She could now untangle her hair without a comb, freshen her mouth without a toothbrush, and paint her nails without polish. When she realized she would never have to shave her legs again, she glowed, thrilled to be rid of razors and their burn.

At Quin's persuasion, she used sorcery to roll up the legs of her jeans and wash her feet, and only then did she let him show her the spell he used to painlessly walk barefoot.

When nine o'clock rolled around, Layla was bursting with enthusiasm, a zest for life she hadn't felt in years. "I still can't believe I've had this in me my entire life and never knew it," she gushed, pacing between the bed and window. "It seems so natural now. Not so natural it's boring." She halted next to Quin. "Do you ever get bored with it? After doing these things for so long?"

"It never gets boring," he answered. "You will get used to it, but it's easy to appreciate the gift of magic. I'm reminded how lucky I am everyday."

"Good, because I don't want it to get old. I haven't been this excited in years. For a while I thought I'd live the rest of my life in a rut, but this is the complete opposite of that."

"I'm glad you climbed out and came to Oregon."

"I was still halfway in the hole when I got here." She paused, cheeks flushing as she looked away. "Until I met you."

Quin's heart ached at the thought of her so depressed, and while he was honored to help, he couldn't find solace in it. Her pain wasn't over. He was surprised she hadn't asked more about her past, but relieved, because he couldn't answer. He also feared the circumstances surrounding her adoption would change her perception of the magical world, and legitimately so. Some of the darkest aspects of magic had already touched her, changed her, and punished her, yet she'd only been in the light for one day. He yearned for more time to show her the positive side of magic, but getting her to the coven held priority.

He watched her absently gaze at the wall, her bottom lip tucked in her teeth as her aura exposed the emotions she tried so hard to hide. "You still have a long road ahead of you," he noted.

"What do you mean?" she asked.

"I mean there are a lot of things you don't know about yourself." He reached for her face then paused with his fingers an inch from her scarlet cheek, watching as she nervously flipped her gaze between his hand and eyes. She didn't object, so he tentatively closed the gap, taking her jaw in his palm. "I know you're curious about why you were adopted, and the truth will be hard to take."

Layla looked away, resuming the abuse of her bottom lip. She hadn't asked too many questions, because finding out the answers would have put a damper on her magical day. But how much longer could she drag it out? If she didn't commit to meeting her family, Quin would leave without her, and that troubled her more than the unknown. In fact, it made her downright queasy. She couldn't deny it, because she clearly felt it. She was squirming from her gut to her throat as she thought about losing sight of the only thing that felt solid in her life.

She tucked her chin in, trying to hide a labored breath, but Quin had one arm around her back, so even if he didn't see it, he'd felt it. Keeping her head down, she looked up, finding his heart then his neck, and her ears buzzed as warmth rushed her veins.

She returned her gaze to his heart, thinking she should run for cover immediately, sever the attachment now rather than later, but she couldn't. She'd finally found her drug of choice. After years of wondering why addicts ached to do the one thing they probably shouldn't, she finally understood. The idea of drowning never to resurface suddenly sounded delightful, as long as Quin's ocean was the one in which she sank. And like a true addict, she went where she never thought she'd go to get a taste of temptation.

Swallowing hugely, she placed her hands on his shoulders and closed her eyes, imagining herself rising from the ground. The magic worked, and a sliver of pride poked through the humiliation. By the time she wrapped her arms around his neck, the pride was gone, and she was caught in a riptide of longing and shame. She tucked her burning face into his smooth throat, hoping her actions weren't proving too desperate, because each time she touched him, her desperation grew.

Despite her mortification, the position felt heavenly and absolutely right. She couldn't imagine it getting any better. Until it did. His arms tightened, firmly pulling her against him, and a purr rose from her chest, vibrating her tingling lips.

The quiver combined with the thrum of Quin's pulse, and he thought his ribs might crack over the forceful pounding of his heart. He swallowed, increasing the pressure of her mouth on his throat, and his muscles tensed. Willing himself to maintain control, he turned his focus to the scent of her hair as it tickled his chin—a bouquet of roses and lilacs . . . with a hint of sweet vanilla.

Their bodies melded nicely, easily, so they stayed that way for a long time, and Layla's blush eventually receded as her regret slipped away. He hadn't rejected her gesture. He stood there like her personal statue, strong and snuggly.

She eventually left his neck, once again embarrassed as she steeled herself to look at him, but the moment she opened her eyes, finding herself in the midst of his rapidly swirling aura, she forgot to be humiliated.

"Wow," she exclaimed, watching bright colors zoom between them.

"Mmm . . ." Quin murmured, smiling as he opened his eyes. Then he saw Layla's stunned expression and sobered. "What?"

"Your aura," she breathed. "It's . . . it's . . ." She couldn't find the right word, because she'd never seen anything like it. "It's magnificent."

He smiled and tightened his grip. "I'm very happy holding you."

She attempted to touch the glowing haze, but while it parted around her fingers, she couldn't feel it. "Can you see it?" she asked.

"No, but I can see yours and it's exquisite."

"It can't be better than this," she argued, trying to catch a strip of luminous silver darting through a rushing emerald river.

"We'll just have to agree to disagree," he replied, "because I've never seen anything more beautiful than what I'm looking at now."

Layla raised her gaze to his, and a lump seized her throat. His aura was magnificent, but it couldn't outshine the man it surrounded. His expression was so sincere and tender, Layla couldn't look away. Not even her flaming cheeks could persuade her to surrender the mesmerizing view.

"I'm ready," she decided.

"Are you sure?"

"No, but I can't put it off forever."

"Sure you can."

"No. I have to know so I can move on. Everything's different now, and I don't want to start a new life with a mystery hanging over my head."

Quin carried her to the bed and smoothly flipped her legs up, sitting down with her on his lap. "There are a few things you should know before we go."

Layla felt cozily secure and uncommonly happy, and wondered what would happen if she imagined him never moving. Curiosity got the best of her, and she closed her eyes, picturing him completely still as he held her in his arms—a more intimate statue, a very detailed statue. She was just about to commend herself on the specifics when the real Quin's muscles flexed.

She quickly opened her eyes, finding his jaw tight and his lids shut. Oh no. Her stomach flipped and tightened. Oh shit.

"You don't have to do that," he said, opening his eyes.

"What did I . . . I didn't mean . . . Did I hurt you?"

"No," he answered, "but it's an uncomfortable feeling when you're not expecting it."

"What did I do?" she squeaked, beyond mortified and so ashamed.

"You used magic on me."

"But I didn't think it would work. I didn't know I could do that." She felt horrible for causing him discomfort, and the reason behind it left her breathless. She'd never been so humiliated in her life.

"It's okay," he assured, laying a hand on her cheek. "I'm not hurt, or the least bit upset, but for the record, yes, magicians can perform magic on other people. But most of us don't unless we're given permission."

Layla burned with a full body blush. "I'm so sorry, Quin. I just thought it felt nice, sitting like this. I didn't think . . . I didn't mean . . . It wasn't supposed to work!"

"Layla," he whispered, touching a thumb to her trembling pout. "It's okay. I promise. I was able to block it when it hit me, and it isn't a harmful spell to begin with. It was merely unexpected. And unnecessary. All you have to do is ask, and I'll stay like this until you're ready to move."

"I'm sorry," she repeated, burying her face in his bicep.

Quin shook his head, sliding his hand from her cheek to her curls. She had no idea how he felt about her, and nothing he said made a difference. He wasn't accustomed to fragile egos, and didn't know how to bolster the one in his arms. "Don't be sorry, Layla. I like that you feel that way, but the next time you want something from me, just ask. I'm pretty sure you'll get it."

"Why are you so nice to me?" she whispered, keeping her face hidden.

Quin scowled, dumbfounded by her insecurities and pissed at whomever or whatever had caused them. If she'd been living the life she was destined for, she would never have such doubts. He gently forced her to look at him, alarmingly moved by the moisture clinging to her long lashes. "You are quickly proving to be the most beautiful, resilient and kindhearted witch I know, Layla. You've been living a nightmare for three years, and I've put you through hell today, yet you're still shining. I look at you, at your aura, and the first things I see are love, compassion, determination and hope. I wouldn't be a very decent man, or a very smart one, if I didn't treat you kindly. And I wouldn't be an honest man if I didn't tell you exactly what I see and feel when I look at you. No matter how much it makes you blush."

A tear escaped, falling to her flushed cheek, and he quickly swept it away with his thumb. "Please don't cry, Layla. What can I do?"

"Nothing," she quietly answered. "You've done so much already. I . . . I don't know why I'm crying. Today was amazing. I'm just not used to this, to feeling this way. It embarrasses me and makes me nervous . . ." Her top lashes fell like black velvet over a stage of emerald. "It scares me."

Quin hugged her close, loving and hating her confession all at once. "I don't want you to be scared, Layla. I want you to feel safe. And the last thing I want to do is make things harder on you. I can't possibly know all the reasons why you're scared, no matter how long I look at your aura, and I'm not going to ask you to explain yourself. But I will say this. I'm not going anywhere. I have nowhere else I need to be, so until you ask me to leave, I'll be right here. Unless you're over there," he teased, pointing across the room.

Layla wanted him to promise, but wouldn't dare ask. He'd known her for one measly day and didn't owe her another. He'd already given her more than any man before him.

She breathed deep, smelling him as she collected herself. Then she boldly met his stare. "What did you need to tell me before I tried to freeze you in time?"

It took him a few seconds to remember what she was talking about. "Oh yeah. I need to fill you in on a few things before you meet your grandparents."

"Like what?"

"Well, your dad's parents, who live in Virginia, they're here. Should be anyway."

"What?" Layla blurted, shocked by the prospect of meeting all four of her grandparents in one night.

"We called them last night," Quin explained, "and they left right away. They were due to arrive this evening."

"From Virginia?"

"Yes."

"I guess they flew?"

"Yes," he answered, flashing a grin.

"Oh . . . " she replied, "you mean they *flew*. No plane."

"Right," he confirmed. "It takes about twenty-four hours to get here from Virginia."

"They flew for twenty-four hours straight?"

"Sure. It's not as difficult as it sounds."

"But that means they flew overnight."

"And all day."

Despite his claims, Layla thought it sounded like an exhausting journey. "They didn't have to do that. They could have waited. Or at least slept. Why did they come so quickly?"

"A few reasons. Most importantly, they want to see you. They've waited a long time for this opportunity, so they weren't going to sit in Virginia and let it pass them by. But there is another reason. When your dad last saw Serafin, he gave him a box and asked him to keep it safe for you."

"My dad left me a box?"

"Yes."

"What's in it?"

"A ring."

"The kind that goes on a finger?"

"Yes. Aedan imprinted his and your mom's memories on her wedding ring. When you wear it, the memories will be yours."

"Let me get this straight," Layla replied. "If I put this ring on, I'll see my parents?"

"Their memories," Quin corrected, "not them."

"Right . . ." Layla mumbled. "Like home movies or something?"

"I can't answer that. The box is sealed with magic only you can break, so no one has seen or touched the ring since Aedan told Serafin about the imprint. The memories might show like home movies or photos. A lot of imprinted objects show that way. But sometimes it's just voices, or images combined with voices, and I've heard of a few that were like out-of-body experiences, but with another person's body. We have no idea which method your dad chose."

The thought of watching any of these things starring her parents excited and scared Layla. The memories would be sad, but the chance to see where she came from, to see who her parents were, was too good to pass up. "When will I see it?"

"That's up to you," Quin answered. "When we go tonight, the minute you enter the community, everyone plays by your rules. We know this is overwhelming, so we do it your way. If you want to see the ring before you meet anyone, that's what you'll do. If you want to meet one person at a time, that's how you'll meet them. If you want a welcome home party, the feast will be prepared before we get there. The call is yours."

Layla understood the enormity of his offer. Twenty-six people were bending over backward for someone they didn't know. "I don't want a party."

"I know," he replied, lips twitching into a grin, "but my point remains. This happens the way you want it to."

"That's really nice of everybody. I know it must be inconvenient."

"Not really. We're a laid back group of people good at rolling with the punches. As you've so beautifully proven today."

"I still appreciate what they're doing."

"I know you do," he assured, playing with a curl.

Layla closed her eyes, absorbing his tingling touch while debating her next steps to the truth. Her dad must have left an explanation, either on the ring or in the box. So whose account of events did she want to hear first? Her parents' or her grandparents'?

Her parents', she decided. No one would know better than they why things turned out the way they did.

Now, did she want to meet anyone before she got her chance with the box? On this she wasn't so sure. She didn't want to be rude and make her grandparents wait, but she would have a better idea how to receive her new family if she knew why they were strangers. Only then could she be honest about her feelings toward them.

Quin patiently waited, watching her face as he twirled a lock of hair around his finger, so when Layla opened her eyes, she immediately found his.

"If I choose to see the box before meeting anyone, where would I look at it?"

"Wherever you'd feel comfortable looking at it," he answered. "You could use your house, your grandparents', or mine. Or we could have someone bring it here."

"Wait a minute. Go back. My house?"

Quin grimaced. "I'm sorry. I forgot I hadn't told you."

"Told me what?"

"You have a house in the community."

"How's that?"

"It belonged to your parents. When they died, the coven decided to keep it for you. I should have mentioned it earlier. I'm sorry."

"Don't be. It's fine."

"Then I'll get back to the point. Where would you like to see the box?"

Layla considered having the ring delivered, but decided it would be more fitting to discover the truth in her parents' house… her house. Besides, she didn't want to ask favors of the family she'd never met. "My parents' house," she answered. "I mean . . . my house."

"Okay. When would you like to go?"

She checked the time—ten o'clock. "Won't they be going to bed soon?"

"Some of them, but your grandparents won't sleep until they know what's going on. If they think there's a chance they'll get to see you tonight, they'll stay up."

"What if I get there, see the memories, then decide to wait until morning to meet everyone?"

"Then that's what you'll do. Is that what you want?"

"Maybe, I'm not sure. I don't know what to expect."

"Then you'll take it one step at a time and we'll follow you. They'll be fine with whatever you choose."

"What about you?"

His dark eyebrows drew together. "What about me?"

"What will you do when we get there?" she elaborated.

His confusion smoothed into thought. "Hmm . . . What do you want me to do?"

Layla took his hand, fidgeting with his fingers as she swallowed a lump and her pride. "I want you to stay with me," she confessed, feeling weak and immature.

Moisture stung her lids, so she squeezed her eyes shut, but a tear escaped anyway, landing in Quin's palm. "That's convenient," he whispered, transforming the teardrop into an emerald green rose petal, "because I really want to stay."

Layla took the petal he offered then found his eyes—dark pools sparkling around her reflection, holding a tenderness previously unknown. "Yeah?" she asked, smiling despite her flaming cheeks.

His dimples deepened as he swept the tip of a curl across her nose. "More than anything."

Chapter 15

As Layla drove into Jewell, a small logging community north of the Sunset Highway, Quin pointed out a dilapidated parking lot bordered by forest. "We live about ten miles northwest of here, but it's surrounded by trees, so you'll need to leave your car."

"How will we get there?" Layla asked, parking between two faded, yellow lines.

"Fly."

"But I don't know how."

"It's easy, but if you're worried, you can fly with me."

"Okay," she agreed, trying to ignore her queasy stomach. "What about my things?"

Quin glanced at the stuffed back seat. "Morrigan made sure your house has everything you need, but if you want your things tonight, I can send them for you."

"Really?"

"Yes, but it might take a while."

Layla hated to ask for more favors, but would be more comfortable having at least some of her clothes with her. She looked at the back seat, searching for the bag containing some old favorites as well as the clothes she bought the day she found out she was adopted. "I don't need them all right now, but can you send that one?"

"This one?"

"Yes."

As soon as she answered, the bag vanished, making her jolt. "I don't know if I'll ever get used to things like that."

"You will," he assured. "Do you want to try flying by yourself, or would you rather fly with me?"

She looked at the dark sky. Learning to fly at night probably wasn't the best idea. "I'll fly with you for now."

His dark eyes twinkled like the stars as his aura brightened like the sun. "Excellent," he approved, pulling his cloak from his bag. "Are you ready?"

She squirmed in her seat, rubbing the side of her neck as her chest and throat clogged.

"We'll land outside of the clearing and walk in," Quin said, pulling her hand from her throat, "to give you more time to prepare."

"Okay," she agreed, but she couldn't calm her swirling stomach.

"You don't have to do this, Layla. We'll wait as long as you need us to."

Layla was tempted to take him up on the offer, but confronting her past would be hard no matter how long she waited. "No. I don't want to put it off."

Quin watched her for another ten seconds before exiting the car, and Layla closed her eyes, trying to steady her unreliable breathing. How was she supposed to fly when she was having such a hard time on the ground?

She jolted when Quin opened her door. Then she rolled her eyes and took his hand, letting him pull her from the car. With a flick of his wrist, he shut and locked the doors. Then he pulled her close, keeping one arm around her as they walked into the surrounding forest.

Once they were shadowed, he opened his cloak, and she slipped her arms in, loving the soothing warmth of luxurious velvet. "You never told me how you keep from freezing," she remembered.

"Magic," he answered, carefully pulling her hair from the collar. Then he covered the tresses with a roomy hood.

"That's all I get?" she objected.

"Are you cold?" he returned, an ornery twinkle in his eye as hooked the platinum clasp.

"No," she answered.

"Then you don't need more," he refused.

She scowled, and he grinned, slipping his hands under the cloak and around her waist. Layla's breath caught in her chest as he lifted her from the ground. Then she was face-to-face with him, lips fluttering around tiny bursts of oxygen laced with his scent, heart thundering as her cheeks burned.

"Is this okay?" he asked.

"Yeah," she breathed. Aside from her embarrassing physical reactions, she was quite content. "It's nice."

"I think so, too," he replied, supporting her with one arm as he reached up with the other. "I'm going to cast a spell to protect your ears from the pressure, but you shouldn't feel any affects. Tell me if you do."

"Okay," she agreed, and he cupped his hand over her ears one at a time.

"Feel normal?" he asked, and she nodded. "Good," he approved. "Tell me if that changes. Are you ready?"

"Yes."

"Don't be afraid."

"I'm not."

She meant what she said, but couldn't help but squeeze her eyes shut and tighten her grip as he shot into the air, darting through a thick canopy of needle covered branches. When they reached open sky, he leaned back, letting her rest on his torso, and she opened her eyes, feeling foolish for closing them in the first place.

She was pleasantly aware of his solidity as gravity pulled her against him, and her cheeks burned brighter as she looked away from his watchful gaze, turning hers to the blur of treetops below. The reality of the absurd situation suddenly seeped in, and excitement replaced embarrassment. They were flying!

Quin ignored the superb view of the stars in the sky, opting instead for those sparkling in Layla's enthused eyes. When her spirals fluttered around the billowing hood of his cloak, softly caressing his cheek, he smiled, mesmerized by the once in a lifetime moment. Nobody else would see the beautiful expression she wore the first time she flew, her aura polished by wonder, shining like the star she was born to be. The moment was his alone.

Captivated by the magic, she didn't hesitate to touch her cheek to his. "This is insane," she whispered, tickling his ear. "Amazing, but completely insane. How do you know where you're going?"

"I've been flying here since I was two."

"That young?"

"Younger, I learned the basics in Alaska."

"That's crazy," she breathed. "And lucky; this is wonderful."

"I'm glad you like it, because I'd love to take you on a longer trip. This one's about to end."

"Already?"

"Yes. I'll be floating upright in about a minute."

"Okay," she agreed, gripping tighter.

Several fascinating seconds later, he floated vertical, and gravity tugged on Layla's legs. He kept her wrapped in a hug as they descended into the trees. Then he lowered her feet to the forest floor.

"That was fantastic," she exclaimed, letting him help her out of the cloak.

"I like your enthusiasm," he approved, stuffing the velvet away. "It's lovely on you."

She barely maintained eye contact as her face flushed with heat.

"Your blush is lovely, too," he added.

"Good thing," she mumbled. "So we just flew ten miles?"

"Approximately."

She glanced around, trying to adjust to the dark. "How far away are we?"

"It's about a five minute walk, but we're within our property line."

Layla scanned him, noting his aura gave the impression he was glowing, but it didn't brighten the area outside of it. "I guess we won't be using a flashlight to get there?"

"Not a conventional one," he answered, raising a palm, and a soft beam of magical light illuminated their way.

"There's one other thing I need to explain before we get there," he said, taking her hand.

"Just one?" she quipped.

He laughed and bowed of his head. "For now. Remember our discussion about soul mates?"

"Yes. You were quite certain they do exist."

"They do, and you're going to meet some."

She came to a standstill. "What?"

"Every magician has a perfect match," he explained, "but it's uncommon for the two to find each other. If they do manage it, they're capable of becoming what we call bonded mates or a bonded couple."

"Bonded mates?"

"Yes," he confirmed, urging her forward. "It's complicated to explain, but I'll do my best. Like I said, it's extremely uncommon, and there are several reasons why. First, the two soul mates have to cross paths. If they do, there's a strong attraction between them, but they have no idea they're perfect mates. The two of them have to make the decision to be together without that knowledge. Then they have to consummate their commitment. Only then do they become bonded mates. Once this happens, a lot of things change for them."

"Like what?" Layla asked, raptly absorbing every word.

"Well," Quin continued, "the moment they bond, they absorb a fraction of each other's magical ability, an increase that lasts until one of them dies. Another change is their perception of each other. What was once beautiful becomes flawless, and it stays that way forever, no matter how much their looks change, no matter how much they change. They might disagree with each other on occasion, or accidentally hurt each other's feelings, but their anger and betrayal won't last long, because their intense love will quickly sweep it away. And neither of them will ever do something to irreparably damage the relationship, which brings me to another change. Bonded mates will never leave each other for an extended period of time. Separation would slowly kill them."

Layla's amazement grew with every word he spoke.

"Another change would be the way they appear to us," he went on. "Not only are they surrounded by auras, they're surrounded by golden hazes we call bonded lights. They're beautiful, and one of the reasons why I'm telling you this, because you'll see them. If you look for their auras, you'll find their bonded lights."

"One of the reasons?" she asked.

"Yes," he confirmed, slowing his pace. "Another difference would be their children. Bonded mates conceive only if they both choose to do so. If one of them has doubts, they won't be able to make a baby no matter how often they make love. Also, their child is capable of more powerful magic than other magicians. They don't possess the amount of power their parents do as a unit, but they're capable of more than their parents as individuals." He stopped walking and extinguished his light. "Am I making sense?"

"Yes," she answered. "So there are bonded mates in your coven?"

"Yes."

"Who?"

"That's another reason why I'm telling you this. Our coven is unusual, because we have two bonded couples, whereas the majority of covens have none. Tonight, however, our community holds three." He brushed her hair behind her shoulders, letting his fingers linger in her curls. "Both your paternal and maternal grandparents are bonded."

"Oh," she breathed, unsure what to make of this. Interesting, sure, but it didn't affect her. "Who else?"

"My parents."

She found this far more interesting. "So you're stronger than other magicians?"

"Generally. I'm what we call a bonded child."

"Hmm," Layla mumbled. "I don't know if I like the idea that there's a perfect match for everyone. It seems unfair to everyone else. I mean, if two people are together, and one of them runs into their soul mate, it's lights out for the relationship."

"Not necessarily," Quin countered. "Remember, a person doesn't know their soul mate when they see them, so if you're in love and happy in your relationship, odds are you'll never know you crossed paths. You just met an attractive and likable person."

"That makes it a little better," she conceded.

"Yes," he agreed. "It keeps the playing field even. You'll see when you meet everyone that the non-bonded couples are very much in love and committed to each other. An attraction to someone else isn't going to end a relationship unless it's already unstable."

"I suppose."

"There's a reason why I've told you this now and not later," he added. "I don't know what exactly is imprinted on Rhosewen's ring, but since she and your dad were bonded children, there will be references to bonded mates. I didn't want you to be confused."

"Oh."

Quin looked forward then back, taking her face in his palms. "There's one more tiny thing to prepare you for."

"You don't say."

"Nothing major," he assured, brushing a thumb over her smirking lips. "I just want to warn you about the size of our clearing. It holds eleven houses with plenty of room for more, and we'll be passing by a few front porches, but there won't be anyone around, so don't feel self-conscious." He watched her nervous eyes, combing his fingers into her hair so he could hold her cheeks. "Are you ready?"

She shook her head no, and he searched the air around her.

"You have questions," he concluded.

"Yes," she confessed, looking down.

"You can ask me anything," he offered. "I promise I'll answer the best I can."

Layla's gaze stayed glued to his torso, like it was stuck with rubber cement. She had no idea what the future held, and despite what he claimed, she had no idea how long he'd be around. The thought terrified her, supplying a dose of bravery.

Utilizing all the pitiful confidence she possessed, she met his stare, ignoring her flaming cheeks and clammy palms. "Why haven't you kissed me?"

Utterly unprepared for the question, Quin tilted his head and searched her eyes, making sure he'd heard correctly. What he found in the emerald pools—intense anticipation and flaring nerves—shattered his willpower.

He eagerly lowered his mouth to hers, moving as slowly as his wounded resolve would let him. Then he parted his lips over her quivering pout, his heart skipping several beats as the tip of his tongue flitted across satiny flesh.

First his kiss surprised Layla. Then it swept her away. One of her hands got lost in his hair, and the other gripped the back of his neck, pulling him closer as her lips pulsed and parted. Their taste buds met, and they both trembled from head to toe. Soon his arms were around her waist, lifting her from the ground, and hers were around his neck, holding him close as her hum rolled over his tongue.

Eyes closed and bodies throbbing, they hungrily tasted each other until they couldn't breathe, and even then they didn't stop. They merely slowed down, leisurely savoring every detail, unabashed by their need for more. When movement ceased, their lips stayed together, spent but definitely not satisfied.

They opened their eyes at the same time, and Layla's pout quivered with a choppy breath. "Wow."

Quin tightened his hug as he softly sucked on her bottom lip, wanting more with every sample. He'd been dreaming about this moment for years, but never imagined it well enough. Nothing could have prepared him for her kiss, for her divine flavor, feel and energy. It had been the most physically and emotionally charged moment of his life. It had been heaven.

"You're amazing," he whispered, finding more in her eyes than before. He was staring into his future.

Layla wasn't ready for it to be over, so she pulled him back for more. She had no idea a kiss could feel so good, so easy and so right, so powerful. It had never been that way before. Not one hormone fueled, teenage moment could compare.

"Why did you wait so long?" she mumbled.

"I've wanted to kiss you longer than you could possibly know," he returned. "But I didn't want to scare you."

"I thought . . ." Her lips stilled as she closed her eyes.

"What?" he urged.

"I wasn't sure if you wanted to."

"Look at me, Layla."

She opened her eyes, and he gave her a soft kiss. "From the moment I met you, I've been thinking about you, thoughts better left in my head . . . for now. I have to be patient, and that's okay. You have a lot on your plate right now, and the last thing I want to do is add unnecessary stress and fear. If I'd come on to you like I wanted to, you would have thought I was crazy, because I would have kissed you within five minutes of meeting you."

Layla carefully searched his gaze. Either he was telling the truth, or he was as good at lying as he was kissing. "I didn't know a kiss could be like that," she whispered.

"Mmm . . ." he murmured, slowly leaning in. "That makes two of us."

Their second make-out session was even better than their first, and it lasted much longer, their minds submersed in bliss and immune to distractions. They didn't have to think, just feel, and it was the easiest thing in the world to do.

When they stopped to catch their breaths for the fifth time, he slid his lips to her neck, kissing and breathing deep. "It's one o'clock in the morning."

Layla had been mesmerized by his touch, but when she heard the time, she stiffened. "Really?"

"Yes. Are you ready to go, or do you want to stay here and kiss me some more?"

She melted back into him. "That's a no-brainer."

He laughed, his lips pressed to her pulse. "You can kiss me there, too. I promise I'll let you."

"I can hardly pass on that offer."

"You can do whatever you want," he disagreed. "I'll stand here 'til dawn if you'd like."

Layla laid her head on his shoulder, trying to catch a ribbon of green darting through his aura. "That's a tempting offer, but I've made you stand here long enough."

"I'll stand longer."

"No," she refused, lifting her head. "We can go, but only if you promise to kiss me again without making me ask for it."

"That's a promise I'm more than willing to make," he agreed. Then he kissed her forehead. "If you'll let me . . ." He kissed her nose. ". . . I'll kiss you every hour . . ." He kissed both cheeks. ". . . of every day."

She giggled, and he flashed deep dimples, finding her lips for another heavenly kiss.

Chapter 16

Layla gasped as she stepped into the coven's clearing, flitting wide eyes over the moonlit community. She'd been warned, but the round glade was larger than she expected—big enough to accommodate a football field with plenty of room to spare—and more beautiful than she could have ever anticipated.

The middle was a wide open expanse, while the perimeter held their houses, each as beautiful and unique as the next, with individualized gardens bursting from their boundaries. The lush green grass grew uniformly throughout and looked alluringly tidy, like it would feel completely natural and quite sensational to roll in it. Suddenly, Layla yearned to be barefoot.

Untouched by the hurried and hectic pace that plagued cities, and unmarred by the scorching sun and tenacious weeds that plagued the countryside, it was like a different world altogether—peacefully ordered and uniquely beautiful.

"You like it," Quin noted.

"It's wonderful," Layla whispered, afraid to disturb the soft tranquility.

She ran her gaze over the houses. Each had the thick forest for a backyard and the perfect glade for a front yard. "Which one was my parents' house?"

"Third from the left," Quin answered.

Layla found it then swallowed an emotional lump.

A pale green, Queen Anne Victorian, it had a circular turret jutting from its right side, resembling a miniature castle, but its spacious front porch was reminiscent of a plantation home. Layla's gaze slid over scalloped, wooden shingles and spotless white shutters, landing on the most attractive garden she'd ever seen. It swallowed the entire front yard save for a narrow walkway of tidy grass—roses of every color and species flowing from its boundaries, somehow maintaining a meticulous appearance as they crept onto the lawn and wrapped around the porch. Never had Layla imagined a more beautiful home.

She looked at the oversized porch swing, and her mind's eye pictured her mom and dad sitting there, so happy and so in love as they watched their baby play on the pristine lawn.

So, this was the life she'd missed.

Her eyes swam with guilty tears, tears that were unfair to Katherine, who'd given everything she had to give. Yet Layla stood there wishing for something different. None of it was fair.

Quin gave her shoulders a supportive squeeze, and by focusing on the cosmetic details of the house, she was able to strengthen her heart and weaken the hurt.

"It's pretty," she whispered.

"Your parents designed and built it," Quin revealed.

For reasons Layla didn't understand, this made perfect sense. "The garden's amazing," she noted, gazing over the vast sea of roses.

"Morrigan takes good care of it," he explained, "the garden and the house. Are you ready to see the inside?"

Layla took a deep breath, letting it out with a firm nod. "Yes."

She was surprised by how easily her feet carried her forward, like they knew right where they were going and were eager to get there. But when she reached the walkway parting the roses, she came to a sudden halt.

Quin furrowed his eyebrows, following her alarmed gaze to the porch. "Damn it, Bann," he sighed. "What are you doing here?"

Layla recovered from her shock and examined Banning's aura, which wasn't as magnificent as Quin's, but by the way it flowed, it gave the impression of happiness and youth—attributes pleasing to the eye as well as the soul.

The haze pulsed as Banning shrugged. "I wanted to welcome Layla with a start off my spearmint plant," he said, holding up a clay pot. "I was bored out of my mind sitting in my room, so I decided to sit here. Good timing, I guess."

"You should have waited," Quin scorned. "You're making a liar out of me."

"Oh," Banning mumbled, nervously watching Quin's aura. "I'm sorry, man. I didn't mean any harm. It's tradition to welcome new members with a sprig of mint, and I didn't want her missing out."

"It could have waited," Quin countered. "And I shouldn't have to tell you that."

"It's okay," Layla cut in, squeezing Quin's hand. "I'm okay."

Quin scanned her face then narrowed his eyes on Banning. "Go home, before your mom figures out you're here. She won't be as forgiving as Layla."

Banning's shoulders sagged as he dropped his head. "Right. Sorry, Layla. I didn't mean to make you uncomfortable."

"It's okay," she assured. "You just surprised me, but I'm fine, really." And she was. Banning was obviously harmless, and his enthusiasm amused her. "So . . . mint?"

"Spearmint," he confirmed, setting the pot next to the door. "They say it's for warmth and welcoming, but its uses go beyond symbolism." His aura had brightened, but when he glanced at Quin, the colors muted. "I'll see you guys tomorrow," he said. Then he took two large steps to the north, vaulted the railing, and disappeared behind the house next door.

Quin sighed, rubbing his jaw as he led Layla onto the porch.

"You didn't have to be so hard on him," she said, examining her new plant. "He brought me a present."

"He knew what was coming," Quin replied, picking up the clay pot. "And I have to respect him for showing up anyway. I'm sure he expected worse."

"You should apologize," Layla pressed.

Quin paused with his hand on the doorknob, grinning as he searched her aura. "He'll laugh in return, but if it makes you feel better, I'll tell him tomorrow."

"Why would he laugh?"

"Because it's already water under the bridge. Banning's my brother in every way but blood. There will be no grudges held over this."

"Oh," she mumbled. "That's good, because I don't want to alienate my family before getting to know them."

"I doubt you could alienate anyone," he replied, opening the door, "least of all this coven."

Layla stepped inside as Quin flipped a light on, illuminating a large living room. Its main elements were pristine and white—the carpet, the oversized couch and padded armchairs, the marble fireplace embedded with sparkling quartz. Even the walls were white, but a much warmer shade and decorated with colorful art pieces, gemstone scattered shelves, and framed photos.

Layla's gaze froze on the biggest photograph, and the next thing she knew she was right in front of it, unable to remember her trek across the room.

The frame was about three feet tall, made of polished silver, and engraved with a vine of roses, each rosebud encasing a cluster of green and blue gemstones. Layla knew the picture well. She'd stared at it for hours at a time on several occasions.

She shrugged her backpack off her shoulders, pulling out the photo of her parents on their wedding day. Then she held it beside the one on the wall. They were identical, but the larger photo was impeccably clear with colors so vivid, the subjects looked real. They stared right at her. No... right through her. Her parents would never look at her that way. Salty moisture blurred her vision as she wondered why. What had ripped their family apart? Now that she was there, where she should have always been, she ached to know why.

She didn't realize Quin had moved beside her until he pulled a tear from her cheek, transforming it into a dark blue rose petal. When he tentatively pulled her into a hug, she gladly tucked into his chest.

"I know this must be hell on you," he whispered. "I'm sorry you're hurting."

"I just don't understand," she returned. "I need to know why."

"The answer to that will hurt as well."

"Probably, but now that I've seen where I came from, where I should have been this whole time, I have to know why I wasn't."

He sighed and leaned back. "The box is in the master bedroom."

"It's already here?" she asked, her wounded heart beating faster.

"Yes. Serafin brought it over before we got here."

She wondered how her grandfather had known to put it there. Then she realized she didn't care. "Where's the bedroom?"

Quin led her down a wide corridor, stopping at the first door on the right. Then he reached inside and flipped a switch, illuminating a crystal chandelier.

Like the living room, the bedroom was huge. Unlike the living room, it was bathed in color, multiple shades of blue and green bursting from linens and walls. But it wasn't tacky or overwhelming. It was impossibly perfect, simultaneously soothing and romantic.

To the right sat a large bed with an ornate, four poster frame stained dark to match the bench at its end, the two nightstands, the dresser, and the armoire and coffee table across the room. The table held a bouquet of emerald green and sea blue roses, and two blue armchairs were arranged on one side, facing a large window hidden by emerald green velvet. Had the drapes been drawn, the view would hold the porch and lawn. These walls were also decorated in art and photos, but of a much different sort. Many of the pieces were erotic, but they were so beautiful, exuding passion rather than sex, that Layla wasn't the least bit embarrassed by their explicit nature.

Her eyes went back to the bed, falling on a box carved from dark reddish-brown wood.

"Are you sure you're ready?" Quin asked, leading her closer.

"No," she confessed, heartbeat erratic, lungs insufficient. "But I have to know."

Despite her burning curiosity, she didn't move to take the box. She just stared at it with wide eyes.

"Do you want me to leave?" Quin asked.

"No," she blurted, tightening her grip.

He reached over, stroking her tense wrist. "It's okay," he assured. "I won't go unless you ask me to. You can relax."

"Sorry," she mumbled, loosening her grip.

"Don't be," he insisted.

Layla stared at the box for another long moment, running her gaze over the long stemmed rose carved into the lid. Then she kicked off her shoes and hoisted herself onto the tall bed, sitting with her legs dangling over the edge.

"Will you look inside and tell me if there's anything in there besides the ring?" she asked.

"I can't," Quin refused, sitting next to her. "It's sealed with magic only you can break."

"Oh yeah," she whispered. Then she sighed and scooted to the center of the bed.

Once she sat cross-legged in front of the box, she took a deep breath and opened the lid, finding a lonely ring glittering from within the soft folds of emerald green velvet.

Layla stared at it for several seconds, too nervous to take in the details. Then she met Quin's stare. "You really have no idea what's going to happen when I put this on?"

"I know some things that will happen," he answered, moving to the spot beside her.

"Like what?"

"Well, you won't be aware of what's happening here, in real time, until the memories are complete. And you probably won't be aware of your body. You'll be seeing things through your parents' perspective, not your own."

"Anything else?" she asked, plucking the ring from the velvet.

"I know what led to your adoption," he confessed, "but it's not my story to tell. It wouldn't be fair for you to hear a secondhand account of your past."

"I see," she mumbled, fidgeting with the heirloom.

When her aura shifted, Quin knew she was gearing up for the dive and offered one more pitiful piece of advice. "You should lie down and get comfortable before putting it on. Like I said, you won't be aware of your body."

"I'll take your word for it," she said, slipping out of her sweater. Then she moved the box to the foot of the bed and uncrossed her legs, lying back on the heap of pillows.

Quin ran his gaze from her head to her toes, trying to steady his heart and lungs. A difficult task when so exposed to her curves. He cursed his suddenly inadequate restraint and looked to her face, finding her staring up at him.

"What will you do?" she asked.

"What do you want me to do?" he returned.

After a moment's hesitation, she took his hand and pulled him down beside her. "I want you to stay with me," she whispered.

"Then that's what I'll do," he agreed.

"Thank you."

He reached over, touching a forefinger to her blushing cheek. "You don't have to thank me for this. I want to be here for you when it's over."

Layla anxiously held his gaze for several seconds. Then she looked at the ring, swallowing an all too familiar lump. After filling her lungs with oxygen, she slipped the wedding band on the third finger of her right hand.

She gasped as her muscles trembled. Then her body faded away as her mind tumbled through a blur of color, landing in an entirely different time and place.

Chapter 17

22 Years Earlier—Virginia

The moist grass reflected the sunlight filtering through a partly cloudy sky, and Aedan lounged on his coven's lawn, celebrating his nineteenth birthday. He was surrounded by family, friends and the woman he'd been dating—Medea Blair of the Blair / Casey community, located about two hundred miles away.

A pretty witch with a sociable personality, Medea was used to attention from men, and she'd held Aedan's for two dates, both of which ended with a polite kiss on her hand. Most wizards would have sealed the deal at that point, if not sooner, but Aedan was restless when it came to women and only stopped to savor them on occasion, usually finding they weren't the flavor he was looking for.

No, he didn't intend to ask Medea out a third time, let alone seal the deal, so when she invited herself to his birthday party, he only agreed out of politeness. As he watched her cozy up to his family, he regretted his consent. It was time to cut her loose.

He scanned the straw colored highlights in her shoulder-length brown hair then slid his gaze down her slender cheeks, watching her defined lips chat with one of his friends. Her eyes were like warm honey—amber in the dark, yellow in the light. And it was that alone that led to their first date. Aedan was confident it would lead her to another, but with a different wizard.

When Medea caught Aedan watching her, she beamed, apparently misjudging his stare for one of fondness. "Are you enjoying your party?" she asked, scooting closer.

"Yes," he answered, looking away. "You?"

"I always enjoy myself when I'm with you."

Aedan's stomach churned and tightened. "I'm glad you're having a good time."

"We should fly to the beach when the party ends," she suggested. "Just you and me."

Aedan watched a bird soar through the clearing as he considered his response. "I doubt we'll have time. You know how these things go. It could be dawn before the last man falls over."

"Yeah," she laughed. "I guess you're right. How about tomorrow? I could stay the night."

Aedan hated lying, but unless he wanted to cause a scene, there was no way around it. Hopefully his aura wouldn't give him away. "I'm busy tomorrow."

Medea's expression fell then brightened. "How about Sunday?"

"I don't know what's going on Sunday," Aedan dodged. "We'll have to wait and see."

Medea slid her fingers to his hair, and the knot in his stomach squirmed. "I need a refill," he mumbled, jumping to his feet. Then he walked away, not giving her a chance to invite herself along.

Aedan avoided Medea the rest of the evening, but she noticed and stuck close, growing increasingly worried with every evasive move he made. By the time the party wound down, she was practically attached to him, and her eyes were pleading loud enough for anyone to hear.

In contrast to his eighteenth birthday party, Aedan stayed sober, determined to keep his common sense. It would be an unpleasant experience—waking up the following morning with her raptly staring at him. And it would only make the inevitable let down more difficult.

When the lawn emptied of everyone save for the two of them, Aedan threw Medea a weary glance then began clearing a table, wondering how much longer she could hold her tongue.

Not long. "What's going on, Aedan?" she demanded. "You've been avoiding me all evening. Even now that there's no one around, you're blowing me off."

Aedan took a deep breath and turned, finding her worried face. This time a lie would be unnecessary. "Let's sit, Medea. We need to talk."

"I don't want to sit," she refused. "Tell me what's going on."

"Okay. You're a lovely witch, but I can't return your feelings for me. It's time to move on."

"You're breaking up with me?" she blurted, honey eyes burning bright gold.

"We're not together," he countered. "We went on two dates to get to know each other better."

"I thought you had a good time," she huffed.

"I did. That's why there was a second date, but there won't be a third. I like you, but not that way. It's time to move on."

She pouted for a moment then relaxed, closing the gap between them. "You're fooling yourself," she challenged, tucking her fingers in his waistband, "trying to pretend you can't be tamed, but you're not fooling me. Tell you what," she added, licking her lips and wiggling her fingers, "keep your wild ways; just let me get closer to the beast. If you'll give me a chance, I'll show you how fun a third date can be."

"I won't take advantage of your feelings for me," he refused.

"What if I said I didn't mind?" she countered.

He swallowed, undeniably tempted to allow himself a birthday romp on the lawn. "I would know better," he resisted, steeling his resolve.

Medea's smile fell as her forehead furrowed. "You need time to think about it," she decided, pulling her hand away. "I'll see you later." She glared at him for another moment then shot into the air.

Aedan watched her go, surprised and concerned by the intensity of her disappointment. Then he sighed and grabbed a jug of wine off the beverage table, magically popping the cork as he headed inside.

Aedan didn't see or hear from Medea for two months, so his worry and guilt ebbed, but then she returned, bringing anxiety with her.

Aedan was in the coven's barn, grooming his horse, when Medea appeared in the doorway, twirling a piece of straw. "Hi, Aedan."

Aedan recognized her voice and halted, taking a moment to smooth his annoyed expression before looking over. "Medea. What brings you here?"

She dropped the straw and walked forward. "You."

"What about me?" he asked, resuming his chore.

"Don't play dumb, Aedan. You know why I'm here."

"Why don't you explain? Just in case."

"I came to see if you've reconsidered," she confessed. "Have you thought about my offer?"

"No."

"Why don't you look at me when you lie to me?"

Aedan stopped what he was doing and faced her. "I'm not lying."

"Then you're in denial."

"No. I'm not interested and I never will be. Give yourself a break and find someone who is."

His rejection floated in one ear and out the other as she took a quick step toward him, smoothly slipping her hand into his pants. By the time Aedan looked down to see if she'd really done what he thought she'd done, she had a firm hold on his manhood. His mouth fell open as he attempted to push her away—carefully—but she stood firm, honey eyes blazing.

"You want this," she insisted, squeezing.

"I really don't," he refused. Nothing about the situation was tempting. She was obviously desperate and entirely too pushy. "Get your hand out of my pants," he simmered. "It's not welcome."

She remained in place, nostrils flaring as her grip tightened. "You're a fool, Aedan. You won't even give me a chance."

"You can call me whatever you want," he tensely warned, "but if you don't remove your hand, I'll remove it for you."

A tinge of fear tweaked her features. Then she relaxed, tilting her chin up as she slid her hand from his pants. "I see you need more time, but don't worry, I'll be back." Then she spun around, whistling as she strolled from the barn.

"Damn," Aedan cursed, turning back to his horse.

Medea clearly hadn't moved on, and he feared things would only get worse.

Like before, Medea kept her distance longer than Aedan expected her to. It had been a month since the unpleasant scene in the barn, and he hadn't seen or heard from her. He didn't dare hope she'd moved on to a different conquest; that might jinx her absence.

His mood was as fair as the weather—sunny with a cool breeze—and he was on his way to a neighboring magical community for a party. He landed outside the lawn, walked in then scanned the large crowd, spotting a few friends lounging on a hillside.

As he headed their way, Medea lithely stepped into his path, flashing a smile that would have looked coy had she a demure bone in her body.

"Are you enjoying the party?" she asked.

One would never know their last meeting ended with his cruel yet necessary rejection. "I just got here," he answered, looking away.

"You can sit with us," she offered, pulling on his hand.

Aedan met her stare and flexed his arm, but he didn't say anything. Words, no matter how they were delivered, flew over her head.

Her expression pinched then smoothed, and she willingly released him. "You are stubborn, Aedan, but I like that about you."

Aedan watched her aura for a moment then sighed, maneuvering around her and walking away. He considered looking back, but didn't want to give her the satisfaction, so he kept his eyes on the ground, hoping she wouldn't follow.

As he neared his friends, he looked up, and his agile steps faltered, forcing him to pause.

Literally breathtaking, the stranger before him was more beautiful than the moon and sun combined. The stars and planets had nothing on her. Her thick, golden hair spiraled past her slender waist, and she wore a pale pink gown that clung elegantly to her svelte body. She moved like fluid, her flawless skin glittering like the surface of a sun-kissed sea. And her aura… it was the most magnificent he'd seen—more colors than he could count swimming with glittering strips of silver, gleefully vibrating, enthusiastically swirling. He had to know her. The sparkling beauty before him was the one thing missing from his blessed life.

As he approached, she turned, looking at him with eyes so blue he could swim in them, drown in them, and he forgot how to breathe as his heart raced. "Hi," he greeted, unsure how he'd managed it.

With that one word, Rhosewen's heart hammered against her ribs, lurching toward the most exquisite man she'd ever seen. Tall, dark and handsome with a lively aura boasting distinct and resplendent colors, he bathed her in both shadow and luminous light. She had to tilt her head back to observe his face, finding first the sun glinting off his straight, black hair, then his emerald gaze, which seemed to bore into her soul.

She took a deep breath to steady herself, truly hoping he wouldn't notice. Then she lightly cleared her throat. "Hello."

So, Aedan thought, his gaze unwavering, that's what an angel sounds like.

One of Aedan friends, a lifelong acquaintance named Keith Ballard, attempted to gain his attention. "Hey, Aedan. Just get here?"

"About five minutes ago," Aedan answered, keeping his eyes on the golden stranger.

Keith must have noticed the exchange, because he promptly introduced them. "This is Rhosewen—my cousin from Oregon. That's Aedan—a fellow Virginian."

Rhosewen smiled, wreaking further havoc on Aedan's heart.

"It's a pleasure to meet you," she said, sending fantastic chills across his flesh.

"The pleasure's all mine," Aedan returned, taking her extended hand, but he didn't shake it; he pulled it to his lips, brushing a kiss across slender knuckles. He knew others were watching, but didn't care. He couldn't look away from her. Her ivory skin had flooded with color, intensifying her radiance.

A shiver ran from Rhosewen's fingers to her spine, and her knees trembled. She'd never had such a strong reaction to a man and struggled to maintain composure. Her heart thumped so hard and fast, the thick material of her satin dress noticeably fluttered over heaving breasts.

Aedan didn't want to let her go, but feared he was embarrassing her, so he let her fingers slide away. "I'm going to find the wine," he said. "Will you join me?" He wanted to get her away from prying eyes, so he could learn more about her, everything about her.

Rhosewen glanced at Keith, who merely shrugged, so she turned back with a smile. "Sure."

Aedan offered his arm, and Rhosewen accepted, letting him lead her along the outskirts of the crowd.

"What's your last name, Rhosewen?"

"Conn," she answered. "Yours?"

"Donnelly."

Aedan spotted the beverage table and aimed a palm at it, summoning two glasses of wine, which soon floated into their hands.

"I want to get to know you, Rhosewen Conn. Will you sit with me?"

"Yes," she agreed. "As long as you reciprocate."

Aedan smiled and led her to an empty spot on the hillside, letting her get comfortable before jumping to the point. "What would you like to know?"

"I get to go first?"

"Sure."

"Okay." She thought for a moment. "What's your element?"

"Fire."

"And your second?"

"Water."

She raised a suspicious eyebrow, and he curiously tilted his head. "Have I said something wrong already?"

"Are you telling the truth?"

"Yes," he laughed. "Why do you ask?"

She appraised him for another moment then shrugged. "It's just quite a coincidence that we're both fire children with water as our second."

"That is quite a coincidence," he agreed. "Maybe we have more in common."

"Maybe. What's your sign?"

"Pisces. I turned nineteen on March 5th."

"You're not lying?" she asked, and he laughed again.

"Why would I lie about that?"

"I don't know, but this is too weird."

"I guess you're a Pisces?"

"Yes. I turned twenty on March 15th."

Aedan considered the similarities as he watched her, fascinated by how perfect she was. "Does it bother you that we have these things in common?"

"No," she replied. "It's just weird."

"I'm sure we'll come up with dissimilar attributes eventually," he surmised, searching for something unusual about himself. "I have one. I'm a bonded child."

Rhosewen froze with her wine halfway to her mouth, flipping her gaze to Aedan's aura. And he froze as well, focusing on the haze around her. He couldn't believe he hadn't already figured it out. No wonder she glittered so brightly.

They stayed that way for several seconds, wondering what to make of their remarkable likenesses. Then Aedan smiled and broke the stunned silence. "You're a bonded child."

Rhosewen took a drink and cleared her throat. "Yes."

"This *is* interesting, Rhosewen Conn."

"Very," she agreed, smiling as well.

They sat in silence for a long time, reading each other's auras while sipping their wine, incredibly content to do so. Then Rhosewen emptied her glass and continued the interview. "What's your favorite animal?"

"Would you feel better if I said cats?"

"Would you be lying?"

"Yes."

"Let me guess, the truth would be dogs."

"Yes."

Rhosewen laid her glass on the ground and turned toward him. "I have another one, but I think we should answer at the same time."

Aedan set his glass aside, in awe of her vivaciousness and amused by her game. "Okay, shoot."

They stared into each other's eyes for five seconds. Then she smirked and asked her question. "What's your favorite color? On three. One . . . two . . . three . . ."

"Green," she answered, right as he said, "Blue."

"See?" he teased. "We're as different as night and day."

She laughed, and it sounded like a heavenly choir singing his favorite song.

"Will you share another glass of wine with me, Rhosewen?"

She nodded her approval, so he refilled their goblets and handed hers over. "Do you work?" he asked.

"Yeah," she answered. "I'm an ecotourism guide. I lead hikes around Mount Hood."

"Do you like it?"

"Yes, but my passion is art. Painting more specifically."

"Do you sell your work?"

"Some of it; my parents own a gallery. But the majority of my work stays in the family. What about you? Are you a painter slash ecotourism guide?"

"No," he laughed. "But I do work with nature. I make wooden furniture for my parents' shop."

"Do you like it?"

"Sure. Woodworking comes naturally to me, so much so a lot of people wagered I'd be an earth child. I carved my first rocking chair at three."

"Did your parents sell it?"

"No. It's on their porch. Mom loves to tell the story of how it was made."

"That's sweet."

"Moms tend to be that way," he agreed.

Their privacy depleted as a crowd gathered on the hillside to watch a game of flame-away—thirty magicians tossing around a fireball as another group of ten tried to extinguish it with water spells. A nearby group of rambunctious children quickly decided to play their own game, but their fireballs fizzled prematurely, and those spraying water aimed at their neighbors more than the puny target.

Rhosewen laughed as she adoringly watched the children, and Aedan's heart stuttered as he intently watched her.

As sunset approached, the flame-away participants lost interest, and only then did the hillside's occupants begin to scatter.

"Do you know that woman?" Rhosewen asked, pointing down the hill.

Until Aedan followed Rhosewen's gesture, he'd forgotten Medea existed, but there she was, glaring at him with burning eyes and pursed lips. He turned his back on her, slightly worried she might literally burn him with those golden eyes, but she was smarter than that; too many witnesses around.

"Her name's Medea," he answered. "She lives about a hundred miles southwest of here."

"Well that's not the first time she's looked at us that way," Rhosewen noted. "Is she an ex?"

"Not by my standards," he replied. "We went on two dates last February and it didn't work out."

Rhosewen raised a curious eyebrow, so he quickly changed the subject. "Would you like to go for a walk?" he asked, vanishing their empty glasses. "There's a river on the other side of the hill with a good view of the sunset."

"Sure," Rhosewen agreed, taking his hand.

As they climbed the hill, he wrapped one arm around her shoulders, and she looked up in surprise. But she didn't resist; the weight and warmth of his arm felt perfect. When they reached the top of the hill, she glanced back, and a shiver ran down her spine. Medea continued to stare, eyes and aura burning.

Rhosewen turned away, looking to the man beside her. Then they were on the other side of the hill and completely alone. Medea didn't exist anymore. In fact, nearly everything was wiped from Rhosewen's mind. All she could concentrate on was Aedan—the arm around her back, the fingers squeezing her shoulder, the hip brushing her side. She swallowed hard, wondering how she would keep her head with him. She'd never been so thoroughly and immediately attracted to a man. The tidal wave of emotions unnerved her.

The river came into view, so Aedan stopped walking, scanning their surroundings as he pulled her closer. "How long will you be in Virginia?"

"A week," she answered, marveling at the coral sky.

"Hmm…" Aedan mumbled. Though he never intended to commit to a woman so soon in life, Rhosewen had him reconsidering. Maybe he could let her leave in a week and move on, but the thought made him nauseous. To think this night would be his only chance to look at her golden hair, ivory skin, and sea blue eyes had his stomach in knots. He was shocked by his immediate attachment to her. He barely knew her, yet she was the reason his lungs transported air. Without her, the vital organs would surely deflate. He needed more of her, all of her, forever. He would have to act fast. If he had any hope of keeping her in his life, he'd have to convince her he was worthy, and he only had a week to do it.

"Stunning," Rhosewen whispered, still watching the west.

"Yes," Aedan agreed, keeping his eyes on her.

Rhosewen looked up at him and had to stifle a gasp. The burst of color on the horizon was beautiful, but he was better. His emerald eyes brimmed with affection as they slowly admired every inch of her face, and the corners of his sensual mouth were turned up, as if he was immensely pleased with what he saw. His warmth emanated through her dress, licking at tingling flesh, and his scent called her name, tempting her to cuddle his neck. When he rested a hand on her hip, she moved closer, like her muscles had a mind of their own. Then he leaned in, sharing the air she breathed, and all her hesitation floated away. She was putty in his hands.

Aedan paused an inch from her face, searching for unwillingness, but there wasn't a refusal to find, only a subtle parting of the plump, pink lips he could no longer resist.

Their first kiss was unhurried, intense and more meaningful than any before it. Eager to accept and prolong, they held each other tightly, memorizing and savoring every taste and feel, every second of every sensation.

By the time they stopped to breathe, they were bathed in moonlight.

"I want to see you again," Aedan whispered, keeping his fingers buried in soft spirals. He wanted to see her everyday for the rest of his life. He wanted to kiss her like that every morning and every night. He wanted to wake up to her aqua eyes forever.

"I'd like that, too," Rhosewen replied, "but I don't know if it's a good idea."

"I think it's the best idea I've ever had," he countered.

"We barely know each other," she argued.

"I'm trying to remedy that," he returned.

"I'm leaving in a week, Aedan."

"Are you trying to convince me?" he asked. "Or yourself?"

She didn't answer, and Aedan took her silence as a good sign. "Have you ever been to the Devil's Den Nature Preserve?" he asked, keeping her pressed against him, terrified to let go.

"No, but I hear it's beautiful."

"It is," he confirmed. "We could make it there in about an hour and a half. Will you let me take you?"

"When?"

"Tomorrow. We could fly over before sunrise and spend the day there." He held his breath, waiting for her answer.

Rhosewen laughed, laying a hand over his expanded chest as she caved. "Okay, as long as my family doesn't mind if I skip out for the day. We only visit once a year."

Aedan was thrilled. Getting her to say yes was the hard part. He'd known Keith's coven his entire life and was certain he'd get their permission. "Good. I'll pick you up at four in the morning, providing, of course, your family can spare you for the day."

"It's a date," Rhosewen agreed, flashing a smile that stole his breath, but his heart soared.

Chapter 18

Aedan arrived five minutes early Sunday morning, but Rhosewen was already outside, waiting on her aunt's porch. She stood from the landing as he approached, and like the first time he'd seen her, his steps faltered.

She was even more beautiful than he remembered. The previous night's dreams hadn't done her justice. Her long, indigo dress contrasted beautifully with her ivory skin, which glittered like snow in the moonlight.

"Good morning," he greeted, taking her midnight blue flying cloak.

He held it open, letting her slip her arms in. Then he carefully pulled the hood over her hair, drifting his fingers down loose spirals to the sapphire clasp at her throat.

Rhosewen was glad he took the liberty; she was paralyzed by his perfect manners and handsome visage. "Good morning."

Aedan smiled and took her cheeks. "You're even more beautiful today than you were yesterday," he whispered.

"Thank you," she breathed, trembling from head to toe.

He leaned in, inhaling her shallow breaths. Then he brushed a soft kiss across her lips. "Are you ready?"

His breath rushed over her tongue, hammering her heart and scattering her brain. How did he do that? The simplest of gestures from him made her legs weak and her oxygen intake inadequate.

"Yes," she barely managed, and he released her face, taking her hand instead.

Having flown these lands before, neither of them watched the scenery. Even when they navigated over Mount Rogers, their eyes stayed on each other, ignoring the red spruce and Fraser fir trees blanketing the mountain slopes. Just before sunrise, they alighted in a large meadow atop a mountain crest.

"You're very graceful in flight," Aedan noted, watching her drop her hood.

"Thank you," she replied, grinning up at him. "Would you believe I was thinking the same thing about you?"

Aedan watched her radiant smile for several peaceful seconds. Then he cleared his throat and pointed east. "We'll see the sun rise in about two minutes."

They silently stood, hand in hand, watching the sky shift from inky blue to pearl gray. When the sun finally breached the horizon, brilliant shades of red and gold bathed them in heat and glittering light.

They took their time exploring the reserve and each other, and the more they learned, the clearer it became—they weren't learning enough. They wanted to know everything.

When no one was around, they compared their magic, finding their abilities evenly matched. And when strangers were nearby, they took the opportunity to close the distance between them, whispering into each other's ears.

Around noon, they claimed a deserted clearing for a picnic, and Aedan summoned their supplies from the bewitched bag at his waist.

"So how did you end up in Oregon?" he asked, taking her hand as they sat.

"Well," she answered, "my mom grew up in Virginia, in the Murray/Hughes coven."

"Murray/Hughes," Aedan repeated, recalling what he knew of them. "Are you Adonia's granddaughter?"

"Yes. She's my mom's mom."

"Then my dad probably knows your mom."

"Probably, if he knows my Grandma Addy."

"So how did your mom end up in Oregon?"

"My dad of course. He met my mom at an art festival in Ireland. The crowd parted and they locked eyes, just like a fairytale. They bonded the next night, but mom says she was ready to uproot her life the second she saw him. She was just relieved he was from the states."

"I bet," Aedan replied, quickly realizing how frustrating distance could be.

"I used to think her move to Oregon was a no-brainer," Rhosewen added, scanning the nature around them. "It's so beautiful there. But the more I visit Virginia, the more I realize how hard it must have been for her to leave. This place is fantastic."

"I've never been to Oregon," Aedan confessed, passing her a sandwich, "but I hear it's breathtaking."

"So is this," she countered, watching a whitetail deer creep into view.

"Yes," he agreed, "but as bonded children, we both know that the land, no matter how beautiful, can't compare to the love of your life."

Rhosewen looked at him, finding his attentive gaze. "That's true."

They watched each other as they ate in silence, completely comfortable with the intense eye contact, and not until he packed away their supplies did Aedan look away.

"So," Rhosewen said, glancing at the doe, which had settled down for a nap at the edge of the clearing. "What's next?"

"There's one more spot I'd like to show you," Aedan answered, "but it's probably crowded right now. If we wait until sunset, we'll have it to ourselves. Unless you're in a hurry to get back?"

"No hurry. What will we do until then?"

"Have you ever spent time with an alpaca?"

"No," she laughed. "I can't say that I have."

"There's a farm nearby that's open to the public," Aedan explained. "They're amazing creatures. Would you like to see them?"

"Sure," she agreed. "Let's go spend some quality time with the alpacas."

Aedan was right. The alpacas were amazing, and too cute. When Rhosewen entered their enclosure, three babies quickly approached, and she knelt, rubbing the tops of their fuzzy heads. The crias' moms followed their young, and Aedan rubbed their necks.

"They're so cute," Rhosewen whispered, in awe of the gentle beasts. "And soft."

"They raise them for their fiber," Aedan explained. "It's softer, stronger and warmer than wool."

Rhosewen giggled as a blonde cria nuzzled her neck. "They're magnificent."

"It seems they feel the same about you," Aedan observed, petting the greedy alpaca nudging his cheek.

After spending nearly two hours admiring the alpacas, Rhosewen said goodbye to the babies four different times then let Aedan lead her to the farm's gift shop. When he caught her admiring a powder blue, sleeveless shirt made of cria fiber, he found it in her size and insisted on buying it. Not that she put up a good fight. She was too busy falling for him to fight him.

By the time they said another farewell to the alpacas and left the farm, sunset was less than an hour away. They flew back to the reserve then landed on a deserted trail, walking toward their next destination.

"Thank you for showing me the alpacas," Rhosewen said, feeling like the luckiest girl in the world.

"You're welcome," Aedan returned. "I'm glad you liked it."

"Very much, but I wish you would have let me pay for the shirt."

"Not a chance," he refused. Then he grinned as he scanned her aura. "You could pay me back."

"Really?" she asked, raising a suspicious eyebrow.

"Yes, by letting me see you in it tomorrow."

The thought of seeing him again made her heart soar. "It sounds like I'm getting the better end of the deal."

"Not possible," Aedan countered. "This is the best deal I've ever made."

Rhosewen glanced at the hand on her shoulder, yearning to pull it further around her, to move into his chest and lose herself there. But there was something nagging her. "So," she said, "that witch from yesterday—Medea. Were you telling the truth about her?"

Aedan sighed and rubbed his jaw. "What I said is true, but there's more to the story than I told you."

"I thought so. Is there still something going on between you two?"

"No," he quickly replied. "It's not like that."

"Then what's it like?"

"I told you the truth. We only went on two dates and it didn't work out. What I didn't tell you is that she wasn't too happy about it. She thinks I'm in denial about my feelings for her, but that's not the case. I took her out to get to know her and quickly realized I didn't want her, so I ended it."

"Hmm . . ." Rhosewen murmured. "Is there more to it? Is she a jilted lover?"

"No," Aedan assured. "Things never got physical. Medea thinks that's the problem—that sex will close the gap between us. But she's deluding herself." He paused, meeting Rhosewen's searching gaze. "Basically, she thinks we have a chance, and she's a little obsessed about making it happen. That's the whole truth. I swear."

There was a long moment of tense silence. Then Rhosewen shrugged. "Sometimes women get overzealous when it comes to gorgeous men. I'm sorry Medea's being such a pain."

Aedan was so relieved, only Rhosewen's hand in his kept him from doing a back-flip. "I haven't convinced you I'm more trouble than I'm worth?" He had to be sure.

"It's not your fault," Rhosewen replied. "But this does mean she won't like me hanging around."

Aedan wasn't sure how far Medea would go to get her way. He hoped he'd never find out. "Does that worry you?"

"No," Rhosewen answered. "I can defend myself."

Aedan had no doubt. Her magic was strictly disciplined and extremely powerful.

"Besides," she quietly added, "I'm leaving in six days."

"Six days," Aedan repeated. Not enough time. He didn't think even a lifetime would suffice.

He looked to the setting sun—a thin line on the horizon surrendering half the sky to soft stars and a distant moon. "We're almost there," he said, squeezing her shoulders. "The park closes to the public at sunset, so we should have it to ourselves."

A few minutes later, they approached the dark mouth of a deep cavern, stopping in the shadow of giant leaning rocks.

"It doesn't look that extraordinary at first," Aedan admitted, "but it feels extraordinary."

Rhosewen understood what he meant. The atmosphere pulsed with energy. She could feel it and smell it, and when she focused, she could see it. A translucent, multicolored haze, much like an aura, rolled from the cave, curling up jagged stone and across cool ground. Having previous experiences with similar mists, Rhosewen knew the rock formation was extremely old.

"It's beautiful," she whispered, moving closer. "How long has it been here?"

"Scientists say six-hundred-million years," Aedan answered, carefully leading her down steep stone to the depths of the cavern. "But only the Heavens know for sure. We do know it was formed by rock collision rather than water erosion, so it's been a dry haven for thousands before us. Do you want to sit?" he asked, finding a smooth slab of granite.

"Yes," Rhosewen agreed, lowering herself toward the stone, but before she could get there, Aedan scooped her legs out from under her.

He smiled at her shock as he sat, making her comfortable on his lap. Then they turned their attention to the cloud of energy slithering along the quartz-laced walls.

After several peaceful seconds, Aedan broke the silence. "You like it."

"Very much," Rhosewen confirmed. "But it's a little overwhelming."

"That's what's so great about it," he countered. "It's incredible how much emotion is packed in here. It's sheltered millions of living things, witnessing life and death, and it retains an impression of every feeling that passes through it. It's swarming with memories that humble the soul and tug at the heart."

"Yes," Rhosewen agreed, clearly sensing what he spoke of.

"Which one do you feel most?" he asked, playing with a golden curl.

Rhosewen looked at him, half confused, half hesitant. "Do you want to know what I'm feeling, or what I sense in the atmosphere?"

"The atmosphere," Aedan clarified, stifling a grin. "There are a lot of obvious emotions floating around. Which one catches your immediate attention?"

Rhosewen smiled, wondering if he'd meant to trap her. She knew which emotion had the strongest hold on her, but she wasn't sure its source had anything to do with the cave's ambiance. "You go first," she insisted.

Aedan stared at her lips, his own twitching with humor. Then he took her hand and entwined their fingers. "Love," he answered. "Passion is a close second, oddly followed by pain then pleasure, but love is definitely the strongest." He looked at their hands then back to her face. "Do you feel it?"

Rhosewen swallowed a lump as she nodded, her lungs stuttering around an expanding heart.

They already loved each other. Somehow, in less than two days, they'd fallen harder and deeper than ever before. The way they felt sitting in each other's arms was foreign and fantastic—pure joy, bubbling anticipation, and sudden dependency. Neither of them ever wanted to let go.

"Thank you for bringing me here, Aedan."

"So you've enjoyed yourself?"

"Definitely."

"Good," he approved, hugging her closer.

As his nose drifted through her hair, he breathed deep, letting the air out slowly before pulling more in. "Does anyone call you Rose?" he asked.

"No," she answered. "Why?"

"Surely someone calls you Rose."

"Not a soul," she insisted. "Why do you ask?"

"Because it would make a fitting nickname, and because you smell like one."

Rhosewen's insides bubbled with pleasure, knees trembling, extremities tingling. She always wondered why nobody called her Rose. She'd tried to start the nickname when she was seven, but while her parents agreed it was fitting, they refused to shorten her name. And for reasons she never understood, it didn't catch on with her peers. Eventually she gave up, figuring she didn't resemble a rose enough to be called one.

Aedan nuzzled her hair, brushing soft kisses across her neck. "May I call you Rose?"

"I would love that," she whispered, pulse quickening as heat stretched from her scalp to her toes.

Aedan found her face then searched her eyes. Every second he spent with her, every word she spoke and every move she made strengthened his powerful attraction. How on earth would he let her go after spending another six days with her? Clearly giving up those six days wasn't an option. Besides, letting her go, even at this point, would knock him down to a place he'd never been. Just the thought of never seeing her again sent his blood into a frenzy, catching his breath and tightening his muscles.

He looked away from her face and raised her hand, sweeping slow kisses along her fingers. "Rose."

"Yeah?" she sighed, savoring the name as it rolled from his lips.

Aedan smiled and kissed. "It worked."

"What worked?"

"You responded when I called you Rose." He looked from her hand to her face. "Rose."

"Are you talking to me?" she laughed. "Or just practicing?"

"Rhosewen is a beautiful name. I have to make sure the nickname compares or it won't do you justice."

"I like the way it sounds when you call me Rose."

"Then it's settled." He returned his gaze to her hand, resuming his kisses. "Would you like to hear something crazy, Rose?"

She sighed again. Yes, the name was perfect when blessed by his lips. "Sure."

"Yesterday afternoon," he revealed, "I was a different person."

"What do you mean?" she asked.

"Well, since I met you, I've experienced things I didn't know exist, and my outlook on life has shifted."

"Oh," she breathed, watching him kiss her pinky.

"All I can see now are roses," he added. "It's safe to say I've fallen for you."

Rhosewen thought her heart might explode it swelled so suddenly, fluttering her stomach and stuttering her chest. She tucked her face in his neck, hiding the salty moisture flooding her lids. How had this happened? How had she fallen in love with someone who lived a country away?

Aedan kissed her palm then her wrist, working his way up her arm. "I know the distance is a problem," he continued, "but I don't intend for Saturday to be the last time I see you." His lips swept across her collarbone, paused on her neck then lightly nibbled. "Providing, of course, you want to see me again."

"More than anything," she purred, trying to deepen her shallow breathing as her lips found his.

Aedan smiled as he wrapped her in a hug, sliding his fingers into waves of hair. Then he firmly pulled her against him, kissing her so passionately, her chest heaved, her fingers flexed, and her toes curled.

When the need to breathe interrupted their zealous kiss, they remained close, staring into each other's eyes as they gasped for air. Rhosewen stifled a giggle, but couldn't quit smiling as she laid her cheek on his shoulder, running her fingers through his racing aura.

"Are you hungry," he asked, touching his lips to her hair.

"You could say that," she answered, physically aching to satiate her thirst.

"For food," he laughed.

"Sure."

"There are a few places nearby that stay open late. If you'd like, we'll have dinner then sneak one more look at the alpacas before heading back."

"Sounds perfect," she agreed.

"Rose."

"Yeah?"

"I just wanted to say it."

"Oh," she whispered, nuzzling his neck. "Okay."

During the flight home, Aedan and Rhosewen thought about their future and what they could do to keep each other in it. When they landed, neither of them were ready to say goodnight, but it was late and Aedan didn't want her family to disapprove.

"What are your plans tomorrow?" he asked, brushing a hungry forefinger across her cheek.

"I'll be in Cape Charles until five," she answered, "at my aunt Ellena's shop. After that I'll be here. You?"

"I'll be at work until six. After that my plans include doing whatever I can to see you." He glanced at the house then back. "I don't think it's a good idea to steal you from your family two days in a row, but if you'd like, if I wouldn't be intruding, I could spend the evening here."

"Would you really?" she asked.

"There's nothing I'd rather do. Besides," he added, pointing to the bag in her hand, "you owe me for that shirt."

"You'll eat dinner with us," she beamed. "It's always an event when one of the families has company."

"They won't mind the intrusion?"

"Of course not."

"Then it's a date," Aedan agreed. "I'll be here tomorrow at six thirty."

"Tomorrow." She didn't want him to leave.

"At six thirty." He didn't want to leave.

He leaned in as she stood on her toes, then their lips met for a sweet kiss.

"Goodnight, Rose."

"Goodnight, Aedan."

His gaze stayed on her face as he stepped back. Then he winked and mouthed the word *tomorrow.*

Rhosewen's grin was a bit cheesy as she watched him fly away, and not until she lost sight of his aura did she happily bounce inside.

Aedan alighted on his coven's lawn to an unwelcome surprise—Medea, who flew from his porch and landed in front of him.

"Where have you been?" she coolly asked.

"That's none of your business," he returned, heading for the house.

"Fine," she huffed, following like a lovesick puppy, "don't tell me. I already know. You were with that witch from the party yesterday, the one from Oregon."

Aedan halted, finding Medea's pleading stare. "Why are you here?"

"Because," she pouted, "I thought we had something special. It's been months and I miss the way I feel when I'm with you. We could be great together, Aedan."

"I've told you every way I know how," he firmly replied, "I don't feel that way about you. You need to move on."

"You're lying. You have to be, because I feel a lasting connection between us."

Aedan scowled and slowly shook his head. "I'm not lying, and there is no us. No connection exists. You and I are nothing, Medea. You have to get that through your head."

She fumed for another few seconds. Then her anger drained away, replaced by doe-eyed innocence. "Look, Aedan, I'm willing to be patient. Maybe you don't feel that way yet, but I can change your mind. We have something to work with or you wouldn't have asked me out. Why fight it? Neither of us is seeing someone else. Why not give each other a chance?"

She stepped closer, raising a hand to his chest, but he quickly grabbed her wrist, returning it to her side. "No."

"Why not?" she demanded, stomping a foot.

"Because I don't want you," he returned, frowning at her immaturity. "And I am seeing someone else."

"Who? The witch from yesterday?"

"Yes."

Medea rolled her eyes, smirking her relief. "She's leaving Saturday, going home to Oregon. I'll still be here. Blondie's a temporary distraction. In six days, she'll be gone."

Aedan disliked that Medea knew so much about Rhosewen. "Not if I can help it."

Medea threw her head back and laughed. "You think she'll stay in Virginia for someone she barely knows?"

"Maybe," he answered, growing increasingly nervous over Medea's roller-coaster emotions. "Or maybe I'll move to Oregon."

Medea froze, narrowing her eyes as her hands clenched into fists. "You lie."

"No," he asserted. "Everything I've said is true. I don't know what will happen Saturday, but I have no intention of letting her leave without me."

"But you just met her!" Medea shrilled.

Aedan shrugged, figuring he would hear that a lot. He might as well get used to it. "It doesn't matter how long I've known her."

He spoke the truth. If Rhosewen were to leave Saturday, he'd leave with her. The decision was made. It didn't scare or worry him. It relieved him. He'd be with Rhosewen next week and the week after, as long as she'd have him.

Medea lost her cool, vibrating from head to toe. "You can't do this!" she shrieked, falling to her knees and clutching his cloak. "Please."

Aedan was shocked, absolutely appalled by her reaction. He knew she liked him and was teetering on obsession, but he had no idea she would take his rejection this hard. "Let go, Medea," he demanded, taking a few steps back, but she held firm and fell to the ground, screaming into the grass.

This is bad, Aedan thought. No, he corrected. An emotionally unstable witch is bad, but he was dealing with an emotionally unstable witch who felt betrayed, which could be disastrous. "Look," he said, keeping his voice even, "I'm no good for you. I can't give you what you want. You deserve someone who can love you, and that's not me."

Medea released his cloak and sat up. "I don't want someone else," she simmered. "I want you."

"You can't have me, Medea."

"I always get what I want," she whispered.

Aedan shook his head, his patience spent. "Not this time. I want you to leave me alone. And you need to leave Rhosewen alone. She has nothing to do with my decision not to be with you. Now leave my lawn. You have no reason to be here."

Medea made no effort to comply.

Aedan watched her blank expression and absent gaze for another moment then sighed and walked home. When he got to his bedroom, he left the lights off and looked out the window. She hadn't budged. Thirty minutes later, once he'd showered, she still hadn't moved.

He cursed as he got into bed. If he'd known things would turn out this way, he never would have dated her. He felt weak and irresponsible for letting an unstable witch into his life.

These and other worrisome thoughts kept him awake for over an hour, and at three in the morning, he was up again, jolting into consciousness.

Rhosewen had been calling to him in his dream, and he'd been searching, dread tightening his gut. When he found her back, he flew toward her, relieved, but then she turned and it was no longer Rhosewen. It was Medea.

Aedan jumped out of bed and moved to the window, scanning the lawn and surrounding forest. He spotted a glow to the south and focused, watching Medea's aura fade into timber. He couldn't prove it, but knew she'd planted the dream in his head.

Aching with worry, he returned to bed, telling himself Medea wasn't stupid enough to hurt Rhosewen. Then he recalled the hysterics on his lawn and realized he didn't know Medea at all. He couldn't count on her to be rational.

Monday morning, as Aedan caught up with weekend orders, he searched for a way to tell his parents he'd fallen in love with a woman he'd only known for two days and was considering a move to Oregon to be with her.

He remained clueless when he sat down to lunch, so he was unusually quiet when his dad sat across from him, summoning a plate of spaghetti and toast.

"What's new with you, son?" Serafin asked. "Anything?"

Aedan eyed him, thinking he might already know. "Yeah, actually, there is something new."

Serafin's nod confirmed Aedan's suspicion, so he continued his confession. "I met a woman at the party Saturday. Rhosewen Conn."

"Pretty name," Serafin replied.

"Yes it is."

"Pretty girl?"

"The prettiest."

"Don't let your mom hear that," Serafin joked. "After all these years of being your number one gal, it would break her heart."

Aedan laughed as he pretended to lock his lips and throw away the key. Then he took a few silent bites, bracing himself to disappoint the man who'd given him everything.

"I may be leaving Saturday," he revealed, preparing for a look of shock, anger or sadness.

Serafin nodded, and Aedan exhaled, furrowing his eyebrows as he scanned his dad's aura. "You already knew," he concluded.

"I saw something," Serafin confirmed, "but I wasn't sure. It wasn't a done deal, too many undecided factors."

"Were you checking up on me?" Aedan asked.

"Always," Serafin confessed, and Aedan experienced a strong rush of affection for his dad.

"So what do you think?"

"I only saw the possibility of you leaving, not the why. You'll have to fill me in on the details. I assume it has something to do with the prettiest girl?"

"You assume correctly."

Serafin scanned his son's aura then went back to his spaghetti. "Where does the blue-eyed beauty live?"

"Oregon."

Serafin frowned, but was quick to smooth his expression. "A beautiful state. You'd enjoy it."

"You're not going to try to talk me out of it?" Aedan asked. "Or lecture me on my haste?"

Serafin met Aedan's stare, their eyes exactly the same save for miniscule wrinkles of wisdom under one pair. "You're a fine young man, Aedan, mature beyond your years, even for a wizard. You're dedicated, determined and responsible, and you've never given me a reason to mistrust your judgment or regret your decisions. You aren't the type of man who loses his head over beautiful women, so if you want to follow Rhosewen across the country, I have to believe it's the real deal. I trust you, son, so does your mom. You'll have our support in whatever decision you make. We'll mourn your move, but we live for your happiness as much as our own. Besides," he added, pointing his fork, "I'm not blind. Your aura is quite clear to me. I'd be concerned if I saw it looking like this and you weren't taking action. I'd think I raised a layabout rather than a man who knows how to get things done."

Aedan was stunned and touched by the vote of confidence. "Thanks, dad. Your support means a lot to me."

Serafin smiled then turned his moist gaze to his plate. "I do think we should get to meet the young lady taking our only child from home. Are you seeing her tonight?"

"Yeah," Aedan answered, going back to his meal. "She and her parents are staying with the Ballard/Lancing coven. I'm joining them for dinner on their lawn."

"That would be a good opportunity to meet Rhosewen and her parents."

"You might already know her mom," Aedan revealed. "She's Ellena Ballard's sister."

"The one who bonded?"

"Yeah, with a man from Oregon—Caitrin Conn."

"That's right," Serafin recalled. "Morrigan. She and Ellena grew up in the Murray/Hughes coven."

"Yes," Aedan confirmed.

"Then I have met her," Serafin replied, "but it's been years. So Rhosewen's a bonded child."

"Yes," Aedan answered.

"Hmm. . ." Serafin mumbled. "I look forward to meeting her. Will it be tonight?"

"I don't know, dad. I haven't said anything to her about the commitment of relocating, and you weren't invited. I don't want to be rude."

"Nonsense. I'll give Ellena an innocent call. If she extends an invitation, I promise not to let the cat out of the cauldron."

"Okay," Aedan agreed. "If you get invited."

"Great," Serafin approved, cleaning up his mess. Then he stood and walked to the door.

"Dad," Aedan called.

Serafin halted, running a hand through his dark brown hair as he turned back. "Yeah?"

"Thanks again. For everything."

"Sure," Serafin replied, his chest noticeably rising and falling. Then he cleared his throat and left the room.

Rhosewen hummed happily as she walked through her aunt's garden, searching for things that didn't belong. She hadn't gone to Cape Charles after all and was keeping herself busy by doing chores around the house. She pointed at a weed pitifully poking from the ground, and it gracefully grew, transforming into a pink belladonna lily. She smiled, but not at the flower. She was picturing Aedan, imagining his tender touch.

Her smile widened as she headed for the back garden. Then the hair at the nape of her neck stood on end and she spun around, finding Medea less than ten feet away.

Rhosewen scanned the witch, focusing on her expression, fingers and aura, searching for threatening signs, but she found nothing immediately dangerous. Only curiosity, jealousy and blossoming instability.

Rhosewen remained wary. She hated confrontation and did her best to avoid it, but she wouldn't hesitate to defend herself. "Medea," she calmly greeted. "May I help you with something?"

Medea took a quick step forward, frowning when her competition failed to flinch. "So Aedan's told you about me," she said, searching Rhosewen's aura. "What did he say? That I'm a crazy witch who won't leave him alone?"

"He never said you were crazy," Rhosewen replied. "But he did say you're persistent and having a hard time letting go."

Medea's upper lip curled. "And you believe him?"

"Yes. Would you like to share your side of the story?"

"It's none of your business," Medea snapped. "You're the outsider here."

"I beg to differ," Rhosewen chided. "It's my family's lawn you're standing on."

Medea took a small step back as fear tweaked her features. Then she hurriedly composed herself, but her aura remained frozen as she scanned Rhosewen from head to toe.

After ten seconds of silence, Rhosewen took a step forward, and Medea took another faltering step back.

"Is there a reason why you're here?" Rhosewen asked. "If not, you should leave. I have things to do."

Medea lifted her chin and pushed her shoulders back. "I want to know when you're leaving."

"Saturday," Rhosewen answered. "Is there anything else I can do for you?"

Medea shook her head no, and Rhosewen took another step. "Then you should go."

Medea sniffed, glared for another ten seconds then shot into the air.

Rhosewen sighed as she watched her go, glad to be done with the meeting and hoping there wouldn't be another. She hated confrontation.

Serafin's plan succeeded. Within minutes of calling Ellena, he and Daleen were invited to dinner, so Aedan and his parents flew to the Ballard/Lancing community together.

Aedan could tell his mom was putting on a brave face. Her aura told him everything she was trying to hide, and it squeezed his heart to see her so sad, but picturing Rhosewen's face was the perfect antidote. He couldn't wait to see the real thing.

The moment he landed, he found Rhosewen's gaze, and their faces brightened with smiles they couldn't contain. She tried to keep her pace casual, but practically bounced across the lawn.

"Hi," she beamed.

"Hi," he returned, scanning her sparkling eyes and curved lips. He wanted to pull her into his arms, kiss her as deeply as he had the night before, but her family was watching, so he merely took her hand, kissing her fingers as he placed a pure white rose in her palm. "A rose for a Rose," he whispered.

She grinned and smelled her gift. "Thank you. It's beautiful."

He winked then turned toward his parents. "Mom, dad, this is Rhosewen Conn."

"It's a pleasure to meet you," Daleen greeted, taking Rhosewen's hands.

"You, too," Rhosewen replied. "Both of you."

Serafin flashed a broad smile as he stepped forward. "We've heard good things about you from your Grandma Adonia. You're even lovelier than your photos suggest."

"Thank you," Rhosewen returned. Then she wrinkled her nose at Aedan. "Good to know Grandma Addy's been telling tales and flashing my picture around."

"She's proud of her family," Serafin laughed.

"And we're proud of her," Rhosewen replied, gesturing toward her approaching parents. "This is my mom and dad—Caitrin and Morrigan Conn. This is Aedan's parents," she announced, flipping the introductions around, "Serafin and Daleen Donnelly."

The two golden couples greeted one another. Then Serafin and Morrigan recalled their last meeting as they accompanied their spouses to the dinner table.

Their conversation faded, so Aedan looked to Rhosewen, sighing as he took her hands. "You look beautiful this evening, Rose."

She wore the shirt from the alpaca farm, which fit her perfectly, begging him to cuddle her.

"Thank you," she returned, grinning from one pink cheek to the other.

Aedan gently touched his forehead to hers, lightly wiggling the tip of her nose with his own. Then he gave it a soft kiss before leading her to the table.

After a long dinner slowed by abundant conversation, Daleen and Serafin returned home, but Aedan stayed behind, waiting for the lawn to clear. When he and Rhosewen were alone at last, he pulled her onto his lap and wrapped her in a hug, burrowing his nose in her hair.

"I've been waiting all day to do this," he mumbled, finding her neck. "Mmm . . . There it is."

Goosebumps stretched across Rhosewen's chest and back, and she sighed, slipping her tingling fingers into his hair.

They silently held each other for several minutes, soaking up the peace. Then Rhosewen shattered it. "I had a visitor today."

"Oh yeah?" he mumbled, sweeping his nose across the hollow of her throat. "Who?"

"Medea."

Aedan jerked his head back. "What was she doing here?"

"She wanted to know when I was leaving."

"You talked to her?"

"Briefly."

"Please be careful around her, Rose. If she comes back, stay cautious. Or just steer clear of her altogether. Let someone else get rid of her."

Rhosewen ran her fingers along his rigid jaw then touched his creased brow. "Okay, but I doubt she'll do anything. She took a long look at my aura today, and I think she figured out I'm a bonded child."

Aedan closed his eyes and smoothed his forehead, so Rhosewen stroked his eyelids. "You're more worried about her today than you were yesterday," she noted.

"Yes," he confessed, opening his eyes.

"Why?"

"Because she was on my porch when I got home last night. She knew I'd been with you. She knows too much about you—where you live and when you're leaving. She didn't come here to find that out. She already knew, which means she went out of her way to gather information on you."

"Is that why you're so worried?" Rhosewen pressed.

"Yes. I don't want her anywhere near you. She's unstable. I saw a side of her last night I've never seen before. When I told her I was with you, she lost it. I'm worried she's gone off the deep end."

"You said she already knew we were together."

"She knew we'd been together, but she didn't know I was serious about you. She thought you'd leave Saturday and that would be the end of it."

Rhosewen completely forgot about Medea as a thousand butterflies swarmed her belly, fluttering with hope and desire. "Isn't it?" she asked, pushing the premature expectations away. "How could it possibly work with an entire country between us?"

Aedan watched her hopeful yet cautious expression as he thought about what he would say, regretting a conversation about Medea had led to it. Ideally, it would be said under far sweeter circumstances. But he needed to know if Rhosewen felt the same. If so, they only had five days to prepare themselves.

He shifted her around, straddling her on his lap. Then he took her cheeks, watching her liquid eyes. "Rose, I've fallen in love with you."

Rhosewen's bones melted. Only Aedan's hands on her face kept her from sinking into him.

"It's only been three days," he went on, "and I'm already dreaming about a future with you. I see it so clearly. It's all I see. I won't ask you to stay here, because I know you don't want to." He paused, searching her eyes and his heart. Yes, he was sure. "But if you feel the same, I'll move to Oregon."

Rhosewen's entire body trembled. Then she sobbed as tears spilled from blue oceans.

"Hey," Aedan soothed, alarmed by her sudden outburst. "Why are you crying? Did I say something wrong?"

"No," she answered. "You've said everything right."

"Then why the tears?" he asked, wiping them away. "Are you sad?"

"No . . . just guilty . . . and so happy."

Rhosewen tried to pull herself together, but couldn't. She'd never felt so many things at once. "I'm in love with you, too, Aedan. I don't want Saturday to be the end, but I don't know if I could leave home. Work is expecting me back, my family and friends are there. It's all I've ever known. And here you are, telling me you'd leave home and everything else to be with me. I feel so selfish and undeserving."

Her tears flowed faster, but Aedan dried them as swiftly as they ran. "You're in love with me, too?"

"Yes," she answered. "I don't understand it, but there's no doubt about it."

Aedan kissed her so hard and so long, her eyes were dry by the time he pulled away. "That settles it," he said. "I'm moving to Oregon."

Rhosewen continued to quake from his kiss, so it took her a moment to reply. "Won't it hurt too much to leave? I don't want that for you."

Aedan's smile stayed in place as he slowly shook his head. "I wouldn't offer if I weren't sure."

"What about your job?" she pressed.

"I plan on opening my own shop," he answered. "Now it will be in Oregon instead of Virginia. My parents' business isn't busy enough for all three of us."

"What about them, and your coven?"

"I'll miss them," he confessed, "but I've always considered a move out of the community a viable option, and if ever there was a reason to go, it's you. I love everything I've learned about you, Rose, and I'm dying to fall in love with the rest. You've done so much to me in three short days, I want to know what else you can do. I want to experience all of it, not just a week's worth. I want to be with you everyday of every year, and there's no denying it. That's just the way it is now."

He'd convinced her. Rhosewen still felt selfish for letting him do it, but he was the only thing she'd thought about for three days, and she couldn't bear the prospect of leaving him. "Come home with me, Aedan. I want you, too."

"You just made me the happiest man on earth," he whispered.

More tears slipped from Rhosewen's lids, and Aedan gently wiped them away, leaning in for another spine-tingling kiss.

Aedan and Rhosewen spent their first sleepover on a blanket in the middle of the lawn, cuddling—mostly innocently—under twinkling stars. The next morning, at precisely the same time, their eyes popped open and met, and smiles stretched across their delighted faces.

"Good morning, my beautiful Rose," he whispered, sweeping his thumb across her cheek.

She closed her eyes and nuzzled his palm, teasing his wrist with her lips. "Good morning."

Aedan's veins pulsed against satiny flesh, and he couldn't deny the urge to kiss her neck, his body light as air yet so full of feeling. "I love waking up with you, Rose. This is already the best day of my life."

He inhaled deeply, sliding his lips to her face, and she turned away from his wrist, finding his mouth as she pulled his hand to her heart. Their longest, most tender kiss yet, it left them vibrating.

They were so wrapped up in each other, they jolted when a door opened. Then they laughed and looked up, finding Morrigan gliding toward them with a tray, her caramel curls and peach eyes glinting in the rising sun.

"Good morning," she greeted, halting beside their bed of blankets.

Aedan and Rhosewen pulled themselves apart and sat up.

"Morning, mom," Rhosewen chirped.

"Good morning, Morrigan," Aedan added. "Did you sleep well?" He couldn't find it in himself to feel guilty for sleeping next to her daughter. Opening his eyes to Rhosewen's had been the most amazing moment of his life.

Morrigan watched Rhosewen's aura as she answered. "I did. Thank you for asking. Did you two sleep well?"

"We slept great," Rhosewen answered, unabashed.

Morrigan smiled as her aura pulsed. "Good. I brought breakfast."

"We could have come inside to eat," Rhosewen offered.

"We already ate," Morrigan replied, "so I thought I'd bring out the leftovers."

Aedan squeezed Rhosewen's hand then jumped to his feet, relieving Morrigan of the tray. "That was thoughtful of you. Thank you."

"Sure," she returned, shifting her attention to Rhosewen. "Do you have plans today?"

"Not really," Rhosewen answered. "Are you and dad going to Cape Charles again?"

"I think we'll lounge around here instead. Would you two like to join us for lunch?"

Rhosewen looked at Aedan, who searched her eyes before answering. "I'd like that, Morrigan, but some other time. I have a lot to do today."

"Oh," Morrigan breathed. "How about you, sweetie? Are you going with him?"

"Nuh-uh," Rhosewen answered, picking through the food. Then she paused and looked at Aedan. "Am I?"

"If you'd like," he offered, "but I'm just running errands around town."

"Looks like I'll be here," Rhosewen said, smiling at her mom, whose face and aura brightened.

"We'll have to come up with something to keep us busy. There's a spot about a mile away that would make a lovely landscape painting this time of year. We should check it out."

"Sounds great. I'll be in after Aedan leaves."

"Take your time," Morrigan insisted. "Have a good day, Aedan."

"You, too, Morrigan. Thanks again for breakfast."

Morrigan offered him a smile. Then she threw Rhosewen one more glance before floating away. Once she was inside, Aedan and Rhosewen abandoned the food, lying back in each other's arms.

"Do you really have errands to run?" she asked, laying her cheek on his chest.

"Yes," he answered. "Why? Did you want me to stay?"

"I always want you to stay."

"I'm sorry. I thought you'd want to speak to your parents alone. I can run my errands tomorrow."

"No, that's okay. I do need to talk to them alone. But I'm going to miss you."

"I'll miss you, too, Rose, but we have a lifetime ahead of us, and there are things I need to do to prepare for it."

She raised her head, flashing a peaceful smile. "A lifetime."

"Yes," he whispered, bringing her lips to his, "a long and lovely lifetime."

As Aedan flew to Virginia Beach, he ran what needed done through his head. His dad would need a new employee, but there were at least three people interested in the job. Packing his possessions would be easy; he didn't have that many. He needed to visit Kearny, his closest friend outside his coven, but he wanted to take Rhosewen along, so he decided to wait.

As he stepped into Virginia Beach's finest jewelry shop, a bell tinkled, signaling a squat, old man from the back. "Can I help you find something?"

"How long would a custom order take?" Aedan asked.

"Well," the man mumbled, scanning an appointment book, "looks like I'm free this week, but I can't give you a time frame without knowing what you want."

Aedan approached, placing a small velvet bag on the counter. Then he unfolded a piece of paper. "I've drawn what I want," he said, sliding the sketch over.

The jeweler perched a pair of glasses on his nose and picked up the paper, examining the drawing under a nearby lamp.

The ring had a dainty band comprised of two spiraling ribbons of gold, and it was set with a round, pink champagne gem encircled by much smaller diamonds.

"I have the stone in the middle," Aedan said, pointing to the bag, "but I'll need the diamonds and the rose gold for the band."

"I generally find custom orders tacky," the jeweler mumbled, still scanning the sketch, "but this ring is quite impressive." He set the paper aside and picked up the bag. "May I?"

"Of course," Aedan allowed, so the jeweler tipped the bag upside down, catching the gemstone in his palm.

His lips parted as he stared at the translucent, sage green stone—at least eighteen carats of pure perfection. He glanced at the pink stone in the drawing then back to the green stone in his hand. "What is this?"

"Zultanite," Aedan answered.

The hand holding the gemstone twitched as the man's eyes widened. "Do you now how rare this is?"

"I do," Aedan assured, "and I'm glad you're aware as well. That will make me feel better about leaving it with you."

The jeweler walked to a window and examined the stone in the sunlight. Then he held it under a lamp, then back up to the overhead lights, watching a few of its many colors make an appearance—khaki, canary yellow, champagne and rose pink. "It's exquisite."

"Yes it is," Aedan agreed, remembering how hard he'd worked to obtain the zultanite, which had only one source—Turkey's Anatolian Mountains. "Do you have the required diamonds and rose gold?"

"Yes," the jeweler answered, "but it's a good thing you brought this, because we're fresh out of zultanite."

Aedan laughed as he tapped the sketch. "That's the size specifications in the upper right hand corner. And I want the finest stones you have. Money's not an issue."

The jeweler looked him over appreciatively then nodded toward the zultanite. "I'd hate to tarnish this beauty with imperfect diamonds. I'll use my best material."

"Great. How long?"

"I usually tell people at least a week, but you're dropping a nice chunk of change and I'm intrigued by the job, so… three days."

"Are you sure? Because I'm leaving town Saturday."

"I'll probably finish Thursday night," the man replied. "You can pick it up first thing Friday morning."

"Do you need a deposit?"

The jeweler chuckled. "I generally ask for half, but this stone is worth more than your bill. I believe you'll be back."

"Thanks," Aedan returned, searching the man's indistinct aura. Then he headed for the door. "I'll see you Friday."

"Yes," the jeweler mumbled, mesmerized by the rare gem in his palm. "Have a nice day."

Aedan arrived at his parents' shop with a heavy heart, but picturing Rhosewen's face soothed him, so that's exactly what he was doing when he walked in. "Hey, dad."

Serafin looked up in surprise. "Aedan. I thought I gave you the day off."

"You did. Where's mom?"

"Checking out a customer's living room. The woman's a chatterbox, so she might be a while. Are you here to work?"

"Only if you need me to. I wanted to take you and mom to lunch. It's clam chowder day at *Charla's*."

"Mmm . . . I haven't had Charla's clam chowder in ages. Your mom's going to be sorry she missed out."

"We'll bring her a bowl."

"We better, or I'll get the look."

"Oh no," Aedan laughed, knowing Daleen could give Serafin any look in the world and he'd love it.

"Hey, Anton," Serafin shouted, "mind the store. I'm going to lunch."

They heard a muffled mmkay from the break room then walked out the door.

Once they sat on Charla's patio, waiting for their order, Aedan broke the news. "I talked to Rose last night. She feels the same way I do."

"That's good," Serafin approved.

"That's putting it lightly," Aedan agreed. Then he took a deep breath, letting it out with his confession. "I'm leaving with her Saturday morning."

"Your mom and I figured as much," Serafin replied. "Seeing you guys together reminded us of ourselves, which led to . . . very pleasant flashbacks." He sighed, his eyes unfocussed. Then he shook his head clear. "What's next, a wedding?"

"Maybe, but it might be a while. I'll make sure she's happy before taking that step. Not that a ceremony will change anything. I'm already committed. I'll stay with her as long as she'll have me. I know that sounds crazy, considering I've only known her since Saturday, but I've been soul searching for three days and all I find is her. If she wants a wedding, she'll get one. If she wants to skip it, we'll skip it."

Charla delivered their soup. Then Aedan waited for her to walk away before resuming the conversation. "I know it's short notice, so I'll find someone to fill my spot at the store."

"Don't worry about it," Serafin insisted. "I already have someone lined up. But there is something else you could do for me."

"What's that?"

"I want you to have dinner with your mom and me, just the three of us. It would mean the world to her."

"Sure," Aedan agreed. "How about three dinners? Tonight, tomorrow and the day after. What will that mean to her?"

"A lot of tears," Serafin answered. "Good ones, though. She'll be thrilled."

Aedan stayed busy over the next three days—finishing projects at his parents' shop, spending quality time with them and his coven, and flying to the Ballard/Lancing community every night so he could sleep with Rhosewen in his arms. By Friday afternoon, he still hadn't found time to visit Kearny. Oh well. He'd have to wait and see him his first trip back. Both he and Rhosewen had roots in Virginia, so they would return soon and often.

Excitement hijacked his veins when he entered the jewelry store, anxious to see the finished product of his imagination—almost finished; it would need to be engraved. He'd considered hunting down the materials and forming the ring himself, easily and expertly. But there was something to be said for items created by physical expertise rather than magical ability. Or, in this case, both—a combination of dedicated hands and a devoted mind. Still, putting his trust in non-magical skill had been a big leap of faith.

"Ahh . . . " the jeweler beamed, "you've come for your ring."

"Yes," Aedan answered. "Is it ready?"

The man chuckled as he disappeared into the back room, talking as he went. "I was so enthralled, I finished yesterday afternoon. I would have called you, but you didn't leave a number." He returned, holding out the velvet bag.

Aedan took it and tipped it upside down, letting the ring fall into his palm. The zultanite glinted pale green under the florescent lights, casting its brilliance across the surrounding diamonds, and the smooth rose gold was professionally polished, displaying Aedan's relieved reflection. The ring was the prettiest he'd seen. His beautiful Rose deserved nothing less.

"What do you think?" the jeweler asked.

"It's perfect," Aedan answered. "You've done a wonderful job, thank you."

"It is perfect," the jeweler agreed, "some of the best work I've done, but since it was your design, I can't take the credit."

"Let's split the credit," Aedan suggested, and the man's smile broadened.

"Deal. Do you mind if I photograph it?"

"Not at all," Aedan allowed, handing it over.

The jeweler arranged it on a piece of black satin, snapped two pictures, then handed it back.

"Thanks again," Aedan said, tucking the ring away.

"It was a pleasure to work with such a rare stone and clever design," the jeweler returned. "I should be thanking you."

"Your fine work is thanks enough," Aedan assured, pulling a thick stack of bills from his pocket. "What do I owe you?"

Chapter 21

Rhosewen's parents took the news about the seriousness of her and Aedan's relationship calmly, agreeing to let Aedan stay in their home until he could build his own. Though they didn't say it, Rhosewen knew they were thrilled with Aedan's decision to relocate, having feared their daughter might stay in Virginia.

Ellena's community hosted a farewell dinner Friday evening, inviting Aedan's entire coven. And Serafin and Daleen were invited to stay the night, an offer they quickly accepted.

Aedan was running late, having just finished engraving the inside of Rhosewen's ring, so the lawn was crowded when he landed. He sighed as he found Rhosewen's smiling face, but then a wizard put his arm around her, and Aedan flipped his gaze over, finding his best friend, Kearny Gilmore.

Aedan smiled and walked forward. "What's this?"

"Well," Kearny answered, squeezing Rhosewen's shoulders, "an angel came to me yesterday, claiming she's taking you to a better place and that this would be my last chance to see you."

Aedan stepped forward, lifting Rhosewen into a hug. "You're amazing," he whispered, kissing her ear. "Thank you."

"It's the least I could do," she countered. "You're giving up so much for me. I'm not the angel here. You are."

"You're wrong," he disagreed, setting her feet on the ground. Only then did he turn to greet his friend.

Rich with eating, drinking, music and games, the evening's tone was one of celebration rather than farewell. Aedan's heart squeezed when he looked at the family and friends he would be leaving, but he was the happiest he'd ever been. To know he would be spending his future with Rhosewen made him feel like he was floating. Nothing could bring him down as long as he had her.

When the party died down and the crowd dispersed, Aedan and Rhosewen stayed on the lawn, tucking into a bed of blankets.

She purred and stretched, feeling more of him through her dress. Then she curled back up. "I can't believe I get to take you home with me. You must be the best souvenir in the history of the world." She pressed her lips to his heart, smiling as his hard body rumbled with laughter. "Thank you for giving me so much."

"If you'll let me," he replied, "I'll give you much more."

"I just might," she hummed, wiggling to his face. Her forefinger traced his brow and nose. Then she stretched her hands over his cheeks. "I love you, Aedan."

He peacefully smiled, watching her eyes as he brushed her hair back. "I love you, too, Rose, for as long as you'll let me."

"Forever," she insisted, her lips curving over his. Then she closed her eyes, melting into his tender kiss.

When it came time to leave, Aedan's chest ached over the impending goodbyes. Seeing his mom and dad so subdued was tough. They were never that way.

"I have one favor to ask," Daleen requested, giving Rhosewen a hug. "Every once in a while, wave a phone in front of Aedan's face and tell him to call his mom. I know he'll be busy staring into your gorgeous eyes, but if you block his view with a phone, he might remember me."

"I promise," Rhosewen agreed. "I'll make it a priority." And she meant it. She hated taking Aedan from his parents. "I'm sorry it has to be this way. I know it must be hard. I..." She wasn't sure what else to say.

"It's okay, darling," Daleen assured. "Aedan's happiness is our priority, and he's found it in you. The distance is worth the peace of mind."

"Thank you for understanding," Rhosewen whispered.

"Don't mention it," Serafin cut in, giving her a hug. "You two take care of each other and come back to see us soon."

"We will," she agreed. Then she turned toward Aedan and laid a hand over his heart, wishing she could offer more support. But with nothing else to give, she merely offered his parents a crestfallen wave and floated away.

Aedan breathed deep, holding the air in as he wrapped Daleen in a hug. "I love you, mom."

"I love you, too, baby," she whispered, burying her face in his shirt.

"We'll come back for a visit soon," he vowed. "Really soon. I promise."

Daleen took a ragged breath, letting it out slowly. "I know you will. Be safe, okay?"

"We will," he assured, tightening his hold as he kissed her onyx hair. Then he let go and turned to Serafin, clasping his hand. "Thanks for everything, dad."

Serafin pulled him into a firm hug then stepped back, meeting his sad stare. "Sure, son. You keep in touch now. We want to hear from you often."

"I'll bug you so much you'll have to screen your calls."

"That would be wonderful," Daleen sighed, leaning into Serafin's open arm.

Aedan smiled as he reached out, touching fingertips to Daleen's heart while watching her pale green eyes. "I'll know I've gone overboard when you change your number."

"Never," they whispered, shaking their heads.

Aedan watched them for another moment then dropped his hand and turned away, unable to say goodbye. Only Rhosewen's eyes and smile kept him moving forward. She made everything better. When he reached her, he took her hand and pulled it to his lips, drawing comfort from her soft skin and lovely scent.

Rhosewen smiled as she touched his cheek, happier than she ever dreamed she could be. Then her expression fell as the hair at the nape of her neck stood on end. She looked up, searching the sky as her stomach tightened into a knot. Then a terrifying scream pierced the air.

Everyone looked north, finding Medea at the edge of the timber—eyes burning, lips twisted, teeth bared. As her scream diminished, lightning shot from her hands, heading straight for Aedan.

He threw a hand out to block it, but Rhosewen had already swept both hands through the air, enveloping Aedan in a foggy blue shield that quickly expanded. Within two seconds, everyone on the lawn was sheltered.

Aedan watched the lightning approach, expecting it to fizzle when it hit the barrier, but Rhosewen had been thorough in her spell work. When the bolt of electricity made contact with the blue fog, it rebounded on its caster.

Medea spun to the left, but not quick enough. The lightning grazed her right cheekbone then struck a tree trunk. The enormous oak toppled forward with an earsplitting crack, threatening to crush the wounded witch into parched, summer earth, but she lunged out of the way, barely escaping death.

Aedan lost her then found her again when she stood from the forest floor, gingerly touching her burnt and bloody cheek. She threw a deadly glance at Rhosewen then fled, her crimson aura disappearing behind thick timber.

Yes, Medea had definitely snapped.

Aedan turned and pulled Rhosewen into a hug, pissed at himself for putting her in mortal danger. The damage was done. "I'm sorry, Rose."

"You didn't do anything wrong," Rhosewen countered, the words vibrating with her body. "Medea's obviously crazy."

"What's going on?" Serafin asked, breathlessly landing next to Aedan.

"Medea just tried to kill me!" Aedan returned. "That's what's going on. And she didn't give a damn about witnesses. She's crazy!" He took a calming breath as he kissed Rhosewen's head. "I'm so sorry, Rose. I hate that this has touched you."

"It's not your fault," she insisted, tightening her arms around his waist.

"Is that witch a girlfriend?" Morrigan asked, narrowing her eyes on Aedan.

"No," he quickly assured, "but she wanted to be. We have to find her, dad," he added, looking to Serafin. "We can't let her get away with this."

"No we can't," Serafin agreed. "You guys go. We'll find her."

Aedan didn't like the idea of someone else cleaning up his mess, but he wanted to get Rhosewen out of there, out of the state, far away from Medea. "Are you sure?"

"Of course," Serafin replied. "We'll head for her coven after you leave."

Aedan couldn't shake the guilt. "I should stay, Rose. You go. I'll fly over once this is taken care of."

"No," she blurted, frantically finding his eyes.

"This is my responsibility," he countered. "I have to make sure it gets dealt with."

"Then I'm staying, too."

"No!" he protested, panicked by the ultimatum. "I don't want you anywhere near her. You need to leave before she comes looking for revenge."

"I'm not leaving unless you leave with me."

"Rose..."

"No," she asserted. Then she rested her cheek to his chest, successfully ending the discussion.

Aedan sighed and looked to his dad.

"Go," Serafin insisted. "We'll deal with this."

"I'm sorry," Aedan whispered.

"Don't worry about it," Serafin replied, slapping Aedan's shoulder. "Your mom and I need an adventure. Don't we, sweets?"

Daleen smiled as she cuddled into Serafin's chest. "Yes. Our lives are dreadfully boring. Get going," she added, waving Aedan away.

"Thank you," Aedan sighed, glancing at Rhosewen's head. "I'll call when we get there, to let you know we made it, and to make sure you've found her."

"Travel safely," Serafin returned. "We'll take care of things here."

Aedan hugged his parents once more. Then the four travelers shot toward Oregon, glad to leave the dangerous episode behind.

Chapter 22

The sun had yet to rise when Aedan entered the skies above Oregon Sunday morning, so he couldn't properly view the thriving terrain he'd heard so much about. He didn't mind. He had plenty of time to discover its secrets, and a beautiful local to whisper them in his ear.

Shortly after bypassing Portland's urban glow, Aedan descended into a dark forest of towering timber, landing on an empty lawn.

"Welcome home," Rhosewen purred, burying her face in his chest. "I hope you'll like it."

"As long as you're here," he assured, "I'll love it."

Once inside, Morrigan showed Aedan to the guestroom. Neither she nor Caitrin had demanded he sleep away from their daughter, but Aedan volunteered, eager to avoid an uncomfortable situation and desperate to make a good impression.

"May I call my parents?" he asked, gesturing toward the phone on the dresser.

"Sure," Morrigan answered, heading for the door. "But it's barely six in the morning in Virginia."

"They won't mind."

"Of course they won't. Join us for a bite to eat when you're done. Then we'll get some sleep."

She left the room, and Aedan picked up the phone, dialing his parents' number.

"Hello?" Serafin answered.

"Hey, dad. We made it."

"Good," Serafin approved, clearing the sleep from his throat.

"Did you find Medea?" Aedan asked.

"No."

"Damn," Aedan mumbled, rapping his knuckles on the dresser.

"We told her coven what happened," Serafin went on, "and you'll never guess what they said."

"What?" Aedan asked.

"That she's been unraveling for a while now," Serafin answered. "They were wondering how long it would be before she snapped."

Aedan ran a hand down his face, wishing he'd been there to give Medea's coven his opinion.

Serafin harrumphed. "I know what you're thinking. Why the hell didn't they do something about it? And believe me, I asked."

"Did they answer?"

"Apparently they tried to cleanse her with gemstones, herbs and some light spell work, but she was resistant and they don't have anyone committed to healing. Their knowledge on the subject is pitiful."

"They could have found at least a dozen people willing to help," Aedan pointed out.

"True, but I think they're ashamed of her. It seems they were trying to keep it to themselves, hoping she would get better on her own. Obviously not the wisest choice, but I think they realize their mistake."

"Too damn late."

"So it would seem," Serafin agreed. "We waited with her family until nightfall, and we called her parents before bed, but she never came home."

"This is bad news," Aedan whispered, glancing at the window. For all they knew, Medea could be creeping into the community.

"I wouldn't worry too much," Serafin insisted. "She's probably hiding out, nursing her cheek and ego. Rhosewen damaged both."

"That's why I'm worried," Aedan countered. "Before, Medea was mad at me. Now she has an excuse to seek revenge on Rose."

"Good point," Serafin conceded, "but try not to drive yourself crazy over it. We'll put out the word that we're looking for her, and we'll keep visiting her community. We should hear something in a day or two."

"Let me know if you do."

"As soon as I know what she's up to, you'll know."

"Thanks, dad. I'm sorry I put this on you. I hate that I didn't see this in Medea before getting involved with her."

A short pause then Serafin spoke. "How involved were you? Did you sleep with her?"

"No. I knew it was a bad idea. Her delusions are based on two dates that ended with a kiss on the hand."

"I'm relieved you didn't fuel her fire."

"Her fire's already blazing. She needs to be found before she hurts someone."

"We'll do everything we can," Serafin assured.

"Thanks again, dad. I feel awful that you and mom are cleaning up my mess."

"This isn't your mess. It's Medea's. Now get some sleep. You have a big week ahead of you—learning your way around and getting to know the people."

"I'm looking forward to it. Tell mom I love her."

"Will do, son. Goodbye."

"Bye, dad."

Aedan hung up the phone with a weighty sigh and a heavy heart. Then he followed the sound of voices to the kitchen. Caitrin sat at the table, reading a piece of paper, and Rhosewen and Morrigan were laughing as they prepared blueberry muffins. When Aedan walked in, everyone paused their tasks and looked up.

Aedan dropped his gaze to the floor, rubbing a hand across the back of his neck as his stomach churned. He'd never felt so guilty or disappointed in himself. "They haven't found Medea," he confessed. "She never came home last night. Dad thinks she's just hiding out for a while, but I think it would be a good idea to let everyone around here know the situation. She knows where you live, and after what she did yesterday, we shouldn't underestimate her." He paused, clearing his throat as he found Caitrin's eyes—blue like the sea, like his daughter's. "I'm really sorry about this, Caitrin. The last thing I wanted to do was put your family in danger."

"History's marred with witches like Medea," Caitrin countered. "The blame rests on her shoulders alone. We'll alert our coven and the others nearby, let them know who and what to expect. We'll know if she gets close."

"Thanks for your understanding," Aedan replied.

Caitrin smiled and looked to his paper. "Your sacrifice has allowed Rhosewen to stay with us. Understanding is the least I can give you."

Sunday afternoon, as Aedan awoke to the realization that the woman he'd been dreaming about was only a shout away, his heart soared. He quickly showered and dressed, then walked downstairs, following Rhosewen's lovely hum to the kitchen.

She was setting the table for two, but looked up with a beautiful grin that pinched her pink cheeks. "Do you like pancakes?"

"Yes," he answered, closing the gap between them, "but not as much as I like your smile." He pulled her into a long and passionate kiss, taking the weight off her wobbly knees by dipping her back. "Can I help?" he asked, pulling her upright.

"Sure," she breathed. "Fix our coffee while I fill our plates."

They sat, and Aedan watched her face as he generously added cream and sugar to her coffee, enjoying every second of the simple experience. "Are your parents joining us?" he asked, sliding her cup over.

"No. They went to let everyone know we're home."

Aedan added a dash of sugar to his coffee and sipped, thinking about Morrigan and Caitrin telling their family that Rhosewen had dragged a man home and that a deranged witch might follow.

Rhosewen finished filling their plates and began eating, taking several bites before addressing the colors in Aedan's aura. "I know how you're feeling, Aedan, and I don't like it."

"I'm sorry, Rose," he replied, shaking his guilty head, "for all of it. It wasn't supposed to be this way. I hate that my lack of awareness has put you in danger, and I hate that I've already made a bad impression on your coven."

"Medea has put a kink in things," Rhosewen conceded, "but I'm not going to let her ruin this for me. And as for your concern about my coven—they're fantastic, Aedan, the most understanding group of people you'll ever meet. You'll sweep them off their feet just like you did me." She set her fork down and reached out, smoothing his frown. "Now stop feeling guilty. I don't like it."

She started to drop her hand, but Aedan grabbed it, pressing his lips to her palm. "I love you, Rose, and I'll do my best not to let Medea ruin this for either of us."

"Thank you," she approved. "And I love you, too." She stabbed another bite. "So, what do you want to do first, see the land or meet the people?"

"Meet the people. We can look at the land along the way."

"Good idea. I'll introduce you to the coven first. Then we'll head to the coast. There are a couple of communities that way."

"Sounds perfect." He was easy to please. As long as he had her, he'd go anywhere.

As it turned out, Rhosewen's coven was fantastic, welcoming Aedan like family. He could tell by their auras that they shared an extraordinary bond, and he fully understood why Rhosewen was so reluctant to leave home. Aedan would miss his old coven, but he was confident the new one would ease the pain.

On their way to the coast, Aedan and Rhosewen detoured to two different communities, where she introduced him to her closest friends. All of them were surprised by the speed and seriousness of the relationship, but supportive just the same, showering Rhosewen with blessings and lighthearted banter.

Once the main introductions were through, Rhosewen led Aedan to Cannon Beach, where they stopped at her aunt's café for coffee then took their time exploring the nearby coast. Aedan looked forward to discovering the area's secrets, but for the time being, he was perfectly content with his beautiful tour guide.

They returned home to find dinner being served by Morrigan, who beamed and added two plates to the table. "Will you join us?"

They agreed by taking their seats, so Morrigan smiled and filled their plates. "How was your afternoon?"

"Great," Rhosewen answered. "I took him to Cannon Beach."

Morrigan sat, and Caitrin tossed his paperwork aside, leaning over to kiss her cheek. "Thank you, my sweet peach," he whispered. Then he took a bite and looked at Aedan. "What did you think of Cannon Beach?"

"Beautiful," Aedan answered. "It might be the perfect place to launch my business."

"A few of our coven members own shops there," Caitrin noted. "Our gallery is north of there, in Seaside. What will you do tomorrow while Rhosewen's at work?"

"I'd like to go with her," Aedan answered, "join one of her tours around Mount Hood. If she doesn't mind."

"I'd love to take you to work with me," Rhosewen agreed.

"Then it's a date," Aedan approved.

Still tired from their long journey, Caitrin and Morrigan went to bed early, but Aedan and Rhosewen stayed downstairs, cuddling on the couch as they flipped through commercial property listings in Cannon Beach. When Aedan caught Rhosewen yawning, he ignored her protests and carried her upstairs, setting her down outside her bedroom door.

"Are you really going to leave?" she asked, puckering up at him.

"I'll never leave you," he assured, touching her pout. "But yes, I'm going to the guestroom."

"Why?" she asked, fidgeting with his shirt buttons.

"Because I don't want things to be awkward with your parents."

"Hmm . . ." she hummed, cuddling closer. "That's noble of you."

He laughed and kissed her head. "You're making fun of me."

"Because you're holding out on me," she countered, rubbing her lips over his heart.

Aedan tilted his head back and closed his eyes, taking a relaxing breath. "Not for long," he assured, pulling her from his chest. Then he softly kissed her lips. "Goodnight, Rose."

"Night," she conceded, taking a step back.

Aedan smiled at the ornery twinkle in her eyes. Then he turned and walked away, thinking he *really* needed to get to work on that house.

When he reached his room, he called his parents, only to find they hadn't located Medea. Every magician in Virginia had been alerted to the situation, but no one had seen her since Saturday morning.

After hanging up the phone, Aedan replaced his worry about Medea with a crystal clear image of Rhosewen then took a shower—a cold one.

He'd only been lying in bed for a few seconds when there was a soft knock on the door. "Yeah?" he quietly called.

The door opened, and Rhosewen slipped inside, flashing a smile as she clicked the latch into place. Aedan smirked at her stubbornness. Then his breath caught in his chest as she stepped into the moonlight.

She wore a wispy, white nightgown with thin straps and a deep neckline, displaying her slender collarbones and firm cleavage.

Aedan swallowed a lump then slid his gaze down her curvy waist, his lips parting with a reverent sigh. The hem of her gown wafted around her upper thighs, giving him his first full view of her legs, which were even better than he'd imagined, and he'd imagined them perfect.

She walked toward him, her ivory skin glittering with every fluid step. "Were you sleeping?" she whispered, climbing into bed.

Aedan rolled onto his side and propped his head on his hand, scanning her from head to toe. "Nuh-uh."

She wiggled closer. "I was missing you."

"What a coincidence," he whispered, drifting his thumb over her cheek. "I was missing you."

He wanted to see the rest of her body, the parts hidden beneath the thin nightgown. They called his name, testing his self-control. "You have a fantastic body, Rose. If you're here to tempt me, mission accomplished."

His fingertips slid into the V of her gown then flitted to her side, trailing over her hip to her thigh. Goosebumps followed, and she giggled, cuddling closer to his warm body.

"How tempted are you?" she asked.

He returned his fingers to her cheek, tilting her head back to find her eyes. "Very, but I don't want to push my luck."

"You're sweet," she whispered, searching his gaze, "and I love that about you, but right now, there's something else I want."

"I'll give you the world, Rose."

"I don't want the world. I want you to stop being so polite to my parents and start making love to me."

"Here?" he laughed.

"Now," she soberly confirmed, wrapping a hand around the back of his neck. Then she pulled him to her mouth, murmuring against his bottom lip. "Don't you want me?"

He grinned, but then she nibbled and his lungs stuttered. "You're a siren," he mumbled, closing his eyes.

"You're making me work for it," she pouted.

He pulled away, finding her shiny gaze. "That's not my intent, Rose. I've wanted you from day one."

"Prove it," she challenged, sliding one of his hands to her breasts.

He closed his eyes and lightly squeezed. Then he sighed and returned his hand to her face. "I'm not prepared for this."

"Hmm . . ." she murmured, pressing her hips closer as she kissed his jaw.

Aedan's heart jolted as his muscles tensed. She was obviously intent on getting her way, and he was lacking the desire to stop her. "Hey," he whispered, jolting again.

Rhosewen halted her seduction and innocently looked at him. "What?"

"You know what," he laughed. "You're very good at this."

"Not good enough," she countered.

"Oh yes, my love, very good, better than I anticipated, which means I'm not protected against pregnancy."

"Oh," she breathed, shoulders sagging.

Aedan frowned, hating the way it felt to disappoint her. "I can fix it," he whispered, gently tapping the tip of her nose. "Right now. If you'll wait for me."

She dropped her gaze, blushing for the first time since walking in. "Nuh-uh."

Shocked by her refusal, Aedan tilted his head, eyebrows furrowed as he stroked her flushed cheek. "Have I ruined it?"

"Impossible," she assured.

"Good," he sighed, "but I'm still confused. Are we waiting?"

"No."

Aedan's lungs expanded as he tried to figure her out, unable to find answers in her aura. "What are you saying, my love?"

Rhosewen knew exactly what she wanted. She'd known the moment she met him. She'd been dreaming about a future with him for eight nights. And she was confident in their relationship, in his love for her. The proof was in his aura every minute of every day; in his eyes every time he looked at her; in his voice every time he spoke to her; and in the way he touched her, constantly and carefully. He gave her everything she needed, yet she yearned for more. She would never get enough of him.

"I'm saying having your baby would make me the most blessed woman in the world," she confessed. "I'm not in a hurry to have a baby, but I would be thrilled to have your baby anytime. I love everything about the idea. However," she added, running a forefinger over his lips, "I understand if you're not ready, and if that's how you feel, please tell me. I'll wait as long as you need me to."

Aedan's heart was no longer his own, not even a little bit. She'd stolen it. His body rippled with emotion and throbbed with desire as he thought about her having his baby. And their child would be amazing, no less than extraordinary. They could create the perfect family and live the perfect life. They could have it all. Boundless bliss was within their grasp.

Aedan had no idea what he'd done to deserve such blessings, but he certainly wouldn't toss them aside. "Close your eyes," he instructed.

Rhosewen bit her lip. "I've scared you."

"No," he laughed. "I have something for you."

"Oh," she breathed, smiling as she closed her eyes.

A few seconds later, he spoke again. "Hold out your hand."

She obeyed, her smile stretching, and Aedan kissed her grin as he placed her ring in her palm. "I love you," he whispered. Then he licked her lips and pulled away, instructing her to open her eyes.

"Oh!" she gasped, glancing between his face and the most beautiful ring she'd ever seen. "It's gorgeous."

"I'm glad you think so, because you're my muse."

"It's perfect," she whispered, running a finger across the pale pink stone. "What is this?"

"Zultanite."

She gasped again, slapping a hand over her mouth. "This is amazing," she mumbled, shaking her head.

"You deserve nothing less," he replied, pulling her hand from her mouth. "I want you to have it now, but if you decide to marry me, I'd like it to be your wedding ring."

She flipped her gaze to his face. "Are you asking?"

"Yes. I know it's soon, so we can wait if you'd like, but I plan on sticking around as long as you'll have me."

"Then yes," she beamed, "I would love to marry you."

Aedan was pleasantly surprised by her quick agreement. "Then that's what you'll do. When?"

"How about tomorrow?" she suggested, only half-serious.

He laughed and kissed her hand. "How about we talk to our parents tomorrow and see what they think? As soon as we can get everyone together, I'll give you the wedding of your dreams."

"You give me too much."

"I told you I'd give you the world," he countered.

"You did," she remembered, taking a closer looking at the ring. Then she gasped again, finding the rose engraved on the gold backing. The bottom of its long stem curved to the left then looped down into cursive letters reading *My Love*. "You engraved it," she whispered, running a finger over the miniscule message.

"Of course I did," he replied. "May I put it on you?"

"Yes," she agreed, quivering with excitement.

Aedan took the ring from her palm, and she turned her hand over, letting him slip the band on her third finger. "Rhosewen Keely Conn, will you make me the luckiest husband on earth?"

Rhosewen tilted her hand left and right, watching the zultanite glimmer through emotional tears. "Yes," she answered, smiling up at him. "I want you forever, Aedan."

"You got me," he assured, lowering his lips to hers. "Forever."

They kissed, slow and sweet at first, but as their heartbeats quickened, passion and need took over. For nine days they'd been engulfed by emotions they didn't understand, experiencing the strongest desire of their lives, struggling with constant temptation. Now they'd unleashed their appetites, and physical urges ran rampant, promising mind-blowing bliss.

Their lips broke apart, and they intently stared at each other, gasping for air as his thumb stroked her quivering lips. "I want you, Rose."

"Then take me," she insisted, pressing her body closer.

Incredibly, Aedan's muscles tightened more than before, and he released her face, casting a spell to ensure no one, particularly the witch and wizard down the hall, would hear what went on in the guestroom.

Aedan's blood ran hot, his arousal begging for release, but he wouldn't rush what was sure to be the most amazing moment of his life. He would savor every sight, sound, feel and smell. And he'd do his part to make the experience perfect and memorable, to make every second count more than the one before.

At first, he just looked at her, intensifying their longing as he focused on each of his favorite features—the smoothness and coloring of her skin, her pouty lips and tiny nose, the long eyelashes fluttering around sparkling blue oceans, and the golden spirals framing her perfect face.

"You're so beautiful," he whispered, trailing his fingertips across her forehead. "I can't believe how lucky I am."

Mesmerized by his sincerity and tenderness, Rhosewen merely swallowed, unable to speak.

Aedan smiled and leaned closer, lifting the strap of her gown as he kissed her clavicle, and Rhosewen gripped his shoulder, uniquely aroused by the mere touch of his lips. Like most witches, she didn't shy away from a little promiscuity, so she was no stranger to physical pleasure. But with Aedan, everything was brand new. Every touch seeped deeper, every kiss lingered longer, and every breath promised to take them higher. Hearts thundering, they were closer to heaven than ever before, and the beautiful journey had barely begun.

After tossing her silk gown to the floor, Aedan looked to Rhosewen's face, searching her wide eyes. "I love you, Rose."

Rhosewen raised a hand to his cheek, smiling like a temptress getting her way, but emotional tears moistened her lashes, exposing her sweet vulnerability—a gift Aedan was the first to receive, no matter how many flings came before him.

Aedan's aura pulsed as he touched a thumb to her temple, catching a tear. Then he slid his fingers into her hair as he lowered his lips to hers. Spasms rocked their bodies, shaking the bed as well, and Aedan laughed, squeezing his eyes shut as he took a calming breath.

"This is going to be amazing," he whispered, finding her gaze. Then he kissed, muffling her breathless reply.

Rhosewen melted into his rhythm, lost in deep emeralds as the rest of the world blurred. Then the world as they knew it flipped upside down.

The moment they joined as one, they adhered together like magnets, electrifying energy tingling their fingers, toes and scalps. Then their lungs emptied as a mystical force lifted them from the bed, suspending them in mid-air. The electricity vibrating their extremities flowed inward—one spine-tingling force colliding with another—and heat exploded throughout their veins, surging from their flesh and brightening the atmosphere. Just as beads of sweat started forming, a wave of cool air rushed over them, followed by a flood of incredibly complete physical, mental and emotional euphoria.

Hearts pounding, they tightened their arms around each other as they drifted to the bed, amazed, stunned and changed. They still held each other's eyes, but saw each other differently, with perfect clarity. What was once beautiful had reached a magical level, and a shimmery golden light surrounded their vibrating bodies, adding to the radiant glow of their delighted auras.

They'd bonded—every intangible piece of them connected together indefinitely.

"Wow," Rhosewen exclaimed. "That . . . was . . . amazing."

Aedan deeply inhaled, nearing a mindless frenzy. Then he slowly exhaled as he took Rhosewen's luminous cheek in his palm, whispering against her smiling lips. "We're not done, my love. Not even close."

Chapter 23

Bonded. Aedan and Rhosewen couldn't believe it. Bonding was so rare, it was quite amazing two bonded children had met and fallen in love. For Rhosewen and Aedan to bond as well was nothing short of a miracle. As far as they knew, it was a first.

"That, my beautiful Rose," Aedan whispered, hugging her languid body close, "was the most amazing moment of my life. I've heard about it, but words can't do it justice."

"I know!" she agreed, grinning up at him. "It was incredible, absolutely incomparable to anything else I've ever experienced. I still can't believe it. Maybe I'm dreaming."

"Well do me a favor—don't wake up."

"If making love to you didn't wake me up, nothing will."

He laughed as he leaned in, drifting his lips across her forehead. "You know what this means, right? You're stuck with me. Forever."

"I wouldn't have it any other way," she assured.

"Good," he approved, nuzzling her spirals, dreading the moment he'd have to let her go. "We need to start working on a house, my love. Our current living arrangement no longer works for me."

"Oh no," she gasped.

Aedan leaned back, finding flushed cheeks and wide eyes. "What's wrong?" he asked. For him, the world was right, so he had no idea what could be upsetting her.

"My parents!" she exclaimed. "They're going to know. As soon as they see us tomorrow, they're going to know what we did and when we did it."

Aedan hadn't considered that yet, but she was right. As soon as Morrigan and Caitrin saw them together, they'd notice their bonded lights. Therefore, they'd know their daughter had sex in their house while they were asleep down the hall. "I'm sorry, Rose. We couldn't have known."

"I know," she breathed, trying to relax. "It's okay. It'll be all right. But that's embarrassing."

"And unnerving," Aedan mumbled, his stomach squirming as he thought about the expression he would see on Caitrin's face in the morning. How many ways could he mess up when it came to his future in-laws? It seemed he was on a fast track to finding out. Never had he put so much effort into staying in someone's good graces, yet every time he turned around a kink was thrown into his plan. Not that he would ever regret bonding with his perfect Rose. He would disappoint the whole world to keep her staring at him like he was the only man on earth.

Rhosewen bathed in Aedan's obvious admiration, her lips curving into a small grin. Then she snuggled into his chest. "If anyone will understand, it should be them, right? They know what it's like."

"Yeah," Aedan laughed. "Maybe your dad will be so impressed with my restraint thus far, he'll forget to hate me."

Rhosewen giggled and nipped at his chest. "I hope so, because if he tosses you out, we'll both be camping on the lawn."

"You'd banish yourself for me?" he asked.

"In a heartbeat," she confirmed, touching her lips to his pulsing pecs. Then they both stilled, saying nothing as they reveled in their newly discovered happiness, love and unity.

Aedan eventually worked his lips through her curls, softly whispering as he kissed her ear. "Will you be returning to your bedroom soon?"

She smiled and turned her head, suggestively raising her eyebrows. "Do you have a better idea?"

"As a matter of fact, I do," he said, taking her with him as he rolled onto his back. And with that, the two of them began making the most perfect love imaginable.

The following morning, in order to get the embarrassing ordeal over with, Aedan and Rhosewen entered the kitchen hand in hand, looking guilty as they paused in the doorway.

When Morrigan glanced up, her mouth fell open and an egg dropped to the floor. "Rhosewen," she breathed, clutching her chest as she swept toward them.

She took Rhosewen's cheeks, intently searching her eyes. Then she showered her face in kisses. "Oh, sweetie . . . I'm so . . . happy for you." She moved to Aedan, kissing him as well. "For both . . . of you."

The crack of eggshell compelled Caitrin to look up, and like his wife, his mouth fell open. He scanned the golden haze around his daughter then flipped his gaze to Aedan, clearing his throat as he rose from his chair.

"Congratulations," he offered, holding his heart as he moved around the table. After shaking Aedan's hand, he cradled Rhosewen's face, searching it with misty eyes. "I'm happy for you, sweetheart. This is an amazing union." He kissed her rosy cheeks then glanced at Aedan. "Not to mention unbelievable."

"We were pretty stunned ourselves," Aedan agreed. "Have you heard of another like it?"

"No. If this has happened before, it's remained a well kept secret. This could be history in the making."

"I don't want to make history," Aedan countered. "I just want to take care of Rose and keep our lives to ourselves. This isn't the world's business."

"True," Caitrin conceded, "but anyone who knows you will know what an anomaly this is."

"Yes, but I'm not worried about them. I'd prefer it if word doesn't spread beyond our friends and family."

"A reasonable request," Caitrin approved. "I'll do my part to make it so, but it would seem the Heavens are already smiling on you—a gift mere mortals like me simply cannot match."

Aedan smiled at Rhosewen. "Rose and I are very lucky—blessed by the Heavens and loved by our families."

Caitrin watched the new bonded mates for a moment then cleared his throat. "Is there a wedding in the stars?"

"Yes," Aedan answered. "I asked Rose to marry me last night, and she accepted. You and Morrigan's blessing would mean the world to us."

"Of course you have our blessing," Caitrin approved, wrapping his arm around Morrigan's shoulders. "We would be fools to think we could keep a bonded couple apart. We wouldn't want to try."

"Never," Morrigan agreed, "lest the Goddess Willa smite us down."

"The goddess of mercy?" Aedan laughed. "If she didn't smite the lord of the underworld, she won't be targeting anyone around here. And thank you for your blessing. We'll keep it close to our hearts."

"Thank you, daddy," Rhosewen added, hovering from the ground to kiss his cheek.

Morrigan was beside herself with joy, bouncing in anticipation. "We have a lot to do if we're going to plan a wedding. We'll need a dress, flowers, a ring…"

"I have a ring," Rhosewen interjected. "He gave it to me last night."

She proudly flashed her ring, and Morrigan gasped as she took her wrist, demanding a closer look. "What is this stone?" she asked, twisting Rhosewen's hand side to side. "It's gorgeous."

"Zultanite," Rhosewen answered, grinning from ear to ear.

Her parents looked at her face, making sure they'd heard correctly.

"I know!" she exclaimed. "Isn't he amazing?" She hovered from the ground and threw her arms around Aedan's neck, planting a kiss on his cheek. "And he's mine."

With no reason to delay, the wedding was planned and scheduled within a month; set for the third weekend in July. The vows would be said on the coven's lawn, and dozens of guests would fly in to witness.

Rhosewen had taken a leave of absence from work, partly because she hated the thought of being away from Aedan every day, and partly to help with wedding arrangements, but her aid proved unnecessary. With so many witches scrambling to offer help, the bride and groom merely made choices, and they agreed on everything, so decisions were made easily and immediately.

With their wedding being organized by others, Aedan and Rhosewen concentrated on building their house. Everything in, on and around it was touched by their hands and magic, reflecting their tastes and talent.

Three days before the wedding, they hung their porch swing, successfully completing their new home. As they stood in the rose garden, admiring their handiwork, Daleen and Serafin arrived, glancing around as they alighted in the middle of the lawn. When they spotted Aedan and Rhosewen, they beamed and flew forward, arms outstretched.

"I can't believe it," Daleen exclaimed, tightly hugging Aedan's waist. "What are the odds?"

"On this," Serafin said, giving Rhosewen a gentle hug, "there are no odds." He stepped back, taking a moment to scan the happy couple. "The bonded lights look lovely and absolutely right on you guys. The Heavens smile on my son and his bride-to-be."

"They bathe us in blessings," Aedan agreed, taking Daleen and Rhosewen under his arms.

After a tour of the community, Aedan showed his parents to Caitrin and Morrigan's guestroom. Then he suggested Daleen view the wedding preparations with Morrigan and Rhosewen while the wizards take a trip to Cannon Beach.

Thirty minutes later, the three men sat in an uncrowded corner of the café owned by Caitrin's sister, Cinnia Giles.

Aedan had led Rhosewen to believe this was a pleasure trip, but it was anything but pleasurable. Ignoring his fresh coffee, he looked to his dad, his jaw and shoulders tense. "Where's Medea?" he demanded.

For two weeks they'd been tracking Medea's movements. She'd turned nomadic, leaving home the same day Aedan had. One week into her solo travels, Serafin received terrifying news.

Aedan vividly remembered his dad's phone call.

"I just got word from south Texas," Serafin had revealed. "Medea was there yesterday."

At first Aedan was relieved to hear Medea was so far away. Three days earlier she'd been spotted twenty miles east of Portland. To hear she was in America's heartland loosened the knot in his stomach.

But Serafin had more to say. "She's searching for the Unforgivables, Aedan."

Aedan's heart had stopped. And forget the knot; his stomach had churned and flipped, its contents licking his swollen throat. "No," he'd croaked.

The sadness in Serafin's voice had revealed far more than his words. "I'm afraid so, son."

The Unforgivables—a villainous coalition assembled in 1947 by a ruthless and determined wizard named Agro; the most feared group of magicians to haunt the continent since the 1600's.

According to rumors, Agro had been a rebellious teenager defiant of morals and self-control, angered by the boundaries placed on his magic. He felt magicians should reign rather than hide, but the majority of covens, his own included, disagreed, so he left home and began searching out individuals who shared his wicked convictions. He sought out unconventionally strong magicians, those with unusual abilities. Then he did everything in his power to spread his gospel. Naturally charismatic and abnormally conniving, he was good at convincing people his cause was just. And if he truly desired the obedience of someone unwilling to fall for his lies, he would simply force them to join, using torture, blackmail or his ever increasing man power. He pretentiously called his clan the Dark Elite, urging them to abuse their magical power and rush to the aid of evildoers. He soon grew fond of welcoming bonded children into his ranks and made a point to search them out, adding as many to his trophy case as possible. His numbers grew until they were too big to safely evade their enemies, so he split his troops, choosing bonded children to lead the others. They stayed hidden, coming out to wreak havoc and spark rumors of magic among the hexless. Then they'd vanish, not to be seen again until the innocents least expected them. Their unspeakable and murderous acts had earned them the title *Unforgivables,* and just the name struck fear into peoples' hearts. Magical families did what they could to protect themselves, which wasn't much. Their only defense was to avoid giving the Unforgivables a reason to come around. Bonded families in particular heeded this advice.

Aedan wasn't able to say anything more than *I'll call you later* to Serafin that day. He'd been too queasy. He could have handled Medea, but the Unforgivables were a different story.

It had been a week since the dreadful phone call, and the only three people aware of the bad news sat in Cinnia's café, discussing it.

Expression grim, Serafin answered the question concerning Medea's whereabouts. "She's dropped off the radar."

"How long?" Aedan asked.

"Four days. She was last seen outside New Orleans."

Aedan dropped his fist to the table, slopping coffee from his mug. "The Unforgivables love New Orleans."

"I know," Serafin whispered, magically cleaning the spill.

Aedan shook his head, his jaw so tight he could barely speak. "This is bad. So bad."

"Yes," Serafin agreed. "This could be bad."

"Let's look at this rationally," Caitrin suggested. "The Unforgivables won't have a use for Medea. She's average at best, so they won't grant her any favors. They could teach her a thing or two, sure, but they're not going to do her dirty work for her. What we need to worry about is Agro being alerted to our special situation."

"Precisely," Serafin agreed.

Aedan was lost in thought and didn't comment, so Caitrin continued. "Agro would love to know you and Rhosewen have bonded, but there's no reason for him to soar right over. It's more likely he'll give it nine or ten months before paying a visit. Everyone knows he doesn't search out bonded couples . . . just their children."

Aedan shifted, resting his elbows on the table as he buried his face in his hands.

After a moment of tense silence, Serafin ominously whispered. "What are you not telling us, son? Is Rhosewen pregnant?"

Aedan leaned back, slowly dragging his fingers down his face. "I don't know."

"What do you mean, you don't know?" Caitrin demanded.

"I mean, I don't know," Aedan snapped, frustrated, worried and unbelievably frightened for Rhosewen's safety. He took a deep breath, trying to pull himself together. Then he leaned forward, calmly elaborating. "The night we bonded, before we even knew, Rose and I agreed we wanted a child together, so we didn't put any protection in place. I know bonded couples don't need any—that we have to consciously decide to have a baby. I know all that, but I don't know what to make of our situation. We made the decision, but we made it before we bonded. So does it count? If so, yes, Rose is pregnant. If it doesn't count, no, she's not. Unless our first time didn't count as a bonded experience, in which case our lack of protection could mean she is. After we bonded, we realized the kind of danger our child would face and decided to wait, but we both know there's a possibility she's already carrying our baby. So you see," he quietly finished, "I don't know." He covered his face again, trying not to lose his mind. He needed it to get them out of this mess.

Caitrin and Serafin silently stared at him for a long time. Then Serafin cleared his throat. "I'm sorry, son. I don't have any advice, because I don't know either. Have you heard of a similar situation, Caitrin?"

"No," Caitrin croaked.

Shoulders sagging, Aedan slid his hand to his chin, meeting their stares with strained eyes. "If Rose is pregnant, and Medea's found the Unforgivables, it could mean . . . it could turn out . . ." He dropped his head into his palm, his throat too tight to talk.

"Listen," Serafin whispered. "We don't know anything for sure. If it turns out Rhosewen's pregnant, we'll take the necessary precautions, but right now you have to pull yourself together. For Rhosewen's sake if not your own. You're getting married to your bonded mate Saturday, and that's something to celebrate. We'll worry if and when the time comes."

"Hear, hear," Caitrin advocated.

But Aedan merely nodded. He'd stay strong for his beautiful Rose, but the knots and worry would remain.

By Saturday afternoon, the lawn was set for a beautiful wedding. White chairs draped in emerald green satin were spread out in curved rows, facing a large archway comprised of sea blue and emerald green roses bursting from twisting vines of gold. Behind the chairs, sat an enormous round table, most of its surface dedicated to a large reflecting pool, yet it could easily hold enough food to serve over two hundred guests. Tropical fish swam in the pool's depths, and its bright blue surface rippled when floating rose petals caught the gentle breeze.

Rhosewen stood in her parents' living room, getting ready to marry the man of her dreams, her perfect love, her soul mate. She couldn't wait.

Morrigan and Daleen fussed over her, but she was serene as she watched Cordelia Kavanagh, her friend and coven member, nurse her baby boy.

"I can't believe those dimples," Rhosewen said, motioning toward the baby. "They're deeper than his dad's, and I swear they get cuter every day."

"I know," Cordelia beamed, dipping a forefinger into the tiny yet defined dimple on her baby's left cheek. "He's gorgeous, isn't he?"

"He's perfect," Rhosewen confirmed.

"I still can't believe how lucky I am," Cordelia sighed. "First I find my bonded mate, now this. Some people have all the luck."

As Rhosewen watched Cordelia nuzzle her baby, she reflected on what she knew of her happily ever after. Cordelia relocated to Rhosewen's coven two years earlier, after bonding with Kemble, one of their lifelong members. They'd met while visiting a mutual friend in Rome, and it had been love at first sight, so Cordelia happily left her home in Alaska. She and Rhosewen found instant common ground, quickly becoming close friends, and now that they were both bonded, they had even more in common. As Rhosewen reveled in the beautiful miracle of mother and child, she laid a hand over her belly, wondering what other similarities she might soon share with Cordelia.

Her view was interrupted when Daleen stepped in front of her, zapping a dress onto her body, but Rhosewen ignored the garment and found the baby again. "Thanks for being my go-to girl, Cordelia. You've been a big help." Not even nursing a four-month-old every two hours had kept Cordelia from tending to even the tiniest wedding errands.

"You're welcome," Cordelia returned. "I'm happy I could help. And Kemble's thrilled to have Aedan around. It's like you and I when Kemble dragged me home."

For what seemed like the millionth time, Rhosewen considered how odd it was that her coven now had three bonded couples. A magician usually had to travel to ten or more communities before laying eyes on one, yet here they had three. It seemed unfair to everyone else. Rhosewen wondered—again, not for the first time—if fate had brought them together, if they'd been deemed worthy of the deities' gazes, touched and guided by them, or if they were simply the luckiest coven in the world.

Cordelia held her baby out in front of her, cooing soft sentiments. Then she switched him to her other breast. "I'm trying to fill him up before the ceremony," she said. "I doubt this is what you have in mind for wedding photos."

"Don't be ridiculous," Rhosewen countered. "It's amazing, watching your beautiful body nourish your beautiful baby. Anyone lucky enough to see it should count their blessings."

"That's what Kemble says," Cordelia replied, "but between us girls, I think he's jealous."

"Of you or Quinlan?"

"Well, I know he would jump at the chance to feed Quinlan, and of course he'd enjoy it, but he would be beyond thrilled to be on a two hour feeding schedule himself, so I'd say it's a little of both."

Rhosewen laughed as Morrigan and Daleen turned her toward the mirror. Then her giggle faded as she scanned her reflection from head to toe.

Everything about her shimmered—her skin, which seemed to be dusted with prismatic glitter; her loose spirals, which were entwined with delicate strands of silver and laced with tiny, sea blue rosebuds; and her silk chiffon Grecian gown, which had thousands of miniscule aquamarines adorning the plunging neckline and empire waist, as well as filaments of silver woven through its soft, layered skirt and the sheer chiffon loosely covering her cleavage. Even her fingernails and toenails sparkled, flashing the exact same color as the zultanite in her wedding ring. When the gem shone pale green, so did her nails. When the gem faded to pink, so did her nails. The entire ensemble was meticulously thought out and designed around her and Aedan's preferences, and she felt every bit the woman he deserved.

"Perfect," she whispered, smiling at Morrigan and Daleen, who'd spent the past two days making her attire. "You've done a beautiful job. Thank you."

Their auras pulsed with pride, and not even their flowing tears could stifle their brilliant smiles.

At three o'clock, the lawn hummed with quiet chatter, soft piano music, and distant birdsong; and Aedan stood barefoot beneath the large archway, waiting for Rhosewen to make her entrance onto the lawn through Caitrin and Morrigan's front door.

His attire was casual—comfortable slacks and a white button-up shirt, which he left untucked. He didn't care what he wore. He'd marry Rhosewen in nothing but a pair of clown shoes if that's what she wanted. Concerning his attire, he had one request—that the top button of his shirt lay open to display the rose gold tag Rhosewen had crafted him. Attached to a braided leather chain and engraved with their names and bonding date, it was the only material object he owned that he considered precious.

He was the epitome of calm, anxious only to see his bride, but that was nothing new. He ached to lay eyes on her every time she stepped away.

When the door opened, their gazes met, and their bonded lights burst loose, mingling with their elated auras. The brilliant combination swirled along Rhosewen's glittering skin and twists of long, flowing hair as she gracefully floated forward, urging her mom and dad to keep up.

As they approached the end of the petal strewn aisle, Rhosewen kissed her parents' hands then let them go, reaching for Aedan instead. He reached as well, and as their fingertips touched, the luminosity of their bonded lights doubled, enveloping them in a glistening, golden sphere.

He pulled her close then firmly held her against him through the ceremony, eyes locked and bodies tingling.

When Aedan grinned and kissed the bride, a hundred white doves swooped through the clearing, dropping heaps of blue and green rose petals, and the guests cheered, shooting colorful spells into the air.

Aedan and Rhosewen listened to their loved ones, but watched each other, unable to stifle their grins. His fingertips brushed across her pink cheek then picked a petal from her shiny spirals. When he softly blew on the bloom's silky surface, it burst into sea blue glitter and formed her name.

Rhosewen's face and aura lit up. Then she pulled him into another kiss, whispering against his lips. "I love you, Aedan."

"You're my life, Rose," he whispered back, sweeping her off her feet. "Forever."

She wrapped her arms around his neck and laid her head on his shoulder, sighing peacefully. "Forever."

Chapter 24

After a fantastic feast abundant with variety, the dinner table was magically swept away, but the reflecting pool remained, lowered to ground level and surrounded by silk covered benches. The chairs were rearranged around a bonfire, and a table of hors d'oeuvres and beverages replaced the arch. Enchanted flutes and acoustic guitars materialized near the north tree line, and soft music began drifting amidst cheerful laughing and bright conversations.

Around midnight, the lawn emptied of everyone who wasn't staying, but the enchanted band continued to play for the coven. Serafin and Daleen remained, as did Aedan's friend Kearny, who decided to stay after meeting Rhosewen's cousin, Enid. The two of them hit it off immediately and were in the surrounding forest, getting to know each other.

Aedan looked at his wife, wondering how on earth he'd gotten so lucky. Then he leaned closer, smelling her hair as he whispered. "Dance with me."

Rhosewen happily turned into him, and he wrapped one arm around her waist, carrying her into sweeping circles.

"Was it the wedding of your dreams?" he asked.

"Better," she answered.

"Good," he approved, picking up the pace.

He didn't have to match the rhythm of the music; the bewitched instruments had been matching his all day, so he was free to concentrate on Rhosewen's entrancing eyes, pink lips, and glowing skin.

"It seems impossible," he whispered.

"What?" she asked, thinking the world was exactly as it should be.

"That you'll be more beautiful tomorrow than you are tonight," he explained. "But it's not impossible, because that's how it is everyday. Every morning, when I open my eyes to your face, you're more beautiful than I remember. You take my breath away every time."

Tears stung Rhosewen's eyes as she clutched his cheeks. "I love you, Aedan. You mean everything to me."

"Sounds like we were made for each other," he quipped, lifting her high into the air. Then he spun once and lowered her lips to his.

They were still kissing when Kearny and Enid shot from the trees, soaring unusually close to the ground. As they approached, their feet flipped out in front of them, catching their breathless bodies, and Aedan and Rhosewen looked over, finding stark white faces.

"The Unforgivables," Kearny warned.

Aedan's embrace tightened as icy fingers gripped his heart. "How long?"

"Thirty seconds. Maybe."

"Shit."

Aedan turned toward the crowd, and Rhosewen spun with him, locked in his tense biceps. The instruments had crashed to the ground, and the lawn was silent, its occupants frozen.

"What are you waiting for?" Aedan shouted. "Go! Get the children inside. Kemble..." he mumbled, searching him out, "take Cordelia and Quinlan and hide, all three of you."

His shouts snapped everyone out of their trances, and many of them scattered. But Morrigan, Caitrin, Serafin and Daleen flocked to their offspring, and several adult wizards formed a united front behind the golden family.

"What's going on?" Rhosewen asked. "Why are the Unforgivables here?"

Aedan met her frightened stare, terror twisting his gut. "Medea," was all he could say, and it killed him to say it. This was his fault. Everybody in the community, everyone he loved most, was in terrible danger because of him.

As if he'd called her name, Medea slowly stalked from the south tree line, her focus on Rhosewen. She looked wild—crazy golden eyes;

matted lackluster hair. Hate and vengeance had consumed her aura, changing not only the hues, but the way it flowed—sluggish and dull, steadily draining of life. Another noticeable change, one that had everything to do with the situation at hand, was the raised, purple scar marring her bony right cheekbone. About half an inch wide and three inches long, it hideously dominated her features.

Fury boiled Aedan's blood as fear challenged his strength. She'd actually done it. She'd sold them out to the deadly Dark Elite. "I can't believe you did this, Medea. And for what? You've doomed yourself as much as you've doomed us."

Medea didn't reply. She just ran an unkempt fingernail down her ugly scar as another thirty magicians emerged from the forest. Wearing blood red flying cloaks, they stalked forward in a perfect V with Agro at its point. When he was ten feet away, he stopped, but the others formed a half circle around the bold yet frightened family.

Menacingly handsome with long brown hair, a sharp face, and glowing orange eyes, Agro cordially stretched his arms out, his gaze sliding over the tight knit group. "Fellow magicians," he greeted, appraising the abundant golden glow. "How nice to see all of you. I've heard wondrous things about your coven."

Caitrin squared his shoulders and cleared his throat, speaking as evenly as possible. "What are you doing here, Agro?"

Agro eyed him with mild interest then glanced at Morrigan. "It is a wedding, isn't it? I'm here to give the happy couple my best wishes."

"You weren't invited," Aedan cut in, muscles twitching around Rhosewen.

Agro narrowed his eyes, scanning Aedan from head to toe. "Tsk, tsk, my boy. Is that any way to treat a guest?"

"You weren't invited," Aedan repeated, flipping his gaze to Medea, who was moving outside the circle, her focus locked on Rhosewen.

Her lips parted and her fingers wagged.

"No!" Aedan blurted, spinning around to shield Rhosewen.

Medea paused then calmly started in the other direction.

"You must be Aedan," Agro concluded. "And this must be Rhosewen, your golden beauty."

Medea bared her teeth and hissed.

"Now, now," Agro chuckled, waving a finger in the air, "let's not be rude." He laughed again, giving Aedan a wink. "You have a way with women, my boy. Tell me—is it natural charisma . . . or trickery?"

This time Rhosewen hissed, and Aedan stroked her hair, but he didn't dare tighten his desperate embrace.

"No matter," Agro went on. "Forget Medea. It's obvious you needed no trickery to achieve this union. I must admit, I didn't simply come to wish you well."

"You don't say?" Aedan countered, watching Medea stalk the outskirts of the circle. When her lips and fingers twitched, he rotated.

"I did want to wish you well," Agro claimed, ignoring Aedan's maneuver. "But it was my curiosity that brought me here. Of course, you must already know that." He intently stared at the newlyweds, scanning their vast golden hazes. "In all my life I've never heard of another case such as yours. Two bonded children bonding themselves. The breed is so rare—an endangered species since the dawn of time. Yet here you are, defying all odds by . . . keeping it in the family." He slowly licked his lips, ravenously, enviously. Then he calculatingly smiled and clucked his tongue, eyebrows arching over an evil grin. "Tell me—are there children in the stars?"

An instinctive growl rumbled in Aedan's chest, rolling up his throat and vibrating his tongue, but his focus stayed on Medea, who continued to look for an opening. She found it, and he quickly closed it, wishing he knew her plan so he could better protect against it.

"Now I've upset you," Agro observed. "My curiosity does tend to get the best of me. But who wouldn't marvel at your situation?"

Caitrin stepped forward, taking advantage of Agro's polite facade. "It's late. If indeed you've accomplished what you came for, you need to leave."

Agro tilted his head, his manners fading as indignation took hold. "Of course," he icily replied. Then he looked to Aedan and Rhosewen, orange eyes flaming red. "The Heavens shower you with gifts. I'm sure your union will prove plentiful. Perhaps my next visit will yield better manners. It's unwise to be rude to guests."

A blatant threat.

Aedan looked over, meeting the stare of a murderous monster that had set its sights on his perfect Rose, his beautiful family.

As everyone watched the intense exchange, no one watched Medea.

Rhosewen's grip on Aedan's waist suddenly tightened. Then a shiver rippled her body from head to toe.

"Rose," Aedan panicked, snapping his head around.

As all eyes shot to the bride, the Unforgivables took flight, quickly disappearing into the night.

Rhosewen was trembling, but seemed unharmed.

"What happened?" Aedan asked. "What did she do?"

"I don't know," Rhosewen replied. "It felt like someone poured ice water on my head."

"Dad!" Aedan shouted. "Examine her."

Serafin stepped forward, laying a hand on Aedan's shoulder. "I'll need you to let go of her, son."

Aedan reluctantly released his grip and took a step back, keeping his anxious gaze on Rhosewen's face. Serafin positioned his hands half an inch from her body then ran them up and down its length, front and back. He did this several times then stepped away, holding a palm to his chin.

"Well?" Aedan and Morrigan urged.

"If they got her with something," Serafin mumbled, "I'm not familiar with it. I didn't pick up anything wrong."

"You check, Caitrin," Aedan insisted.

Caitrin moved forward and kissed Rhosewen's forehead. Then he repeated Serafin's routine. "Nothing," he concluded, slowly shaking his head.

Aedan wasn't satisfied, so he stepped forward and began running his hands over Rhosewen, actually touching her as he searched for an energy that didn't belong. He slipped his hands up her skirt and ran his palms down her bare legs. Then he slid her silk straps aside and gently wrapped his hands around her neck, gliding them over her upper chest, shoulders and arms. When he got to her back, he unbuttoned her dress and laid the material aside, running both hands up and down her spine. As he focused on a spot right behind her heart, he stiffened.

"Here," he said, giving his dad access to the afflicted area.

Morrigan clutched Daleen for support as Serafin placed a palm to Rhosewen's back. When he sadly bowed his head, Morrigan sobbed and collapsed in Daleen's arms. Caitrin quickly checked for himself. After a moment's concentration, he dropped his head, squeezing his eyes shut as he took a shaky breath.

Rhosewen turned toward Aedan with big, frightened eyes. "What is it?"

"We don't know," he whispered, pulling her into a hug.

"But I feel fine," she countered. "Maybe they tried and it didn't work."

"Maybe," Serafin agreed, raising his head.

Aedan looked up, desperate for hope. "Do you think that's likely?"

"I wouldn't say it's likely," Serafin replied, "but it is possible. Only time will tell. I've never felt anything like it, and I don't understand why she hasn't experienced any after affects. This is either something unusually advanced and completely foreign to me, or it's a botched spell."

The vague answer wasn't what Aedan wanted, so he looked to his beautiful Rose, an ever welcome sight. "Are you sure you don't feel any different?" he asked. "You're not hurting anywhere? Or experiencing any odd sensations?"

"No," she assured. "I feel fine. It didn't hurt earlier either. It was just cold and tingly."

Aedan scanned her aura then looked to his dad. "I'm not satisfied. I want to know why her back feels that way, whether it has an affect on her or not."

Serafin nodded as he squeezed Aedan's shoulder. "I can't promise answers, but I'll steep myself in research."

"I'll join you," Caitrin offered, pulling Morrigan from Daleen. Then he laid a hand on the back of Rhosewen's head.

Aedan looked at his wife, begging the Heavens to keep her safe from the unidentified magic. He couldn't consider the alternative. It tormented his insides, practically cutting off his air supply. The alternative would kill him.

Over the next few days, Aedan performed nightly physical exams on Rhosewen, asking her multiple times if she felt any different, but the answer was always no, and his inspections always yielded normal results. Deciding it must have been a botched spell after all, everyone began to relax.

They remained guarded against possible visits from the Unforgivables, and assumed they were being watched from a distance, which was a huge inconvenience for Cordelia and Kemble, who hadn't left the house with Quinlan since the wedding. But for the most part, life returned to normal. For a day or two.

Rhosewen had just finished showering for bed and stood naked in the bathroom, examining her body inside and out. She was three days late for her menses, something she'd never been in her life, so she'd been performing self-exams after every shower, but so far they'd been fruitless. She'd found nothing but her own familiar body.

Eyes closed, head clear, she held her palms to her lower abdomen, focusing, feeling, searching . . . searching . . . search . . .

She found it. Her soul wasn't alone. Another had joined it.

Her eyes popped open as she pulled her hands tighter against her belly. "Baby," she breathed, looking down.

Emotion bubbled in her chest as elation fluttered from her toes up, making her feel light as air, consumed by the purest love she'd ever experienced. But the euphoria didn't last. It shattered as pain clutched every bone in her body, buckling her knees. She grabbed the edge of the vanity, squeezing her eyes shut and clenching her teeth, trying not to scream.

What was going on? She was disoriented and scared, awash with the onslaught of burning, prickling torment.

As suddenly as it hit, the pain subsided, leaving behind a dull, throbbing ache. She straightened, steadied then opened her eyes, perplexed but so happy. She'd always wanted a baby. To have one with Aedan was a dream come true. Her life would be impossibly perfect now.

She took a deep breath, making sure the pain was under control. Then she walked from the bathroom, receiving an unpleasant, squeezing sensation with every step. She had no way of knowing if her aura reflected the pain.

"Aedan?"

He looked up from his book then tossed it aside, scowling as he flew from the bed and scooped her into a cradle hold. "What's wrong?" he asked, scanning her body.

"I . . . I'm . . ."

"You're what?" he urged. "Are you hurt?"

As Rhosewen watched his panicked expression, she decided not to tell him about the painful episode. A baby should mark a happy occasion. Complaining to Aedan about pain would overshadow the joy, and she refused to ruin this for him.

She did her best to look as happy as she felt as she touched a reassuring hand to his cheek. "I'm pregnant, Aedan."

Emotion consumed him, spinning his head and swelling his heart. Every feeling possible bursting into bloom—love, happiness, anticipation, wonder, worry, fear, and upon finding Rhosewen's eyes, love again.

"Rose," he whispered, his gaze roaming to her stomach—a lovely and wondrous haven keeping their baby safe and warm as it grew into a tiny person. "A baby."

"Our baby," she said, laying her palms on her belly. The ache in her bones sharpened, but she forced herself to lie still.

Aedan flew to the bed and gently laid her down, placing his hands on top of hers. "Our baby," he repeated, resting his head on his hands, but he quickly popped back up. "Is that too heavy?"

Rhosewen hurt, but not from the weight on her belly. "No, but get closer." She moved her palms, replacing them with his cheek. Then she slid her fingers into his hair, trying to ignore the mild ache that wouldn't go away. "How's that?" she asked. "Better?"

"Perfect." He kissed her belly then lay back down, pulling one of her hands to his lips so he could kiss her fingertips. "I love you, Rose. And I already love our baby."

The pain throbbed, but not enough to stifle her joy. "Me, too," she breathed, watching the top of his head through happy tears.

She closed her eyes, and after a long stretch of silence, the pain subsided, letting them fall asleep with each other and their baby on their minds and in their hearts.

First thing the following morning, Aedan called his parents and asked them to return to Oregon right away. They'd only been home for three days, but they agreed without hesitation.

Now that Rhosewen knew she was pregnant, other magicians would know as well, just by looking at her aura—the tell-tale colors of love and concern congregating around the womb, its vigilant flow of maturity and responsibility. She was baking, and her oven light was on, so she couldn't leave the house. She didn't mind too much and would never risk a trip outside if there was a chance the Unforgivables were watching.

Morrigan and Caitrin's worry weighed heavily on them, but they did their best to smile around their daughter, unwilling to compound her stress. They weren't fooling anybody. Morrigan rarely left Rhosewen's side in the twenty-two hours it took Serafin and Daleen to arrive.

Once the family of six had gathered, they sat in Aedan and Rhosewen's living room to discuss their options.

For Aedan, there was only one. "We have to leave," he announced, stroking Rhosewen's dainty knuckles.

Daleen dabbed her eyes with a handkerchief, Serafin kissed his wife's silky hair, and Morrigan buried her face in Caitrin's bicep.

"You could be followed," Caitrin noted. "Then you'd be alone in facing them."

"We'll have to take the risk," Aedan replied. "If we stay, they'll find out and no one in the coven will be safe, particularly our baby. Our best chance is to hide and hope they never find out Rose conceived. We'll change our names and integrate into a non-magical community. As long as we're together with only ourselves to worry about, we'll have the edge against intruders. We can disappear in less than a second, get out before anyone knows we're there. We could hide that way for a long time. Until it's safe."

"What do you think of all this?" Caitrin asked, looking at Rhosewen.

She slowly shook her head, jarring a few tears loose. "I don't see any other way, dad."

The sadness in her aura grasped Aedan's heart and twisted. "I'm sorry, Rose," he whispered, brushing a thumb over her tears.

She grabbed his wrist and held tight. "Don't be sorry," she insisted, moving his hand to her stomach. "Not about this."

He ran his hand under her shirt, finding soft skin. "Never about this."

"They're right," Serafin cut in, briefly meeting Caitrin's stare. "The best we can do is get them to safety without being seen. At least there's a chance for them that way. Agro would do anything to get his hands on their baby. If they stay here, he'll quickly discover the truth. Then there will be no hope . . ." His voice broke, and sad silence held the room, leaving everyone breathless.

By that evening, the plans were made, the farewells were said, and Aedan and Rhosewen were as prepared as they would ever be to leave their home. For how long, no one knew.

Daleen had been gone all day, hunting down a place for them to stay, and had met a nice woman living in Ketchum, Idaho. Thirty-one-year-old Katherine Moore was single and childless, a secretary by day and a loner by night. As luck—or fate—would have it, she had a fully furnished, garage apartment with activated utilities and phone service. Daleen softened her up with two years rent, telling her the truth mostly —the apartment was a gift for her son and daughter-in-law who were expecting a baby. She gave Katherine their new names, Chris and Sarah Callaway, and told her they'd be arriving late that night, insisting she not wait up for them.

Daleen had worked out the where while Aedan, Serafin and Caitrin had worked out the how. Morrigan was a mess, unable to tear her attention away from Rhosewen for more than a few seconds at a time, so she didn't take part in the planning.

The six of them would leave together after sun down, lowering their bodies' visibility with the same spell they used when they flew during the day. Hiding their auras and bonded lights, however, was something none of them were accustomed to, so Aedan and Rhosewen practiced throughout the day, finding it fairly easy to do. Combined, the concealment spells would provide excellent cover, but an alert magician standing in the right place at the right time could easily spot a shimmer of evidence, so several coven members patrolled the surrounding lands and skies, making sure the Unforgivables weren't close enough to witness the family's departure.

Inside their house, Rhosewen and Aedan said sad goodbyes to their parents. The six of them wouldn't be landing together. In fact, each couple would be landing in a different time zone.

The witches cried, and the wizards flexed, eyes shiny and red.

"Keep in touch," Serafin insisted, grasping Aedan's shoulders. "We'll make sure no one hears our side of the conversation."

"We will," Aedan whispered, his throat too tight to do more.

As nightfall approached, someone knocked on the door, and Aedan sluggishly moved to open it, wishing the task would distract him longer than a few seconds. "Kemble," he greeted, scanning his aura.

"Everything's clear," Kemble reported. "We haven't seen a soul."

"Thanks," Aedan mumbled, starting to turn away. Then he paused and looked back. "Will you leave as well?"

Kemble shrugged as he glanced at his house. "We haven't decided."

"You should," Aedan insisted. "If Agro drops in looking for us and sees your lights…" He swallowed and shook his head. "Just go, get away for a while. Maybe stay with Cordelia's parents."

Kemble thoughtfully nodded. "Cordelia and I have discussed our options. If we decide to go, we have places to stay." He glanced at Rhosewen's tear-streaked face then met Aedan's sorrowful stare. "I'm sorry, Aedan," he said, clasping his hand. "I have a pretty good idea what you're going through, and I hate that such hard times have fallen on you. Be safe, be strong, and come back to us sooner rather than later."

"We'll do our best," Aedan agreed. "Take care of Cordelia and Quinlan."

Kemble nodded and stepped away. "Goodbye, Aedan."

"Until next time, Kemble."

"Until next time," Kemble repeated. Then he shot toward his post.

"Everyone knows the plan," Caitrin hoarsely announced. "Call when you safely arrive."

Aedan and Serafin nodded, but the women continued to cry, and Rhosewen was gasping for air.

Aedan took her face and leaned close, touching his nose to hers. "Breathe," he whispered.

She nodded, keeping her gaze glued to his as they inhaled and exhaled together, and her eyes eventually dried as her shaking quieted.

"Ready?" he asked.

"Yeah," she squeaked.

He watched her for another moment then turned to his parents, concealing their bodies and lights while Rhosewen did the same for Morrigan and Caitrin. After Aedan and Rhosewen performed their spells on each other, only hazy shimmers occasionally caught the light, revealing the location of the six magicians.

Each couple clutched hands. Then they stepped into the warm, night air, shooting into the sky as one. They flew east for thirty minutes then south for two hours. When they turned east again, Caitrin and Morrigan slowed, their silhouettes appearing over the bright moon then dropping out of sight. The two of them planned to retrace their path to the community, keeping their senses alert to signs they'd been followed.

The others flew east for another hour and a half. Then Serafin and Daleen appeared out of nowhere, but they didn't slow down or turn around. They merely held each other close as they continue east. Aedan and Rhosewen were no longer with them. They'd turned north.

An hour later, with Rhosewen wrapped in a hug, Aedan landed in the quiet backyard of a two-story, country home. He scanned his surroundings as he climbed the stairs outside an old garage. Then he used the key Daleen had given him, opening the door to a small, one-room apartment.

After checking the bathroom and closet, they released their concealment spells and appeared in each other's arms, but they didn't speak. They just held tight, catching each other's hot tears and labored breaths.

Once the tears ran dry, Aedan called Caitrin. Then he and Rhosewen crawled into their strange bed, drained by their long and emotional day.

Chapter 25

Katherine Moore—tall and slender with long brown hair and bifocals over large, milk chocolate eyes. She was sweet, instantly likable, with an aura that shone brighter than most non-magical auras. The haze was laced with saddening colors, indicating a troubled past and a deep hesitancy to trust the world around her, but it also held an exceptional amount of optimism and compassion.

Katherine adored Rhosewen from day one, doting on her every chance she got. Within six weeks, Rhosewen had found true friendship in Katherine, albeit based on lies.

One evening, as Aedan ran errands, Katherine joined Rhosewen for tea. She'd been thrilled to accept Rhosewen's invite, and was in an excellent mood as she refilled their mugs, raving about a baby crib she'd seen at a flea market.

"It was so pretty," she said, adding heaps of sugar to Rhosewen's tea, "all white with spindly rails. You would have liked it."

Rhosewen stirred her beverage then sipped, watching the pulsing haze surrounding her company. "It sounds pretty. You should have bought it."

"You can't get a crib without seeing it first," Katherine countered.

"Not for me," Rhosewen laughed. "For you. You like kids, right?"

"I love kids," Katherine confirmed.

"Then you'll probably have one someday."

Katherine's aura darkened as her expression fell, making her look older, sadder and wiser. But then her lips curved into a hopeful smile. "I can't carry a baby, but I would like to adopt one. Someday soon, I hope."

"Oh," Rhosewen whispered, eyes moistening. "Adoption is a special commitment. It takes a special person to do it. I think you'd be perfect for the job."

Rhosewen believed what she said, yet her heart ached for Katherine—an outwardly average, inwardly amazing, beautiful woman, who would never know what it feels like to carry a baby, to know her body was responsible for the most precious, miraculous, magical thing possible.

Sharp pangs suddenly ripped through Rhosewen's bones, and her mug shattered on the floor. She squeezed her eyes shut, grasping at air before finding the edge of the table, her knuckles and face painfully tense.

"Sarah!" Katherine shouted, rushing around the table. "What's wrong? What happened?"

"I'm fine," Rhosewen rasped. "I just . . . need . . . a second." She forced herself to breathe through the subsiding pain, which quickly ebbed to a tolerable ache. "I'm better now," she said, peeling her hands from the table as she willed her smarting body to stand.

"What are you doing?" Katherine gasped.

"Cleaning up my mess," Rhosewen answered, waving a shaky hand toward broken glass.

"I don't think so," Katherine protested, urging Rhosewen to sit. "I'll clean up your mess while you tell me what that was all about."

"It's nothing," Rhosewen assured. "I've just been achy since I got pregnant. Sometimes it flares up."

"You should see a doctor."

"It's not that bad," Rhosewen countered. "I don't know why I dropped my cup. Clumsiness, I guess."

Katherine halted, suspiciously eying her hostess. "You're the most graceful woman I've ever met, Sarah. Whatever that was hurt you more than you're letting on. You need to see a doctor." She dumped the broken glass in the trash then turned back with raised eyebrows. "Does Chris know about this?"

"No," Rhosewen mumbled, thinking about how much energy she devoted to keeping Aedan in the dark. Of course she felt guilty—an unending, gut wrenching, stomach flipping kind of guilty. But she hadn't found the courage to destroy his happiness. When he performed physical examinations on her and the baby, she worked her own magic, shielding the sore areas of her body when his hands moved over them, and she'd learned how to manipulate her aura, which took constant concentration.

"That's what I thought," Katherine sighed, "because he wouldn't let this go on without getting you medical help. He loves you and that baby too much."

"I know," Rhosewen conceded. "I'm going to tell him."

"Soon?"

Rhosewen was deciding how to answer when Aedan walked in. Katherine glanced at him then shot a meaningful look at Rhosewen, but she didn't say anything more on the subject.

Aedan covered the distance to Rhosewen in two strides, pulling her out of her chair and into his arms. "Hello, my love," he breathed, doing so easily for the first time since he'd left. He kissed her lips then knelt, nuzzling and kissing her stomach. "Hello, my other love."

Rhosewen's pain pulsed, but she held perfectly still. She'd become quite skilled in her dishonest quest.

Aedan straightened and looked to Katherine, who'd been leaning against the counter, admiring the family reunion. "How are you, Katherine?" he asked.

Katherine shook her head clear and smiled, scanning the room for her purse. "Good, Chris. Thanks for asking. Did you get by the bank before they closed?"

He hadn't gone to the bank. He'd flown to a nearby town to call his parents. They couldn't achieve a magical connection at these distances, and something as non-magical as phone records could easily lead to their discovery, so they kept their phone calls from the apartment down to two a week.

"I did," he lied. "Just barely."

"Better late than never," Katherine returned, grabbing her purse off the sofa. "Well, I have things to do around the house. Call if you need anything, Sarah."

"I will," Rhosewen replied. "Thanks for having tea with me."

"Anytime. See you guys later."

"Bye," they said in unison, waving as she walked out the door.

"She's sweet," Rhosewen whispered, burying her face in Aedan's chest.

"Not as sweet as you," he countered, nuzzling her hair.

"What did your dad say?"

"They've spread the word that we're on an extended honeymoon, but Agro's smart enough to figure us out. We just have to hope our hiding place stays safe."

"It will," she assured. "It has to." The alternative was unthinkable. "Maybe I'll try to commune with the Heavens in my dreams. Mother Ava led me to you. Maybe she'll lead me to answers."

"You believe the Goddess of the Heavens brought us together?" Aedan asked.

"Who else besides Ava could deliver heaven on earth?" Rhosewen countered. "If I can commune with her in my dreams, perhaps I can persuade her to guide my fairytale down safer paths."

"You aim to sweet-talk the Heavens," Aedan laughed, "woo them with your wily charm?"

"Not wily wooing, just . . . humbly requesting."

"If anyone can sway the Heavens," Aedan conceded, nuzzling her ear, "it's my golden Rose."

"Mmm . . . " Rhosewen murmured, leaning into his lips. Then she grinned and pulled away. "Where are the gemstones we brought? Maybe there's something in there that will sharpen my perception and deepen my meditation."

Aedan laughed as he dug into his satchel, very willing to humor the magnificent mother of his child.

The next few months passed uneventfully, with Aedan and Rhosewen taking full advantage of their idle time, spending days and nights in each other's arms, singing lullabies to their baby, and getting to know each other's souls.

Rhosewen's pain steadily increased, but so did her resistance to it. She'd come to consider it a mild annoyance. It was only fair after all. Everything else was perfect. Not even hiding from the world bothered her too bad. As long as she had Aedan and her baby, she would hide forever. She dearly missed her parents and coven, but the separation was a small sacrifice to make to ensure the safety of her baby and maintain her husband's peace of mind.

Though she hadn't received any enlightening visions from the Goddess Ava, she continued to sleep with a bag of gemstones under her pillow. Having them there helped her maintain hope if nothing else, and perhaps someday they'd bring her the courage and wisdom she needed to confess her unexplained aches and pains to Aedan. He was so happy and peaceful not knowing, it made her happy and peaceful as well, so she kept her mouth shut, telling herself the pain wasn't so bad it should overshadow this joyous time in their lives. But deep in her squirming gut she knew it was wrong. She was harboring a lie that got heavier with each passing day.

Four months into their retreat, they were lying naked in bed—something they did more often than not—and their hands were on her growing belly as Aedan sang a lullaby.

Moments like these were Rhosewen's favorites, and not even the slight increase in discomfort could prevent her from enjoying them. Occasionally the pain kept her from singing the words, but she could easily sweet-talk Aedan into taking over the lyrics while she hummed along.

Tonight, as she lay aching but happy, humming an upbeat tune, Aedan held his lips to her stomach, singing the song he called *Angel's Lullaby*.

"How special you are, my love.
How special you'll always be.
How much you have touched our lives,
your beautiful mom and me.
We'll see you soon, sweet child.
How happy we will be
when we look into the eyes
of our angelic baby."

That's when it happened—the softest, little thump beneath their fingers. Their beautiful, amazing, wondrous baby was moving. Their eyes met, wide and shiny as grins stretched across their faces. Rhosewen was so thrilled, she had no problem ignoring the flaring burn sliding over her body.

Another tiny thump.

Rhosewen giggled, heart soaring as her toes danced, and Aedan replaced his fingers with his lips, quickly kissing when he felt another kick.

"Wow," Rhosewen breathed. "It's amazing, Aedan. I can feel our baby moving inside me."

"Now can I check?" he asked, tapping anxious fingers on her belly.

Since the beginning, he'd wanted to know the gender of the baby, but Rhosewen made him promise to wait until they felt movement.

"Now you can check," she agreed.

Aedan grinned and closed his eyes, lightly pressing his palms to her stomach as he searched for the baby's energy. When Rhosewen laughed and wiggled, his concentration snapped, and he peeked at her with one eye.

"I'm sorry," she giggled, wiggling again. "I'm just so excited."

"You need to lie still if you want me to know for sure," he teased.

"Okay. I promise." She took a deep breath then held perfectly still.

Aedan focused on her belly, and she eagerly watched, but his expression stayed neutral. After a very long fifty-three seconds, he opened his eyes, a serene smile creasing his chiseled cheeks.

"Well?" she urged, body trembling. She couldn't wait one second longer.

"It's a girl," he answered, his voice impossibly tender. "We're having a baby girl."

Rhosewen froze as reality washed over her, flooding her with an intense maternal instinct and an incredibly fierce devotion to her daughter. A baby girl, made up of her and Aedan, created by the love they'd shared, was growing, kicking and living inside her body.

Her body . . . her burning—breaking—body.

She screamed as the worst pain she'd ever experienced consumed her. She arched and clawed at the bed. A thousand daggers stabbing her, a massive boulder crushing her, flames licking every inch inside and out.

"Rose!" Aedan shouted, trying to stifle her thrashing. "Rose!"

Her head flung back, neck flexed, veins bulging as she willed herself to endure. "Aedan."

"What?" he blurted, sweeping his gaze over her body. "What's happening?"

"Hurts . . ."

"What hurts?"

"Everything . . ."

"Shit." Hysteria spiking, Aedan blinked back moisture and forced himself to breathe. "What can I do, Rose? Help me make it better. Please."

She found his hand, wrapping it in stark white fingers, but she didn't answer. She couldn't. If the words were to make it through her stretched throat, they wouldn't get through her clenched teeth.

"Rose," Aedan choked, checking her pulse—rapid, but not fatally so. In fact, he couldn't find any reason for her pain. Every organ he examined was stressed but working. "I can't stand seeing you like this, Rose." It sucked his breath away and pulverized his heart. "Give me a clue, love. Please."

He pried her other hand from the sheets and firmly held on, begging for the pain to take him instead, employing magic, willpower and faith to make it so. He would gladly take all of it, every last drop, anything to give her relief.

His hands began prickling, like an army of fire ants had suddenly swallowed them, and while instinct told him to cringe, undying love and devotion welcomed the burn. As it stretched up his arms and throughout his torso, Rhosewen went limp.

Muscles rigid, Aedan struggled to breathe through clenched teeth, but he was winning the battle, absorbing then pushing the pain away with relative ease.

Rhosewen breathlessly watched his face as tears streamed from her bloodshot eyes. "How did you do that?"

"I don't know," he mumbled, shaking away the last of the burn. He released her hands and took her face. "What was that? Do you have any idea what just happened?"

Her features twisted as more tears slipped down her temples.

"You do know," he realized. "You have to tell me, Rose. What's going on?"

"This . . . this wasn't the first time."

"What? This has happened before?"

"Never that bad."

"Damn it, Rose. How could you keep this from me?"

"I'm sorry," she sobbed. "I didn't know what was happening . . . and I . . . I didn't want you to worry."

"Ssh . . ." he whispered, laying his cheek to hers. "Calm down. I'm sorry I cursed at you."

"No, Aedan... you're right. I should have told you... but it's never been this bad." Her tears and sobs were relentless, breaking up her speech.

"It's okay," he assured, sweeping her hair from her clammy face. "Don't worry about that. It's as much my fault for not seeing it."

"But I hid it, Aedan. I've been using magic to keep it from you."

Aedan turned his face into his bicep, closing his eyes and breathing through his nose. He had no idea how much it would hurt to find out she'd been lying to him. He smoothed his expression and met her stare, gently stroking her moist cheek. "Let's forget you hid it. We'll never talk about it again, but you have to tell me everything now. All of it. Okay?"

She pulled in a ragged breath, trying to calm herself. "Okay."

"When was the first time you hurt?"

"When I realized I was pregnant, but it was nothing like this. It was mild compared to this."

Damn. This was bad. "How long did it last?"

"Most of it went away after a few seconds."

"Most of it?" he repeated, narrowing his eyes.

She squirmed. "Well . . . it never went away completely. I just got used to it. It's kind of an achy feeling."

Aedan's features twisted with a different kind of ache. She'd been suffering in silence for five months while he'd been an ignorant fool. "Have there been other times like the first?"

"Yes," she confessed.

"How often?"

"Two . . . three times a day."

"Shit," he muttered, shaking his head. "I'm sorry, Rose. So sorry."

"Why? You have nothing to be sorry for."

"I'm sorry you're in pain and I can't help."

"But you did help. You took it from me."

"What about now? Are you hurting now?"

She shifted and swallowed. "Yes, but I can handle it."

"You shouldn't have to. I'm calling our parents. We have to figure out what's going on before it gets worse."

"Okay," she mumbled, pulling his hand to her heart. "I'm sorry, Aedan. I should have told you, but everything was so perfect. You were happy, which made me happy . . ." She dropped her gaze, ashamed of her suddenly inadequate defense. "That's no excuse. It was wrong. You should be furious with me."

"Never," he countered, touching his lips to hers. "I could never be furious with you. But no more secrets. You have to tell me about every little thing, no matter how insignificant you think it is. And please don't manipulate your aura anymore. I want to see everything that's supposed to be in it, so I can help."

"Okay," she agreed, desperate to redeem herself. "I promise."

He gave her a kiss then started to get out of bed, but she pulled him back, more tears springing from her eyes. "I love you, Aedan."

He dried her tears then gave her another kiss. "I love you, too, my beautiful Rose. You and our baby girl are my life."

He watched her eyes for another long moment then got out of bed, walking three feet to the phone. Now that he knew what she was going through, he wouldn't leave her alone, so he embraced the risk of calling their family from the apartment.

He called his parents first, reaching Serafin on the second ring.

"Hello?"

"Hey," Aedan greeted.

"Hey, son. Everything okay?"

"No."

Aedan relayed what he knew of Rhosewen's affliction, which wasn't much. "I've never seen or felt anything like it," he finished, remembering the pain he'd absorbed from her hand. "This isn't a complication stemming from pregnancy. It's something else."

"You think the Unforgivables' curse hit its mark."

"I'm afraid so."

Aedan watched Rhosewen walk to the bathroom then waited for her to close the door. "It seems her pain has something to do with the baby," he quietly suggested. "It started the second she found out she was pregnant, and it's only gotten stronger. The worst one yet happened right after the baby kicked and we found out she's a girl. I can't know for sure, but it's as if . . . it would seem . . . it's like the more she loves our baby the more she hurts. And if that's the case . . ." He swallowed and squeezed his eyes shut. "If that's the case . . . having our baby could . . . it could . . ." He couldn't say it.

He didn't have to. "I understand, Aedan. I'll call Caitrin and fill him in on what's going on. Now that we have an idea of what the spell is doing to Rhosewen, we can research its origins and perhaps learn how to counter it."

"Have you ever heard of a spell like this?"

"No, but that doesn't mean anything. Give us time."

"We may not have much."

"We'll do everything we can, Aedan. It's our number one priority."

The bathroom door opened, and Aedan looked at his love. She was so beautiful, even with a pale face and weary eyes. "Call when you know something," he mumbled, watching her crawl into bed.

"Of course," Serafin agreed. "Give Rhosewen a kiss for us."

"I will," Aedan assured. "Talk to you later."

"Bye, son."

Weighted with worry, Aedan replaced the receiver, quickly crawling into bed with his sweet and sorrowful Rose.

Chapter 26

Rhosewen's pain continued and worsened so by her seventh month of pregnancy, she was extremely ill. Every move enhanced the torture; therefore she barely moved at all. Her dull, sagging skin clung to bone, veined and ghastly white, and her limp spirals were losing their luster. The only parts of her body that hadn't paled were her bright blue eyes, which were always shiny with moisture, and her big, round belly, which was only big in comparison to the rest of her frail form. Aedan held her hand around the clock, absorbing a fraction of her agony, but Rhosewen endured the bulk of the physical misery.

Their parents put their lives on hold to search for answers, going so far as to visit dangerous and dark covens, seeking information on the wickedest spells, but they'd found nothing pertinent to their situation. Not even the soothsayers they'd paid exorbitant deposits to could divine useful answers.

The idea of seeking out the Unforgivables and asking them to remove the curse had been broached several times, but Rhosewen wouldn't allow it.

"That would defeat everything we've gone through," she argued after hearing the idea. "Our number one priority is keeping our baby safe."

Of course Aedan wanted to keep his daughter safe, but watching his beautiful Rose wilt was killing him. Nevertheless, they decided to stay away from the Unforgivables.

Aedan was sure the actual caster had been Medea. He'd taken his eyes off her for mere seconds; that's when the curse had hit. He suggested locating Medea and getting her alone. They could make her talk. He would make her talk, and he'd have no problem silencing her.

But Caitrin had gathered information that Agro was keeping Medea under his thumb, which meant they'd have to breach an army to capture their mark.

So Rhosewen and Aedan suffered, awaiting their fate.

Through all the desperation and gloom, Katherine had been a godsend, nothing short of an angel. When the curse began taking a toll on Rhosewen's physical appearance, she told Katherine she'd been diagnosed with a rare, untreatable heart condition. Though curious and suspicious, Katherine kept her questions to herself, going the extra mile to make her renters comfortable. She even did their grocery shopping, taking payment for her trouble only because Aedan placed the money in her purse. He suspected she gave it back by buying extra groceries, and he knew she spent more money on their baby than she did herself. She'd already stocked one of her guestrooms with every newborn necessity imaginable; the apartment had a corner devoted to gifts she'd bought the baby; and she'd ordered a crib, measuring every inch of the apartment to make sure it would fit.

Aedan and Rhosewen watched Katherine's avid preparation and found it sweet, amusing and depressing. They wanted to join her in the planning, share her enthusiasm, but due to Rhosewen's health, they couldn't reach Katherine's level of excitement, so they settled for watching it. She brightened their moods, kept them entertained, and gave them a glimpse of the outside world, which they hadn't seen in months. Yes, Katherine was an angel.

"Have you decided on a name?" she asked during one of her frequent visits.

"It depends on what she looks like," Rhosewen answered, lying on the couch with her head in Aedan's lap. "We have one for if she's dark and beautiful, like her daddy, and one for if she's fair and beautiful . . ."

"Like her mom," Aedan finished, caressing Rhosewen's white knuckles.

"I guess you're not going to tell me the two options?" Katherine concluded.

"Nope," Rhosewen grinned. "We want to surprise you."

Katherine lifted a hand to her heart, obviously touched by the sentiment. "Are your parents going to visit soon?"

"Two weeks," Aedan answered. "They'll stay until the baby's born. My dad's a doctor and will perform the delivery."

"That's nice," Katherine approved. "I'm sure you guys miss them."

"Yes," they confirmed.

"Hey!" Katherine exclaimed, her face and aura lighting up, "I have an idea. Why don't you guys stay at my house for the rest of the pregnancy? I have two extra rooms, so your parents can stay, too. I'll take the apartment while they're here."

"That's kind of you, Katherine," Aedan replied, deeply moved, "but we won't impose on you like that."

"Nonsense. I want you to impose. Please."

Aedan and Rhosewen looked at each other, considering the cramped apartment and its tiny bathroom.

"Okay," Aedan decided. "We would love to stay, but we won't have you living out here. When our parents visit, mine will take the apartment."

"But I really don't . . ."

"That's the deal," Aedan interrupted. "Take it or leave it."

"I'll take it," Katherine agreed, shooting up from her chair. "I'm going to get the rooms ready. I'll be back once everything's in order."

"We'll be here," Aedan dryly quipped, and Katherine laughed as she walked out the door.

"That was really nice of her," Rhosewen whispered, rubbing her stretched abdomen.

"Yes," Aedan agreed. "Katherine has a positive and active energy that would give most witches a run for their money, and her heart's extraordinary." He leaned over, kissing Rhosewen's clammy forehead. "Almost as golden as yours."

Two weeks after settling into Katherine's largest bedroom, Aedan reluctantly left Rhosewen's side to meet their parents in the front yard.

He introduced them to Katherine as Jack and Susan Callaway and Paul and Diane Klein. Then Katherine made an excuse to leave.

As Aedan led his parents inside, they watched his expression and the air around him, not saying a word. The moment they entered the house, Morrigan sobbed and slumped toward the floor. Caitrin quickly caught her with magic then hugged her to his chest, burying his red face in her hair.

Daleen wrapped her arms around Aedan's waist, and Serafin took his shoulders, searching his eyes. "Is it really that bad, son?"

Aedan wasn't crying. His Rose still had petals. "Yeah," he confirmed, clearing his tight throat.

Morrigan shook her head in denial, her wail muffling into Caitrin's shirt, and Aedan took a deep breath, struggling to go on. "She's in bed. That's where she stays . . . hurts her to move." He looked from the faded hardwood to Morrigan's trembling back. "She wants to see you guys, but you have to keep your composure around her. I don't want her feeling guilty."

Everyone nodded save for Morrigan.

"I know it's hard," Aedan added, touching Morrigan's shoulder. "And I don't expect the tears to stop, but you can't break down in front of her."

Morrigan took several deep breaths then left Caitrin's chest. "I won't," she agreed. "If I can't handle it, I'll leave the room."

"Thank you," Aedan whispered. "And... I'm sorry... for everything."

"Me, too," she returned, squeezing his bicep. Then she grasped for Caitrin's hand as she followed Aedan down the hallway.

When they entered the bedroom, Morrigan stumbled to a standstill, gripping Caitrin so fiercely her entire arm turned white.

Rhosewen's body was emaciated, absolutely pitiful, all but the big, round belly brimming with life. Her dilapidated muscles convulsed and flexed as she looked at her parents, her pallid lips curving into a weak smile.

Aedan rushed to the bed, quickly taking her left hand. Then his muscles tightened as hers melted into the blankets.

"That's better," she sighed. "Thank you."

He kissed her hand then laid his cheek in her palm. "Of course, my love."

"You guys are just in time," she said, looking at their company. "Your granddaughter's kicking up a storm. Come feel."

Morrigan and Caitrin flew to the bed, gently hugging and kissing their daughter. Then they moved aside, letting Serafin and Daleen do the same. Soon all four of them had their hands on her twitching stomach, sighing as they reveled in miraculous peace.

Once the baby stilled, Serafin performed examinations on mother and child. Though Aedan did this multiple times a day, he demanded additional opinions, hoping they could disprove his dire assessment.

After Serafin and Daleen finished, they took each other's hands and looked at Aedan. "Let's give them some privacy;" Serafin suggested, "go talk in the kitchen."

Aedan didn't like this suggestion and looked away, searching Rhosewen's eyes.

"Go," she insisted. "I'll be fine."

After another long moment of watching her, Aedan looked to Caitrin. "Let me know if it gets worse."

Caitrin nodded, keeping his sober gaze on his daughter, and Aedan leaned in, kissing her forehead. "I love you," he whispered, kissing her lips. Then he let go and followed his parents.

Once they sat at the kitchen table, he turned to his dad. "Well?"

"You're right," Serafin lamented. "Her organs are failing her."

Aedan dropped his head to the table as an anguished cry scraped his throat.

Daleen stifled a sob, wrapping one arm around Aedan's back, and Serafin cleared his throat before going on. "Her heart, liver, kidneys, bones, even her skin, it's all in terrible shape. The only healthy thing about her is the baby, who's thriving despite Rhosewen's condition."

"Isn't there something we can do?" Aedan croaked. "Anything? There has to be something we haven't thought of yet."

"We've hit dead ends at every turn," Serafin replied. "We know the curse was designed to target her and not the baby, and it would seem our theory is correct—the spell's catalyst is her love for the baby. We've figured out the curse's intention, but it doesn't do us any good. A spell like this involves thorough detail, details we can't possibly know. And we haven't found anyone with a similar experience, no one to clue us in on the specifics. Without knowing the actual spell work involved, we can't remove it or reverse it. We could guess for years and not get it right. There are far too many components incorporated. Furthermore, if our theory is correct, as long as she loves her daughter, we can't heal her body."

"I've tried healing her," Aedan whispered. "It doesn't work."

Serafin reached over, resting a hand on his son's back. "I'm sure you've done everything you can, Aedan, but this is out of your hands. It's my belief this will end in one of two ways. The first, the most hopeful, is that we're dealing with a temporary spell, designed to affect Rhosewen only while she's pregnant. Once she gives birth, the curse will cease to exist, which means we could heal her… if she makes it through the delivery." He paused, sliding his hand to Aedan's shoulder. "But if the curse is everlasting, our hands are tied. Rhosewen's body can't take much more. If this goes on, she will die."

The word hung in the air like a veil, smothering Aedan as he slowly raised his head. "Which scenario do you foresee?" he asked, his voice raw and raspy, his lungs empty and burning, his heart breaking—constantly.

"We're talking about the Unforgivables," Serafin whispered. "They're merciless. I'm sorry."

Aedan abruptly stood, knocking over his chair. He couldn't sit still, drowning in the agony of a broken heart, but there would be no swimming to the surface. The surface was gone. "I'll be back in ten minutes," he said. Then he turned and left the house.

Sadness, pain, anger and love—sweet, perfect love—had him gripping his heart as he walked to the garage apartment. Once he was through the door, he fell to his knees, a tormented roar bellowing from his chest as he buried his face in the shag carpet.

She was going to die. His love, his Rose, his life, it was all coming to an end. She would never see her friends, family or home again. She would never celebrate another birthday, or spend another day on the beach. She would never walk another forest trail, or feel another waterfall's spray. She would never know her daughter—the precious babe she loved so much, the life she was dying for. She deserved the world, yet everything was being ripped away from her.

Rage filled him, boiling his blood and vibrating his body. He wanted to rip open his chest and yank his heart out. He wanted to tear every last fiber from the carpet. He wanted to scream until his lungs exploded. But he didn't. He merely whispered one word.

"Medea."

It wasn't an easy decision to make, and he didn't make it lightly. It would mean leaving his little girl, leaving the only piece of Rose he would have left. But he wouldn't be able to keep her safe without Rhosewen. If Rose died, so would part of him—the biggest part of him. Their daughter's best chance would be to hide in the non-magical world, oblivious to her heritage, and he had to give her that chance. He owed it to her. He owed it to Rose.

He lifted himself off the floor and walked to the closet, emerging with a large jewelry box made of cocobolo wood. Hinged by pink gold, it had a long stemmed rose carved into the lid. He'd made it with the intention of placing his daughter's first ring inside and giving it to Rose on the day of the birth. He'd never gotten the chance to fill it and would never get the chance to present it to his love.

He sat down at the table, sadly staring at the box for several heart-wrenching seconds. Then he sealed it with magic. Only his daughter would be able to open it now.

That night, after their parents had gone to bed sad and defeated, Rhosewen lay in Aedan's arms, thinking about the day's events. "I'm glad our parents are here," she whispered, "but it's making mom sad."

"Everyone's sad," Aedan replied. "It's hard to see someone you love in so much pain, but we're not the ones who have to feel it."

"You do."

"A small fraction, my love. I hate that I can't take it all."

"I wouldn't want you to."

"I know, but I would anyway."

Using his chin, he brushed her hair from her face and touched his cheek to hers. With such a short amount of time left to them, he didn't want to talk about the end, but there was something that had to be done. "Rose?"

"Yeah?"

Dread weighed on his chest like a boulder as he searched for inner strength. "You understand, right? That your body might not . . . that there's a chance . . ." Why was it so hard to say out loud? He was furious with himself for being so weak when his wife and child needed him so badly.

"It's okay," Rhosewen whispered, laying a frail hand on his face. "You don't have to say it. I know what the odds are."

A tear slipped from the corner of her eye, and he quickly kissed it away. "I'm sorry, Rose. We don't deserve this. It shouldn't be this way."

"No, but it is. The most important thing to do now is make it all worthwhile by giving our baby girl the chance she deserves."

"Yes," he agreed. "And I'm going to make sure she gets that chance. No matter what happens to us."

"I know you will. You're the most amazing man in the world. Our baby and I are very lucky to have you."

He kissed her cheek then looked at her left hand. "There's something else I want to do for our daughter. I want to give her the opportunity to know her mom."

"I'd like that, too," Rhosewen squeaked, more tears streaming from her eyes.

Aedan lifted their hands, gently wiping her face dry with a knuckle. "I've been working on a spell that could provide that for her . . . if things go wrong."

"What kind of spell?"

"I want to imprint memories of our time together on an item, something symbolic of our relationship. Your wedding ring would be perfect. We're both connected to it, which will make the images clearer, but if you'd rather, we could use something else."

"No. I want to use the ring. How will it work?"

"I'll take care of the spell work. All you'll have to do is hold the ring close to your heart while focusing on the memories you want her to see."

"That sounds easy," she approved. "I focus on those memories daily."

"Me, too," he whispered, rubbing his lips across her bony cheek. "I'll be adding my own recollections later, so don't feel pressured to remember everything. I don't want you to feel overwhelmed."

"I won't. This is a really good idea. How will she get it?"

So she knew. She knew he wouldn't be staying after she was gone.

He considered her question for a long moment before giving the best answer he had. "I can't promise she will get it. I haven't figured everything out yet, but I hope to provide her with information that will lead her home. I'll lay the clues, but it will be up to her to follow them. If she does, the ring will be waiting for her. I don't know any other way to do it without putting her in danger or risking her well-being."

"I have faith in you, Aedan, and in our little girl. If this is our best chance to safely share our lives with her, I want to take it." Her gaze roamed to her wedding ring. "When should we do it?"

"Whenever you're ready, but we don't want to wait too long. I'm afraid the weaker you get, the weaker the imprint will be."

"That makes sense. Can I wait a couple of days, though? I want to make a few more memories before I do it."

"Of course, love."

She laboriously turned her head, finding his devoted, emerald gaze. "Thank you."

"You don't have to thank me for this, Rose."

"Not just for this. For coming into my life, for loving me and our baby, and for taking care of us."

"I love you guys so much, Rose. I'd do anything for you. I would die for my two beautiful girls."

"I know. That's why I love you. For that and so much more. You're my everything, Aedan."

"Forever," he whispered, touching his lips to hers.

They laid together for a long time that night, not talking, not sleeping, just feeling, just being together, both brokenhearted, both in pain, both deeply in love.

Chapter 27

Aedan and Rhosewen's nights were devoted to lying alone in their borrowed bed, but they spent their days with their parents. So over the next week, during daylight hours, one could find the family of six in the largest bedroom of the old, country house. Rhosewen remained in bed. Aedan held her left hand while Morrigan held her right. Caitrin did his best to keep his wife and daughter comfortable. And Daleen sat to her son's right with one arm wrapped around his back. Serafin was the only magician who rarely held still. When he wasn't performing examinations on Rhosewen and the baby, he was busy meeting the needs of the healthy occupants of the room.

Their conversations remained light and focused on family. Kemble, Cordelia and Quinlan were staying with Cordelia's parents in Alaska. Cinnia was expanding her café in Cannon Beach. And Kearny was spending an ever increasing amount of time in Oregon, sweeping Enid off her feet.

"There's something about those Oregon girls," Serafin teased. "Our Virginia boys keep disappearing."

"We grow beautiful women," Morrigan whispered, brushing a spiral from her daughter's forehead.

"Yes," Aedan hoarsely agreed.

He rarely spoke anymore. He just listened and stared at his wife, soaking up every move and every word. They were in constant agony now, but the pain had become as much a part of them as anything else. For the most part, they silently endured, but when Rhosewen felt a surge of increased love for her daughter, often triggered by the baby's movements, their torture intensified, throwing them into flexed fits of agony. When this happened, Morrigan had to leave the room.

Katherine sporadically popped in to ask if anybody needed anything, and she always stayed a while, visiting with Rhosewen and doting on the unborn baby. An eternal ray of sunshine, Katherine brightened the atmosphere, reminding them that life thrived outside the melancholy bedroom.

Early Wednesday morning, she brought in a breakfast of pancakes, bacon, toast and jam, and Rhosewen insisted she stay and dine with them. All of them ate save for Aedan, who wouldn't let go of Rhosewen's hand. He would force down a piece of toast the next time he used the bathroom.

Katherine finished first and set her plate on the dresser, moving to Rhosewen's side. "May I talk to the baby while you eat?"

Rhosewen laboriously swallowed and smile. "You don't have to ask."

Katherine beamed as she looked at Rhosewen's stomach. "Hi there, baby girl," she cooed. "Are you getting a full belly? Should be; your mommy loves pancakes. Know what else your mommy loves?" she asked, gently tapping Rhosewen's tummy. "You. Your mom and dad love you so much. You're a very lucky girl."

The baby moved, rolling beneath near translucent skin so clearly, they could discern the shape of her tiny hand and its five tiny fingers. That's when things went from bad to worse.

Rhosewen screamed as her tormented body bucked, and her breakfast plate flew from her chest, shattering against the nightstand. Aedan tightened his grip as he groaned into his bicep, and their parents jumped from their seats, their breakfast plates disappearing into thin air. Startled, Katherine had fallen from the bed and was lying on the floor.

"You should leave," Serafin said, helping her to her feet. "You shouldn't see this."

Horrified, Katherine backed out of the room, closing the door as she went, and Serafin moved to the bed, contemplating how to examine Rhosewen's thrashing body.

Morrigan rushed to take Rhosewen's right hand, and Aedan squeezed his eyes shut, trying to master the pain in a desperate attempt to provide mental, physical and emotional support for his wife. But it was the longest, most painful episode yet, and his smarting body was hard to ignore.

Rhosewen's screams faded into wails as tears flooded from her closed lids, and her legs curled and flexed, her feet drilling into the bed as her head dug into pillows. Aedan opened his eyes, finding her biting a hole in her lip, and he choked back a sob as he buried his face in her neck.

She was in so much agony; he couldn't stand it. He had to do something. He had to help her. Through clenched teeth he spoke, rubbing pursed lips across tight tendons. "Rose . . . remember that cave I took you to? The one at Devil's Den? How we sat reading the emotions in the atmosphere?" He felt a slight change in her body and forced his own to move, climbing into bed with her. "I was already in love with you," he whispered, scooting as close as possible. "I'd already decided to follow you to the ends of the earth. Everything you said, everything you did, exuded beauty, compassion and grace. You were the most captivating woman I'd ever met. From the very beginning." He was able to unclench his jaw, and her moans had quieted, but tears still ran from her closed lids as her flexed feet pushed at the covers. "As I watched you play with the baby alpacas," he continued, softly kissing her stretched throat, "I was already scheming on ways to keep you in my life. You forever became my perfect Rose that day."

"Aedan," she sobbed, popping her eyes open.

He left her neck, finding her teary gaze. "Ssh . . . . You don't have to say anything. Just let it get better. It's getting better."

As his warm breath washed over her lips and cheeks, her legs stilled, sinking into the blankets. She let go of her mom's hand then rolled onto her side, lifting her palm to Aedan's cheek. "You had me . . . the moment . . . you met me..."

Their faces came together, cheek to cheek, and tears streamed from their bloodshot eyes—sad rivers running down the contours of her sunken features. Aedan didn't mean to cry, but once he started, he couldn't stop, so they cried together, treasuring what they loved and what they'd lose, while fighting the agony holding their bodies captive.

❧

By the time Rhosewen and Aedan regained control, Serafin had performed seven examinations. Aedan stayed in bed, lying close to Rhosewen as they listened to Serafin's update.

"You've been dilated to two centimeters for three days," he explained, "including first thing this morning. Now you're at a three. The baby looks great—around six pounds, fully developed and healthy. She could be safely delivered at a moment's notice. Your body, however, is a different story. The deterioration is increasing in speed. Your health has declined more in the past four hours than it did in the first three days we were here." He paused, lightly clearing his throat as he glanced at the floor. "Particularly your heart. It's struggling to keep your blood pumping, and I fear another episode like that will have it stopping altogether."

Rhosewen calmly nodded her understanding. At this point, she wasn't afraid of dying. The two things she feared most were a separation from Aedan and a risk to her child. She knew the separation wouldn't last long, so her number one priority was her daughter's safety.

"Do you think it will make it through the delivery?" she asked, speaking of her heart like it was a rusted component on a piece of old machinery.

"I can't promise anything," Serafin replied, "but the longer this continues, the smaller the chances."

Rhosewen's bruised lips dropped into a frown. "What can we do to speed up the delivery?"

Aedan winced. Speeding up the delivery meant shortening his time on earth with her.

Serafin glanced at his son then bowed his head. "There are things we can do to invoke an early birth, but you've already progressed from a two to a three this morning. I think we should wait a while, see how you do naturally. If you don't dilate anymore today, inducing labor might be our wisest option."

Rhosewen considered his suggestion, contemplating every possible scenario. "Okay," she decided. "We'll wait and see how it goes, but I don't want my baby ripped from her dead mother."

Everyone closed their eyes, moaning at the visual she'd put in their heads, but she couldn't let that deter her. "If it looks like it might come to that, I want to have her early."

Serafin ran a hand down his face and shook his head clear. "Okay, dear. We'll examine you and the baby every thirty minutes unless your pain increases, in which case we'll do them every ten minutes."

"Do them every ten anyway," Aedan insisted.

"Of course," Serafin conceded. "Whatever you think is best."

"May Aedan and I have a few minutes alone?" Rhosewen asked, scanning everyone's weary faces.

"Sure, sweetie," Morrigan agreed, grabbing Caitrin's hand. Then she pulled him from the room, immediately followed by Serafin and Daleen.

Aedan watched the door close then looked to Rhosewen, ardently staring into her swollen eyes. "You're the most amazing woman I will ever know, Rose. Our time apart will be hell on me."

"Me, too," she whispered, "but we'll be together again soon."

"Very soon," he confirmed, giving her a soft kiss.

"I'm ready to imprint the ring," she said, glancing at their hands. "I'm afraid to wait any longer."

"Sure," he agreed. "Just let me tell them to wait a while before coming back in. We'll be naked during the spell work."

"Goody," she approved, smiling sweetly.

Aedan watched her grin as he tried to mentally communicate with his dad, but the connection was too fuzzy, and Serafin soon entered the room.

"Your mind searches aren't discernable," he said.

"I gathered as much," Aedan replied. "We need some time alone. Don't come back in until I call you."

"Sure," Serafin agreed. Then he left, closing the door behind him.

After removing their clothes, Aedan instructed Rhosewen to roll onto her right side. Then he formed his body to the back of hers, pressing her left palm to her heart so the ring's band made contact with her skin.

"Ready?" he asked.

As his breath whispered across her cheek, she sighed, aroused yet peaceful. "There's something I'm not sure about," she confessed.

"What's that, my love?"

"Well, I'm not sure if I should include our bonding. I want to share the experience with her, show her how amazing and fulfilled we are together, but I'm afraid it will embarrass her."

"When our daughter finds her way to the ring," Aedan replied, "she won't be a child; she'll be a woman—mature enough to handle the idea of her conception. But if you're worried about it, you can filter what she'll sense. Just give her the song without the dance."

"Good thinking," Rhosewen approved. "I can show her how you make me feel without showing you naked. Plus, it will save time. If I include all the ways you've loved me, she'll be experiencing the imprint for months."

Aedan managed a small smile as he kissed her cheek. "They were the most amazing moments of my life, Rose. I'm going to miss fulfilling my earthly desires with you."

"Me, too," she whispered. "We gave new meaning to the words making love. We were perfect together."

Aedan closed his eyes. It had been months since he'd made love to her, but he recalled the magnificent moments with perfect clarity.

"Okay," she sighed, pulling him back to their grim present. "I'm ready."

He kissed her cheek, letting his lips linger as he whispered. "Close your eyes and focus on what you want her to see, feel and hear of your memories. I'll do the rest."

Rhosewen closed her eyes and took her mind back to the day she met him—the love of her life, the father of her child, the perfect provider, protector and lover… her soul mate.

As she did, he began chanting next to her ear, so softly and quickly she couldn't understand what he was saying. She wasn't trying to understand. She'd immersed herself in a replay of the last nine months of her life, delving into the danger as well as the adoration.

They lay that way, Rhosewen remembering and Aedan chanting, for over an hour. When at last she reached the present, she opened her eyes and the ring grew hot. When Aedan's murmuring ceased, the ring cooled. The spell had worked.

Rhosewen slid his hands to her protruding belly then held them there as she hummed a sweet and slow melody. Aedan raptly listened, savoring every last drop of the bittersweet moment. Then he added soft lyrics to her soulful serenade.

"Our sweet, precious child,
you'll soon be in the world.
You'll bring it so much joy,
our beautiful baby girl.
Mommy and daddy love you,
and wish you all the best.
Just be your precious self,
and your heart will do the rest."

By that afternoon, it was clear invoking an early birth wouldn't be necessary. Rhosewen progressed at a normal rate and had dilated to six centimeters by five o'clock. She didn't notice the pains of labor. Her body had been in worse agony for too long. Only the tightening of her abdomen confirmed her contractions.

The family kept constant vigil at her bedside, knowing it might be their last chance to spend time with her, but a curtain of dread kept the room quiet and sober as time flew on supernatural wings.

When Aedan looked at the grandfather clock across the room, finding the short hand approaching the twelve, he shook his head and refocused. "Is that the right time?"

"Yeah," Caitrin answered, checking the timepiece on his wrist. "It's 11:17."

As Serafin performed an examination, placing his hands on Rhosewen's bare belly, the baby kicked and Rhosewen wailed. Aedan lurched into action, brushing swift kisses across Rhosewen's tight jaw.

"She's ready," Serafin announced, and Rhosewen cried again, tightening her grip on Aedan.

"Mom . . ." she gasped, blindly reaching out with her right hand, ". . . dad . . . I love you . . ."

Her parents immediately responded by leaning closer, and Morrigan buried her face in golden spirals as Caitrin tenderly wiped away Rhosewen's tears.

"We love you, too, sweetheart," he rasped. "You're the best thing that's ever happened to your mom and me. And we're so proud of you… for being so strong for your baby girl." He touched his forehead to hers, squeezing his eyes shut on fat teardrops. "I love you, Rhosewen, with every beat of my heart. Always." He kissed her wrinkled brow then backed away, literally choking on grief.

Morrigan stroked Rhosewen's hair as she touched her lips to her ear, murmuring a gentle proclamation of devotion that only a mother could execute correctly. "You'll be with us forever and always, my sweet child, in our hearts and on our minds. I love you with every ounce of my being, and until I see you again, I'll miss everything about you every second of every day." She pulled away, staring deep into Rhosewen's eyes for a long, heartbreaking moment. Then she gave her a lingering kiss, whispering *I love you* over and over again. Instead of backing away, she fell away, landing in Caitrin's open arms.

Rhosewen's features twisted as she squeezed her eyes shut. Then her body cringed as her eyes popped open, frantically searching the room. When she found Daleen, she tried to speak, but screamed instead.

Daleen moved closer, touching her lips to Rhosewen's clammy forehead. "You don't need to say anything, darling. You've made our son the happiest he's ever been, and you've done a wonderful job keeping our granddaughter safe and healthy. You're an amazing daughter, wife and mother, and special things await a person like you, wherever you're heading."

"Thank you . . ."

"No, Rhosewen. That's our line. We love and appreciate everything about you. Please know that."

Rhosewen managed a small nod, and Daleen soothingly smiled as she moved away. But as soon as she was out of Rhosewen's sight, she quietly sobbed into her hands.

"It's time," Serafin insisted, holding a hand to Rhosewen's lower abdomen. "Your body's too weak to do it alone, so Daleen's going to give you a magical hand, but I'll need you to push during contractions."

Rhosewen and Aedan found each other's eyes and searched each other's souls, trying to recall every detail of their journey, every second they'd spent together. But time was too short.

"I love you, my beautiful Rose," he whispered. "More than my own life. We'll be together again soon. I promise."

"I love you, too . . ." she sobbed. "I won't be complete without you." She squeezed her eyes shut then forced them open, finding his gaze once more. "I'll be looking for you every second until I find you . . . but please . . ." she pleaded, tightening her grip, "please make sure our daughter's safe before you come to me. Please."

"I swear, Rose. I'll give our baby what she needs, but then I'm coming to find you."

He touched his burning forehead to hers, fighting red hot tears. Then they kissed, so passionately their bonded lights reached their full potential for the first time in months, bursting from their trembling forms like a heavenly explosion. All too soon their lips broke apart, severed by Rhosewen's bucking body, and the golden hazes retracted.

"We have to do it now," Serafin advised.

Aedan glanced at his dad's forlorn expression then looked to his wife's sea blue eyes. "Ready, my love?"

"Yes," she answered, squeezing his hand.

"Then let's meet our baby."

"Our baby," she breathed, and Aedan inhaled the sweet sigh as he gave her another kiss.

Aedan held her hands, Morrigan braced her back, and Daleen placed her palms on her stomach, murmuring with her eyes closed. Serafin would deliver the baby with Caitrin's assistance.

After thirty minutes of unbelievable effort on Rhosewen's part, Serafin announced he could see the baby's hair. "Just a few more pushes," he encouraged. Then he lowered his voice as he glanced at Daleen. "Release her womb and check her pulse."

Daleen obeyed, choking back an alarmed squeak as she touched Rhosewen's chest.

Aedan heard his mom's muted terror, but ignored it, keeping his eyes on Rhosewen as she pushed again.

The grandfather clock tolled midnight, echoing in Aedan's ears like a death knell as Rhosewen's emaciated shoulders lifted, shuddering over desperate gasps. The second bell chimed, and Rhosewen squeezed her eyes shut, giving her daughter all the strength she had left. As the clock's third strike faded from the air, a tiny cry filled the room with miraculous music. Serafin worked quickly and had the baby on Rhosewen's chest before the clock's fifth signal.

Rhosewen and Aedan stared at their little miracle—tiny, red and raw, but healthy and so perfect. She had her daddy's dark skin and onyx hair, her mommy's curls, and a shiny white aura swimming with wispy rivers of pearlescent silver and soft pink. Clutching her teeny fists to her chin, she stared at them with blurry, emerald green eyes, confusion creasing the features of her petite face.

"She's beautiful," Rhosewen breathed, running a quaking thumb across her daughter's wrinkled forehead. "Our perfect . . . Layla." She gripped Aedan's hand like never before, pulling it to her cheek as she lowered her lips to Layla's matted curls. "I love you guys." she rasped, her aura swelling with proof. "So . . . much . . ."

Darkness suddenly washed over Aedan as the worst physical pain he'd ever experienced shot from Rhosewen's hand, pulverizing his insides, stealing his breath and sanity. But as quickly as it came, the agony drained away, all of it, and he knew.

He opened his eyes, finding his baby girl lying on his wife's idle chest, the heart inside no longer beating. It had burst with love.

Aedan slipped her wedding ring off her finger then folded her hands over her flat stomach. After carefully closing her lids, he whispered across her lips. "I love you, my perfect Rose. Forever."

After one last kiss, he left her lips and wrapped his hands around his daughter, gently pulling her into a warm, cradle hold. His Rose was gone, but a piece of her lived in their baby, their beautiful, perfect Layla. He bowed his head over her, closed his eyes, and cried like never before.

Chapter 28

Aedan wasn't able to sit beside Rhosewen's empty body for long. Morrigan and Caitrin had already left the room, and as soon as he was composed enough to safely carry his baby, Aedan left as well.

He walked dazedly down the hallway, finding Rhosewen's parents sitting on the couch in the living room, crying in each other's arms, and Katherine sitting in an easy chair by the fireplace, looking lost and helpless as she twisted a tear-soaked tissue.

When Aedan tried to speak, his voice failed him, so he cleared his achy throat and tried again. "She needs a blanket."

Katherine jumped up and disappeared down the hall, returning in a flash with a pink blanket. "May I?" she asked, motioning to the baby.

Aedan drifted the tip of his nose across his daughter's soft cheek then gently handed her over.

Katherine cooed and whispered as she wrapped the baby in a cozy cocoon. "Hello there, you precious, little girl. It's so good to finally meet you." She kissed her tiny forehead then passed her back to Aedan. "What did you name her?"

"Layla," he answered, watching his baby's eyes. "It means dark beauty."

"Layla," Katherine whispered. "It's beautiful. Does she have a middle name?"

He and Rhosewen hadn't discussed middle names, but for him there was only one. "Love," he answered. "Layla Love. Do you like it?"

"I love it," Katherine approved, eyes shiny like melted chocolate. "I think it's perfect."

"Good. Your approval's important to me."

Katherine's eyebrows furrowed, displaying her surprise and confusion. Then she sobered and bowed her head. "I'm sorry about Sarah, Chris. She was . . . such a beautiful person, in every way. She'll be missed."

"Yes," Aedan rasped. "Do you mind fixing Layla a bottle?"

"Of course not," Katherine agreed. "Did we decide on a brand?"

"Whatever you think is best," Aedan replied, knowing absolutely nothing about baby formula.

"Okay," Katherine replied. "I'll be back in a few minutes."

Aedan watched her leave the room then walked to Morrigan and Caitrin, sitting between them so they had a clear view of their granddaughter.

"She's beautiful," Morrigan whispered, struggling with continued sobs. "I can see Rhosewen so clearly."

"Yes," Caitrin croaked. "She holds a striking resemblance to both her parents."

"Would you like to hold her?" Aedan asked, turning toward Morrigan.

"Yes," she answered, jarring tears loose with an avid nod. "Very much."

Aedan passed Layla over, and Morrigan stifled a sob as she pulled the newborn's cheek to her bosom, squeezing her eyes shut and tucking her chin in. "I can smell Rhosewen," she breathed.

Aedan's heart squeezed as he looked at his empty hands and flexed his idle fingers. "Why don't you take Layla to your bedroom, Morrigan? I'll have Katherine meet you there with the bottle. I need to speak with Caitrin and my parents."

Morrigan's tears paused as she looked at him. "Are you sure?"

"Yeah. I need to deal with a few things. Then I'll be able to hold her the way I want to."

"Okay," Morrigan agreed, lips curving into a small smile. "She'll be yours when you're ready."

"Thanks. Caitrin will join you soon."

Katherine entered the room as Morrigan was leaving and was thrilled with the invitation to watch the newborn drink her bottle, so both women set off down the corridor.

Aedan's eyes stayed on the doorway for a moment then turned to his father-in-law. "I'm sorry for your loss, Caitrin. Our loss."

"Our loss," Caitrin repeated. "I'm sorry, too."

"Will you take her home? She would want to be laid to rest at home."

"Yes, if that's what you wish . . . what she wished."

"Will the four of you be able to get her there without being seen?"

"Yes."

"Nobody outside the coven can know the details of what happened here," Aedan stressed. "For Layla's safety."

"Of course," Caitrin agreed. "Layla's safety comes first. Rhosewen died for her. We're willing to do the same."

"Yes," Aedan mumbled, glancing at the hallway.

Caitrin looked, too. "When will we take her?"

"Soon," Aedan answered. "I need to talk to my parents, and I want you guys to spend some time with Layla." His throat tightened, cutting off his air supply. "There's no guarantee you'll see her again."

Caitrin swallowed as he looked at his fisted hands. "I figured you'd choose this route—the safest . . . the hardest." He raised his knuckles, choking into them. "It's what my baby girl wanted, yes?"

Aedan closed his eyes, clearly picturing Rhosewen's face. "She knew of my intentions."

"Then yes," Caitrin sighed, running flexed fingers down his face, "we'll want to spend some time with our grandbaby. We'll leave an hour before sunrise."

"Thanks, Caitrin. Will you tell my mom and dad to meet me in the apartment when they're done in there?"

"Sure," Caitrin agreed, rising with much less energy than usual. "I'll let them know on my way to hold my granddaughter."

After sitting in the apartment for ten minutes, simultaneously mourning and planning, Aedan looked up to find his parents in the doorway. He lethargically stood, and they rushed forward, pulling him into a familiar family hug.

"I'm so sorry, baby," Daleen whispered.

"Words can't convey," Serafin added. "I can't imagine the pain you're in. I wish I knew a way to help you bear it."

"The pain's there to stay," Aedan countered, "but there's something else I need your help with."

"Name it."

"I'm leaving here, sometime soon, and I'm certain I won't be coming back. Not here or anywhere else."

Daleen's arm tightened around his waist, but she didn't object.

"I'll make the necessary arrangements for Layla to hide in the non-magical world," Aedan continued, pushing the words through an achingly tight throat. "But if all the pieces fall into place like I want them to, she'll eventually receive information that could lead her to our coven in Oregon."

"Eventually?" Serafin asked.

"Once she's grown," Aedan explained. "Children need stability, which she won't get if she's chasing down her family or running from magicians who want to use her. She needs time to mature and explore her heart with clear understanding before being told the circumstances of her birth, which would pollute anyone's sense of self, especially a child. Nothing about this situation should be thrust onto a child, so I'm not going to give her the truth until she's had time to be a kid and graduate high school. Besides, the longer she stays out of our world, the longer Agro has to forget about her."

He paused, retrieving the homemade jewelry box from the coffee table. "Which brings me to the favor I need to ask. I'm leaving this box with you. Should Layla find her way home, I want her to have it. At the moment it's empty, but I've enchanted Rose's wedding ring to hold our memories of each other." He raised his right hand, displaying the ring halfway down his pinky. "Rose imprinted hers yesterday, but I'm not done with mine yet. I need you to perform a spell that will transfer this ring from my finger straight into this box the moment I die, not a second later, and it has to work. Otherwise Agro will get his hands on a treasure map that will lead him straight to Layla. Once the ring reaches the box, it will stay secure. Only Layla can open it, and the wood won't bust or burn."

His parents looked at each other then back to their son. "It doesn't have to be this way," Serafin insisted. "I know you'll miss Rhosewen. I know every second without her will decrease your quality of life, but you can find her in your child. Layla will help fill the hole in your heart. At least give it a chance."

"I can't," Aedan refused. "If I sit around and do nothing, Layla may not make it past her first birthday. But if I can find Agro, I can make it safe for her. I promised Rose I would give our baby the best chance I possibly can, and this is it. If I could kill Agro and his army, I would. Then I'd take my baby home, where she belongs, and I'd stay with her as long as my broken heart would allow. But it's a dream. I can't dispose of an army, so I'll settle for filling their heads with lies. This is the last thing I can do for my wife and daughter, and I'm going to do it. Preferably with your help."

Daleen burst into sobs, burying her face in Aedan's bicep, and Serafin ran a shaky hand down her long mane, his own sadness clear in his watery, green eyes, down-turned mouth, and sagging shoulders. "You're very brave," he whispered. "I expect nothing less. Of course we'll help."

As Aedan scanned his dad's despondent posture, the vast hole in his heart widened. "I'm sorry, dad."

Serafin shook his head as he slid his hand to the side of Aedan's neck. "Don't apologize, son. We understand, and we'll keep Layla's possessions safe until her awaited return."

"Thank you," Aedan replied. "I'll miss you guys. All of you . . ." His voice broke as he clutched his throat, willing it to loosen. "My Layla Love," he choked, tears flooding his strained eyes.

He dropped his gaze to the jewelry box, thinking it a pitiful gift to leave his daughter. Then he set it aside and raised his head, taking his dad's shoulder. "If she finds you, make sure she knows how much Rose loved her, how much I love her. And keep her safe once she's close. Show her all the love she's going to miss, give her the family she deserves, and make sure she's happy." His head fell again. "Please."

"We promise," Serafin vowed. "Our lives are hers."

Aedan watched as Layla's grandparents shared her throughout the predawn hours, but all too soon it was time for them to leave with Rhosewen's body, which lay undisturbed in the room she left it. Aedan wouldn't watch them carry her out. The woman he loved was elsewhere, waiting for him to complete his purpose on earth.

Each grandparent held their grandbaby one last time, telling her to be safe and happy and asking her to come see them as soon as she could. Then they laid her on the bed so they could say goodbye to Aedan.

Morrigan embraced him first, wrapping one arm around his waist and touching a hand to his heart. "Thank you for loving our daughter so much, Aedan, and for easing her pain. We'll always be in your debt for making her life better."

"The debt is mine," he disagreed. "I'm eternally grateful to you for giving my precious Rose life."

Morrigan reached up, touching his cheek as moisture slid down her temples. Then she dropped her hand and moved away.

Caitrin stepped forward, clasping Aedan's hand and shoulder. "Give Rhosewen our love when you see her. Make sure she knows we're already missing her."

"I will," Aedan agreed.

"Good luck, my son. May the Heavens be with you."

"Thanks, Caitrin. Give the coven our love and goodbyes."

Caitrin nodded as he let go. Then he pulled Morrigan into a hug. As they left the room, they briefly turned back, catching one last glimpse of their sleeping grandbaby.

Daleen had thrown herself into Aedan's chest and was weeping uncontrollably.

"I love you, mom," he whispered, hugging tightly. "I'm sorry I'm leaving you like this. Please understand."

"I do," she sobbed. Then she took several shaky breaths, attempting to talk clearly. "I love you, Aedan, with my whole broken heart. And I trust your heart . . . and your beautiful soul. Someday, when my life is through, we'll be together forever."

"I'm counting on it," he whispered, inhaling her familiar scent.

She looked up, taking his face in her quivering palms. "Goodbye for now, baby boy."

"For now," he returned, placing his palms over hers.

She choked on a sob as she pulled away, flashing her gaze to Layla. Then she left the room in tears.

Aedan sucked in a heavy breath as he turned to his dad, mirroring his mournful expression.

"Do you have a plan?" Serafin asked.

"Not a detailed one," Aedan confessed. "Where's Agro's last known location?"

"He was near Duluth, Minnesota two weeks ago, but he's cleared the area now. If someone knows where he went, they weren't telling me. Perhaps you'll have better luck."

"Then I'll start there," Aedan decided.

He looked at Layla, raising a hand to his tormented heart. "I'm going to spend some time with her before I go. It seems unfair . . . that I get that chance when Rose didn't . . ." He closed his eyes, picturing Rhosewen's smiling face. Then he returned his gaze to their baby. "I won't leave until I know she'll be taken care of. I don't know how long it will take, but it doesn't matter. There are requirements to fulfill before I go. One of them is relocation. I don't want her staying in Idaho or anywhere else connected to our family. If you get an itch to find her, and I know you will, don't bother coming here. And if locating her can't be done in complete secrecy, don't do it. At least wait until she's grown. If she doesn't find you at that point, safely search her out, but remember, she may not want you to find her. Her lack of knowledge may leave her bitter, and if staying in the dark about her birth family is what she desires, that's her choice to make."

"The temptation will always be there," Serafin confirmed, "but we play by your rules. Layla's safety and happiness are what matter most."

"I'd die a thousand times to ensure her safety and happiness," Aedan whispered. But he couldn't die a thousand times. What he had to give was pitiful. "I'm leaving her all the money I have, including the cash you and Caitrin gave us, so she'll be financially set. She won't have a coven to lean on, but she'll be loved and cared for. I'll make sure of it."

"Good," Serafin approved. "She deserves the world."

Aedan nodded, his jaw and fingers flexing as he looked from his baby to his dad. "Once that's taken care of, I'll start searching for Agro and Medea. I don't know how long it will take, or if I'll even succeed, but it will be my final gift to my girls to die trying."

"If you need me for anything," Serafin offered, "or if you change your mind, please come home."

"I can't change my mind, and I won't drag you and mom any further into this mess."

He reached up, untying the necklace Rhosewen had given him. Then he pressed his lips to the rose gold, kissing their engraved names. "Put this around Rose's neck," he said, handing it over. "I won't get a proper burial, so I'd like to be considered buried with my Rose. This is the only way I know how to do that. I hope Morrigan and Caitrin will understand."

"They will," Serafin assured, morosely examining the necklace.

He looked back up, and they both swallowed, staring at each other through salty moisture. Then they tightly embraced.

"Remember, dad, if Layla finds you . . ."

"We'll take care of her, son. I promise."

"Thank you," Aedan whispered. "For everything."

"I love you, Aedan. You're my life's most precious achievement."

"I love you, too, dad. I am who I am because of you. You and mom."

"Goodbye," they choked in unison, fiercely squeezing. Then Serafin swept from the room.

Aedan watched him go, and truly understood the word heartbroken. His was shattered, and it hurt like hell.

He walked to the bed and lay beside Layla, running his gaze from the top of a corkscrew curl to the tip of a teeny toe. The redness from her birth had faded, leaving her skin velvet soft and olive toned, and her jet black hair was clean and dry, lying against her head in the most perfect spirals imaginable. Her petite fists were curled up against her puckered mouth—a mouth like her mother's. And her round cheeks were naturally rose colored—just as her mother's had been. As she slept, her long, black eyelashes fluttered, and her pink lips suckled at delicate fingers. She was perfection in the flesh.

Tears began flowing as Aedan watched her—so beautiful and purely innocent, brought into the world by perfect love, blessed with life by a perfect woman, his perfect Rose. He could only hope that, one day, their angelic Layla Love would know exactly how perfect it had been.

Chapter 29

The grandfather clock signaled noon as Layla stretched in Aedan's arm, awakening him with a panicked jolt. Newborns weren't supposed to go that long without eating.

He scanned his daughter, looking for signs of distress, but her healthy body leisurely stretched, and her big, green eyes alertly gazed. She was fine. Better than fine. Her bright aura sparkled as it swirled around her little body, clearly exuding a sense of calm wonderment.

"Hello, my Layla Love," he greeted, his voice strained, but filled with a gentle sweetness and serene adoration that came as naturally as breathing. "You slept for a long time."

At his voice, her mouth formed a little o of surprise, and her hand reached for his face. He kissed her palm then lowered his lips to her soft curls, inhaling her sweet scent. Somehow familiar and brand new all at once, her bouquet was perfectly subtle in its potency, yet incredibly powerful in its objective. As it rushed up his nose and down his throat, peace washed over him, lightening his dreadfully heavy heart for a brief and blessed moment. She smelled of roses and lilacs, with a hint of vanilla.

His heart sighed as he scooped her off the bed and headed for the kitchen, constantly staring at her and talking to her. "You have so many people who love you, baby girl. I hope you'll get a chance to meet them, once you're all grown up."

She responded, and her coo and gurgle were the sweetest sounds he'd ever heard. "You have a very beautiful voice, my angel. Your mommy sounded like an angel, too. Remember? You'd be kicking like crazy, but then your mom would hum her lullaby and you'd quiet right down."

Layla squirmed, letting out a tiny cry that tugged at his heart. "I know you're hungry, baby. Daddy's fixing your bottle right now."

He looked at the pan of cold water he'd placed on the stove. Then he looked at the empty bottle and the can of formula on the counter. After a moment's hesitation and a glance around, he waved his empty hand, watching as Layla's meal prepared itself. When it floated toward him, he held the underside of his wrist out, catching a few drops of warm milk. Then he plucked the bottle from the air.

"There we go, Layla Love. That's what we call magic. Maybe someday you'll get to try out your magic, but it's okay if you don't, because you're perfectly magical without it."

As he entered the living room to get comfortable, the front door slowly opened, and Katherine poked her head in.

Aedan halted, looking up from the tiny toes he'd been counting. "Hi, Katherine."

"Hey," she returned, lingering in the doorway. "I don't want to intrude. I just need to get some coffee."

Aedan walked over, gently nudging her inside and closing the door. "This is your house, Katherine. You can't intrude on what's yours."

"I know, but I wanted to give you some privacy."

"You've done a lovely job of respecting our privacy," he commended, moving to the easy chair. "You've been a godsend for my family. I can't thank you enough."

Katherine blushed, but finally relaxed, moving closer to admire the baby. "Hello, little Layla."

Aedan set the bottle aside and lifted one of Layla's hands, giving Katherine a tiny wave. "Say hello to Katherine, my love."

Katherine smiled and leaned over. "You are the most precious thing I have ever laid eyes on," she whispered, brushing a curl from Layla's forehead. Then she kissed it. "Where are your parents, Chris?"

"They left this morning," Aedan answered, following her gaze to the hallway. "They took Sarah with them."

"Why didn't you and Layla go?"

Aedan scanned Katherine's shocked expression then sighed. "There are some things I need to tell you. Do you have time to talk?"

"Sure. I took the day off when I found out Sarah was in labor."

Layla gave a tiny cry that stole Aedan's undivided attention. "I'm sorry, baby," he soothed, grabbing the bottle as he sat. "You've been so patient with your daddy. Here you go."

For a while he just rocked and admired his baby, listening to every sound and watching every move. When he wondered what it would have been like to watch her nurse at Rhosewen's breasts—the way it should have been—a pang pierced his bleeding heart. He fought the moisture blurring his vision. He didn't want anything obstructing his beautiful view.

When Layla was ready for a burp, Aedan moved her to his shoulder, patting her back as he looked at Katherine. "We weren't completely honest with you," he revealed. "I'm sure you've already figured that out. Like I said, you've done a lovely job of respecting our privacy. But that doesn't make our actions right, and I'm sorry we made you feel like you had to keep your questions and opinions to yourself. We generally don't live that way, and it was never our intention to make you live that way, but it was necessary. Even now there are things I can't tell you, and I'm sorry for that as well. I hope you can continue to display the understanding you've shown so far."

He returned Layla to his arm, placing the bottle's nipple to her eager lips. Then he looked up, finding Katherine confused but listening intently. "We told you our parents live in Florida, but that's a lie we used to explain their absence. Sarah's parents really live in Oregon, and she and I had a home there before coming here." He paused, trying to figure out how to phrase his half-ass confession. "What I'm about to tell you might frighten you, but you're perfectly safe right now, so try to stay calm." He searched her face—still confused and curious, but unafraid. "Sarah and I moved to Idaho to hide from a group of . . . people . . . who want to take Layla away."

"What?" Katherine gasped, clapping a hand over her mouth.

"It isn't government authorities," Aedan quickly elaborated, "or anything like that. These . . . people, they're very dangerous and capable. Sarah and I were capable as well. Until she got sick."

"I don't understand," Katherine objected. "What people?"

"I can't go into detail, Katherine. I'm sorry. Just know they're the worst kind of people, and Layla absolutely cannot get anywhere near them. I know this is confusing, but I beg for your patience and understanding."

"But . . ."

"Please, Katherine, try to trust me."

Her eyebrows furrowed. Then she purposefully smoothed them. "Okay, I'm listening."

"Thank you," Aedan returned, watching Layla eat as he resumed his confession. "We came here because this is one of the last places they would expect us to be. Our plan was for the three of us to hide until it was safe to go home. That's why our parents stayed away, to keep our location a secret. But the situation has changed. It's still not safe for Layla to go home—it won't be for a long time—and now her mom's gone . . ."

His throat tightened as he squeezed his eyes shut on tears, but one escaped, falling to Layla's rosy cheek. She stopped sucking and stared at him with wide eyes, her hand grasping at thin air. No, not thin air; his aura. He wondered what it must look like to her.

He tenderly dried her cheek then soberly looked up. "There's something I have to do, Katherine, somewhere I have to go, and I . . . I won't be coming back." He could tell she was confused, but relaying the whole truth would do more harm than good. "I know this must sound insane, but it truly is my only acceptable option."

"I understand if you need to move," Katherine offered. "I didn't expect you and Layla to stay in the garage apartment forever. And I have no problem returning the extra rent money."

"No," Aedan refused. "That money's yours. You've earned every penny my mom gave you. Like I said, you've been a godsend, and no amount of money can buy that."

"I don't know about all that," she murmured, cheeks flushing.

"I do," Aedan countered. "You've been a blessing too many ways to count."

"Then why are you moving?" she teased, trying to lighten the mood and divert his attention.

"Well," he replied, taking a calming breath, "you've misunderstood what I'm trying to tell you."

"You're not leaving?"

"I am," he confirmed. Then he cleared his throat, squarely meeting her gaze. "Sarah once told me you can't carry a baby and that you hope to adopt." He watched as tumblers began clicking into place. "I know you love Layla, and I know you loved Sarah." He paused, pulling in another calming breath. Then he exhaled his heartbreaking request. "So I want you to adopt our baby and treat her as Sarah would have if given the chance."

He observed Katherine's raised eyebrows, gaping mouth, and frozen posture. Then he looked down, pulling the bottle from Layla's puckered lips. Once she was on his shoulder, he returned his attention to Katherine, who hadn't moved an inch.

"I know it's a big commitment," he added, "raising a baby by yourself, but I also know you're capable of making it. You'll be a fantastic mother. If I didn't think so, I wouldn't ask you to keep my Layla Love."

A long moment of stunned silence passed before Katherine responded. "I don't have a problem with the commitment, Chris. I have a problem with taking a baby away from her dad. How can you even consider it? I mean, I can help. You'll be a single dad, but you won't be alone. You can live in the apartment, and I can be Layla's Aunt Katherine."

"It's not about that," Aedan cut in. "Being a single father is well within my capabilities. There are few things I want more than to stay with Layla forever."

"Then stay with her."

"I can't," he breathed, blinking back tears.

Katherine shook her head. "I don't understand, Chris."

"I know you don't," Aedan conceded.

"Wouldn't Sarah want you to stay?" Katherine argued.

Aedan pulled Layla from his shoulder and examined her serene face—a mini Rhosewen, just colored different. "Sarah knew my plans, and she understood. She loved you, too, Katherine. I know she wanted you to do this for us."

Katherine didn't respond. She merely sat there, staring at the perfect baby in his arms.

"Katherine," he whispered, "this is something I have to do. I have no other option. I want you to be Layla's mom, but if you can't, I'll find someone else."

"No!" she blurted, eyes widening. "Please don't do that. I'll keep her. I'd hate not knowing where she is or who she's with."

"Thank you," Aedan sighed. "I know she'll be in good hands with you, but before you commit, there are a few stipulations to consider." He laid Layla on his chest, and she pulled her knees and arms in, cuddling into him like she belonged there. He closed his eyes, memorizing everything about the moment—the feel of her skin, the smell of her hair, the rise and fall of her tiny torso. Then he looked at Katherine. "Keeping her means you'll have to change your last name and leave Idaho without telling anyone where you're going."

"Change my name?" she whispered.

"Your surname," he confirmed. "I know it's a lot to ask, but I'll pay for everything, so money isn't an issue."

"Will we be in danger if we stay?" she asked, finally displaying a hint of fear.

"I don't expect it," Aedan answered, "but I want to make sure, and moving will only increase your safety. I'll buy you a more dependable vehicle and a new home wherever you choose. All I ask is that you stay away from the coastlines—east, west and the gulf—and away from the northern border, particularly the Great Lakes. Is that something you're willing to do?"

Katherine silently considered his request for over five minutes. By the time she gave her answer, Aedan's nerves were on fire.

"Yeah," she agreed. "I'll do whatever you need me to do."

"Thank you," he sighed, but he could never truly express his vast appreciation for the wonderful way she'd handled everything. "Aside from the money I'll give you for the move, I'll give you money for Layla. If she needs anything, use it. When she turns eighteen, she can have what's left."

"You don't have to do that," Katherine countered, but Aedan shook his head.

"Where I'm going, money's worthless. I want everything I have to go to you and Layla."

"Oh," she mumbled, obviously speculating about the underlying meaning of his comment. "Will she ever meet her true family?"

"She has to believe you are her true family," he insisted. "For now. Once she's grown, it should be safe enough for her to search out Sarah's parents. I want her to, if that's what she wants, but not until she's matured and finished high school. That's very important, Katherine. She has to wait. If she starts searching as a child, before she's grown into the amazing woman she'll undoubtedly be, her safety could be greatly compromised, so enjoy the next eighteen years with her before exposing her to this heartbreak. Hopefully by then she'll have the tools she'll need to deal with whatever comes her way."

"So I'm to lie to her for eighteen years?" Katherine blanched.

"Yes," Aedan confirmed. "That's part of the deal. I can't risk having her out there as a child, exposing herself to danger, and I don't want her carrying this burden through adolescence."

"Oh," Katherine breathed. "I hadn't thought about how she might react to the truth."

"She'll be hurt," Aedan predicted, "which is why you need to make sure she's equipped to handle the news before laying it on her."

"Yes," Katherine agreed, but she was lost in thought, probably trying to figure out how she'd break the news.

"For reasons I can't properly explain," Aedan went on, pulling her attention back, "we've given you false names. I can't give you the real ones, not even to pass on to Layla, nor can I give you our families' addresses. I'll leave you a picture of Sarah and I, and I can tell you we lived somewhere near Portland, Oregon. When Layla's old enough, hopefully that will help her find her grandparents."

"That's it?" Katherine blurted. "How will she ever find them?"

"I know," he breathed, "it's pitiful."

He dropped his gaze to his daughter, searching for a way to safely lead her home. The answer came quickly, and he experienced the first rush of hope he'd had in . . . well, he couldn't remember.

"There's a little town on the coast," he explained. "Cannon Beach. It's about an hour west of Portland. Sarah and I spent a lot of our free time there, and we always stopped at a place called *Cinnia's Cannon Café.* Tell Layla that if she makes it to Oregon, she should try Cinnia's coffee, because it's the best there is."

"*Sinya's Cannon Café*?"

"Sin-nee-a," he corrected. "C-I-N-N-I-A."

Katherine grabbed a pen and wrote the name on her hand. "Okay, but how is that going to get her anywhere?"

"I don't know if it will, but it could prove more useful than you think, so don't leave it out."

Perplexed, Katherine sighed and nodded her agreement. "When will you leave?"

"That depends. I could leave as early as tonight, but if you need me to help with the move, I'll stay."

"Do you need to leave so soon?"

"The sooner I leave, the easier my objective will be. And I assure you, my objective is vital. If I could tell you about it, you'd agree, but you'll just have to trust me."

"I do," she whispered, "and I can handle the move, but you must want to spend more time with Layla before you go."

"I would spend eternity with my Layla Love if I had the option, but it would be selfish of me to stay longer than necessary. Will you promise to move as soon as you're able?"

Katherine wracked her brain for a long moment then nodded. "Yes. As long as I have the money to go, I can be gone within a couple of weeks."

"Thank you," he replied. "You have no idea how much your sacrifice means to me. What surname will you take?"

"Hmm . . . How about Callaway?"

"Yes," he approved, raising his eyebrows. "It's perfect. I'll have everything gathered by this evening. Then, once I leave, you'll be Layla Love Callaway's only family until fate deems otherwise." He paused, nuzzling his daughter's curls as he breathed deep. "Promise me one more thing, Katherine."

"Sure, Chris, anything."

"Love her more than anyone's been loved in the history of time. Love her like her mom loved her, like I love her . . ." His throat tightened, strangling his request.

"I promise," Katherine whispered, wiping away a tear. "She deserves it all."

"Yes," he breathed, squeezing his eyes shut, "she does."

Katherine spent the day running errands, while Aedan spent the day holding Layla, not once laying her down. He needed to use the bathroom, but willed his body to wait. He would let his bladder burst before sacrificing time with his daughter.

When Layla wasn't eating, Aedan would hold her out in front of him, memorizing her features as he softly spoke. Her eyes widened when he talked about his hopes and dreams for her; her lips puckered when he talked about her mother; and when he sang Rhosewen's favorite lullaby, Layla's eyelids grew heavy, closing the curtains on shiny emeralds.

In reverent wonder, Aedan watched every bittersweet second, in awe of her purity and flawless beauty. His heart soared, riding high atop the wind that was the miracle in his arms. But as it soared, it bled, irreparable gashes splitting further each second he looked at her. He embraced the pain, knowing it wouldn't ease until his heart stopped beating altogether. And he wouldn't sacrifice these moments for anything in the world, let alone a temporary dose of relief.

Determined to devote himself to Layla when she woke, Aedan spent her nap getting things ready for his departure. He called a local bank and a few government officials, using a clever combination of mind magic and charm to trick the system. Then he used one hand to magically prepare official documents for Katherine and Layla Callaway.

It seemed time had been cursed to quicken, and Aedan sighed heavily and so sadly when the clocks struck nine. He wondered how he was managing to put one foot in front of the other, but then Rhosewen's face appeared in his mind's eye as he looked at Layla, and his dread warped into determination. The heartache, however, strengthened. He could only hope his anguish would work to his advantage once he found the Unforgivables.

He entered the living room to find Katherine waiting for him, so he soberly led her to the coffee table. "I opened a bank account under your new name," he said, passing over a folded piece of paper. "The funds will be available by tomorrow, and everything's in order with the bank personnel, so there won't be any red tape, paperwork or explanations to deal with."

Katherine unfolded the paper and straightened her glasses. "Oh!" she exclaimed. "That's . . . that's a lot of money."

"That's your money," he insisted. "Yours and Layla's. I want you to use it for everything you guys need. A car and a house, and all the things Layla will need growing up. Neither of you should ever go without. And I want you to have fun, so don't save all of it. Splurge once and while."

Katherine nodded her agreement, eyes wide and watery, and Aedan scanned her face and aura, making sure she was absorbing everything.

"I've prepared the necessary documents," he went on, retrieving an envelope from the table. "Birth certificates, social security cards, a driver's license, and they're valid with the government, so don't hesitate to use them."

"How did you . . ." she mumbled, but then she shook her head. "Never mind."

She took the envelope and glanced over its contents, halting when she got to the birth certificate listing Katherine Anne Callaway as Layla Love Callaway's only parent.

"Here's the picture of Sarah and I," Aedan said, holding out the photograph. "It was taken on our wedding day."

Katherine slipped the birth certificate back into the envelope then took the photo. "Wow," she whispered. "Sarah looks like a Greek goddess. You're both so beautiful."

"Sarah made everything more beautiful than it was before," Aedan agreed, staring longingly at the mere memory of his Rose.

Katherine looked up, and Aedan cleared a lump from his throat. "Don't show that picture to anyone," he instructed. "It's for Layla's eyes only. If she chooses to search for Sarah's parents, she should be very selective about who she shows it to. It could lead her to her grandparents, but it could also lead her to danger."

Stunned by the turn of events, Katherine merely nodded.

"I know this is overwhelming," Aedan sympathized, "but you're handling everything great. I can't imagine a more perfect person to set this on."

Katherine silently nodded again, and Aedan squeezed her shoulder. "Remember, if Layla wants to find Sarah's parents, she'll need to start near Portland, Oregon."

"I'll remember," Katherine assured. "Portland, Oregon, and she should check out the coffee at *Cinnia's Cannon Café* in the coastal town of Cannon Beach."

"Yes," he confirmed. "*Cinnia's* may be the most useful tip I've given you. Furthermore, Cannon Beach is a safe area. Her odds of finding danger there are low." He looked at Layla, and Layla looked at him. "I know it's pitiful, but that's the best I can do for her. Please take care of her in the meantime. It's my sincerest hope that the two of you will share a life of happiness and love."

"Are you sure you have to leave, Chris?"

"Yes. It's what's best for Layla."

Katherine sighed as she straightened her glasses with a shaky hand. "Well, if you can come back, or if you change your mind, I'm pretty sure we'll be in Oklahoma. I've wanted to visit since I saw the musical, and it's about as far from the coasts as you can get."

"Thank you for doing this, Katherine. I know it's a sacrifice."

"No, Chris. The sacrifice is yours. I'd move a million times for Layla."

Aedan sadly nodded as he looked at his baby. "May I have a moment alone with her?"

"Of course," Katherine agreed. "I'll be in the kitchen."

She left the room, and Aedan sat on the couch, holding Layla out in front of him. He closed his eyes, making sure he had every part of her memorized. From her corkscrew curls to her teeny toes, she was as perfect in his mind as she was in his arms.

He raised his burning lids, fighting the tears misting his vision. "You're so beautiful and special," he whispered, lowering his face closer to hers. "And I'm so sorry I have to leave you, but it's what's best for you. Hopefully you'll understand when it's time to learn the truth." He swallowed, trying to loosen his throat, but it didn't work, and he nearly gagged as he continued. "I know you won't remember this, and that's okay. I just want you to hear it. At least once. Your mommy's name was Rhosewen Keely Donnelly. I liked to call her my Rose. She was so beautiful, Layla, and she loved you so much. I wish things had been different. Then we could have stayed with you forever. That's what we wanted, what we dreamed about from the moment we met, and it breaks my heart that we're not getting it. But you'll be safe with Katherine. She's your mommy now, and she'll take good care of you, because she loves you very much." He softly kissed her button nose. "I have to leave, baby, but you'll always be in my heart." He kissed her wrinkled forehead. "Hopefully, someday, you'll know who I was." He kissed her rosy cheeks. "I'm Aedan Dagda Donnelly, your daddy, and I love you more than life itself." He pulled her to his chest, freely weeping into soft spirals. "Be safe, Layla Love, and find us when you can."

The pain was horrendous, but the love was pure, and he cried into her curls for an hour before forcing himself to his feet.

He sluggishly made his way to the kitchen, constantly kissing her petite palm. Then he held his breath as he passed her to Katherine. "Keep her safe," he whispered.

"I promise," Katherine vowed, shedding salty rivers.

"Thank you, Katherine. For everything. From beginning to end."

She solemnly nodded. "Goodbye, Chris."

Aedan looked at his daughter once more, slowly running a finger across her cherub cheek. Then he dropped his hand and turned away, reluctantly leaving her for the first and last time.

Chapter 30

Aedan let the tears flow as he flew toward Duluth, Minnesota, and every salty drop reinforced his purpose.

After spending thirteen hours along the western shores of Lake Superior, he found out Agro had gone to Maine, so he headed east.

Two weeks and seven states—a few of them twice—and not once did he waver from his quest. He'd land, eat, sleep then search for the Unforgivables, trying to tap into Medea's mind. He didn't know if it would work since his powers had dwindled, but he kept trying. The attempt, whether successful or not, wouldn't go unnoticed. If he got near her, she would know he was coming. He wanted her to know.

The midnight sky twinkled as he flew over Colorado Springs, scanning the lands moistened by passing storms. When the city lights faded, he finally got a fuzzy read on Medea. He knew it was a trap. The Unforgivables were reeling him in. He readily took the bait.

He couldn't read Medea's thoughts or see what sights her eyes beheld, but he sensed her presence. He was close.

Several large, sandstone formations appeared in the distance, like arthritic fingers reaching for the starry sky. Aedan knew the area, having hiked its trails when he was fifteen. How fitting it would be to meet his end in the Garden of the Gods.

He landed and looked around, finding Pikes Peak looming on the horizon, and the large and prominent North Gateway Rock dominating the forefront.

Breathing slow and steady, he stripped down to his pants, twitching from head to toe as the brisk breeze contrasted with his boiling blood. Rhosewen's and Layla's faces flashed through his mind.

Then he locked the gorgeous images away, determined to guard them from outside intrusion.

He made his way to the renowned Balanced Rock—a huge chunk of sandstone precariously poised on its smaller end—and scanned its earthen platform. At first it appeared deserted, but he soon found what didn't belong. Medea was crouching in the rock's shadow.

Temptation twitched Aedan's fingers. One spell would bring the boulder crashing down. But Medea's ruin wasn't a priority. Besides, Aedan had no desire to destroy something so beautiful—not the witch, but the natural phenomenon she lurked beneath.

Aedan couldn't see the other Unforgivables, but sensed them there. He wasn't afraid. After all the heartbreak he'd suffered, death would be sweet release. He filled his lungs with crisp oxygen, determined to stay levelheaded and strong for his two beautiful girls, but no amount of meditation would extinguish the fire in his veins.

"Medea," he simmered. "Why don't you stand and let me get a better look at you?"

She hesitated then straightened, revealing her aura as she slinked to the edge of the grainy platform.

Aedan observed every move, pleased to see she looked like hell. Apparently life under Agro's careful watch didn't agree with her. Grotesquely hollow, her pallid face had a skeletal appearance, and her hooded, yellow eyes were bloodshot and lusterless. Haunted by a melancholy mixture of maroon, blue and gray, her stagnant aura revealed a lost soul, an expired spirit begging for release.

"You look like shit," he noted, and her top lip curled with a hiss.

"You don't look so hot yourself."

True, but Aedan didn't care. "I can thank you for that."

A wicked grin stretched across Medea's gaunt face. Then she feigned a sympathetic pout. "Ahh . . . Did something happen to your precious *Rose*?" The lovely name slithered through her teeth, desecrated by her disdain, sullied by her sickening spite.

Aedan's muscles rolled. He wanted to kill her. He wanted to wrap his hands around her scrawny throat and watch every ounce of life drain from her revolting body. Hate dislocated another piece of his shattered heart, but he wouldn't mourn that piece. If ever there was righteous hatred, he held it.

"She's dead," he confirmed, "but you already knew that."

"I figured," Medea confessed, tapping her scarred cheek with a jagged fingernail. "That is why you're here after all. Vengeance? Well you're on a death mission. Did you really think you'd be able to kill me and live to see another day?"

She looked around, and Aedan followed her gaze, finding thirty-eight crimson cloaks encircling him.

"No," he answered, unperturbed by their sudden appearance.

"You don't wish to kill me?" Medea scoffed.

"Oh, I'd enjoy watching you die," Aedan corrected, "and I'd love to do it myself, but I don't expect to live."

Medea's eyes narrowed, and Aedan focused on filtering his aura and blocking his mind.

"In fact," he went on, "you've ensured I have nothing to live for."

Terror twisted Medea's ugly features as she opened her mouth to speak, but she screamed instead, falling to her knees and curling into a ball.

Aedan knew the kind of torture she was experiencing, because he knew that agonizing expression well. Rhosewen wore it often throughout the last four months of her life, but she'd worn it with beauty and grace. Medea just looked wretched and strung out. Aedan intently watched, waiting for the pain to hit him as well, but it didn't come.

One of the Unforgivables lowered their hood and walked forward, and Aedan glanced over, unsurprised to find Agro's orange eyes.

"Aedan," he greeted, waving a hand toward Medea, who went limp, her screams fading into sobs. "It's a pity we always meet on such unfriendly terms."

"Are there any other kind with you?" Aedan countered.

"Some would say no," Agro confessed.

"I'd agree with them," Aedan scorned.

Agro's eyes flashed red, but his posture remained casual. "As I said, pity." He looked at Medea then back. "Your wife is dead?"

"Yes," Aedan answered, jaw set.

"I'm sorry to hear that."

"I bet you are."

Agro scanned every inch of Aedan and the air around him, trying to find a hole in his persona. "Perhaps you think it was I who cursed your mate, but I assure you, I had no part in that one. I would have preferred to handle the situation myself, but that was Medea's handiwork. I was led to believe she would merely make your mate's hair fall out, or stain her teeth green, something inconvenient yet insignificant. I had no idea she'd come up with something so . . . creative. I've already disposed of the disloyal magicians who helped her work out the details."

Agro's lack of involvement surprised Aedan, but he made a point not to show it. It was his word against Medea's, and he had to play his part convincingly. Everything he had left on earth depended on it.

He looked at Medea, genuine hate and anger burning his body and aura. "You."

She met his stare, head bobbing as tears streaked down her withered cheeks.

"You once claimed to care about me," Aedan seethed, "yet you destroyed my life. You deserve a punishment far worse than death, because what I've lost was more precious than air, and it was you and you alone who stole it from me. Your soul is wretched, Medea. Your life means nothing. You're merely a shit stain on an otherwise beautiful foundation."

Agro stepped closer. "Where's your child, Aedan?"

"What child?"

"No!" Medea screeched. "He lies! I swear I did it right . . ." A bloodcurdling scream ripped from her throat as she once again curled into a ball.

"Are you saying Rhosewen didn't conceive?" Agro pressed.

"My love was pregnant," Aedan confirmed, "but breath was stolen from her before her third trimester, taking my baby's beating heart with it."

"No," Medea sobbed. "He's lying . . . He has to be lying."

"Silence!" Agro barked, raising a hand, and Medea's mouth slammed shut.

Agro's palm turned toward Aedan, who was ready for the icy feeling that gripped his bones. He'd endured so much pain in the past four months, his body merely jolted.

Agro frowned. Then the ice gripped tighter, threatening to grind Aedan's bones into frozen dust. He fell to his knees as a groan gurgled in his throat, but his body stayed upright and his eyes stayed open.

Agro curiously tilted his head, raising an appreciative eyebrow. "Your endurance for pain is amazing."

Aedan couldn't reply. If he opened his mouth, he would scream.

"Now," Agro whispered, stepping closer, "I'm going to ask you again. Did Rhosewen give birth?"

The cold barely eased, and Aedan roughly filled his lungs. "No, she was only five months pregnant . . ."

The pain spiked, more than before, and Aedan fell forward, his palms slapping red earth as a tormented roar vibrated his clenched teeth, swirling sand into his nostrils.

"Are you absolutely sure about that?" Agro asked.

When the agonizing force ebbed, Aedan breathed deep, laboriously pushing himself up to meet Agro's stare. "Do you think I'd be here, facing my doom, if my baby lived? If I still had a precious petal from my Rose?" He sucked in another ragged breath. "I'm not strong enough . . . to leave what I want most in the world in order to procure justice, impossible justice. No, I'm desperate . . . lost without my love and broken without the child I couldn't save. I came here to meet my end, so I can join my family in the afterlife. Just let me take the witch down with me." He breathed through his nose, trying to ignore the pain so he could focus on hiding the truth.

Agro considered him for several tortuous seconds before lowering his palm, and Aedan slumped to the ground, gasping as icy cold gave way to raging heat.

"Well, well, Medea," Agro bristled.

Aedan quickly composed himself, bringing his torso erect so he could see Medea's pleading eyes. He didn't want to miss this—the last guilty pleasure he'd fulfill on earth.

"It seems you've made a mistake," Agro fumed, ruthlessly staring at the witch. "Perhaps Rhosewen loved her baby more than you expected her to."

Medea's lips were magically sealed, but a muffled noise grated her throat as she tried to plead her case, begging with bloodshot eyes.

Agro wasn't interested in judging the accused. He was the executioner. "You understand how angry that makes me," he rumbled, voice and temper rising. "You've robbed me of the most powerful bonded child to ever be conceived."

Aedan flexed, truly sorry it wasn't in his power to destroy Agro before making his exit. But an attempt could compromise the lock on his thoughts, and many of the surrounding vultures were waiting for him to lose focus so they could crack him open. He wouldn't give them the chance.

"This is unacceptable!" Agro boomed. Then he spoke much quieter, deadlier. "You must pay the consequences." His right hand swept into the air then came down in a nonchalant gesture of farewell.

Medea's yellow eyes widened as four hooded figures stepped from the surrounding circle. Then four different spells hit her at once. Fire, water, earth and air combined in a burst of chaos and color that lifted her from the rock, contorting and twisting her like putty.

Wind-whipped sand and humid heat spattered Aedan's face as he watched Medea's last haunted dance—a macabre and sickening scene, but undeniably satisfying.

By the time the evil storm lifted, Medea was a smoldering pile of twisted limbs. The four casters made the motion of dusting off their hands, and the mutilated corpse turned to ash, drifting into the Garden of the Gods.

Agro turned toward Aedan, clearly disappointed, yet greedily intrigued. "I'm sorry for your loss, Aedan."

"You lie," Aedan spurned, shaking his head. "You're sorry for *your* loss. You can't see past your wicked agenda enough to realize my wife's and baby's deaths are a loss for the masses, not the few."

"Medea was out of line," Agro conceded.

"You brought her there that night," Aedan countered, "and even if she hadn't cursed my wife, you would have hatched your own evil plot to tear my family apart."

"You speak sharp words for a man with few options, Aedan. I'm offering you a deal. You won't be leaving by yourself, but you'd make a fine asset to the Dark Elite."

"Go to hell," Aedan refused.

"You answer without even considering," Agro rebuked.

"I disagree with your ethics," Aedan explained, breathing in the cold, night air, appreciating everything about it.

He was ready. He'd succeeded, and his baby—his perfect Layla Love—was safe. Just one more loose end to tie up before leaving this life in search of another. He laid his right hand over his heart, making sure the band of Rhosewen's wedding ring touched thumping skin.

"You might as well get it over with," he whispered. "If you don't kill me, I'll spend the rest of my life trying to kill you."

"I'd rather use you than kill you," Agro reproached. "I wish you'd reconsider."

"Not a chance," Aedan sighed, a serene smile curving his lips.

He was going to see his Rose, his beautiful, golden Rose. He could already feel the grief lifting. Soon he'd feel light as air.

Agro curiously watched him for a full minute then took three steps back, raising his right hand.

Aedan's eyes drifted shut as he performed one last bit of magic, and the happiest and saddest moments of his life filled his heart before finding their way to Rhosewen's ring. *Goodbye, Layla Love, my sweet angel. I'll miss you . . .*

Unbelievable pain. Then darkness. Then . . . nothing.

Aedan had joined his love in the afterlife.

Present Day—Oregon

Layla was dead. She'd died with her father. Or had she?

Nothingness enveloped her, suffocating body and mind, stripping away her sense of being and replacing it with her parents'. Their memories played again and again. Layla couldn't shut them out or let anything else in, so she repeatedly witnessed her mom and dad meet, bond, then continue down a path of pure love and saddening destruction, culminating in the ultimate sacrifice—death.

The memories abruptly ceased, suspending Layla in a dark pool of unattached realization where she dissected and retained the facts like a thirsty scientist. Then the nothingness crept away, leaving a disaster in its wake.

Layla's lungs expanded, her fingers and toes awakened, and her wounded heart echoed in her eardrums. A sorrowful wail bubbled in her swollen throat, growing louder as emotional turmoil—a pain as physical as any she'd ever felt—gripped and squeezed, pulling her into a ball.

"No!" She wanted to go back to the nothingness. The pain of reality was too much, breaking her down and grinding the pieces to dust.

She clawed at her heart, trying to rip the agonizing organ from her chest, but a large hand encircled her wrist, pulling her frantic fingernails away. She gasped, appendages flinging out as her eyes popped open, wet and disoriented. Then warm air floated over her left cheek.

"It's okay, Layla. You're safe."

"Quin," she sobbed, curling into his chest. "Oh, god . . ."

Quin wrapped his arms around her and squeezed, but she barely felt it. The sorrow squeezed so much harder.

Her cries grew louder as her body cringed, at the mercy of unrelenting emotion. So many emotions—overwhelming awe at how deeply her parents loved her; unbearable grief for the sacrifices they made to keep her safe; utter sadness for the way things turned out; and love . . . heart-gripping love for the people who'd given her life, the mom and dad she never knew. Love for the parents who were gone. Dead.

"Oh, god," she whimpered. "They were perfect . . . and I'll never know what it's like . . . to touch them and to let them touch me."

Regret churned her stomach, throbbing her aching head and heart. She'd been harboring anger about her adoption—resentment toward her father and the disconnect she felt with her mother. Now the anger rebounded, smothering her in remorse, punishing her for daring to disrespect those who had blessed her with breath before forfeiting their own. And atonement was nowhere in sight. She'd never be able to look at her parents and tell them how much she loved them, how much their devotion meant to her. After everything they went through, they deserved to know—to hear it from their daughter's lips that their undying love touched her; that she felt it pulse in her broken heart and course through her thriving veins. They hadn't abandoned her; they'd saved her, and she'd give anything to let them know she understood the enormity of their sacrifice.

She sobbed harder, shoulders shaking. Then her ears started humming as her mom's wedding ring quivered, expelling waves of vibrations up her arm. She opened her eyes, shocked and confused. Then a cooling sensation washed over fluctuating flesh, melting her tense muscles.

Quin's shirt slipped from her grip, and he leaned back, running his bewildered gaze from her head to her toes. Layla looked down as well, and only then did she realize she was glowing. And singing! The humming wasn't in her ears, but all around her, flowing from the ethereal mist that poured from the ring and blanketed her body.

Salty moisture blurred the beautiful sight, so Layla closed her eyes, sliding her vibrating hand to her chest. When the ring found her heart, warm affection and tranquility flooded her senses, and she unfurled, losing herself in the magic.

For a splendid moment in time, her broken heart and its aching shell vanished, and she was merely a soul, blissfully floating in her parents' love. She could feel them as clearly as she felt anything else. They were more real than the bed beneath her. And while they didn't speak, she could hear them. The mesmerizing mist and its magical message told her more than words could portray. Furthermore, if she could feel *them*, receive *their* message, surely they could feel her.

True or not, it brought Layla peace to believe it, to imagine her parents floating in her soul, absorbing all the love and appreciation she had to give, taking sublime comfort in knowing their hopes for their daughter had come true—she remained safe from wicked magicians and had found her family.

While Layla drifted on hope and love, as peaceful as a sleeping angel swaddled in fluffy clouds, she vowed to live her life in a way that would never forsake her parents' sacrifices. They'd given her a gift beyond measure. No longer would she spend it in a rut. She'd find at least one thing to be thankful for every day, and she'd recall the undying love that paved her way.

Rhosewen's ring stopped vibrating, the heavenly hum faded, and the feel-good magic ebbed, returning Layla to her liquid body, but she didn't move or open her eyes. She just lay there with her hand over heart as silent tears streamed down her temples.

Despite her new lease on life and her vow to appreciate it, the emotional pain returned the moment the magic departed. Not even the strongest spells could make her forget the affectionate expression her mom wore when her heart burst with love, or the sorrowful and sweet goodbye her dad had given her before dying in a flash of agony. Those memories and many more would always be with her, and they would always hurt.

Layla knew the permanence of loss well. The day after Katherine's passing, as she'd rocked in an old recliner that smelled of memories,

Layla had realized with certainty that death was final, that no amount of wishing, hoping or praying could reverse what doctors could not. If ever she held faith, she'd lost it that day—the day she realized Katherine was gone, never to return, and she was alone, stuck in a world with no one to love.

Now, as she lay mourning those who'd given her life, realizing with certainty that they were gone, never to return, the hopelessness once again threatened to engulf her, to strip away any trace of faith she'd managed to retain. But this time Layla had something she'd lacked before. She had a family—a beautiful and kind family. No longer was she alone with no one to love.

She swallowed a lump and opened her eyes, finding her first reason to be thankful. Exquisitely stretched out beside her, his chest unobstructed and perfect for cuddling, Quin searched her face, his dark gaze shiny and deep.

"Hey," he whispered, playing with one of her curls.

Layla tried to say hey back, but her throat was swollen shut.

"Do you need anything?" he asked.

She shook her head no, jarring more tears from her lids, and Quin reached over, softly wiping the moisture away. His tender touch intensified the emotions plucking on her raw heartstrings, and she turned her face into his hand, bursting into more sobs.

"I'm sorry," she gasped, making a slobbery mess of his palm.

"Don't be," he replied, sliding his free hand under her head. Then he curled her into a ball and pulled her close, tucking her into his chest.

Layla continued to struggle with a never-ending supply of tears, but Quin's alluring scent, strong heartbeat, and firm embrace cuddled her like a cozy cocoon, keeping her safe and warm as she mourned her old life and embraced the new—a life full of magic, family, and if she was really lucky . . . Quin.

Epilogue

Present Day—Oklahoma

The mundane neighborhood was silent—only a light spring breeze rustling the soft white blooms of Bradford pear trees, feathering manicured lawns and shadowed shrubs.

Dark and deserted, stood a small house with a covered porch, a *for sale* sign posted near the tidy walkway. The moonlit lawn ruffled in waves. Then five crimson cloaks appeared out of thin air, casting long shadows across the whispering grass. Glaring from the cape closest to the porch, were flaming orange eyes.

Agro's nostrils flared as he scowled at the dark windows. He could sense the witch's lingering energy, but she was gone. He soared to the porch, opening the front door with a wave of his hand. Then he floated inside, halting when he reached the witch's deserted bedroom. The tiny closet and particle board dresser were empty, and the bed was bare, its mattress askew from the box-spring.

Agro landed beside the bed and leaned over the place she once slept, breathing in the sweet floral bouquet of pure power. His body tightened as his lungs quickened, drowning in her essence, and he burned to get his hands on the source, to inhale the flower at its freshest.

After memorizing every element of her scent, he straightened and started to turn, but paused when he noticed a streak of color poking from beneath the crooked mattress.

He waved his left hand, tossing the mattress aside. Then he froze, staring down at a dark-haired siren like no other. The way she gazed from the photograph—big, round emeralds deeper than the sagest soul yet swimming with innocence—made Agro shudder, simultaneously awed and aroused. Even through glossy paper he could tell she possessed the powers of the Heavens. Molded in their empyreal image, she could have been birthed by the Goddess Ava—Mother of the witches, the first of the breed.

Agro gingerly lifted the photograph, wondering why such beauty would hide under a mattress. Then he noticed an old crease running across the lower half of the portrait, obscuring the words *Class of '07*. The graduation photo had been shoved under the mattress to flatten a fold. Lucky for him, it had been forgotten.

He ran a forefinger over the crease, magically repairing the damage. Then he carefully rolled it up, tucking it in his cloak as he returned to his guard. They stood where he left them, alertly scanning their surroundings, so Agro moved to the *for sale* sign and crouched.

"Farriss," he hissed.

"Sir?" the henchman replied, kneeling beside him.

"Tell me again what you learned," Agro demanded.

For the past week Farriss had been exploring Oklahoma, seeking information on a witch living a hexless life. He eventually made contact with a coven in southeast Oklahoma that knew of such a person. Two of their members had encountered an unaware witch while dining in Gander Creek—a tiny town near the Kansas border. One of the members had been more than happy to tell her story, claiming the witch held unusual beauty, both body and aura, and had looked and acted as though she knew nothing of magic.

Following the vague tip, Farriss ended up in Gander Creek's lone watering hole, quickly learning his target—twenty-one-year-old Layla Callaway—had left town. He easily obtained her former address and place of employment, along with a brief rundown of her life. Then he delivered the bad news to Agro, who insisted on visiting Gander Creek himself.

"This house and the diner," Farriss answered. "That's all we have. The witch has been a recluse for three years. The locals in the tavern claim to know her as well as anyone, but they know nothing of her current whereabouts or activities. They didn't even know she was leaving town until she was gone."

"You'll visit the diner," Agro decided, "question her boss. Then you'll pay this broker a visit—Gerald Greene."

"Yes, sir," Farriss agreed. "The diner's open twenty-four hours. Would you like me to go now?"

"Yes, but I don't want the witch hearing about your visit. After talking to the boss, convince him to keep his mouth shut. He's not to tell his staff the subject of your interrogation. Tomorrow you'll intimidate Mr. Greene. If his office is closed on Sundays, you'll find his home."

"Yes, sir."

Agro looked at the abandoned house, a menacing growl rolling in his chest. Then he raised a palm, watching with pleasure as the insipid structure burst into raging flames.

Plain, dingy and too bright for the dark field surrounding it, the all night diner sat off a deserted highway, catering to local hell-raisers, early birds, and the occasional trucker.

Farriss descended behind the building and released his concealment spells, hovering an inch above cracked cement as he curled his lip at the overflowing dumpster. He transferred his cloak to his satchel, summoned polished leather shoes onto his feet, then adjusted the diamond cuffs of his Armani suit—the one he used to intimidate the hexless. After straightening his tie, he slicked his long hair into a low ponytail and secured it with a magical band. When facing down the powerless, he preferred to keep their focus on his saffron yellow eyes rather than his copper red hair.

Staying in the shadows, he headed for the front of the building then walked around the corner, surprised to find a line at the door. Apparently the local boozers had flocked to the diner after last call.

Farriss slowed his pace, hesitant to draw a crowd's attention. Then he relaxed, realizing the circumstances could work in his favor. The intoxicated wouldn't remember him, and the employees would rush to get him out of their hair.

He continued along his course, easily clearing a path through the wasted patrons, who ceased their carousing and stared with blurry eyes.

"Who's this asshole?" one guy murmured, and the girl beside him speared his ribs.

"Shut up, ya dumbass. Dude looks like a fed."

"Whadya know 'bout feds?" the cocky drunk returned. Then he and his friends burst into laughter, forgetting the sharp dressed man who entered the diner.

Farriss glanced around, taking a few seconds to assess the situation —multiple customers at every table, and only three servers, none of whom dressed like a boss. Through a metal framed window stood a cook, and behind him a dishwasher, but no manager.

A frumpy, spectacled woman with fly-away hair rushed behind the bar, stopping to stack condiments on a tray.

Farriss stepped forward, placing a hand on her platter. "I need the boss."

"Don't we all?" the woman snorted, crouching out of sight. Then she popped back up, tossing a handful of straws on the counter. "The boss ain't here. If ya got a complaint, come back tomorrow."

She tried to take her things and go, but Farriss kept his hand on the tray. "I need to see the man in charge," he pressed.

The waitress paused, raising a skeptical eyebrow at Farriss' sleek jacket. "The *man* called in sick today," she countered. "Better luck next time."

"Listen," Farriss replied, glancing at her nametag, "Phyllis, I have business with your boss..."

"Do I look like I care 'bout your business?" she interrupted. "Sure, you're fancy and all . . . and kinda handsome in a weird way, but I ain't got time for this. I'm in the middle of a bar rush."

Farriss narrowed his eyes. The old biddy wasn't the least bit intimidated by him. "Perhaps there's someone else I can speak with," he suggested, struggling to keep his cool. "Who's the man in charge when the boss is gone?"

"Lord, help us," Phyllis sniffed, rolling her eyes. Then she yanked her tray away and turned, speaking to a passing waiter. "Deal with this chauvinist pig, Travis. I ain't in the mood."

"Yes, ma'am," the waiter agreed, digging under the counter, but when he spotted Farriss, he straightened, raising one eyebrow as he scanned the Armani suit. "You must be Mr. Pig."

Farriss scanned the scrawny excuse for a man from head to toe. "Give me a break," he grumbled, grinding his teeth.

The waiter shrugged his skinny shoulders and turned to the till. "Don't have one."

"I need your boss," Farriss repeated, exhausted by the inadequate staff.

"That'd be her," the waiter replied, nudging the frumpy old woman, who was rattling orders to the cook. "He's all yours, Phyllis," Travis added. "I'm not man enough."

The waiter walked away, and Farriss' jaw tightened as his nostrils flared. "Enough," he said, reaching over the counter. The waitress tried to back away, but Farriss caught her apron, retrieving her notepad and pen and slapping them on the bar. "Your boss' name and address," he demanded, pointing to the paper. "Right here."

The waitress scowled, but Farriss could tell he'd rattled her. About damn time.

"Go to hell," she snapped, lunging for the phone. "You got three seconds to leave or I call the sheriff."

Farriss stiffened, taken aback by the woman's rebuff. "Listen, lady," he seethed, "I've been in this shit-hole diner long enough. Give me your boss' address and I'll get the hell out of here."

Phyllis replaced the phone, and Farriss thought he'd finally gotten through to her, but then she smiled and propped her hands on her hips.

"This diner may be a shit-hole, but it's the only one open for fifty miles, which explains why Sheriff Jenkins is walkin' in the door."

"Shit," Farriss cursed, spinning around.

Sure enough, the sheriff and his deputy were strolling through the crowd, making sure the drunks weren't causing trouble. The sheriff made eye-contact with Farriss then turned to Phyllis, who'd emerged from the bar to greet him with coffee and complaints.

"If you're lookin' for troublemakers," she snitched, "I got one at the counter."

"The guy in the suit?" Jenkins asked, looking toward the bar, but there was no one there.

"Where'd he go?" Phyllis mumbled, scanning the room. Then utter chaos erupted when someone screamed *Fire!*

"Shit," the stranger whispered, hovering fifty feet above earth as he watched flames leap from the diner. Two miles north, smoke continued to curl from the embers of the witch's former residence. The stranger could hear sirens as the fire department rushed from one hopeless mess to another, and screams occasionally reached him from the frightened patrons pouring out of the restaurant.

The stranger searched the sky, glimpsing a shimmer as Farriss made his exit, and he wondered if Agro had ordered the fire or if the barbarian had lost his temper.

"Foolish," the stranger scorned.

Agro and his dogs were fools. Burning down the witch's former home was bad enough. By destroying the diner, the Unforgivable had hoisted two red flags. They might as well have phoned the witch to tell her they were coming.

"Unacceptable," the stranger mumbled, soaring clear of smoke.

This was *his* project, damn it. Not Agro's. *He* was the wizard who discovered the witch, and it was *his* careful planning and magical expertise that set things in motion. He couldn't let Agro flaw his scheme. He had special plans for the special witch, and it would not do for Agro to change them. Perhaps bringing the Unforgivables into the plan was a mistake.

Well, if Agro continued to act like an obsessed head case, the stranger would adjust his path, avoid the consequences of his erroneous judgment.

The diner was crumbling, and he knew Agro's intentions, so there was no reason to stay in Oklahoma. The stranger flew higher then soared over smoke, heading for Oregon.

Now Available

About the Author

B. C. Burgess is a small town girl born and raised in Oklahoma, where she still resides with her devoted husband and their young son. She's addicted to coffee and writing and thinks the combination is heaven. Inspired to write by her love of reading, she feels fiction provides a healthy escape from the hardships of life, and hopes her stories touch the hearts of her readers, just as she's been touched time and again. Though most of her visions flower in the form of fiction, she dreams of the day her passion for writing, along with determination and hard work, will prove to her son creative dreams can come true.

If you like the tales B. C. weaves, let her know.
She loves hearing from her readers.

Follow B.C on her website:
www.bcburgess.com

Made in the USA
Lexington, KY
18 April 2013